PRAISE FOR *THE LAST TRUE VAMPIRE*

"Full of sexy vampires, strong women, and excitement."
—*Fresh Fiction*

"The chemistry is electric . . . Kate Baxter has done her job, and masterfully." —*San Francisco Book Reviews*

"A jackpot read for vampire lovers who like sizzle . . . brimming with heat!" —*Romance Junkies*

"Mikhail and Claire's love story ha[s] that combination of romance, steam, and suspense."
—*Book-a-holics Anonymous*

"If you like the Black Dagger Brotherhood . . . pick up *The Last True Vampire*, you won't be disappointed."
—*Parajunkee Reviews*

"Kate Baxter has done a remarkable job of building this paranormal world." —*Scandalous Book Reviews*

ALSO BY KATE BAXTER

The Last True Vampire

The Warrior Vampire

The Dark Vampire

The Untamed Vampire

The Lost Vampire

THE WICKED VAMPIRE

KATE BAXTER

St. Martin's Paperbacks

This is a work of fiction. All of the characters, organizations, and events portrayed in this novel are either products of the author's imagination or are used fictitiously.

THE WICKED VAMPIRE

Copyright © 2017 by Kate Baxter.

All rights reserved.

For information address St. Martin's Press, 175 Fifth Avenue, New York, NY 10010.

ISBN: 978-1-250-12543-9

Our books may be purchased in bulk for promotional, educational, or business use. Please contact your local bookseller or the Macmillan Corporate and Premium Sales Department at 1-800-221-7945, ext. 5442, or by e-mail at MacmillanSpecialMarkets@macmillan.com.

Printed in the United States of America

St. Martin's Paperbacks edition / December 2017

St. Martin's Paperbacks are published by St. Martin's Press, 175 Fifth Avenue, New York, NY 10010.

10 9 8 7 6 5 4 3 2 1

CHAPTER
1

Sasha Ivanov was a killer.

At least, she had been. In another life. Now, her existence was devoted to frivolity. Revelry. Pleasure. Oh, the pleasure. Drinking, dancing, touching, kissing, heated words and touches . . . She'd been a devoted servant of her coven for far too long and she was finally free of responsibility and living her life. On her terms. Free of obligation and attachment.

The deep bass echoing through the club thumped in her chest, a pleasant pulse that vibrated outward through her limbs. Her tongue flicked out to close the punctures on the throat of the male she'd latched onto and she rocked back on her heels before turning away. The male—a shifter who obviously thought he was the shit—reached out and grabbed her arm to turn her so her back pressed against his chest as he thrust his hips, grinding against her ass in time to the music.

He dipped his head to hers and said, "Baby, that was intense."

Eh. She'd had better. The shifter's hands wandered from

Sasha's torso, around to her stomach and down her thighs. He gave another thrust of his hips and his erection pressed against her ass. Again, not all that impressive. He'd already given her what she wanted. Sasha wasn't interested in his body or anything else.

"I need a drink."

The shifter spun Sasha around in his arms so she faced him. A spark lit behind his eyes, revealing a glimpse of his animal nature. He tilted his neck to one side, a brash invitation as he lowered his head to hers. "I've got what you need, baby. Take as much as you want."

Ugh. She fought the urge to roll her eyes. She'd had her fill of this male, thank you very much. He cupped the back of her neck with his palm to urge her closer. *Idiot.* She could drink him dry and leave him for dead in the middle of the dance floor without even batting a lash. And if he didn't quit trying to force her to his throat, she might do just that. Sasha braced her palms against his chest and pushed away with enough force to let him know she meant business.

"Unless you've got Jose Cuervo running through your veins, you don't, in fact, have what I need." Sasha stepped back. "Go find some other ass to grind against. I'll catch up with you later." *Try never.* Sasha kept her thoughts to herself as she turned and left the shifter on the dance floor. She didn't know his name, and frankly, she wasn't interested in learning it.

"So. Bored."

Sasha collapsed onto the bar with dramatic flair to emphasize her words. It was still early, only two in the morning, and she was nowhere close to calling it a night. The L.A. club scene never slowed down—especially in the supernatural world. It's not like there was a shortage of entertainment, but she'd grown restless of the party scene and of males like the shifter she'd left out on the floor who thought they were special because they'd managed to hook up with one of a handful of vampires in existence. The thrill was gone. It had lost its appeal months ago. Sasha needed something new to excite her.

"Have another drink." Ani, the sylph who tended bar at Onyx—one of three exclusively supernatural bars in the city—had become Sasha's closest friend. Ani's carefree, wild streak appealed to Sasha. She was always up for anything, any time.

"Ugh. My eyes are floating."

Sasha had been guzzling cocktails for most of the night and had glutted herself on enough blood to keep her sated for at least a week. Thanks to her supernatural metabolism, the alcohol burned out of her system before she could reap its benefits. The blood, on the other hand, gave her a nice buzz that left her feeling pleasantly lightheaded. Even with all the feels, Sasha couldn't drink another drop. She could find someone to fuck or go to another club or hit a quiet bar or two, but what was the point? She didn't have the energy to kick anyone out of her bed at sunrise and she wasn't going to find any entertainment anywhere else that was better or worse than what she could find at Onyx. Gods, she was restless.

"I'm so tired of this scene. There's got to be something more entertaining than drinking, dancing, and hooking up."

Ani gave her a wry smile. "Are you telling me you're tired of gorgeous males throwing themselves at you every night?"

Huh. She guessed she was. Sasha had always been the quiet one. Reserved. Responsible. Dead serious in her role as head of security for her coven and then later, co-ruler. When her maker, Saeed, had left on his quest to find his mate, it had been Sasha's breaking point. For too long she'd put others' needs and happiness before hers. Not anymore.

She'd decided it was time to be selfish. To live her life for herself. She had a lot of time to make up for, damn it. She refused to live with any more regrets.

Sasha didn't reply to Ani's teasing question. She just didn't have the energy. She loved the club scene. Enjoyed being a carefree party-girl. But the thrill was sort of gone. She'd jumped from one rut to another and it was time once again for a change.

Ani let out a long-suffering sigh. "Gods, you're hard to please." She followed up the comment with her trademark snarky smile. "I'm off in an hour. If you don't think it'll kill you to wait, someone told me about an underground scene that's picking up a ton of traction. We could go check it out."

Sounded promising. "What kind of underground scene?"

Ani grinned. "Supernatural Thunderdome."

Sasha snorted. "Like a fight club? I thought that sort of thing quit being edgy when MMA went mainstream."

Ani slid a shot, a Stella, and the cocktail she'd just mixed across the bar to the waitress, who loaded it all on her tray. "Please. No one cares about a bunch of humans knocking each other around. This is like MMA on steroids. Fight to the death."

High stakes for sure. But as creatures who could take a ton of damage without feeling so much as a pinch, Sasha figured it wouldn't be worth it without raising the stakes. No doubt the atmosphere would be wild and dangerous. She needed something to shake her out of her comfort zone. Something to get the blood pumping in her veins. Something that made her feel a little unsafe.

"I'm in."

"Good." Ani grabbed a shot glass and artfully poured three levels of different liquors into the glass before sliding it toward Sasha. "Tastes just like an oatmeal cookie."

Sasha downed the shot. It was okay. A little too sweet, but it did taste a lot like an oatmeal cookie. "Not too bad."

"Go dance and kill some time," Ani said with a laugh. "We'll be out of here in an hour."

Sasha pushed away from the bar and turned toward the dance floor. No sign of the shifter she'd blown off, which was good. Rather than hit the dance floor, though, Sasha headed for the door.

The sidewalk was almost as crowded as the inside of the club. Eager partygoers lined up down the street, waiting for an opportunity to be let inside. At the corner, a guy with a guitar belted out his version of Ed Sheeran's "Shape of You," nodding as passersby dropped bills or coins into his open guitar case. At the opposite end of the block, a couple of hookers fought over something. Thanks to her supernatural hearing, Sasha could have easily eavesdropped, but really, why bother?

The affairs of humans didn't interest her. They never had. Even as a dhampir, Sasha had kept herself separate from humans, careful not to form any entanglements. They were too fragile, their lives too short. Survival had been more important than bothering herself with the rest of the world. Even now, she was an endangered species.

Maybe she wasn't so different from the humans after all. A few centuries ago, when the Sortiari had waged war on the vampires in their misguided quest to manipulate Fate, the vampire race had nearly been eradicated. If not for Mikhail Aristov—the last true vampire—surviving the attacks, the dhampir race would have died off as well. The two races were symbiotic. They needed one another to thrive. When Mikhail finally found his mate and ascended to power, he was able to turn dhampirs into vampires and to replenish their ranks. Sasha was one of ten vampires currently inhabiting the planet. To say their resurgence was tenuous was a bit of an understatement. Especially when rumors circulated that the berserkers who had once been under the Sortiari's control had broken free of their bonds and continued the Sortiari's abandoned quest to obliterate the vampire and dhampir races.

Her existence was far more fragile than she wanted to admit.

And yèt, Sasha went out night after night, blatantly flaunting what she was. She drank from the throats of others in the public view, her fangs extended and lips stained crimson. She enjoyed the curious stares, the wonder, the whispered words, and even the fear she instilled in those around her. Sasha lived her life without restraints. Without shame. Without a single thought as to how her brazen actions would affect those in hers and other covens.

Wow. She really had become a selfish bitch. Then again, the soulless had little reason to worry about things like selflessness, duty, or love.

"Ready to roll?"

She turned to find Ani standing at the edge of the sidewalk a few feet away. She'd been so lost in her thoughts, she hadn't realized she'd managed to whittle an entire hour away on the street.

"Ready." Yep, Sasha was totally selfish. Soulless. And she didn't see her attitude changing any time soon.

Adrenaline coursed through Ewan Brún's veins. His heart thundered in his chest and his skin tightened on his frame. Power surged through him, anxious for an outlet to release its fury on and he was more than ready to free that power on the poor bastard who was about to fall beneath the weight of his fists.

A berserker didn't need a weapon to be deadly. Ewan himself was a weapon.

"If Gregor or any of the others find out what you're up to, you'll get more than a sound beating."

Ewan glanced at Drew, and let out a derisive snort at his cousin's words of warning. When in the grips of full battle rage, a berserker warlord was nearly invincible. The only creature who stood a chance at an equal fight was another berserker. "You're probably right." Ian Gregor, the self-proclaimed king of their clan, didn't approve of any activities that fell outside of his agenda. Gregor was consumed with his need for vengeance. And he expected every single male who answered to him to be as equally consumed.

Unfortunately, Ewan had lost interest in their leader's vendetta years ago.

"That's why no one's going to find out." Ewan trusted Drew. He wouldn't utter a word about his extracurricular activities.

Beyond the confines of the tiny room they occupied, the raucous cheers of the crowd reached a crescendo. Looked like a winner in the current fight was about to be determined, which meant some miserable son of a bitch was about to take a dirt nap. Ewan didn't subscribe to any particular religious belief. God . . . gods . . . a higher power . . . He didn't believe in any of it. Nature made them what they were and when they kissed their asses good-bye, all that awaited them was nothingness.

Bleak? Maybe. But Ewan's soul was shrouded in bleak darkness.

Tonight was about blowing off some steam and walking away with some cash. The supernatural fighting arena wasn't for the faint of heart. If you entered into its confines you were either confident you'd win, or you had a death wish. Ewan wasn't interested in dying. Nor did he doubt his ability to win. He'd take a hefty purse with tonight's win, and after he gave Drew a small cut—after all, familial obligation was only part of earning his loyalty— Ewan would add it to his stash and be one step closer to his goal.

Freedom.

And not the bullshit version of freedom Gregor had promised them. For centuries they'd been indentured to the Sortiari. The so-called guardians of fate had promised Gregor his revenge if he swore allegiance and fought their war for them. He'd gladly accepted the Sortiari's shackles— bringing what was left of their race with him—only to find the Sortiari's promises were as fickle as Fate itself. They'd done the Sortiari's bidding for centuries until Gregor decided they'd been slaves long enough. The revolt had been quiet and free of violence. No doubt, the director of the Sortiari, Trenton McAlister, didn't want the word to get out that his guard dogs had broken their leashes. Still, rather than gift his brethren with their freedom, Gregor had replaced their collars with shackles of his own making. Each and every remaining member of their clan had pledged his undying loyalty to their clan and their leader. Gregor demanded nothing less.

"You keep winning, Gregor's going to know something's up without either one of us telling him. Word's going to spread. And then what?"

Ewan turned his attention from the roar of the crowd to look at Drew. "Fuck Gregor."

"Big talk, cousin." Drew gave a sad shake of his head. "But if he finds out what you're up to, he'll make you watch as he guts you."

Probably, but neither pain nor Gregor's wrath frightened Ewan anymore.

"I keep winning, and I'll finally have enough money to live my life on my own terms. We both will."

Indentured servitude to the Sortiari hadn't exactly been

a lucrative gig. Now free of their so-called *protection*, the berserkers lived in poverty. Squatting wherever they could find shelter and practically begging for scraps in order to feed themselves. Every spare cent they had went to Gregor to fund his ridiculous vendetta. There were rumors Gregor sat on a small fortune that he refused to share in order to make their lives better. It was rarely talked about, however. No one dared to incite their leader's infamous wrath.

Ewan didn't give a shit about whatever money Gregor did or didn't have. He was on the path to independence and there was no turning back. ·

"Who am I fighting tonight?" Ewan usually gave little thought to who he'd go up against. Berserkers sat at the top of the supernatural food chain. That he'd come out the victor was practically guaranteed. His mind was restless tonight, though. His nerves stretched taut as a tingle of anticipation raced down his spine. And he didn't like it one fucking bit.

"Fae," Drew replied with disinterest. "Not sure what kind."

At least his opponent would give Ewan a challenge. Shifters and werewolves were strong, but he'd yet to find one stronger than him. Magic wielders were certainly tricky, but without their magic lacked the physicality necessary to overpower him. Fae, in most instances, possessed both magic and strength. They could be both quick and nimble. Ewan's prize money wouldn't be easily won tonight. He liked that.

"At least it'll be interesting." When the crowd was entertained, it raised the stakes. More money changed hands, which meant more cash in Ewan's pockets.

Drew chuckled. "You've got that right."

Ewan did little to prepare himself for the fight. No wraps to cover his knuckles, no protection of any kind. Why bother? He healed almost instantaneously and he didn't feel pain in the same way other creatures did. As far as the supernatural world was concerned, he was a freak of nature. Beyond their comprehension. Feared. Reviled.

And he liked it that way.

Beyond the confines of the room, the crowd broke out into another round of chaotic cheers that refused to wind down. Ewan brought his gaze up to meet Drew's and held it for a moment. A renewed rush of adrenaline raced through his bloodstream, triggering his body's natural response to the impending fight. A resiliency that made him nearly indestructible.

"Looks like you're on."

Ewan bucked his chin in acknowledgment. "Looks like it."

Drew's lips spread into a wry grin. "Well, what are you waitin' for? Get out there and kick a little ass."

He'd do more than that. Ewan headed for the door. Drew held out his fist and Ewan knocked it with his own. He didn't know if the fight would be over quickly, but he did know it would end with him coming out on top.

Ewan walked up the incline of a narrow concrete tunnel that led from the basement of the building to the ground floor where the fights were being held this particular night. The location changed regularly. Each building was protected by magic to deter humans, and likewise reinforced with darker magic to shield them from supernatural authorities who might be interested in shutting them down. Those wards weren't as foolproof, however, which was why secrecy was key. Ewan didn't care about getting busted. He hated to admit it, but his only concern was Gregor finding out. He took his beatings in the battle arena. He wasn't interested in facing off with the most infamous berserker warlord to ever live.

Pomp and circumstance didn't exist in this place. There

were no flashy introductions, no grand entrances. No posturing and crowing for the bloodthirsty crowd. They simply dragged the dead from the arena, lauded the victor, and moved on to the next fight.

Ewan wasn't a hero. Never had been. He was a killer, plain and simple. And it was time to go out there and show the eager crowd exactly what he was capable of.

CHAPTER
2

A surge of electric anticipation raced through Sasha's veins. It tightened her stomach and caused her heart to pick up its pace with every step she took toward the arena. Ani led the way, winding a path through the shoulder-to-shoulder packed crowd so they could get a front-row view of the action. The L.A. club scene—supernatural clubs included—was tame in comparison to the world they'd just immersed themselves in.

The very atmosphere was charged with violence. Heavy with it. Magic thickened the air to the point that it pressed in on Sasha's lungs, making it difficult to breathe. A diverse variety of supernatural creatures were present, but Sasha was certain she was the only vampire in the building. Curious eyes followed her, some brazen in their admiration, others narrowed with suspicion or outright aggression. Sasha didn't cower from their open stares. Instead, she met them look for look, her head held high, her demeanor proud. She invited their lust, their hatred, and even their fear. She enjoyed the attention almost as much as she enjoyed the thrill of this new and dangerous place.

Ani turned back to look at Sasha and grinned. "Well, whaddya think?"

"I'm definitely not bored." They'd barely walked through the door, and already Sasha knew she'd be back.

"Hell yeah, you're not." Ani grabbed Sasha's hand and pulled her close as they reached the webbed silver fence that formed the cage of the battle arena. "Buckle up, Buttercup. Because shit's about to get real."

A new match was about to begin. The crowd cheered, agitated and eager for violence. The scent of blood from the previous fight reached Sasha's nostrils and she inhaled deeply as her own thirst was awakened. She welcomed the dry burn at the back of her throat and the gentle throb of her fangs in her gums. The discomfort kept her on edge and some small masochistic part of her liked it.

Self-destructive? Maybe. But Sasha no longer possessed the depth of emotion necessary to care.

A willowy female with waist-length, blush pink hair wandered through the crowd, a tray balanced perfectly on her palm. It was laden with champagne flutes filled nearly to the rim with a seemingly thick liquid that swirled like molten gold. Ani plucked two flutes from the tray and handed one to Sasha.

"Faery wine," she remarked. Her full lips spread into an indulgent smile. "It's illegal to serve to even supernaturals. It can be highly addictive if you drink too much. But it gives you one hell of a buzz."

"Nice." One of Sasha's biggest complaints with drinking alcohol was the fact that it had no effect on her. For once, she wouldn't have to drink blood to experience a pleasant high. She brought the glass to her lips. The faery wine smelled like flower nectar. Sweet. Floral. Heady. She took a tentative sip and her eyes drifted shut for an indulgent moment.

"It's the tits, right?" Ani said with a grin.

Sasha took another drink, deeper this time, before letting out a soft chuckle. The wine slid smoothly down her throat to settle as a warm glow in the pit of her stomach. Its effects were almost instantaneous as a giddy lightheadedness settled over her. Sasha swayed on her feet and her friend leaned in to steady her. Laughter bubbled up Sasha's throat and refused to stop.

"It's totally the tits!" Sasha's hand came up to cover her mouth. "Oops! Am I shouting?" Her voice boomed in her ears and she took another deep drink from her flute before crumbling into another round of silly laughter.

"Okaaaaay. I'm thinking no more than one of these for you tonight." Ani brought her own glass to her lips and sipped. The faery liquor didn't seem to have the same effect on her and Sasha wrinkled her nose.

Gods, she was a little embarrassed she was such a lightweight!

"Only one? Come on, I have to build up a tolerance!" Was she still shouting? Were her words slurred? She really couldn't tell. Another round of giddy laughter threatened, and Sasha swallowed it down. She didn't want to come off as an innocent newb. She was a badass vampire, damn it! She had to at least pretend she had her shit together.

"Take it easy, Tiger." Ani wrapped her arms around Sasha's waist to keep her upright. "One's enough, trust me. You're going to have one hell of a hangover in the morning."

Sasha responded with spluttering laughter. "I'm a vampire! I won't be up in the morning!"

Ani rolled her eyes. "Morning, evening, whatever. When you wake up, you're going to feel like you've been hit by a truck."

Sasha had never had a hangover before. *Cool.* "Bring it

on! I'm ready to be hung over!" She pumped her fist in celebration.

Ani chuckled. "Uh-huh. We'll see how you feel about it tomorrow."

The crowd broke out into rowdy cheers, signaling the start of a new match. Sasha's gaze was drawn to the caged arena and her breath stalled in her chest as she waited for the competitors to enter. Anticipation danced up her spine, a sensation unlike anything she'd ever felt. A side effect of the faery wine? Or something more?

A tall, muscular fae entered the arena first. Most of faery kind wore their hair long, but this male had clipped his short. The style accentuated his otherworldly features, elongating the square line of his jaw and making his cheekbones appear sharper, as though they protruded from his face. Sasha took him in from the fine points of his ears, past his broad shoulders and too-narrow torso, to his sturdy thighs and bare feet that were planted firmly on the concrete floor. If she had to judge by appearance alone, she would consider the fae quite formidable. Whoever faced him in the arena certainly had his or her work cut out for them.

The second competitor entered the arena and in unison, the crowd went deathly silent. Still considerably buzzed, Sasha was slow to react, taking her time before she pulled her attention from the fae to the competitor that had caused such a dramatic stir. A delicious scent hit Sasha's nostrils, awakening each one of her senses, and sobering her in an instant. Dry heat ignited in her throat, the thirst so intense that it rivaled what she felt upon her turning. Her secondary fangs punched down from her gums, throbbing almost painfully.

Dear gods. If she didn't find the source of that delicious smell, she'd go out of her mind.

"Sasha? Are you okay?"

Ani's words barely registered. Sasha's eyes went wide as a second male entered the arena. Tall, broad, impossibly thick with muscle. He'd yet to fight but sweat already glistened on his bare chest and shoulders that were lightly dusted with freckles. Her gaze wandered past the ridges of his abs to where a pair of loose workout pants hung from his hips. He stood rooted firmly to the floor, his feet bare as well. His toes flexed against the concrete floor and even that simple act exhibited more strength than Sasha thought possible. She dragged her eyes back up the length of his body to settle on his face. Hard. Rugged. His square jaw was rough with light auburn stubble, the exact same shade as the mop of hair on his head. His expression was cut from stone. Serious. Deadly. Void of any hint of emotion. Her eyes met his, and his golden brown irises went dark as night, causing Sasha's breath to stall in her chest as an inexplicable force slammed into her.

"Sasha?" Ani gave her a rough shake. "What's going on? Talk to me!"

Sasha drew in a gasping breath as her soul was returned, filling her body close to bursting. She clutched at her chest as though to banish the sensation. How was this possible? Her soul had been returned to her! By the terrifying male who'd stepped into the arena.

"Sasha, come on! You're scaring me."

She gave a violent shake of her head as though somehow she could wake herself from this nightmare. Words formed and died on her tongue. How could this have happened? How was it even possible? His scent . . . so inviting and delicious. It shouldn't have been so. He should have smelled like death, and rot, and . . .

Sasha took a deep breath to calm the tremor in her voice. "I . . . I'm okay." She couldn't tell Ani what had just happened. She couldn't tell anyone. She gave a nervous laugh that she hoped didn't sound too fake. "That wine hit me a little hard, that's all."

Ani's brow furrowed as she gave Sasha a look. "Are you sure that's all? You looked pretty damned shaken up."

Sasha offered up a weak smile in response. "I'm fine." Truth be told, she couldn't be further from fine. She'd left fine about ten miles back and had entered into holy-shit-I'm-so-fucked territory. A low murmur spread through the crowd and by slow degrees elevated to an excited roar. Sasha's gaze slid back to the dangerous male and she swallowed against the insistent burn of thirst in her throat.

She'd been tethered.

By a berserker.

Ewan stretched his head from side to side and his neck cracked. He brought his arms high above his head and swung them down. Out in front of him, and behind. His muscles were warm, his body loose. The anticipation of the coming fight vibrated through him but no longer caused him to tense. Instead, he relaxed into a fighting stance and let out a slow, even breath. Completely unflappable.

The crowd had gone silent upon his entrance into the arena. He was used to it. The supernatural community feared his kind and rightfully so. They were hardened killers, each and every one. Genetically designed for battle, predisposed to violence. He felt more at home in this arena than he'd felt anywhere in a long damned time.

Including the company of his own brethren.

A female's voice caught his attention and Ewan scanned the crowd. At the far end of the arena at the edge of the silver cage that kept them contained within its confines, he spotted her. His gut knotted as a strange thrill chased through him. She wobbled on her feet and another female helped to steady her. Who was she? And why did he suddenly feel as though he were about to be tossed ass over teakettle?

Without warning, the battle master's voice rang out to signal the start of the fight. "Choose your weapons!"

He opened a large case that contained two of each weapon: daggers, machetes, short swords, knives, silver cords, and iron maces. The fae stepped forward, his moss-green gaze hard as he chose two delicate daggers. Light and easy to wield with razor sharp blades and pointed tips guaranteed to do a little damage. Ewan grinned as the fae spun the daggers artfully in his grip, giving the crowd something to cheer about. The battle master turned to him and offered up the case for Ewan to choose a weapon. He simply stared back and shook his head.

The crowd quieted for a moment as the realization spread that he'd refused any weapon with which to kill or defend himself with. The quiet was short-lived as everyone present hollered and shouted their approval. Ewan had just guaranteed them all a grand finale to tonight's fights. Their entertainment meant more money in his pockets. He was happy to oblige. Besides, choosing a weapon would only give him more of an advantage in an already unfair fight.

The battle master closed the case and stepped out of the arena. Anticipation thickened the air and Ewan's attention wandered back to the female who watched the goings-on with wide eyes. Her dark hair cascaded over one shoulder, polished mahogany against the pale backdrop of her bare skin. He couldn't bring himself to look away. He wanted her.

Ewan's opponent capitalized on his momentary distraction and went after him, landing a solid blow to Ewan's jaw. He reeled backward and the fae advanced, spinning as his leg came around in a roundhouse kick that connected with Ewan's chest.

Motherfucker. He blew out a forceful breath to clear the cobwebs from his head. The bastard had gotten lucky, but Ewan wouldn't be caught off guard again. He put the female to the back of his mind. She was inconsequential, a distraction he couldn't afford. There was too much at stake—his reputation, for starters—and he wasn't about to lose face. Ewan was here for one reason and one reason only: money. And he wasn't going to earn a penny if he didn't keep his head in the gods-damned game.

The fae came at him once again, but this time Ewan was ready. Anger and aggression turned to power. It flooded his limbs, his muscles, and centered his focus. Nothing mattered but the fight. The female who'd drawn his attention faded to the back of his mind as well as the bloodthirsty crowd that cheered them on. His surroundings blurred until nothing remained but him and his opponent. His vision shifted from full-color to shades of black, white, and gray. His senses sharpened. Every minute motion made by the fae translated into sound, allowing Ewan to anticipate his movements at the exact moment he executed them. It made Ewan's reaction time instantaneous—as though he knew what his opponent would do before he did it.

Ewan blocked a wide sweep of the fae's arm, knocking the dagger from his grip, and countered with a jab to the male's face. The fae took several stumbling steps back but recovered quickly and retrieved the discarded dagger in a graceful blur of speed as he rushed at Ewan once again. He was certainly formidable. Strong, quick, surefooted. Ewan still couldn't determine what faction of fae the male happen to be, but it didn't really matter. Whether he was elemental or one of the powerful *bean sidhe*, he'd beat the bastard either way.

The fae's lip curled into a sneer. "I'm going to do the world a favor by making sure there's one less berserker in the world."

Big talk. Ewan expected nothing less. What the fae didn't realize was that Ewan couldn't be fazed. It was impossible to get into a berserker's head. Ewan grinned as he easily swept aside another attempted blow aimed at his throat with his right hand and followed up with a sharp left uppercut. His fist connected with the male's chin, whose head whipped back. The fae recovered quickly, showcasing his quick reflexes, and swiped at the blood that trickled from his nose.

Big mistake, you fastidious bastard.

His opponent's vanity worked to Ewan's advantage. Usually, he liked to drag out a fight. Give the crowd a good show and encourage money to change hands. For some reason though, Ewan felt the urge to end this quickly. As though his time tonight would be better spent elsewhere. He knew of nothing a berserker enjoyed more than fighting. His curiosity burned, only adding to his impatience.

"Going to do the world a favor, are you?" He didn't usually engage with his opponents. Tonight had him all kinds of thrown off. "Well then, you'd better get the fuck on with it." Ewan's taunting words were enough to spur the fae to action. He'd been playing coy before, holding back, prolonging the fight, perhaps for the same reasons Ewan did. Now though, the fae unleashed his fury on Ewan in a blur of movement that required every ounce of his concentration and skill to defend against. The male was a warrior. A fighter worthy of Ewan. Finally.

It was almost a shame he had to kill him.

Another surge of power shot through Ewan, this one more intense than the first. The prospect of an evenly matched fight ignited his bloodlust and triggered the battle rage that stirred fear in the hearts of immortals and fueled the legends of humankind. His body moved as though on autopilot, no longer in his control. Ewan gave himself over to instinct and shut his mind down completely. The crowd outside of the silver cage went wild and he knew how he looked to them. Eyes black as night, with inky tendrils bleeding out onto his cheeks. Muscles bulging, veins engorged and standing out on his flesh, pulled tight over his frame. His lips pulled back into a snarl to reveal his teeth as he let out a roar that vibrated his vocal cords. The fight would be over soon. The fae would be dead. And Ewan would have virtually no memory as to how any of it happened.

He entered another state of awareness. One where he merely existed, shrouded in shadow. His body moved, his arms and legs swept out, to kick, parry, and jab. His breath left his chest as he took a blow, and then another. He felt nothing. Yet, he fought. He raged. And he decimated his opponent.

Ewan dragged in a sharp breath as he came back into himself. He stood over the broken and bleeding body of the fae, the daggers still clutched in his fists. A supernatural creature was hard to kill. With nothing more than his fists, he'd beaten the fae bloody and ripped his head from his spine. Perhaps it was a blessing that he had no recollection of what he'd done.

The crowd went deathly silent once again before breaking out into wild shouts and cheers. Some cursed his very existence and that of every berserker on the planet, while others celebrated his victory as cash exchanged hands. Ewan's breath sawed in and out of his chest. His shoulders dropped as his fist relaxed at his sides. The sensation of his skin tightening on his frame abated with every exhaled breath and color bled into his vision to banish the shades of gray.

The battle master approached. The male's fear burned

Ewan's nostrils and he let out a rueful snort. The world was afraid of him, and rightly so. He was a fucking monster. "The victor!" The battle master reached out with a tentative hand and gently took Ewan's wrist before raising his arm in the air. Just as quickly, he released his hold and took several cautious steps back. Ewan paid it no mind. He was used to fear. He'd been on the receiving end of it his entire life.

His gaze scanned the crowd before he even realized what he was looking for. His eyes found her, and Ewan went still. Her dark, haunting beauty called to him and he was helpless not to answer. The web of silver that constructed the dome began to slowly rise from the battle arena. Brave supernaturals flooded the concrete floor, eager to congratulate him and perhaps gain a powerful ally. He paid them no mind, pushing his way past the bodies that stood between him and the female. Her gaze locked with his and her full lips parted to reveal the razor sharp points of her fangs.

Vampire.

Ewan nearly tripped on his own feet. By all rights, he was required to kill her on sight. Gregor would accept nothing less. To let her live would be the ultimate betrayal, one that would cost Ewan his life. But with every step he took to close the distance between them, Ewan knew that he wouldn't kill her. Couldn't.

Why?

Within seconds he stood before her. Close enough to touch. He breathed in deeply of her sweet cinnamon scent and held it in his lungs before letting it out in a slow, measured breath that did nothing to temper the white hot lust that overtook him.

"Your name, vampire." He barked out the demand without an ounce of pleasantry. He stood face to face with a mortal enemy and all he could think of doing was running his nose along the creamy flesh of her throat in order to savor her delicious scent.

The vampire bucked her chin defiantly as she squared her shoulders and further closed the gap between them. Brave. Fierce. Seductive. "Sasha Ivanov. And your name . . . *berserker* . . . ?" She let the question hang but Ewan didn't miss the challenge in her tone. One delicate brow arched over her eye and he fought the urge to smile.

It appeared as though he would have one more secret to keep from their leader. Because he'd be damned if he raised so much as a finger against her. She fascinated him. And he was no longer interested in playing by Gregor's rules.

CHAPTER
3

The berserker didn't offer his name. Instead, he flashed a smile that was almost cruel. Sadistic. Did he know what he'd done to her? What he'd inadvertently done to himself? Sasha studied him for a quiet moment. He was one of the most reviled creatures in the supernatural world, and yet, she was drawn to him unlike any other. His scent—sweet when it should have been rancid—ignited her thirst. The sight of him drove her mad with want. She'd watched his display of violence with morbid fascination, not even a little scared. Okay, maybe a little. But it only added to the thrill.

He seized her by the wrist and turned to walk away. At the same moment, Ani reached out to grab Sasha's other hand. "Are you crazy, Sasha?" The sylph's eyes practically bulged out of her head with disbelief. "You can't go with him!"

No, she probably shouldn't. But that's exactly what Sasha was going to do. She disengaged her hand from Ani's grip. "I'll be all right. I'll catch up with you later."

"Sasha."

The urgency in her friend's voice gave her pause. "It's okay." She didn't have time to explain her situation. At this point, she didn't even know if she wanted to explain it. "I'll text you later. I promise."

The berserker gave an urgent tug on her wrist and Sasha followed his lead through the crowd. She had no idea where he was leading her and she didn't care. She was a slave to her thirst. To her desire. To this dangerous male who'd tethered her soul without even realizing it. For all she knew, he was about to take her to a back alley where he would kill her. If that were the case, Sasha hoped he'd do it quickly. Because honestly, what other option was there for two mortal enemies who'd been inexorably bound together by fate?

No matter what, Sasha knew she was on the road to disaster.

The berserker paid no mind to those brave enough to congratulate him on his victory. His grip tightened around Sasha's wrist as he led her down the narrow concrete hallway. They came to a stop where the corridor branched off into two hallways. It only took a moment for him to come to a decision and he pulled Sasha to the left and into the nearest bathroom. He didn't utter a single word as he spun her to face him and backed her up to the counter.

Sasha's heart raced in her chest. Adrenaline dumped into her bloodstream, the fight-or-flight reflex at war with her own raging thirst and desire. The berserker closed the space between them, leaning into Sasha's body. His arms came to rest on the countertop on either side of her to pin her in place. Long moments passed and he simply stared. There was nothing soft in his expression. Nothing tender. So void of emotion it caused a chill to race down Sasha's spine. There was heat, though. Intensity. Something so foreign to her that she didn't really know how to interpret it.

"I should kill you." His voice was a low, dangerous

growl. Sasha's stomach muscles contracted and a warm, wet rush spread between her thighs. The very vulnerable position she'd put herself in shouldn't have been a turn-on and yet, every inch of her vibrated with anticipation. The berserker leaned in close until his lips brushed the outer shell of her ear. "But I'm going to fuck you instead."

Oh gods. Sasha's lids drifted shut at his heated words. She didn't know what to think, how to feel. Instinct and the tether that had instantaneously bound her to him guided her. Heat unfurled within her like a length of fiery ribbon. Her breaths were quick and tight, and her eyes remained closed as she waited for him to act. He dropped his nose to her throat and inhaled. A low growl gathered in his chest and Sasha swore she felt its vibration over every inch of her skin.

The suspense continued to ratchet to the point that she didn't think she could take another second. Her arms remained braced on the counter behind her, fingers flexing as she gripped the edge. She swallowed against the dryness in her throat, desperate to pierce his skin and glut herself on his blood, and yet unable to do so. A tremor settled in her thighs as her body went rigid with anticipation. No male had ever affected her in such a visceral way after having done so very little to arouse her.

Sasha drew in a surprised gasp as he seized her by the hips and spun her around. He reached in front of her to unfasten her jeans before jerking them, along with her underwear, down around her ankles. Sasha allowed her eyes to open to find him watching her reflection in the bathroom mirror. Once again, the dark intensity of his gaze caused her heart to stutter in her chest and the Formica countertop cracked beneath her fingernails as she tightened her grip.

He reached between them. His hand brushed her bare ass as he yanked down the loose-fitting workout pants past his hips. He laid his palm to her back and pressed her down, not roughly but with insistence. Sasha had never been so ready to be taken. Her body trembled, her thighs slick with arousal. Her own heartbeat thundered in her ears and silver overtook her irises as she held his gaze in the mirror.

He put his hands to her hips and jerked her backward, angling her exactly how he wanted her. The heat of his erection probed at her opening and Sasha sucked in a sharp breath. He drove home with every ounce of urgency she felt and she let out an indulgent moan of relief as he filled her completely. Sasha expected this to be nothing more than a quick, urgent interlude that would end before it even had a chance to begin. Instead, the berserker took his time with her. He fucked her slow and deep, every thrust executed as though he'd carefully planned it out. Sasha couldn't tear her eyes away from his reflection. His auburn brows bunched together on his forehead, his jaw squared, and his nostrils flared with every labored breath. She waited for the moment when inky black would overtake his beautiful dark gold irises and fan out in terrifying tendrils over his cheeks. That moment never came. The monster she'd been taught to fear never showed its face. He reached between her legs and slid his fingers over her pussy until he found the swollen nerves of her clit.

His touch broke her apart in an instant.

Sasha cried out as pleasure radiated through her. The deep pulsing waves crashed over her, battered her, and left her raw and shaken. Her gaze never left his. The intimacy of it betrayed the casual way they'd ended up here. His eyes became hooded as he dragged his fingers through her wetness before pulling his hand back to her hip as his thrusts became faster, wild and disjointed.

He let out a low moan as he thrust hard and deep one last time. His body trembled against her as he held her tight and his head fell back on his shoulders. Sasha's head dropped to rest on her arms as she fought to catch her breath. His hands left her hips to once again brace his weight against the countertop and he remained buried inside of her for several moments before pulling out.

Sasha let out a shuddering breath as she was overtaken with emotion. The hinges of the bathroom door squeaked and groaned with the berserker's passage and Sasha looked up into the mirror to find herself alone. Tears pricked at her eyes moments before their wet warmth slid down her cheeks. She had no idea why she cried. It could've been the return of her soul, or her own misfortune that prompted her tears. More likely, it was the sheer intensity of the past moments that prompted such an emotional response. Even now, she was raw, shaken, and so weak she wasn't sure she could support her own weight. Thirst burned in her throat, unquenched. The berserker's scent lingered on her skin and Sasha drew in a deep breath and held it in her lungs. She didn't dare move. Couldn't. There was too damned much to process and she couldn't wrap her head around it all. She swiped at her cheeks and forced herself to quell the sudden burst of emotions that she wasn't prepared to deal with. She'd gotten used to not having a soul. Enjoyed her watered-down feelings. In a single moment the berserker had taken everything she'd made herself into over the past several months and decimated it.

He hadn't killed her. But he might've damned well destroyed her.

Ewan's legs were as sturdy as Jell-O as he rushed down the corridor toward the tiny room where Drew waited for him. They'd agreed early on that if Drew didn't actually watch him fight he still had a certain amount of deniability that would protect him if Gregor found out what they were up to. He took several deep breaths in an attempt to slow his racing heart and scrubbed a hand over his face.

Gods. What in the hell had he just done?

Sasha's face was burned in his memory. He still felt the tingle of sensation from where their bodies touched. Her cries of passion echoed in his ears and he reached down to adjust his erection that jutted out from his gods-damned pants. He was hard as a fucking stone and ready to have her again. His step faltered as he considered turning around and burying himself to the hilt in all of that tight, wet heat once more. But fighting and killing for money was an offense worthy of a slap on the wrist compared to what he'd just done.

Taking the vampire—and likewise, walking away afterward—was beyond treasonous. The ultimate betrayal. Ewan couldn't muster an ounce of guilt, however. He'd wanted her. He wanted her still. And now that he'd had her he didn't experience the sense of relief—of release—he thought he'd feel. Instead, the sultry vampire had managed to work her way under his skin in an instant. Ewan knew that once would not be enough.

"What took you so long?" Drew pushed himself up from the bench as Ewan entered the makeshift locker room. "From the sounds of it, the fight was over a half hour ago."

Had it been that long? He raked his fingers through his hair and let out a forceful breath. "The crowd was rowdy tonight. Lots of sore losers and ecstatic winners."

Drew smirked. "I thought you'd drag it out longer. Must've been antsy tonight, huh?"

That was one way to put it. His focus had been shit, his brain too full of Sasha to concentrate on anything else. He was still rattled. Still preoccupied. He might've been in this room talking to Drew, but his mind was back there, with her.

Ewan shrugged. "Wasn't much of a challenge. I didn't see any point in dragging it out."

"As long as you get paid, I guess it doesn't matter, right?" Drew folded his arms across his chest as he regarded Ewan. "You look a little on edge, cousin. What happened up there?"

He swallowed down an amused snort. It's not like Drew would believe him if he told him the truth. "Lost myself deep in the fight tonight. That's all."

He didn't have to explain himself further. Drew knew exactly what he meant. "You'll sleep it off and feel fine in the morning."

Giving themselves over to mindless battle rage took its toll. Drew was right. In most cases Ewan would sleep it off and be right as rain the next day. It wasn't the fight that had him on edge, though. And a good night's rest wasn't going to do shit for what plagued him. He settled down onto the bench that Drew had occupied a moment before and rested his elbows on his knees as he let his head hang between his shoulders.

"When's the next fight?" The only thing that might have a chance of distracting him from the vampire was the opportunity to make a shitload of fast cash. If he was too busy fighting, he wouldn't be tempted to go looking for her. The only thing that would get him was a world of trouble.

"Day after tomorrow," Drew replied. "They're switching venues again. An abandoned gym somewhere in the Valley. The address will be texted to me the day of."

"Good." The chances of the vampire finding him at a new venue might be slim. He needed to do everything in his power to ensure he didn't see her again. He'd played with fire tonight and enjoyed the lick of flames far too much. He had enough to worry about, he couldn't afford to pile one more thing on his plate.

"Did you collect the purse?"

Ewan looked up at Drew. "Not yet." He'd been too ob-sessed with the vampire to give a single shit about the money he'd won.

"Get it and let's go," Drew said. "Gregor's got a bug up his butt tonight and wants everyone front and center."

Great. What could he possibly want now? Gregor's san-ity—as well as his temper—balanced on a razor's edge lately. If any of them was unaccounted for when he snapped his high-and-mighty fingers, there'd be hell to pay. "An-other wild goose chase, no doubt."

For months, they'd been doing Gregor's bidding, one unreasonable task after another, all of them seemingly without rhyme or reason. They'd had a brief reprieve while Gregor and a few of his most trusted soldiers had gone to Seattle to find . . . Hell, Ewan had no idea. But now that he was back, there would be no rest. At least, not until Ewan made enough money to get the fuck out of here and as far from Gregor—and his own past—as possible.

Drew shrugged. "Not sure. At any rate, I'm not inter-ested in keeping him waiting."

Honestly, neither was Ewan. Ian Gregor was the last male on the planet he wanted to piss off. "I'll get our money and meet you out front." He pushed himself up from the bench. Gods, it was going to be a long night.

"All right." Drew cut him a look. "You sure you're okay?"

Not by a long fucking shot. "Yeah." He made his tone as light as possible. "We better get our asses in gear. I don't want to give anyone reason to question where we've been."

"You and me both, cousin," Drew said. "I'll get the car."

Ewan waited for Drew to leave the locker room before settling back down on the bench. He blew out another slow breath that did nothing to calm the storm that brewed within him. He didn't have the energy or presence of mind for one of Gregor's insane missions tonight. His eyes drifted shut and his mouth went slack as he relived the memory of fucking Sasha. He'd only scratched the surface of what he'd wanted to do with her. Had yearned to put his lips to her satin-smooth flesh. He'd wanted to touch her. To let his palms roam freely over every inch of her. He'd wanted her naked. Completely exposed to him and on display for his gaze to admire. He was far from satisfied.

He'd lost himself so easily to her. It stung his pride as much as it piqued his curiosity. He should've wanted to kill her. Should've gladly carried the burden of Gregor's vendetta. He could have led her away tonight and run a silver dagger through her heart. One look at her, however, and causing her harm was the last thing on his mind. Was she a vampire, or a gods-damned witch? Because he'd fallen easily enough under her seductive spell.

He'd wasted enough time. Ewan once again pushed himself up from the bench. He rolled his shoulders before swiping up his discarded T-shirt and gym bag from a nearby shelf. Funny how these moments spent in the silver cage made him feel more normal than any other in his miserable existence. He lived a shadow of a life, one constructed by a madman hell-bent on vengeance. And until he won his freedom, nothing was going to change.

CHAPTER
4

"Late night?"

Weren't they all? The night was all they had until the sun rose and they were forced to hide and succumb to the oblivion of sleep. Sasha fixed Diego with a narrow eyed gaze. "Don't you have anything better to do than spy on me?"

Diego leaned against the doorjamb and hiked a casual shoulder. "Not really. Now that Saeed has reassumed leadership of the coven, I find myself in need of a distraction."

Sasha snorted. As Sasha's one-time co-ruler of the coven, Diego might've sounded put out, but she knew he was happy to have handed the reins back over to Saeed. "You need a hobby. Have you considered taking up knitting?"

Diego chuckled at the not-so-gentle barb. "Are you saying I'm boring?"

Her eyes went wide with feigned innocence. "Of course not! I mean, you bought full-sugar soda the other day. You're totally living on the wild side."

Before her transition, Sasha would never have even considered being a smart-ass. In fact, she wouldn't have been adventurous enough to drink whole milk, let alone the sugary Coke Diego loved. She'd been the epitome of boring. Safe. Uninteresting. Regimented. It was why Saeed had put the coven's security, and later, leadership, in her hands in the first place. Diego was none of those things she'd once considered herself. She was simply in a foul mood and misery loved company.

"Sorry." Sasha let out a slow breath. "I had a shitty night."

Diego pushed away from the doorjamb and walked farther into her room. "Want to talk about it?"

Suuuure. She'd love to tell him how she'd been tethered by a berserker in the middle of an underground supernatural battle arena and then promptly let one of their mortal enemies bend her over a bathroom sink and fuck her after watching him rip the head from the shoulders of some poor fae in cold blood.

"Not really."

Diego pursed his lips. His dark eyes roamed over her, contemplative. "You've been going pretty hard lately, Sasha. Maybe it's time to slow down a little."

Indignant fire ignited in her belly. She was so sick of everyone telling her how to live her life. "What I choose to do in my free time is no one's business." She gave him a pointed look. "Including you."

There had been a time when Sasha's two closest friends had been Saeed and Diego. There wasn't anything she wouldn't have done for either of them. But Saeed had abandoned her in favor of his search for his mate, and Diego hadn't seemed interested in Sasha's downward spiral until she'd stopped being responsible and no longer concerned herself with the well-being of the coven. So much for undying loyalty. It seemed that door swung only one way and those Sasha had pledged herself to hadn't been interested in returning the favor.

She'd come to the conclusion that the only person she could rely on was herself. And that those around her who so greedily took of her generous and caring nature weren't interested in reciprocating. So, screw everyone. She wasn't interested in Diego's false concern or anything else.

"It's my business if it interferes with the safety of this coven."

Sasha averted her gaze. The safety and security of the coven had been her responsibility for centuries. Ever since she'd proved herself to Saeed as formidable. Diego had since taken over the responsibilities she'd shirked. She couldn't help but feel like a wild teenager who'd just been caught hanging out with the local drug dealer. Well, in her case it would be more like hanging out with the local crazed-predator-slash-assassin, but she wasn't about to admit to anything. Likewise, it wouldn't do her any good to behave like a teenager and further stir Diego's suspicions. She needed him out of her hair about ten minutes ago. Ani was waiting for her to text and check in and Sasha seriously needed a few minutes alone to decompress and get her head straight. The berserker had approached her in plain view of hundreds of sets of eyes. Something as scandalous as that wouldn't go unnoticed—or untalked about. Gods, she was so wound up she was making up words! Seriously, she needed Diego to get the hell *out*.

"Look, I'm being a good girl. Is that what you want to hear?"

Diego's eyes narrowed and his lips pursed, painting the perfect image of disappointed parent. "It would be if that were the truth."

Sasha rolled her eyes. She hated that Diego and Saeed held her to a higher standard than anyone else. Totally not fair. As though everyone else in the world was allowed to make mistakes and be forgiven, but if Sasha so much as stepped a toe out of line, she'd be as good as excommunicated. Banished and forgotten. Cut off without so much as an ounce of leeway.

"You know what? If you're going to stand there and give me grief till the sun rises, you can do us both a favor and leave me alone. I'm in for the night so you won't have anything to worry about. The precious coven will be safe from whatever nefarious things I'm apparently up to."

She was too angry to feel any guilt about the fact that tonight, her wild extracurricular activities might actually have put the coven in danger. Too hurt to act anything other than indignant. Diego let out a slow breath and his posture relaxed as though in defeat. "If I didn't care about you, I wouldn't ride you so hard. You know that, right?"

Sasha snorted. "If you say so." She was so over this conversation. Diego didn't move an inch as she brought her gaze up to meet his. She held it as she forced a pleasant smile to her face and infused her voice with saccharine calm. "May the rest of the night treat you well, Diego."

His expression fell like a deflated balloon. A twinge of regret tugged at Sasha's chest and she forced the unwelcome emotion away. "May the rest of the night treat you well, Sasha." He returned the formal words of parting and left without another word.

Sasha sank back onto the sofa and allowed her head to fall back onto the cushions. Unspent adrenaline pooled in her limbs and her unquenched thirst raged like wildfire eating dry grass. The berserker's scent still swam in her head, an intoxicating aroma that made her mouth water and her body hum. He shouldn't have smelled so delicious. He should have repulsed her instead of enticing her. She ached with want. Could still feel the grip of his strong hands at her hips and the powerful thrust of his hips as he drove into her. Her heart pounded in her chest and the influx of emotions that besieged her left Sasha weak and shaken.

She dragged a hand across her mouth and the point of one sharp fang pierced the skin near one of her knuckles, coaxing a drop of blood to form and run in a rivulet toward her thumb. She licked the blood away but it did little to sate her. Nothing but the berserker's blood would calm the fire that raged in her throat.

Fuck.

The situation was beyond catastrophic. The tether was absolute. Unbreakable. The only thing that could sever it was death and if Saeed found out what had happened, Sasha was certain her soul would be freed from her body once again. A tether between a vampire and berserker wouldn't be tolerated. And without her mate, Sasha would be doomed to spend eternity as one of the soulless.

Empty. Forever.

It was a fate of unimaginable suffering. A torture she didn't think she'd be able to endure. If anyone found out about her bond with the berserker, they might as well do her a favor and run a stake through her heart. Because she knew without a doubt that she wouldn't survive losing her soul a second time.

Tears stung at Sasha's eyes but she willed them to dry. She was still far too raw to give the impression she had her shit together and said a silent prayer of thanks that the sun would soon be up to carry her away to the blissful oblivion of daytime sleep. Before she could escape reality, though, she needed to let Ani know she was all right.

Sasha shifted on the couch and fished her cell from her back pocket. She could have texted but she simply didn't have the energy to type out answers for every question Ani would undoubtedly have. The sylph answered on the first ring. Eager much?

"What the actual fuck did I see tonight?" Ani's incredulous tone coaxed a smile to Sasha's lips despite her dire situation. "A berserker coming on to a vampire? Did the apocalypse start and no one told me?"

Incredulous with a dash of eager and a splash of alarmist. Sasha didn't think she had the energy to deal with any more drama tonight. It wouldn't do her any good to lie about what had happened though, or try to gloss it over. She needed to confide in someone or she'd go out of her mind. Ani was the only person she could tell.

"He tethered me." The words left her lips in a guilt-laden whisper.

She was answered with a space of silence in which she imagined Ani's head exploding. "He what, now?" Her voice squeaked as it reached a decibel only werewolves could hear. Yup. She'd definitely short circuited.

"He tethered me." Sasha still couldn't believe it herself. "The berserker returned my soul. He's . . ." Gods, was she really going to say it out loud? "He's my . . . mate."

Having her fangs pulled out with rusty pliers would have been less painful than making that admission.

"I'm coming over."

Ugh. No. The last thing she needed was for Diego to blow a blood vessel over Ani hanging around the house. "The sun will be up in a few hours and I'll be out. So it's not like there's going to be any gossip going on." Honestly, Sasha didn't think she wanted to give Ani any more information than she'd already given her. "I'll see you at sundown tomorrow."

"Fine." Ani sounded put out but she'd live. "I'll be there the *second* the sun goes down."

And not a moment later, Sasha was sure. "Tomorrow." Already the weight of sleep tugged at her limbs and eyelids. She felt like she'd gone through the wringer. She needed to rest. "Bye." The word left her lips a little slurred as she ended the call.

Sasha couldn't help but think that tonight was the beginning of the end.

Ewan's brain was a dark mass of brambles, so tangled he barely had the presence of mind to put one foot in front of the other. He'd made a right fucking mess tonight. One that was bound to bring undue attention to his extracurricular activities. He couldn't afford for Gregor—or anyone—to find out what he was up to. Not when he could practically taste his damn freedom. He snorted. Who was he kidding? After tonight's spectacle, the only freedom he'd know was death.

There was no way he could keep what had happened a secret. Of course, no one had seen him drag the vampire into the bathroom. No one knew he'd bent her over the countertop and fucked her soundly. Ewan sucked in a breath. The memory of her soft skin and tight heat was a sweet torture he wanted to relive again and again.

"Did you hear the rumors circulating around the arena?"

Drew's voice broke into the heated images of Ewan's memories and he scowled. "What rumors?" His gut knotted tight. As though he had to ask.

Drew glanced at Ewan from the corner of his eye as he drove through downtown. "There was a vampire there, watching. A female. Did you see her?"

He could lie to his cousin, but what would be the point? "Aye. She kicked up a bit of a stir."

"You went after her, didn't you?" Well, that was true enough. Though Ewan suspected not in the way his cousin meant. "I heard two shifters talking as I was leaving to get the car. They said you got right to business and put the fae down. When you were done, you headed straight for the female."

The animosity between the berserkers and vampires

was legendary. A feud that spanned centuries. No doubt any onlookers that saw Ewan approach the vampire assumed it was an act of aggression. He could only hope if Gregor found out, he'd make the same assumption.

Ewan cleared his throat. Drew would smell the lie on him if he wasn't very careful with his words. "The vampires are becoming brazen." Of course, he couldn't speak for other vampires, but Sasha certainly wasn't afraid. Of anyone or anything. Gods, that bravery heated his blood and only served to further spark his curiosity. "They're not afraid of us anymore."

Drew turned to face him. "Is anyone afraid of us anymore?"

Ewan snorted. Drew had a point. Without the backing of the Sortiari, were the berserkers any more threatening than any other supernatural creature that inhabited the earth? Gregor seemed to think they were, but that was the disillusionment of ego. Sure, they sat atop the food chain due to their strength, cunning, and ability to heal from any wound. The only way to kill a berserker was to sever their heads. That made them damned near invincible. But they weren't gods. Without the Sortiari's power, they were just one more faction living among the masses. Ewan held no misconceptions as to what they were and likewise, what they weren't.

Gregor would be wise not to fall victim to his hubris. Then again, when did their self-proclaimed king ever listen to reason?

"Did you speak to her?" Drew's curiosity about the vampire wouldn't be easily quashed. Ewan swallowed down a territorial growl. For some reason, his cousin's interest caused his hackles to rise.

"Aye." There was no point in denying it.

Drew's eyes widened. "What did you say?"

Ewan shrugged a casual shoulder. "Asked her name."

Drew broke out in disbelieving laughter. "Holy fuck! Gregor's going to shit a brick if he finds out." Drew continued to stare as a space of silence passed. "Well? Did she give it to you?"

Ewan nodded. Again, it would do him no good to lie, but he wasn't thrilled about divulging any detail about her to even Drew, who he trusted implicitly. "Sasha."

Drew let out a low whistle. "Pretty damned cordial, aren't you? Jesus, Ewan. Why didn't you just ask her out for dinner while you were at it?"

Ewan rolled his shoulders. He'd cut dinner out of the equation and gotten right to dessert.

"What else did you talk about?"

Ewan didn't appreciate Drew's amused tone. There hadn't been much time for talk, as he'd been preoccupied with getting Sasha's ass bare as quickly as possible. "Not a damn thing." That at least was the truth. Whatever else happened was none of Drew's—or anyone else's—business.

"I don't have to tell you this isn't good." Apparently, Drew had taken it upon himself to state the obvious. "This sort of attention . . ." He gave a rueful shake of his head. "Gregor's going to know."

He wasn't wrong. Ewan had been so careful the past several months to keep his bouts in the battle arena a secret. A feat in itself, considering Gregor's uncanny ability to know what every member of their clan was up to at any given time. All of that hard work and secrecy was shot to shit thanks to Sasha's seductive charm. Ewan had never wanted anything like he'd wanted her. She'd drawn him like a magnet and he'd had no choice but to give himself over to her pull.

"Aye." Ewan was only capable of monosyllabic grunts of agreement. If he let himself dwell too much on it, his temper would get the better of him and that certainly wouldn't do him any favors.

"What are you going to do?"

Ewan didn't miss the worry in Drew's tone. "He won't know you're involved. I'll make sure."

Drew let out a visible sigh of relief. "You know I've got your back—"

"I know." Ewan didn't bother to let him get to the "but." He wasn't a complete asshole. Ewan never expected Drew to take the fall with him if they ever got caught.

"So . . . ?" Drew grinned. "Do you think she's dangerous?"

Without a doubt Sasha Ivanov was the greatest threat to Ewan's existence. And that was saying something, considering the battles and creatures he'd fought. Whether or not she posed a threat to the rest of his clan was yet to be seen.

"As dangerous as any vampire."

Drew laughed. "Given the chance, Aristov will turn the tables on us and have his revenge."

Ewan would never admit it, but some part of him believed that Mikhail Aristov was entitled to his pound of flesh. "Would you blame him?"

Drew shrugged. To agree was as good as treason.

Centuries ago, a vampire lord and his dhampir child had caused so much hurt. And instead of meting out his justice on those two, Gregor had decided to declare war on an entire race. With the Sortiari's backing, he was unstoppable. The berserkers' strength coupled with the Sortiari's purpose had made them a formidable force that had nearly eradicated the vampire race. Had Gregor managed to kill Mikhail Aristov centuries ago, they would have been successful. But Mikhail was stronger than anyone had given him credit for. And now, the fledgling vampire race thrived. A species returned from the brink of extinction. Mikhail would no doubt crave vengeance just as Gregor had. When would it stop? An eye for an eye, for an eye,

for an eye. . . . Until there were no more vampires or berserkers left on the face of the earth.

Foolish. And a waste of fucking time.

Drew pulled into the driveway of the run-down apartment complex in the Valley Gregor had claimed as their
temporary home base. The place was a total shithole. Big
enough to accommodate the fifty berserkers currently oc-
cupying the city. The remaining two hundred fifty berserkers were strewn around the world, stationed at various
locations by the Sortiari.

Gregor's group was the first to break their bonds. One
by one, the remaining cells had followed suit. It wouldn't
be long before they were three-hundred strong in L.A. and
ready to wage war against Aristov's meager numbers.
Ewan scrubbed a hand over his face. Gods, was there to
be no end to the fighting?

"Pray the gods show you favor that Gregor hasn't gotten wind of what went down tonight."

Ewan's hand froze on the door handle as he turned to
face his cousin. "There are no gods. No fate. No mysterious hand that guides us. We're either fucked or we're not.
And we won't know until we walk through that door."

Ewan got out of the car without another word. He'd
know soon enough if the gossip had reached Gregor's ears.
Ewan had no more fucks to give either way. Because he
was already thinking of how to track Sasha down.

He had to see her again.

CHAPTER
5

"For how much longer are you going to give that piece-of-shit vampire, Saeed, quarter?"

Ian Gregor's gaze slid to the side for the barest moment. Gavin, his cousin and second in command, shifted uncomfortably in the passenger seat of the beat-up Subaru they'd stolen a few months ago. Ian hated to be questioned. He expected those under his command to do two things: keep their mouths shut, and obey. He demanded unwavering loyalty.

"As gods-damned long as I want to," he barked. "You have a problem with that?"

Gavin cleared his throat. "No."

"Good." Ian's gaze narrowed as a sleek Audi R8 pulled into the driveway. Fucking vampires and dhampirs never did waste an opportunity to flaunt their wealth. They were frivolous, extravagant creatures. Self-serving and vain. The world would be a better place without them in it. And Ian planned to make sure not a single one of them survived to populate the earth.

A female exited the car and headed toward the house.

Vampire. Another one of Mikhail's fledglings? He couldn't help but wonder to which coven she belonged. She could be one of Saeed's, but Ian wouldn't put it past the vampire king to be populating L.A.'s thirteen covens with as many new vampires as possible. Fortifying their ranks and building their strength one abomination at a time. Gregor rolled down his window and inhaled deeply to commit her scent to memory. His brow furrowed. Another scent mingled with hers. Reminiscent of one of Ian's own. Interesting . . .

Who was she? Newly turned, that much was certain. Then again, weren't they all? Fledglings created as a result of Mikhail Aristov's ascension to power. Ian's lip curled. Only one other creature plagued his existence more than the supposedly "unkillable" father of the resurrected vampire race. If things went according to plan, all of the thorns in Ian's side would soon be removed. Permanently.

At least one vampire had the good sense not to break faith with a berserker. Several months ago, Ian had been in Seattle searching for a particular fae. An *enaid dwyn*. A soul thief. This particular one was the slave of a crafty mage by the name of Rinieri de Rege. Ian's plan had been to take the mage hostage and use his slave as bait to lure his true target out of hiding. His strategy had been thwarted, however, when he learned that a vampire, Saeed Almasi, had also gone to Seattle in search of the same fae.

Ian let out a disgusted snort. Vampires were ruled by their insufferable mate bonds. Tethers as they called them. It overrode common sense and reason. It was their greatest flaw and at the same time, their greatest strength. Saeed's tether with the soul thief had changed the course of Ian's plans, though thank the gods, it hadn't completely derailed them. He'd helped to free the fae's soul from slavery and in return, Saeed had agreed to bring his mate back to Los Angeles. Close to Trenton McAlister and right where Ian wanted her.

The vampire was upwind of him and Ian took another deep breath and held it in his lungs. Her scent confused him. Desire, fear, excitement, adrenaline . . . it was both sour and sweet. He couldn't wait to find out what the fuck had happened tonight. And he would find out. Secrets never stayed hidden for long. Ian always discovered the truth.

Gavin glanced Ian's way. "Do you smell that?"

"Aye." Ian wasn't about to divulge his thoughts on the matter. He played everything close to the hip. He had no confidants. No one he trusted implicitly. Trust was a luxury Ian Gregor couldn't afford.

"What do you make of it?"

Ian shrugged. "Not a thing. Yet."

Gavin sighed. Ian didn't give a single shit if the male was put out.

"What if the soul thief's sister never shows? She might not ever come out of hiding."

It was a possibility Ian hadn't discounted. Yet, some instinct urged otherwise. Fear could be a hell of a motivator. And with her sister free and in the same city as the mage she'd betrayed, Ian was banking on that knowledge to be enough to coax Fiona Bane out of hiding.

"She'll show." His faith was solid.

"Yeah," Gavin snorted. "But when? Five years from now?"

"I don't give a fuck if it's five hundred years from now," Ian snapped. His patience, like his faith, had no end. He'd wait till the end of the gods-damned world to have his revenge if he had to.

He was answered with another long-suffering sigh. Gods, was there no end to the melodrama? "All right. But you can't possibly think she'll waltz right up to the front door."

Ian had considered the possibility that if Fiona had come to L.A., she'd be keeping a low profile. No use in alerting those she'd wronged to her presence in the city. Especially if she expected retribution. Still . . . the sense of instinct that tugged at Ian's gut told him otherwise. Somehow, he *knew* Fiona would seek out her sister. And eventually, Trenton McAlister as well.

"I'm keeping my enemies close." Gavin didn't need any more explanation than that. "Only a fool turns his back on those who mean to do him harm."

Gavin chuckled. "Amen to that."

Ian knew some of the members of his clan had grown weary of the fight. Their memories dimmed with the passing centuries, but not Ian's. His need for vengeance burned as hot and bright today as it had when their females had been slaughtered. He'd heard the whisperings of his brethren over the years. Felt the weight of their doubt and exhaustion. Some considered the debt paid. A mad vampire and his dhampir child had exacted first blood. The berserkers had paid it back ten-fold as they'd annihilated the vampires for the Sortiari. They were even. Blood for blood. So what if a few of them survived? Who cared if they replenished their numbers?

Ian cared. And as long as that need for retribution burned within him, that's all that mattered.

A momentary swath of light cut like a blade through the darkness as the vampire opened the front door and disappeared inside the house. Ian relaxed into the seat and wound his fists around the battered steering wheel as he let out a slow breath. A tingle of trepidation raced down his spine. Change was coming, and whatever it was, it wouldn't be good.

He turned the key in the ignition and the engine reluctantly sparked to life. The car was a total piece of shit.

Time to ditch it and steal something a little more reliable. The rest of the supernatural community might have liked to flaunt their wealth, but every last cent Ian had managed to collect over the years was already spent. Dedicated to the cause. Whether or not everyone agreed on the allocation of those funds was another matter. One on a long list of things Ian didn't give two fucks about. *He* was in charge. *He* made the rules. Those who chose to disobey or express a differing opinion could prepare to suffer the consequences.

Ian Gregor didn't take betrayal lightly.

The sun would be up soon and there was no use watching the house when all of the vampires inside would be dead to the world until sunset. Gods, the temptation to ambush them when they were weak and slaughter them all was almost too great to resist. But for now he needed this coven alive and intact. At least, until he got what he wanted. After that, he'd run a stake through every single one of their hearts and raze the sophisticated mansion to its foundation.

"I take it we're done for the night?"

Ian glanced Gavin's way. "Not quite." There was no rest for the wicked and Ian's black heart was the wickedest. "We have a couple of stops to make before we head for downtown. I want to be at McAlister's shitty office, waiting, before the bastard shows up for the day."

It had been a while since Ian had rattled Trenton McAlister's chain. The director of the Sortiari had received a nice reprieve and Ian needed to make his presence known. If anything, to remind the director that he was still alive for no other reason than Ian willed it so.

Gavin fumbled for the lever beside him and released his seatback to let it recline. "Well, if this is the only rest I'm going to get tonight, I'd better take advantage of it while I can."

Ian snorted. Gods. When had they gotten so soft? Doing the Sortiari's bidding had made them compliant it seemed. Perhaps it was time to remind those in his ranks exactly what they were and what was expected of them.

"You have a lot of nerve showing up here."

Nerve had nothing to do with it. A wide grin split Ian's lips at the director of the Sortiari's outraged tone. Ian had Trenton McAlister by the balls and the bastard knew it. He settled into a chair that faced the director's desk and propped his feet up on the polished surface. McAlister's steely gaze dipped briefly to Ian's feet and his lips thinned. Gods, how Ian loved to ruffle his sanctimonious feathers. McAlister's attention moved from Ian's offensive feet, to the door of his office. A large shadow passed in front of the open space and Ian bristled.

Fucking Caden Mitchell.

The bear shifter was so damned big he took up the entire space. Ian had hoped the son of a bitch had headed back to his multimillion-dollar estate in upstate New York. Unfortunately, it looked as though the male was going to be hanging around for a while. A couple of years ago, Caden had caught Ian off guard and delivered a sound ass-beating. The memory of it still stung. It wouldn't happen again.

"Don't be shy, Mitchell," Ian drawled without taking his gaze from McAlister's. "Come in and have a chat, yeah?"

McAlister's gaze narrowed. He inclined his head, giving the shifter permission to come in. Ian snorted. For all of his strength, money, power, and clout, the mighty Caden Mitchell was nothing more than another one of the Sortiari's slaves.

Pathetic.

Caden stepped deeper into the office. Besides taking up all the space, the big bastard also took up most of the breathable air. Ian's hackles rose and a low growl gathered in his chest as the shifter came closer. He wasn't here to start a fight. Or to finish one. He needed to keep his temper in check and his hunger for violence at bay.

"I thought I needed your oracle." There was no point in mincing words. McAlister knew exactly what Ian was talking about. "I was wrong."

Ever since Mikhail Aristov had found his mate, McAlister had been obsessed with a human girl who had fallen under the vampire king's protection. It had taken a while for Ian to figure out exactly what her worth to McAlister was, and he'd found out several months ago, when he'd tried to ambush a meeting between Mikhail Aristov and McAlister in which the girl was present. Thanks to a stubborn Alpha werewolf and Caden Mitchell's interference, Ian had missed his chance to snatch the girl. It hadn't mattered, though. He'd heard enough of her conversation with McAlister to point him in the direction he needed to go. She'd sent him to Seattle. To the soul thief. And that's why Ian was in McAlister's office today. To put a little fear into the smug bastard.

McAlister didn't utter so much as a word and that was totally fine with Ian. He'd planned on this being a mostly one-sided conversation. "A little hard to make out her riddles, but I figured it out eventually. Seattle is a promising city. Full of all sorts of interesting supernatural creatures. Shifters, werewolves, *bean sidhes.*" Ian grinned. "Mages . . . *enaid dwyn . . .*"

The director's eyes widened the barest fraction of an inch but it was as good as a disbelieving gape. Ian chuckled. Getting a rise out of him was considerably more entertaining than he thought it would be.

"I'd always thought soul thieves were a myth," he mused. "This one, though . . ." Ian let out a low whistle.

"She was something else. Powerful. Hell, she scared the fuck out of me."

McAlister's heartbeat kicked into high gear. Music to Ian's ears. His scent soured with anxiety and his pupils dilated as adrenaline dumped into his bloodstream.

Ian shot a superior smirk Caden's way. "I think I rubbed the mage she kept company with the wrong way, though. Guess I have a tendency to do that, huh, Mitchell?"

The bear shifter let out a derisive grunt.

"Does your endless rambling have a point, Gregor? Or did you come here to attempt to bore me to death?"

Finally, a few words from the self-important director. He turned his attention back to McAlister. Power sparked the air around them and settled on Gregor's tongue with an electric tang. For so long, he'd feared that power and marveled at McAlister's self-control, never knowing that all this time, the bastard's magic had been bound. The only power he possessed was what his position within the Sortiari lent him.

"No point." Ian wasn't ready to show his hand just yet. McAlister was smart enough to read between the lines. "Just wanted you to know I had a nice vacation." He grinned even wider, showing his teeth. "That's all."

McAlister folded his hands together and rested them on the surface of the desk. His gaze hardened and his jaw squared. Anger boiled under the surface of his calm façade and Ian couldn't help his own superior smirk. A slave no longer, he'd show the guardians of fate what it meant to be under another's thumb. When he was done with them, they'd all bow at his feet, including their haughty director.

"You have two minutes to remove yourself from Sortiari property before Caden removes you."

Ian let out a chuff of laughter. McAlister had obviously forgotten who he was speaking to. Didn't matter. Soon enough, Ian would remind him. He lifted his legs from the pristine desktop and set them firmly on the aging industrial carpet before pushing himself out of his chair. Why McAlister chose to hold court in this run-down office when the Sortiari had a fancy-as-fuck, state-of-the-art building on the outskirts of the city was beyond him. They certainly liked to play their games. This illusion of poverty, though, was a fucking joke.

"No need to get your pet involved, McAlister. I know where the door is."

Ian turned to find Caden so gods-damned close he could practically feel the son of a bitch's breath on his face. Berserkers sat atop the supernatural food chain. Not much frightened them. But bear shifters could definitely cause a bit of unease. A corner of Caden's mouth quirked into an arrogant smirk and his light blue eyes flashed with feral gold.

"Careful he doesn't pull that leash of yours too tight, Mitchell." Ian brushed past the shifter, his spine straight and shoulders thrown back. "I'd hate for you to choke."

"If I were you, I'd worrying about my own neck, Gregor." Caden's deep voice resonated in the tiny office. For a second there, Ian had wondered if the male had gone mute. "You're not as omnipotent as you think you are."

Ian chuckled. He loved it when those around him underestimated him. Made his job so much easier. He paused at the door and turned his attention back to McAlister. "Give my regards to Aristov the next time you see him. Tell him I hope to see him soon."

The director didn't bother to respond. He simply met Ian's gaze and held it. The bastard didn't cower. Ian could at least respect that. He cast one last amused glance Caden's way before leaving the office. A great start to the day.

CHAPTER
6

"Is this some sort of contest to see which one of us is the most crazy self-destructive?"

Sasha rolled her eyes at Ani's comment. Ani was wild, but hardly self-destructive. Sasha, on the other hand . . . ? Yeah, she definitely had some kind of mental defect. Or death wish. Or both.

She had to see him again.

"I'll go by myself if I have to. Just tell me where tonight's fights are going to be held."

The battle arena moved from location to location so as not to draw undue attention. The supernatural world had its rules just like the mundane world did. Cage matches to the death for the sole purpose of making a little money was definitely frowned upon in both worlds.

"You got lucky last time, Sasha. I think it's best not to tempt fate."

Ani had that backward. Fate had definitely tempted *her*. "I'm not tempting anything." That was the truth. The damage had already been done. The tether was irreversible. "Like

I said, I don't need a wingman. Just point me in the right direction and I'll go alone."

"What you need," Ani began, "is a smack to the head to jar some sense into you. A berserker tethering a vampire is the worst omen I can think of. No good will come of it, Sasha. Be grateful your soul was returned to you and *walk away*. It's the only option."

Sasha knew Ani had her back but it wasn't so simple. It wasn't that she didn't want to walk away. It was that she didn't think she could. The tether connected her to the berserker. It drew her to him. Fighting it was like trying to stop the changing of the seasons.

"I can't walk away. I don't expect you to understand."

"That's a cop-out, Sasha and you know it." For someone who'd been so eager to hear the gossip about her initial encounter with the berserker, Ani had sure changed her tune. "You're inviting disaster. There's no scenario in which this ends well other than you keeping your distance. If he doesn't kill you tonight, it will only be a matter of time before a member of his clan gets the job done."

Sasha couldn't explain it, but instinct told her otherwise. He wouldn't hurt her, and she didn't think he'd let anyone else hurt her, either. Of course, Sasha was a pro at lying to herself. For years, she'd eaten her own spoon-fed lies as she'd made herself believe Saeed had felt something more than friendship for her. Maybe this was the same thing and that "instinct" she was listening to was nothing more than her own hopes telling lies her ravenous heart eagerly devoured.

"I'll keep my distance." It was a promise she actually didn't think she could keep. "I need to satisfy my curiosity or it's going to eat me alive." That much, at least, was true. Her first thought upon waking to the sunset was of the ruggedly magnetic berserker. Dry heat scalded her throat and she swallowed as though to soothe the burn. It wouldn't be long before her thirst got the better of her and she went out in search of the berserker whether or not Ani helped her to find him.

Ani's expression turned wary. "First sign of trouble— we're out of there."

Sasha nodded. "Deal. Do you know where we're going?"

She was answered with a rueful sigh. "Yeah. I do."

Sasha knew her friend had been holding out on her. She wasn't going to complain about it, though. The more time they could shave off, the better. "Okay, good. Let's get out of here before Saeed pins me down for a talk." She'd been avoiding her maker for weeks. She wasn't interested in talking to Saeed about anything right now. Especially when her heart was still so raw and hurt from being cast aside.

"I'm ready whenever you are." Ani was always ready to roll at a moment's notice. Just one of the many things Sasha loved about her.

"Lead the way." Sasha fell into step behind Ani and headed for the door. Behind her, she sensed a presence and her step faltered. *Shit.* Not fast enough, it seemed.

"Sasha." Saeed's deep, soothing voice drove through her chest like a spear. Since his return to the coven, she'd avoided him. Desperate to escape his piercing dark eyes and his beautiful, petite, red-haired mate who was nothing more than a reminder of Sasha's own heartache. "Going out again?"

She owed him nothing, least of all an explanation. "I am." She didn't bother to turn and face him. Didn't want to meet his gaze. "Don't bother waiting up."

Sasha forced one foot in front of the other as she

followed Ani out the door. She wouldn't give Saeed the satisfaction of seeing her undone. Not that he'd care. His soul was tethered and he had his mate. For that matter, so did Sasha. And she wasn't going to waste another second in this house when she could be near him.

The drive to the Valley seemed to take hours. Impatience pulled Sasha's muscles taut and her thirst raged at a nearly unbearable level. Not that she expected that to change anytime soon. She doubted she'd get close enough to the berserker to exchange two words with him, let alone sate her hunger. Tonight wasn't about contact. She simply wanted to satisfy her curiosity. Get a glimpse of him and see if her reaction to him was as powerful as it had been upon her tethering. Maybe she'd get lucky and not feel even a tiny spark of interest. In which case, she could do as Ani suggested and walk away with her life and her soul intact.

"Man, this place is a real shithole."

Ani pulled into the parking lot of an abandoned Kmart and killed the engine. Sasha got out of the car and made her way across the lot. The glass doors had been blacked out with paint and looked like the sort of place where last-minute raves popped up. It wasn't the most elegant venue and definitely a step down from the last building the fights had been held in, but no one came for the ambiance.

Magic sparked the air, an indicator of the glamour cast over the building and parking lot to keep curious humans at bay. The faint sound of cacophonous cheers reached Sasha's ears and she picked up her pace toward the doors. Who knew how long the fights had been going on? The berserker could have already been here and gone.

"Hey! Wait up!"

Sasha didn't even realize she was running until Ani called out. She stopped dead in her tracks. Her heart pounded and her breath raced in her chest. Electricity raced through her veins and a spark of anticipation danced along her skin. She'd tried to play it cool. To act as though her curiosity over the berserker was superficial. Her own behavior betrayed her words. Gods, how pathetic. Over the past several months, she'd coached herself to be strong. To take no shit. To depend on no one. To have her own back because she knew no one else would. And one cruel, brooding male had undone all of that hard work with a look?

Bullshit.

Sasha refused to fall victim to her own bleeding heart ever again.

She felt Ani at her back but didn't turn to face her. Instead, Sasha walked slowly—almost mechanically— toward the entrance of the building. A mantra ran through her head, one she'd be damned if she didn't heed. *Guard your heart. Feel nothing. Protect yourself.*

"In a bit of a hurry, are you?" Ani's sarcasm went ignored. "You promised you'd keep your distance, remember?"

"I remember. And I will. I just don't want to miss any of the fights."

Ani clucked her tongue. "Worried he'll slip through your fingers?"

Something like that. *Guard your heart. Feel nothing. Protect yourself.* "No one's slipping through anything." Sasha refused to lose herself yet again to a male. "I just want to see what I'm up against."

"Tethered to a berserker." Ani's disbelieving tone echoed Sasha's feelings exactly. "You sure took keeping your enemies close to an extreme."

Heh. She supposed she did.

Sasha took several cleansing breaths. It was stupid to get so worked up over someone she didn't know. The butterflies that swirled in her stomach were an unwelcome reminder of how soft her heart could be and the damage that softness could cause. She was here to sate her curiosity and nothing more. She couldn't afford for it to be anything more.

In and out. That was the plan.

As the crowd roared once again, Sasha reached for the door handle. She hoped her stupid heart wouldn't do anything tonight to derail her mind.

Guard your heart. Feel nothing. Protect yourself.

Ewan's gaze roamed the crowd for any sign of Sasha. He'd hoped she'd be here. Front and center. Her dark, expressive eyes trained on him, her full lips slightly parted with awe. Oh, it was a grandiose image to paint. One that made Ewan aware of his own ego. A thrill rushed through him but it wasn't the impending fight that excited him. It was the prospect of seeing her again. Feeling her wet, silken flesh glide against his. The fight was nothing more than a pretense to get her here. Front and center with all eyes on him.

"We're never coming back to this place." Ewan cast a sidelong glance at Drew. "What? It's a dump. They have the fighters queued up like fucking cattle. You deserve more respect than this."

Arrogance was definitely a trait common to all berserkers. They demanded respect. Commanded fear. Ewan didn't give a shit about being treated like a king, however. He'd let those delusions of grandeur fall to Gregor and the others. Impatience was his only complaint at the moment. Impatience for the fight. Impatience to see her. Impatience for what might happen in the next couple of hours. Gods. Ewan couldn't remember a time when he'd been so damned antsy and on edge. He wanted something—anything—to happen before he crawled right out of his own gods-damned skin.

The blacked-out doors opened, bringing with it a waft of air. Ewan inhaled deeply the scent of warm cinnamon and held it in his lungs before letting out a slow breath. His gaze went to the entrance, where the object of his obsession stood shoulder-to-shoulder with the same female she'd been with two nights ago. Her mahogany hair cascaded over her shoulders and her dark eyes scanned the room. The intensity of her expression sent an electric thrill chasing through his veins.

"Ewan."

Drew's voice barely registered. His attention didn't stray from her as she wound through the crowd of onlookers. Closer. Closer . . .

"Ewan!" Drew gave him a hearty shove. "You're up."

Fuck. The timing could've been better. Focus was near to impossible when his thoughts were all over the place and his head was so full of her heady cinnamon scent. His keen senses weren't doing him any favors right now. Not when he could pick out her scent among thousands and see every detail of her expression in a sea of faces.

"Are you afraid, berserker?" Ewan looked up to find his opponent already in the cage. "Come on, tonight's as good a night as any to die!"

As if the werewolf even stood a chance. The full moon was a couple weeks off, which meant he wouldn't be at full strength. He couldn't take on his animal form, which meant he'd heal much slower from any damage he sustained. The scale was so tilted to one side, Ewan almost felt bad for agreeing to step into the cage with him in the first place.

Someone was going to die tonight, but it wouldn't be Ewan.

The werewolf was obviously mouthy and interested in providing the crowd with a good show. Ewan could at least give him that. He'd ended his last fight too quickly in his preoccupation with the vampire. He couldn't lose sight of why he was here. This was about making money. Period. A bored and restless crowd did nothing to line his pockets.

Ewan might not have wanted to keep the vampire waiting, but neither could he risk the possibility of not being invited back into the arena to fight. If he didn't provide the necessary entertainment, there'd be no use for him. Ewan couldn't have that. Sasha had to have known he'd be here tonight, which meant she wasn't going anywhere anytime soon. He could afford to dedicate his attention to the werewolf and appease the bloodlust of the crowd.

He'd put on a show and then some.

Ewan crossed his arms over his torso and stripped his T-shirt from his body. The simple act sent the crowd into a frenzy as he stepped up to the webbed silver cage and stepped inside. Berserkers had few vulnerabilities. Most supernatural creatures couldn't tolerate silver but it didn't affect Ewan in the slightest. The magic woven within the silver webs was a different story, however.

Berserkers were magic sensitive in that its very presence was sometimes enough to agitate them. While beheading was the most effective way to put a berserker down, magic could get the job done, too, if wielded by an adept. Not many—if anyone—outside of their ranks knew that little tidbit. Always best to keep potential enemies guessing. Never reveal the chinks in your armor. Don't give your adversaries ammunition against you. Always strong. Always determined. One mind, one goal, one clan. Gregor had pounded those values into their heads for as long as Ewan could remember.

His obsession with the vampire was bound to land him

in deep shit with Gregor. And the male didn't tolerate betrayal. Too late to do anything about it now, he supposed.

The door to the cage closed behind him and Ewan rotated his hands and examined the silver cuffs that circled each wrist. They didn't offer any support, but the spikes that protruded from each cuff would aggravate the hell out of his opponent. He stretched his neck from side to side, rolled his shoulders. Shifted his weight from one foot to the other and forced his mind to focus on the task at hand and not the scent that filled his head as though she were the only other being in the building.

"Not much of a talker, are you, berserker?" Ewan couldn't help but wonder if the werewolf's strategy was to talk him to death. "Do berserkers even know how to speak? Or do you communicate with grunts and growls like the animals you are?"

Ewan rolled his eyes. He'd heard it all before. Hopefully the werewolf was a better fighter than he was an insult slinger. Otherwise, there wouldn't be much he could do to prolong the fight.

Ewan didn't bother to set the werewolf straight on his assumptions. Instead, he let out a low growl as he adopted a fighting stance. He wanted tonight's fight to be a performance. For an audience of one.

The werewolf took a swing that Ewan dodged with ease. Power gathered within him as he sensed the battle rage rise from the pit of his stomach like a writhing, living thing. Ewan wanted to give in. To let it consume him completely and send him to that dark place where he checked out and couldn't be held accountable for his actions. An effective warlord killed indiscriminately. The battle rage allowed him the freedom from memory or guilt. It let him do what had to be done.

Ewan swiped his arm upward and caught the werewolf in the face with one of the spikes of his silver cuff.

The scent of burning flesh singed his nostrils as the silver scorched the werewolf's cheek, opening a wide gash. Blood scented the air and a renewed sense of power surged through Ewan's veins. The crowd went wild, chanting for more bloodshed, eager for death. The battle master stepped between Ewan and the werewolf, arms outstretched. There weren't many rules in the arena, but the werewolf had tried to strike before Ewan had been afforded the opportunity to choose his weapon.

All the interruption served to accomplish was to ignite Ewan's temper and impatience.

"Will you take a weapon for this bout, berserker?" The battle master's voice echoed with the spark of magic and the crowd fell silent. "And one free shot against your opponent."

The crowd erupted into shouts and cheers once again. Ewan's breath heaved in his chest as the battle master faced him and presented the case full of weapons.

"Get out of my way and let me fight." Ewan forced the words from between clenched teeth. "I don't need any of that to kill him."

If the atmosphere had been full of excited anticipation before, it was positively electric now. Ewan's arrogance, his defiance and hostility, his sheer aggression sent the crowd into a frenzy. The werewolf was weak. It wasn't even close to a fair fight.

"Let them fight! Let them fight!" Angry voices called out from the groups of onlookers, as eager as Ewan to get on with it.

Ewan leveled his gaze on the battle master and held his attention. "I'll fight as I am. Now, get out of the way unless you want to die as well."

The battle master took a quick step back and exited the ring without another word. Rowdy cheers echoed in Ewan's ears, his opponent's lip curled back in a determined snarl.

His own focus became laser sharp and he tuned out everything around him.

Everything but the vampire who stood at the edge of the ring, watching him in just the way he hoped she would.

CHAPTER
7

Gods, he was magnificent. It bothered Sasha more than she wanted to admit that she didn't know his name, but it didn't dull his charisma in the ring. A cold finger of fear stroked down her spine as she watched him fight and it only seemed to heighten her excitement. The berserker was the ultimate forbidden fruit. A sworn enemy. Deadly. Dangerous. Violent. Cruel. Unforgiving.

And he belonged to her.

He moved faster than any creature she'd ever seen. Each blow delivered landed with amazing precision. The werewolf wouldn't last long in the silver cage. Sasha almost felt sorry for him. He'd walked in of his own volition, though. Both males knew the rules and both knew only one would make it out alive. There was no doubt the berserker would be the one left standing. No one could best him.

He was . . . invincible.

Heat coiled low in Sasha's belly and spread outward. She shouldn't want him. Hell, she should have been shaking with fear and running the other direction. But all she wanted was to get closer. To flirt with the flames in hope of getting burned. Gods, how could she possibly be tethered to this male who fought with such wild ferocity?

The berserker toyed with his prey for the benefit of the crowd. It worked the eager onlookers into a frenzy and money changed hands all around Sasha. Anyone who bet against him deserved to lose their money.

"Honey, close your mouth. You're starting to drool." Ani reached over and lifted Sasha's chin with her fingertips.

Sasha didn't dare drag her eyes from the arena. She didn't want to miss a second of her mate's impressive display of strength, stamina, and skill. She wiped at her bottom lip as though there were actually something there to clean up and Ani laughed.

"You do realize how bat-shit crazy this is, right?" Sasha still didn't bother to look at her friend. "I mean, look at him!"

Oh, she was getting an eyeful. Ani didn't need to worry about that. Adrenaline coursed through Sasha's veins, causing her limbs to quake with unspent energy. Anticipation pulled her muscles taut and she squeezed her thighs together to keep them from trembling. She knew she should be disgusted by the violent exhibition. She should turn away. Put her back to him. Walk out the door and never try to find him again. But Sasha stood rooted in place. Her gaze was trained on the berserker. She was captivated. Mesmerized. Nothing, not even the barbarism of this moment could force her attention away.

Thanks to supernatural healing and stamina, these fights could last hours. The werewolf was armed with a dagger and a wicked-looking mace but he'd yet to deliver a single blow to the berserker. The battle dance encouraged the crowd. Loosened pockets. How much money did her mate stand to gain by putting on a good show tonight?

Gods. Her mate. The more she thought about it, the

more unbelievable it seemed. She took a step toward the silver cage as though drawn to him like metal to a magnet. His attention wandered from the fight for the barest moment. His gaze met hers. Wild and intense. Sasha let out a quick gust of breath and sucked it in just as quickly as the werewolf capitalized on his distraction and landed a blow to his shoulder with the studded mace.

Sasha flinched as though she'd been hit by the heavy weapon. The berserker let out a grunt, but other than that gave no outward show he'd been harmed. His dark gaze narrowed as he turned his attention back to his opponent and focused once again on the fight. Inky black bled into his eyes and he fought with a ferocity that stalled the breath in Sasha's chest. He was nothing more than an animal now, operating on base instinct and rage. Unarmed, save the silver cuffs at his wrists, he needed no other weapon to be deadly. He was a weapon. And Sasha stood in awe of him.

He no longer played with the werewolf. Wasn't interested in prolonging the fight for anyone's entertainment. The werewolf would die in a matter of moments and a ripple of fear vibrated through Sasha at the realization. Their world was a violent one. Sasha was accustomed to death. But it was of little comfort to her as she watched, wide-eyed, as her mate spun in a blur of motion to snatch the silver dagger from the werewolf's hand and drive it through his heart.

The berserker turned to look at her. The midnight black retreated from his gaze but did nothing to diminish the intensity of his expression. His chest heaved with labored breath, sweat glistened and ran in rivulets over the hills and valleys of his muscled chest. He jerked his chin toward the rear of the building. Sasha didn't need words to know he just given her a command, and fool that she was, she obeyed.

She tossed Ani her key fob. She wasn't about to leave her friend stranded. "I'll find my own way home."

Ani didn't seem to be the least bit surprised. She gave Sasha a disapproving look, her lips pursed. "At least promise to be fucking careful."

"Promise."

Sasha turned and pushed through the crowd as she made her way to the back of the building. Another fight was about to begin, but in the meantime, those who'd made good money were eager to congratulate the berserker on his win. Sasha didn't wait for him to make his way to her. Instead she rushed toward the back of the building to find a private space, away from prying eyes.

A set of double doors led to a large stockroom. The space was empty now except for a few random cardboard boxes and an old metal desk at the far end of the vast space. She was surrounded on all sides by concrete. The walls, the floor. A large docking bay door had been left open to allow a chilly breeze to circulate through the space. Sasha hugged her arms around her midsection as she looked up to the ceiling at the exposed ducts and wiring. Goose bumps rose on Sasha's flesh and she suppressed a shiver.

"Back for more, vampire?"

The brogue of his voice resonated through her. The berserker's left arm wound around her waist. He hauled her against his chest as his right hand reached up to brush her hair away from the nape of her neck. His touch was a brand in comparison to the cold air that surrounded her. His open mouth came to rest where his hand had just been and Sasha's stomach clenched tight with lust. His teeth grazed her sensitive skin and Sasha let out a quiet whimper. A rush of wet heat spread between her thighs as she reached for his arm at her waist and gripped it tight. He was one-hundred-percent predator, and Sasha thrilled at the prospect of becoming his prey.

"Yes." The word left her lips on a breathy whisper. He bit down on her neck again, a little harder this time, and she swore if she wasn't holding on to him her legs would've given out beneath her. "Don't disappoint me this time."

His low laughter coaxed a fresh round of chills over her flesh. "Don't worry, pet. I don't plan to disappoint you."

The bathroom where they'd had their first encounter had been more accommodating than this fucking stockroom. Ewan didn't know why it bothered him. It was as good a place as any to fuck. That's all this was, after all. An emotionless fulfillment of need. Nothing more, nothing less. She was an itch he wanted to scratch. Soon enough, he'd be bored with her and move on. Until then, he planned to enjoy her in any way he damn well pleased.

He brought his mouth to the nape of her neck once again. She tasted like honey fresh from the comb, almost too sweet. His left hand dove beneath her shirt and he jerked down the cup of her bra to fondle one full breast. Sasha gasped at the contact and hardened Ewan's cock to stone. He rolled her nipple between his thumb and fore-finger and she cried out with pleasure, the sound echoing off the stark concrete walls.

For the past couple of days he'd thought of nothing but having her again. His erection throbbed between his legs almost painfully. He needed to be inside her like he needed his next fucking breath. Driven by his own desperation, Ewan spun her and pressed her body up against the near-est wall as he reached for her pants, unbuttoned them, and jerked them along with her underwear down to her ankles. She kicked off her shoes and toed her pants the rest of the way off. The scent of her arousal hit him and Ewan let out a low growl.

"Spread your legs."

She did as he asked without so much as a pause. She

braced her arms against the wall, fingers splayed. Her breath raced and her heart pounded, music to his ears. The scent of her desire bloomed around him and he breathed in deeply of the heady perfume. He reached between her thighs and found her dripping wet. Slick and ready for him. Such a brazenly wanton little creature. He gripped her by the hips and jerked her backward, angling her pert ass toward him. He took an indulgent moment and stroked between her thighs, once again circling the tight knot of nerves at her core before slipping one finger inside. She let out a low moan as he pulled out and let his wet fingertips caress down and back up her inner thigh. Gods, how he wanted to tease her. To play with her until she begged him to take her. But that required time they didn't have. Drew would come looking for him soon and Ewan would hate to have to beat the shit out of his cousin for the interruption.

Ewan pulled down his workout pants. He'd taken her from behind in the bathroom during their first encounter. This time, he wanted to see her face as he fucked her. See the expressions that went along with those tempting moans and whimpers. He turned her in his arms before cupping her ass and lifting her. For a moment, Ewan stared. Her beauty damn near stole his breath. There was a darkness in her that called to him. Captivated him. Held him rapt. Her full, dark-pink lips parted and he leaned in as the temptation to kiss her overtook him. The tip of one fang became visible and Ewan stopped short. He couldn't let himself forget what she was. What he was. He could enjoy her. But nothing more.

He drove home in a single thrust. Sasha shuddered and her head fell back as she let out a low, indulgent moan. Her eyelids fluttered. Ewan swore the rapture in her expression was enough to make him come. Gods, she was wet. Warm. Tight. So responsive to every touch. Every thrust. He could fuck her for hours and it still wouldn't be enough to satisfy him. He could watch her for days and his eyes would still want more.

Her pleasure was exquisite.

Ewan lost himself to the moment as he fucked her. His mind went blank and he was left with nothing more than blind sensation and raw need. He reached up with one hand and gripped the back of Sasha's neck, forcing her gaze to meet his. Silver rimmed her irises and bled into the darker brown, yet another reminder of what she was. Taboo. Forbidden. *Mine*. The word resonated in Ewan's mind with such clarity. As though it had been planted there. Had she done that? Vampires had the power to bend others to their will, but could they do it with a thought? Ewan gritted his teeth as a wave of agitation crested over him. But that suspicion and worry did nothing to stop him.

Ewan brushed his thumb against her jawline as his pace increased. The pad moved to her bottom lip and dipped inside her mouth, dangerously close to one sharp fang. Her tongue lashed out as her lips closed around his thumb and she sucked. Ewan's gut tightened as he imagined those supple lips wrapped around his shaft, her teeth—her fangs—scraping over his sensitive flesh . . .

He jerked his thumb from her mouth the second the thought struck. Gregor would rip out his heart and feed it to him if he found out. This was the last time with Sasha. It couldn't happen again.

"Don't stop." Sasha's silvery gaze met his and her pleading tone vibrated through him. "I want it hard. Deep. I need to come."

Her heated words banished the thoughts that gave him pause. Ewan buried his face against her fragrant throat as he pounded into her. "I want you to say my name when you come." The words left his lips unbidden, but what did it matter? He needed that ownership of the moment. For her to know who had pleasured her.

"I don't know your name, berserker." The husky timbre of her voice vibrated down his spine and tightened his sac. A few more deep strokes and he'd go off. He refused to come until she did.

"Ewan Brún." He put his mouth close to her ear and pulled her lobe between his teeth before pulling away. "Say it."

Her moans became tighter, louder, echoing around them. So close. He drove hard into her, harder. Faster. His jaw locked down as he fucked her without mercy. Sasha's nails dug into his shoulders, breaking the skin, and he relished the bite of pain. "Say my name, Sasha." It wasn't a suggestion by any stretch of the imagination. He demanded it of her. "Say it."

"Oh, gods." Her body went rigid in his embrace. "I'm coming. Ewan. Gods, Ewan!"

Her pussy squeezed his shaft with powerful contractions that sent him over the edge. She buried her face against his throat and he let out a grunt at the sharp bite of pain where his shoulder met his neck. Heat suffused him, threading through his limbs and veins. Tiny tendrils of pleasure unfurled that intensified his orgasm to the point that his thighs shook and a growl gathered in his chest. His thrusts became disjointed. He pressed his body tight against hers, allowing the wall to help pin her against him. Shuddering breaths shook him as the blinding pleasure began to ebb and clarity blew in to take its place.

Her mouth. At his throat. A sharp sting. Gentle suction.

Gods. She'd bitten him!

Ewan couldn't think of a more forbidden act. To have allowed it at all invited disaster. Before she could close the punctures he pulled away with a violent jerk. Her fangs tore the tiny holes deeper and blood scented the air as it trickled down his neck to his chest. Sasha's brow furrowed and the silver drained from her wide-eyed stare. Fear chased across her delicate features and a momentary pang of guilt tugged at Ewan's chest.

"You have to let me close the punctures. My saliva—"

"You bit me!" Ewan did nothing to temper his seething tone.

Sasha's legs fell from his hips as he deposited her on the floor. The absence of her warmth sent a chill down Ewan's spine but he forced the sensation away. Sasha's brow remained furrowed, but she didn't cower from his spark of anger. Didn't shy away or act demure. Instead, she bucked her chin and her jaw took on a defiant set as she bent down to shove her legs back into her pants and pulled them up to her waist.

"What in the gods' names makes you think you have the right to bite me?" As far as Ewan was concerned, fucking the vampire wasn't an invitation to have her fangs at his throat. In their known history, no berserker had ever allowed a vampire to do such a thing. The consequences would be worse than death if Gregor found out. Ewan didn't dare contemplate the possibilities.

Sasha's eyes flashed brilliant silver and her breath heaved in her chest. One pale hand came up to brush her long, dark hair behind her shoulder as she fixed him with her hypnotic gaze. "You've tethered me, berserker." The words spilled from her full lips in an angry rush. "You're my *mate*."

Ewan took a stumbling step back. The words were as unbelievable as they were plausible. He'd never known vampires to take mates outside of their own species. And whereas he had no idea what a tether was, it had to have been the cause of the instant and visceral attraction between them.

"Magic?" He couldn't manage more than a single angry word. His interaction with the vampire seemed to create layer upon layer of trouble. "You've used some sort of enchantment on me?" It wasn't a question, more of an accusation.

Sasha's expression transformed into one of angry disbelief. "Enchantment?" The word was spoken with so much force that it pricked at his skin. "You think I've put some kind of spell on you?"

"Well, haven't you?"

Her palm cracked across his cheek. *Damn.* The vampire packed a punch. Ewan loosened his jaw and gave a violent shake of his head as a wave of anger crested within him. His fists balled at his sides as white-hot rage gathered in his chest. His nostrils flared as he dragged in several deep breaths in an attempt to keep himself calm.

Truth be told, Sasha didn't appear to have her temper in check any better. "Fuck you."

Her anger made her appear even more feral. More dangerous. More beautiful. And gods help him, even more irresistible.

CHAPTER
8

"Funny. Thought we just finished up with that."

Sasha's jaw hung slack. Her outrage had no effect on him. In fact, it only seemed to egg him on. She wanted to hit him again. This time, lay her fist against his other cheek. What good would it do, though? He obviously enjoyed the fight, as evidenced by his return to the arena.

"Sorry to disappoint you, but I don't have the power to enchant anyone or anything." Her fingers shook as she zipped and buttoned her pants. She bent down and slipped her shoes on. "So you have no one to blame but yourself for coming on to me."

He let out an amused snort that did nothing to calm her temper. "Don't try to cast the blame on me, as though you had no part in this."

"Contrary to what you might think, berserker, I have no control over the tether. What's done is done and there's no taking it back." Sasha pushed away from the wall and headed for the open docking bay at the rear of the stockroom. She didn't have to explain herself to him or anyone else. And she'd be damned if she let him blame her or make her feel guilty for something that was completely out of her control.

Sasha's wrist was seized in an iron grip a moment before she was spun around. The berserker's eyes darkened with his anger, giving him an almost sinister appearance. Under the cover of shadow, his face became more angular. Harder. His cheekbones sharp enough to cut. He didn't frighten her, though. It probably would've been better for her if he had.

"I want to know what this tether is," he demanded. "I want to know what you've done to me."

Sasha let out a disbelieving bark of laughter. "I haven't done a damn thing to you, berserker," she said with a rueful shake of her head. "It's you that's done something to me."

"I've got a name. You know it now. Use it."

Bossy SOB. Sasha let out an aggravated sigh. "Fine. I haven't done a damn thing to you, *Ewan*. Is that better?"

For a moment, his expression softened. He quickly recovered, however, and maintained his façade of barely controlled rage. "Better. Tell me about the tether."

Gods, he was infuriating. Sasha decided she liked him a lot better when they were simply fucking and not talking. Giving him any information would be tantamount to treason. But at this point, what did it matter? The damage was done. He was her mate and nothing would change that. Perhaps she could give him just enough to whet his appetite. Satisfy that annoyingly demanding curiosity and shut him the hell up so she could get out of there.

"Every vampire instinctually knows their mate on sight." Wasn't exactly a lie. She was simply mincing words. "It's something we feel in every fiber of our being. That first night, at the warehouse, I recognized the mate bond the second you crossed the arena toward me."

He fixed her with an unwavering stare, as he searched her expression for any sign of deceit. He made a show of breathing in deep and holding the air in his lungs before letting it slowly out. Sasha rolled her eyes. She didn't frighten easily. And she wasn't stupid. She knew what she could and couldn't get away with. He wasn't going to catch her in an outright lie.

"You expect me to believe that?"

Sasha shrugged as though she couldn't care less. "I don't expect anything from you. It is what it is. I'm just laying out the facts for you."

"You call those facts? You didn't give me one single piece of useful information."

Sasha's head canted slightly to the side. His accent became thicker, more pronounced, when he was agitated. Reminiscent of his native Scotland. She would've found it entertaining had she not been so monumentally annoyed. She couldn't help but wonder if he were truly this hard-headed or if he were simply working an angle. "The majority of supernatural creatures recognize mate bonds." This couldn't possibly be news to him. "Are you seriously going to stand there and argue over the legitimacy of mine?"

For two days, she'd been operating under the assumption that Ewan had sensed the bond between them. She knew little about berserkers, but what other explanation could there have been? As sworn enemies, she couldn't imagine him going to her willingly. He'd managed to shoot that theory to shit, though.

"Berserkers don't recognize the mate bond." His gaze hardened to onyx. "All of our females were executed by *vampires*."

Sasha flinched as though stung. Their combined histories weren't pretty. She'd heard the stories, though to her they'd merely been legends. An excuse for the berserkers and Sortiari to wage war against them. Either way, she didn't appreciate the accusation in his tone. She'd had no part in what had happened to their females, and yet, she and every dhampir and vampire on the face of the earth had apparently been made to pay for it.

"As was every vampire executed by berserkers." She could give as good as she got and she wasn't about to stand there and take his insults.

Ewan's dark gaze narrowed. "Not every vampire. Otherwise you wouldn't be here right now."

She let out a disbelieving chuff of laughter. Tethered mate or not, she wasn't going to listen to another second of this bullshit. So typical of a berserker to think that two wrongs would make a right. She jerked her arm free of his grasp. A hundred angry retorts sat at the tip of her tongue but Sasha swallowed them down. It would do no good to speak another word. Besides, she had a feeling he'd enjoy arguing with her all day, given the chance. She turned on a heel and kicked her supernatural speed into high gear, crossing the stockroom to the docking bay in the space of a second. It would've been nothing for Ewan to catch her if he'd wanted to give chase. Sasha stopped just outside the docking bay and glanced over her shoulder at the empty opening. Emotion tugged at her chest, half relief and half disappointment that he hadn't pursued her. She rubbed at her sternum as if it would somehow banish the sensation as she turned away and continued to run.

Preternatural stamina aside, Sasha regretted letting Ani take her car. The trek back to L.A. from the Valley only served to aggravate her already boiling temper. Plus, being alone gave Sasha plenty of time with her thoughts, allowing her to replay everything that had happened over and over again in her head. The images of the range of emotions that had passed over Ewan's expression when he realized she'd bitten him were seared in Sasha's mind. Her chest ached as though someone had hollowed it out with a spoon and she feared the dull pain would never go away.

Not even Saeed in his emotionless detachment had hurt her as badly as Ewan just had.

If this was what it meant to be tethered, Sasha wanted no part of it. She wanted to send her soul back into oblivion where nothing and no one could touch her. Where her heart would be guarded from those who could so carelessly rip it from her chest. Gods. She'd forgotten how ridiculously sensitive she could be. The beauty of being without her soul for all those months was that it had given her the opportunity to harden her heart. Or at least to have created the illusion of it. Before her turning, she'd feared that emptiness. Had dreaded the prospect of becoming numb.

Sasha stopped dead in her tracks. She doubled over, wrapping her arms around her torso, and let out a scream of frustration that echoed off the buildings around her. It did little to release the tension built up inside of her and did nothing to ease the dull ache in her chest. Tears stung at her eyes, but she refused to let them spill. The berserker was nothing more than a means to an end. A way to reclaim something she'd lost. There were plenty of males who would give a limb for the opportunity to have her fangs at their throats. So what if this one didn't want her? She had her soul back. She needed nothing further from him. She could let this be the end of it and move on.

In fact, it was what she had to do. The reality of the situation was, she had no other choice.

"Fuck!"

Ewan laid his fist into the cinderblock wall and it cracked from the force of the impact. The skin split at his knuckles and four crimson drops formed there before the wounds closed almost instantaneously. A surge of anger rose inside of him so intense, the flood of power caused him to sway on his feet. He'd wanted to chase after Sasha. To grab her by the arm once again and haul her against his body. To strip her and fuck her until he was too gods-damn tired for anything other than sleep.

Inside the building proper, the crowd cheered on two new fighters. The night was far from over and tonight's audience was particularly bloodthirsty. It would be nothing for Ewan to pull in several thousand dollars tonight. He could fight until he was too fucking exhausted to stand and Drew would be forced to drag his ass home. He had to do something. Because if he didn't, his own tortured thoughts would drive him out of his fucking mind.

The hurt in Sasha's expression was burned into his damn retinas. It stabbed through him sharper than any blade and cut deep. It was the sort of wound that supernatural healing couldn't mend. The type of wound that left a scar. Ewan had hurt many creatures over the course of his long life. Physically. Emotionally. Mentally. None of it had ever weighed on him until now.

Until her.

If she hadn't enchanted him, why did he feel this way? If she hadn't done something to him, why did hurting her matter when none of the others ever had? What made her so gods-damned special? What made her different? Ewan raked his fingers through the tangles of his hair, pulling at the strands. Nothing short of an ice pick through his cranium was going to get Sasha out of his head.

A growl built in Ewan's chest as he marched out of the stockroom and headed back toward the arena. Frustration, anger, want, need, and blind rage pooled in his gut. The power it created circulated through his limbs until he shook from the force of it. A dark haze fell over his vision, drowning out all color until his world became nothing more than shades of black and white. His thoughts slowed and became cottony until he was reduced to a creature of instinct. Driven by violence. Hungry for the kill.

He pushed his way through the crowd, past the battle master, and into the arena. It didn't matter that there were already two competitors inside. He'd kill them both. The crowd went wild until the sound of their eager shouts drowned out the last remaining shreds of Ewan's conscious mind. The battle rage took hold completely and he went to that dark place where nothing mattered. He didn't exist. His body moved without instruction from his conscious mind. There was nothing but empty black.

Freedom.

He came to with a spluttering gasp. His arms flailed, fists flying out to fight an invisible foe.

"Ewan!" He latched onto the sound of Drew's voice and let it pull him toward lucidity. "You're okay. It's over. There's no one left to fight."

No one? Jesus. From the way Drew made it sound, he'd killed off half of the gods-damned city. His head pounded like someone had driven a railroad spike through his brain. Another indicator of how completely he'd given himself over to the battle rage. He imagined it was the supernatural equivalent of a hangover, only he hadn't been afforded any of the fun to get to this place.

"What happened?" Ewan swallowed. His tongue stuck to the roof of his mouth. He couldn't have been out of it for more than a couple of hours, but his throat was dry enough to convince him he'd gone months without a sip of water.

"What happened is that you kicked serious fucking ass." Drew's wide grin caused Ewan's stomach to curl into a knot. He must've put on one hell of a fucking show for his cousin to look so smug. Drew pulled a large roll of bills from the front pocket of his hoodie and handed it over to Ewan. "Ten grand." He laughed. "I've never seen anything like it. You had the crowd so amped they were practically throwing their money at you."

Great. Like that wasn't bound to draw a hell of a lot of unnecessary attention. There was no way Gregor wouldn't find out about this. Ewan was fucked. "Go home, Drew. Right now. Don't wait for me. If Gregor asks where I am, tell him you have no idea and haven't seen me since this morning. Got it?"

Drew gave a determined shake of his head. "No way. I'm not hanging you out to dry."

"That's exactly what you're going to do." From the beginning, he'd planned to take all the heat whether Drew wanted him to or not. "Do as I say. If he asks, you're going to look him straight in the eye and lie like you've never lied before."

"He'll see right through it."

"No, he won't." They'd been working on their story for months just in case something like this happened. It was difficult to lie to a supernatural creature, but not impossible. If you owned the lie, truly believed your own bullshit, it could be done. Drew could pull it off. "It's too late for a change of heart now." From the beginning, Drew had been reluctant to help Ewan find the underground fighting ring and set up the matches. But his cousin was well connected in the city and trusted by those in the know despite what he was. Ewan had practically pressured him into it and there was no way in hell he was going to let him be punished for it.

"We go back together, or not at all."

Hardheadedness was a trait all berserkers shared. That stubborn streak got them into trouble more times than not.

"I'm not going to argue with you, Drew. This is what we agreed on. This is the way it has to be."

"He might not know. He's so damned preoccupied with other things he might not be paying attention to any of the gossip. It could be days before he hears anything about what happened tonight."

Wishful thinking. Ewan knew better. He'd obviously been in rare form tonight, burning off the anger and frustration from his fight with Sasha. Returning to the arena had been a mistake no matter how much cash it had brought in. He'd let her get under his skin and now he was going to pay the price for it.

"He's going to know, and he's going to be waiting for me. I can talk my way out of it but only if I'm not worried about covering your ass as well. Do us both a favor and stick to the plan." It was going to cost him a chunk of change and an even bigger chunk of his pride, but he'd do what had to be done. "I've got this under control, but you need to trust me."

Drew studied him for a quiet moment. "Never in a million years is he going to believe you're working alone."

It was true that berserkers behaved more like pack animals. They usually worked in small groups; even pairings were rare. Gregor would assume there were others involved and Ewan was prepared for that. He never did anything without a backup plan.

"Whether he believes it or not is immaterial. All I need is to distract him."

Drew's gaze narrowed. "From what?"

Ewan gave a shake of his head. Sometimes his cousin could be a little dense. "You. Me." He threw his hand up and swirled around. "This." He hated that he'd have to give up tonight's winnings, but the one thing he knew Gregor would never turn away was money. Not when he needed so much of it to fund their cause.

"No. No way." The light bulb finally clicked on inside Drew's head. "It's a fucking fortune. The biggest purse you've won yet. And you're just gonna hand it over to him?"

"It's good money, but hardly a fortune. And offering it up to Gregor is worth the sacrifice if it buys us some time." Ewan wasn't about to take his eyes off the prize. He wanted out. As far as possible from this centuries-old vendetta and Gregor's ego-fueled power grab. Now wasn't the time to lose focus. He could still pull this off. He just needed Drew to cooperate.

His cousin gave a sad shake of his head. "You deserve every penny of that money. You more than earned it."

Ewan pulled five hundred-dollar bills from the role and slapped them into Drew's hand. It was far less than what his cut should've been, but he was owed something for his trouble.

"I'm not taking this." Drew held out his hand but Ewan refused to take the money. "If you're handing your cut over, I'm handing mine over, too."

Ewan hesitated but he could tell by the set of his cousin's jaw that he wasn't about to back down. He appreciated the solidarity and took the money back without another word of argument. "I'll make it up to you." When Ewan made a promise, he kept it.

"I know you will." Drew's lips quirked in a half smile.

Anxious energy skittered down Ewan's spine. It had been one hell of a night, and it was far from over. "Go home." The sooner Drew got back, the better. Besides, he needed a few moments alone to clear his head.

Drew gave a curt nod and turned to leave without another word. Berserkers were creatures of action. Once they agreed on a plan, they followed through. Always. At least for that, Ewan could be thankful. The gods knew he had little else to be grateful for.

He let out a slow breath as his thoughts inevitably circled back to Sasha. He let out a chuff of rueful laughter. Funny to think, Ian Gregor was the least of his problems.

CHAPTER
9

"Ewan, Gregor wants to see you. Now."

Ewan couldn't say he was surprised to find an escort waiting at the door to take him straight to their fearless leader. No doubt it had been orchestrated as a sort of ambush. Gregor's favorite tactic. Unfortunately for him, Ewan was more than prepared for an attack. Sort of tough to get the upper hand on one of your own when they already knew the playbook.

Gavin stared Ewan down as though anticipating defiance and since Ewan loved to disappoint people, he headed straight toward Gregor's apartment without so much as a grunt in response. He kept his posture relaxed, his breathing even, and his heartbeat slow. Ewan knew exactly what to do to make his body cooperate. He'd spent years training his physical reactions to obey his conscious thoughts. Ewan wouldn't be betrayed by quickened breath, dilated pupils, tense muscles, or anything else. For all intents and purposes, Gregor would find him calm and amicable. Completely trustworthy.

He stopped in the hallway at Gregor's door. The

abandoned apartment building wasn't fit for rodents, but Gregor insisted they live here. Ewan's lip curled with disgust. He hated it here. Hated the disrepair. The smell. The lack of electricity or running water. He hated living like a fucking animal and foregoing even the smallest comfort for the supposed greater good. Gregor expected sacrifice and complete loyalty without offering a gods-damned thing in return. The bitter tang of resentment burned Ewan's tongue and he swallowed against the sensation that formed a tight knot in his throat. His eyes drifted shut for the barest moment as he drew in a deep and even breath, held it in his lungs, and released it just as slowly. Calm settled over him as the anger ebbed from his body.

"Get in here."

Ewan didn't even have to knock. Gregor was shrewd, his senses keen. It was tough to get one over on the self-proclaimed berserker king but Ewan was about to give it his best shot. He turned the knob on the door and stepped inside the dark and dingy run-down apartment. Gods, what a shithole. He still couldn't believe Gregor found this existence preferable to working for the Sortiari.

Not even a candle illuminated the living room. Ewan was sure Gregor preferred it that way, as though the dark would somehow make him even more sinister than he already was. Instead, Ewan found it unnecessary and melodramatic. These sorts of theatrics might've worked on other supernatural creatures, but it was a waste of energy for him to use it on his own brethren.

"You've been a busy son of a bitch, haven't you?"

This wasn't the first time Ewan had been on the receiving end of that angry, abrasive tone. It didn't faze him in the slightest. He shrugged, knowing full well that Gregor would see the casual gesture through the dark. "I wouldn't say busy, so much as preoccupied."

Gregor attacked in a smear of darkness, shoving Ewan

so hard against the wall that the plaster cracked and the drywall gave way. Chunks of it landed in his hair and he gave a shake of his head to dislodge the debris, sending a cloud of grayish white dust around them. Anger pooled in his gut and threatened to overtake him. Ewan commanded his body to resist the pull of anger and focused his thoughts. An image came to mind of lush pink lips and he calmed.

"What the fuck makes you think you can speak to me in that way?" Gregor wrapped his fist in the neck of Ewan's T-shirt as he leaned in close.

It was a rhetorical question not meant to be answered, simply a reminder that Gregor was—as he'd always been—someone not to be fucked with. As if Ewan, or anyone else for that matter, needed a reminder. Instead, he reached into his pocket and pulled out the roll of bills he'd earned tonight and held it aloft for Gregor's inspection.

"What the hell is this?"

"For the cause." It took every ounce of willpower Ewan had to keep the sneer from his tone. "I have been busy. Earning money for you."

Gregor's lip pulled back into a snarl. He gave Ewan a rough shake that rattled his jaw and embedded him deeper into the drywall. "You expect me to believe that shit?"

"Would I be giving you the money otherwise?"

Gregor laughed. "You might. If you'd been found out and were trying to save your own gods-damned neck."

No one could say Ian Gregor was stupid. Ewan had known this was going to be a hard sell but a little skepticism and a couple of body slams weren't going to deter him. "You were gone. It was stagnant as fuck around here. I needed to do something." That much at least, was the truth. "You're going to get down on me for being proactive?" It might've been stupid to poke the bear, but berserkers were aggressive by nature. It would be more suspicious if Ewan didn't try to pick a fight.

"I'm going to get down on you for going behind my back!" Gregor railed. "And . . ." He tightened his grip on Ewan's shirt. His voice went low and dangerous and a flicker of fear shot through Ewan's veins. "For keeping company with a gods-damned vampire. Who the fuck is she?" Gregor demanded with another rough shake. "And why isn't she dead?"

Fuck. Ewan had been hopeful that little bit of gossip had yet to reach Gregor's ears. He should have known better. A protective instinct rose within him at the mention of Sasha. Ewan didn't want Gregor to know a gods-damned thing about her. She was a secret he wanted to keep all to himself. He could try to lie. Tell the crafty warlord king that the gossip was wrong. That whoever saw what they thought they saw had been wrong. But lying would only insult Gregor's intelligence. Ewan had known that if he were going to pull this off, his plan would have to be set on a foundation of truth.

Despite Sasha's confession that Ewan had somehow tethered her, he didn't owe her anything, least of all his protection. She'd bitten him. Without his permission. Taken his blood as though it was something due her. The offense was still fresh in his mind. Still stung his pride and tarnished every belief that had been ingrained in him. Ewan had to look out for himself because no one else would. He had to look out for Drew because he'd given his cousin his word. He'd made no vows to Sasha. His throat tightened as though resisting the words he was about to speak. Resisting the betrayal. There was no help for it. Ewan had no choice.

He knew what he had to do.

"The vampire thinks I'm her mate." The truth burned his tongue as though to punish him with it. "She said . . ." He let out a breath. "Nothing that made any sense."

Gregor loosened his hold on Ewan's collar and he

braced himself for the blow that was sure to come. Instead, Gregor threw his head back and his robust laughter filled Ewan's ears.

"Aristov must be breeding madness in his fledgling flock. Her mate?" His incredulous tone caused Ewan's hackles to rise. "It's impossible!"

He didn't know why Gregor's words got on his nerves so much. Hadn't he thought the exact same thing when the affirmation left Sasha's lips? A mate bond between a vampire and berserker wasn't simply unheard of; it went against everything they knew about themselves. But Gregor couldn't believe it simply for those reasons. Believing would undermine the very foundation of a centuries-long vendetta and the revenge he so desperately craved.

"What did you say to her when she told you this nonsense?" Gregor asked between bouts of laughter.

Perhaps it was Gregor who was mad and not the vampires. He sure as hell didn't seem to have his shit together. Ewan had come here expecting to receive a sound beating. He didn't like shifting gears, but here he was, foot to the pedal. "I told her to get the hell out of my sight." Honesty was the best policy, but there were some things even Ian Gregor didn't need to know. The last detail Ewan planned to divulge to anyone was that she'd bitten him. He still hadn't taken the time to fully process what had happened himself.

"And she obeyed?"

Honestly, Ewan was just as surprised about that as Gregor was. "She did. I told you, she thinks there's a bond between us. Her certainty is unflappable."

"I can use this," Gregor said more to himself than to Ewan. A tremor of anxiety rippled through him. "And you, Ewan Brún, are going to help me."

Ewan's situation had definitely just gone from bad to worse. The last thing he needed was to have Gregor's undivided attention. And thanks to Sasha, he was going to get it.

"Sasha, I'd like you to meet Lucas."

Gods, why had she agreed to this? Sasha extended her hand. Lucas took it in his and gave it a firm shake that nearly pulled her elbow free of her arm. The male was *huge*.

"Nice to meet you."

She smiled at Lucas and then at Bria before stepping aside to invite them inside the house. Shortly after Sasha had been turned, Bria—Jenner's mate and a sort of vampire community outreach representative—had come to the house to check up on things. Saeed had left on his quest for his mate and put the coven in Sasha's and Diego's care. The vampire king hadn't been thrilled about Saeed jumping ship and had sent Bria to do a "new vampire" welfare check. Bria had sensed Sasha's loneliness and despair, and had offered to introduce her to her friend Lucas so that the two might keep each other company. That had been before Sasha had decided she'd had enough of her mopey existence and had gone out to do something about it. Now, she was stuck in what she could only assume was a blind date. *Awesome.* Like this wasn't bound to be awkward as fuck.

Lucas stepped inside and gave her a sheepish smile. Despite his size and imposing appearance, Sasha could tell that Lucas was gentle and kind. Eyes didn't lie and his soft blue gaze hid nothing. There was an innocence to Lucas that softened Sasha's heart. She didn't even have to know him well to sense it. It surrounded him like an aura.

Sasha led the way to the media room at the south end of the house. Diego had left a half hour ago, and Saeed and his mate had left for Mikhail Aristov's house at sundown. The other members of their coven were either gone for the night or occupied elsewhere, which was fine by Sasha. The last thing she needed was a bunch of curious dhampirs nosing in on her business to report back to Saeed.

"So, how's it going?"

If anyone other than Bria had asked, Sasha would've responded that she should mind her own damned business. But Bria was as kind and sincere as they came. She didn't have a fake or malicious bone in her body. And Sasha knew anything she told her would go straight to the vault. She wondered if the same went for Lucas? The gods knew Sasha could use a few more allies.

"Oh, it's going." She flopped down on the sectional and motioned for Bria and Lucas to join her. "Same old, same old."

Bria studied Sasha for a quiet moment. A wry grin spread on her lips. "You've definitely loosened up since the last time I was here, so some things must be going all right."

The beauty of being an emotional bottler was the ability to pretend that your life was sunshine and rainbows even when it was a complete shit show. Sasha's new carefree, don't-give-a-fuck lifestyle had little to do with being happy. More to the point, it only served to prove she had wicked self-destructive tendencies.

"Sure." Sasha shrugged. "I decided to embrace change instead of fight it."

"It's okay to need an adjustment period. Change is hard for everyone."

Sasha really did like Bria. But her calming presence was as disturbing as it was reassuring. Rather than put Sasha at ease, it reminded her of the turbulence of her own life. For the past several days she'd tried to get the berserker out of her head. Tried to forget the sensation of his touch, the intensity of his gaze, the heat of his body against hers, his rough exterior, gruff voice, and his cruel words that bit into her flesh like barbs. She didn't understand how someone she knew so little about could already claim ownership over her emotions. When Bria had asked if she and Lucas could come over, Sasha had seen it as an opportunity for a much needed distraction. But she was starting to think that nothing short of a lobotomy would banish the berserker from her mind.

"Change is a pain in the ass." Sasha didn't bother sugarcoating it. "But it doesn't do any good to fight it."

Bria laughed. "True."

Sasha shifted in her seat. The walls of the media room felt like they were closing in on her and she cleared her throat. Bria was being nothing but nice and so far, Lucas had adopted a don't-speak-unless-spoken-to approach to the conversation. This wasn't the distraction that Sasha needed. Not by a longshot. She could sit and nod her head and pretend to hear every word Bria said while her mind wandered inevitably to Ewan. Despite his obvious disgust at having her fangs at his throat, Sasha craved yet another taste. Everything about him should've turned her off. She should have found him nauseating. Unsavory. Foul. His stench, his taste, should've repelled her. Instead, she longed to breathe in his heady musk. And she craved his blood like junkies craved their next fix. In the space of two encounters he'd managed to ruin her. He'd pleasured her. Insulted her. Excited her. And hurt her. It showed just how little pride Sasha had that the only thing she could think about was how she might be able to find him again.

"Hey." Sasha brought her gaze up and focused on Bria's concerned expression. "Are you okay, Sasha? You seem a little preoccupied."

That was an understatement. "I know it's rude, and this is going to make me a horrible hostess, but I seriously feel like I'm about to crawl out of my own skin. I really need to get out of here, Bria." If she thought about Ewan for another second, she'd go out of her mind. "I'm sorry, Lucas. Can I get a rain check?"

Bria's brow furrowed but she didn't press Sasha to talk about what had her so keyed up. "Of course. Don't let us stop you from getting a little air, especially when you need it."

Sasha wanted to laugh. Her life was so pathetically tragic it was almost embarrassing. She pushed up from the couch and at the same time, Lucas stood. "If you want some company, I'll go out with you."

Why couldn't she have found herself tethered to a male like Lucas? He was seemingly perfect. Good-looking, sweet, gentle, polite. She doubted he'd ever grab a female by the arm and bend her over a bathroom sink without so much as a proper introduction. Sasha cursed under her breath as a thrill chased through her at the memory of Ewan doing just that. He reviled her. Found her bite disgusting, and still, she wanted him.

"I'd love some company." The last thing Sasha wanted was to be alone. She could've called Ani to go out with her, but she wasn't looking for a lecture from her, either. She didn't think Lucas was interested in talking her ear off or offering up any judgment. He'd make a great wingman. "If that's okay with you, Bria?"

"Hey." Lucas's light blue eyes sparked with amusement. "I don't need her permission to go out. Last time I checked, I didn't need her permission to do anything."

Huh. Sasha smiled. Looked like gentle, quiet Lucas wasn't quite so meek after all. She liked that there was a little mystery to him. Her gaze slid to Bria who wore a wide grin. "He's right. You two have fun, and I'll catch up with you later."

Bria pushed up from the couch and headed for the door to the media room. She gave Lucas a quick wave in parting before she left. Sasha couldn't help but wonder if it had been her plan all along to throw the two of them together. Too bad Bria didn't know that Sasha had already been tethered, not that it would matter.

Sasha turned to Lucas. She needed a distraction and she needed it now. "Well, Lucas? Ready to get into a little trouble?"

He flashed a wide smile, which wasn't quite as innocent as she'd anticipated, that showcased the dual points of his fangs. "Absolutely."

Perfect.

CHAPTER
10

A few days ago, Ewan might've counted himself lucky that the vampires had become scarce. Out of sight, out of mind and all that. Though really, Sasha could've taken up residence on another planet and it wouldn't have been far enough to keep her out of his thoughts. Ewan didn't know much about Sasha, but one thing he knew with certainty: she was chasing a thrill. He wouldn't find her in some nightclub or coffee shop. She wouldn't be hanging out at a concert, or a bar, or any other mundane, overdone, tired location. Sasha craved danger. Excitement. She wanted to push the boundaries of her comfort zone and maybe even scare herself a little. She wanted to feel alive. He knew because he had the same wants and needs. It was part of what had sent him to the battle arena in the first place. He'd find her. Eventually. He simply needed to look in the right place.

Ewan should have known Gregor would use the information he'd given him to his advantage. Rather than take Ewan to task for not killing Sasha on sight, Gregor found an opportunity to infiltrate his enemies from the inside. He planned to use this notion of a mate bond to his advantage in the hopes that Sasha would somehow trust Ewan enough to allow him entrance to her world. Knowing the location of her coven would afford Gregor the opportunity to ambush it and kill every vampire and dhampir within its confines. Ewan's gut soured at the thought even though it was an optimistic plan, one that was more likely to fail than succeed. Sasha might have claimed some mystical force bound her to him but that didn't mean she was going to bring Ewan home to meet the fam.

None of it mattered, however, if he couldn't find her first. She'd abandoned the fighting venues. Ewan hadn't fought since the night he'd come clean to Gregor, a fact that had Drew cranky and on edge. His cousin was already in too deep and Ewan refused to bring him in any deeper. He told Drew simply that he had to put fighting on the back burner until things cooled down with Gregor and his attention wandered elsewhere. Drew wasn't buying it. He was convinced Gregor was setting them up, allowing for a false sense of security, in order to take them down nice and hard later on. It had taken Ewan a good day to convince Drew that he'd be fine as long as he kept his nose to the ground, business as usual. In turn, Drew had insisted on coming along as backup for whatever tasks Gregor had set out for Ewan. Of course he'd refused, telling Drew that for now, keeping his zero accountability status was more important than anything else.

But damn it, finding Sasha might've been a hell of a lot easier with some backup.

In reality, supernatural creatures had very little to fear. With their virtual immortality came very minimal risk. They were impervious to most hurts, were incredibly fast and strong. The battle arena drew crowds and participants alike because the stakes were high. Wherever Sasha chose to spend her nights now would carry the same sorts of risks. Anything else would bore her.

Gods, he wished he knew what he was looking for. High-stakes betting? Contests? Tests of strength or stamina? Where would she go? What would she do if, like Ewan, she was trying to forget the electricity that sparked between them?

Perhaps the thrill Sasha sought had nothing to do with violence at all. Ewan's jaw squared with anger and his teeth ground together as realization struck. Sex. That was the thrill she'd sought the night they met. What better way to banish an old lover from your mind than to take a new one?

Motherfucker. If any male so much as laid a finger on Sasha, Ewan was going to gut him.

There were plenty of sex clubs in Los Angeles but few that catered to specifically supernatural clientele. Power flooded Ewan's bloodstream as anger transformed to rage. The unfamiliar jealousy was like fire in his veins. He'd never experienced anything like it before. Unnerving. And a damned nuisance.

Why should he give a single shit who the vampire fucked? Despite her assertion to the contrary, Ewan had no claim on her. He cupped his right palm over his throat. The sensation of her bite was branded in his memory, still so visceral it caused his cock to stir behind his fly. He'd turned her away. Treated her with disgust and disdain. Why wouldn't she go in search of another male in order to put Ewan out of her mind? He wouldn't blame her for the retaliation, but he sure as shit didn't have to be happy about it.

Ewan climbed into the beat-up Honda Civic that was barely big enough to accommodate his large frame. He knew of a place in West Hollywood that was bound to draw Sasha's attention. A pang of guilt tugged at his chest. He should leave her alone and let whatever this was between them wallow in its death throes. Instead, he was letting Gregor use him and their supposed bond in order to protect his real secret from being found out.

So yeah, he was a total piece of shit. Then again, Sasha would be wise not to expect anything but betrayal from someone that for all intents and purposes was an enemy.

Ewan tried not to think too hard about the path Gregor had set him on as he pulled into a parking space on Santa Monica Boulevard. His knuckles turned white as he gripped the steering wheel. Some small part of him hoped he wouldn't find Sasha inside the club, while the rest of him knew without a doubt he'd see her. And when he did, the gods help anyone that was within touching distance of her.

Ewan got out of the car and walked across the street to North La Brea. He walked a block or so, toward what appeared to be a clothing boutique. The signage read *Sugar Plums* and looked like the sort of place trendy starlets came to blow a few thousand dollars on a fucking blouse. The boutique was closed but Ewan knew it was only a front. He walked around to the back of the building and knocked at the service entrance. He was greeted by a lithe, buxom fae dressed in tight black leather and combat boots. Her bright violet eyes raked him from head to toe and a wry smile settled on her full crimson lips.

"Pay to play, berserker." She held out her hand, palm up.

Ewan's lip curled. Of course this would cost him money. "How much?"

The fae rested her shoulder against the doorjamb as she continued to study him with interest. "Two hundred."

Great. Ewan fished inside his pocket and retrieved four fifty-dollar bills. He slapped them into the fae's waiting hand and her grin widened.

"Have fun." Ewan stepped forward and she placed the pad of her index finger against his chest, pressing into him as her expression became serious. "But not too much fun. Behave yourself down there and don't play rough." The smile returned to her face. "Unless someone asks you to, that is." She lowered her arm and stepped aside to allow Ewan entrance.

She might've played it cool, but Ewan recognized the anxious tang of her scent. He doubted a berserker had ever frequented the place and that was bound to make anyone nervous. They weren't exactly known for their even tempers and gentle ways. Berserkers were killing machines and good for little else. Some of the rumors that circulated about them suggested they were celibate and behaved as priests under the Sortiari's direction. Others thought them to be unequipped for anything but fighting and killing. Smooth like a Ken doll. Ewan let out a disdainful snort. He'd fucked his way across the city when they first came to L.A. His equipment worked just fine. It was simply a matter of his partners not wanting it out that they'd fucked a monster.

From the stockroom, a set of stairs led down into a basement. Lights flickered and music played from the secret supernatural sex club that operated beneath the boutique. With every step he took, Ewan's gut clenched tighter. His nerves were raw, his senses on edge. He couldn't afford to lose control, but if he found Sasha down there, all bets were off.

Ewan reached the bottom step and took in his surroundings. The air was thick with lust. Heady to the point that the scent nearly made him drunk. A long, dark corridor stretched out toward a central lounge and from there, two more corridors jutted off at either end that led to private rooms and smaller lounges. The individual scent signatures of all the creatures present mingled into one, confusing Ewan's senses. He tried to pick Sasha's spicy cinnamon from the mix but came up short. Frustration tightened his muscles as he walked deeper into the club.

On a raised stage in the center of the main lounge, females danced and twined their naked bodies around poles, dipping and twisting toward onlookers, eager for their outstretched hands and gentle touches. At the far end of the main lounge, partially shrouded in darkness, naked bodies writhed as couples, and even small groups, fucked for the entertainment of those around them.

Ewan's blood pumped hard and fast through his veins as he scanned the crowd for any sign of Sasha. A vampire would be a rare prize in this place. He suspected that wherever she was, she'd no doubt gathered several eager admirers. Ewan let his instinct guide him as he wound his way through the lounge toward the corridor that jutted off to the right. The faintest hint of cinnamon mixed with something deep and musky hit his nostrils and he said a silent prayer that his nose was wrong even though he already knew the truth.

Sasha was here. And she wasn't alone.

Sasha had started out the night with Lucas but she hadn't finished it with him. They'd hit several downtown clubs, danced, drank, flirted, and laughed. They'd had a great time and Sasha truly liked him. But she grew too restless for what she now considered mundane entertainment. Her mind was too full of Ewan to settle down. Lucas wasn't quite as innocent as Sasha had first assumed, but he was still far too tame for this place. And so, they'd parted ways so she could go out and find a distraction that would once and for all banish the dangerously attractive berserker from her thoughts.

Sure, she could've hooked up with some random male

at Onyx or the Dragon's Den, but an encounter like that would've lacked the thrill Sasha had quickly become accustomed to during her brief encounters with Ewan. She'd only been with him twice but already he'd ruined her for other males. *Gods.* Fate really did have it out for her. She had one goal tonight: get that big, muscled, gruff, asshole of a sex god out of her system. Period. She'd fuck every last male in the city if that's what it took. The berserker couldn't possibly be the only good lay in the city.

"What sort of fun are you looking for tonight?"

Sasha turned to the source of the deep rumbling voice and smiled wide to showcase her fangs. The male wasn't bad looking. Shifter. A few inches taller than her with a lean, sculpted frame, strong jaw, and high cheekbones. His hair was a few shades darker than Ewan's, and his eyes blue instead of light, haunting brown. Neither did he tower over her or make her feel small with his bulk. And he didn't carry himself with the same brazen arrogance. The shifter might've thought he was a badass, but Sasha had yet to meet anyone as menacing, dangerous, and completely thrilling as Ewan. This male was like a shitty carbon copy from an obsolete Xerox machine. All he'd manage would be to disappoint her. Time to move on.

Like everyone Sasha came into contact with, the second the shifter took stock of her fangs his demeanor changed. His smile grew. His eyes widened a fraction of an inch and shone with a greedy light. His scent intensified with desire and he took a step closer. One of the problems with being unique.

"Whatever it is," Sasha replied, "it isn't going to include you. Sorry."

The cool rebuff did little to deter him. He took another step closer and reached out to seize her wrist in his hand. Moments like these made Sasha second-guess her decision to live her life out in the open. She was desirable because she was different. Exotic. An endangered creature rarely seen in the wild. A prize for any hunter, and make no mistake, the supernatural world was populated with predators. Her uniqueness didn't make her public property, however. It didn't give him—or anyone—the right to touch her, demand a piece of her, or anything else. If he thought he was entitled to any little bit of her, he had another think coming.

"I think you've forgotten where you are tonight, little vampire." The shifter leaned in close and put his mouth to Sasha's ear as he spoke. His grip tightened on her wrist as he guided her hand to his cock. "Everyone plays. Or you go home."

Sasha's muscles tensed as a wave of angry annoyance stole over her. "I'm not sure what you think you're entitled to"—she jerked her hand from his grip—"but it sure as hell isn't me. I said I don't want you. I'm not sure how much clearer I can be. Leave me alone before I'm tempted to sink my fangs into your throat and drink you dry."

The threat of violence only seemed to encourage him. *Great.* He reached for her again, this time wrapping his arms around her waist and hauling her body roughly against his. "Perfect." He reached up and wound his fist in the length of her hair to keep her immobile. "I like it rough, and I don't mind a little fight."

Oh, he was going to get more than a little fight. Before Sasha could swing out with her fist, the shifter turned and put her back to the nearest wall. It was the same tactic Ewan had used in the stockroom, but the shifter lacked her mate's charisma, finesse, and raw sexual allure. Was he really so stupid as to think he could force her? Or maybe he thought she was playing some sort of game? Did she need a safe word? Gods, she didn't know. Either way, the male was about to receive a serious wake-up call.

Time to show the unruly shifter what happened when you tangled with a vampire.

Before Sasha could act, the shifter was ripped away from her. Strong arms pulled him from her body and tossed him against the far wall like he was nothing more than a rag doll. Sasha turned toward her high-handed rescuer and her breath caught in her chest. Ewan was magnificent in his rage, eyes dark and inky black, muscles bulging, chest heaving, and his full lips pulled back in a menacing snarl.

"Touch her again and I'll rip your arms from the sockets."

His accent thickened with his anger and a thrill chased through Sasha's bloodstream. Gods-damn it, why was he the only male on the face of the earth who could affect her in this way? It was completely unfair.

The shifter dragged in several ragged breaths. "Take your hands off me, you disgusting piece of shit. Do you think I'm scared of you? You're the dregs at the bottom of the supernatural barrel."

Sasha wanted to tell the male that it probably wasn't a good idea to insult a berserker warlord, but it looked as though Ewan was about to get the point across on his own just fine. Sasha hung back, her shoulder blades still pressed against the wall, hands splayed beside her. Her heart beat a mad rhythm in her chest and her breath raced. Ewan excited her like no other male could.

Rather than give the shifter what he wanted, Ewan smiled at the insult. Somehow the expression was more frightening than an angry scowl. The calm before the storm. Black bled into his irises and the inky tendrils reached out into the whites. When possessed by rage, Ewan truly was a terrifying sight. The shifter's scent changed, the first indication that his cocky show was nothing more than bravado.

Ewan wrapped his hand around the shifter's throat. The act was done with such measured calm—almost lovingly— that it sent a chill over Sasha's skin. His fist contracted and the shifter squirmed and clawed at Ewan's hand as he tried to free himself from the unyielding iron grip. Sasha had seen Ewan kill. She'd bore witness to his cold, cruel determination. But in those cases, both participants had been willing parties, aware of the consequences. If Ewan killed the shifter, it would be cold-blooded murder.

"Don't." Sasha kept her tone calm and even. She pushed away from the wall and moved to stand behind Ewan. Her hand came to rest on his shoulder and the muscles there flexed beneath her palm. The shifter was a son of a bitch, no doubt about that, but Sasha had been holding her own before Ewan intervened. He didn't deserve to die.

The shifter's face turned red as desperate gasps died in his chest. His eyes rolled back in his head as Ewan's fist constricted tighter. Tighter . . . Sasha's fingertips dug into his shoulder as the tension stretched out for another moment. Ewan released his hold and the shifter crumpled to the floor. He massaged his throat as he sucked in frantic gulps of air into his lungs. Gold sparked in his blue gaze that narrowed on Ewan and then Sasha. He didn't say a word, though. Didn't move. After a moment, his gaze dropped to the floor in a show of submission.

Sasha let out a slow, shuddering breath as the tension drained out of her body. Gods. That could have been a disaster.

Ewan turned and seized Sasha by the wrist. He looked from one open doorway to another and steered her in the direction of the first available room. She was getting pretty damned tired of high-handed males hauling her around without at least first asking how she felt about it. Sasha resisted his pull and he turned to bestow upon her a look that was part lust, part unchecked anger, and part stunned disbelief.

"We can do this in that room"—he jerked his chin toward the doorway—"or right here in the fucking hallway. Take your pick."

Gods, what did he plan to do to her? A pleasant rush fanned outward from Sasha's stomach through her limbs. He shouldn't have excited her like he did. She should have been annoyed. Angry. Repulsed. Even a little fucking scared! But when it came to the rough and demanding berserker, Sasha found that she had no self-control. No pride. No fear. Not an ounce of damned sense. And it needed to stop.

"You insult me, turn me away, treat me like dirt on the bottom of your shoe, and you expect me to fall into line and obey your orders without question?" Sasha let out a disbelieving bark of laughter. "Sorry, but it's not going to happen."

Ewan's gaze narrowed but it remained the beautiful tawny golden brown that she loved so much. His finger jutted out toward the doorway. "Get in that room, Sasha. Now."

She folded her arms across her chest. "No."

"All right." He took a step toward her. "You asked for it."

Well, shit. She had asked for it, hadn't she?

CHAPTER
11

Ewan grabbed Sasha and threw her over his shoulder. If she was going to act like a stubborn child, he was going to treat her like one. She let out a squeal of enraged surprise followed by a forceful whoof of air. Ewan stepped to the left, into the nearest available room, and kicked the door closed behind him. This was where the shifter intended to take Sasha. And it was certainly equipped for all sorts of erotic play.

Anger rose fresh and hot in Ewan's chest. She'd come here tonight looking for this. He stood, feet planted on the floor, and took in the sight of the room. A sex swing hung from one corner of the ceiling, one wall was adorned with bondage gear. The king-sized bed in the middle of the space was equipped with a sturdy headboard and footboard complete with leather cuffs, long scraps of silk, blindfolds, leather crops and others with feathered tips. It was a room designed for pleasure and the realization that Sasha had willingly sought this out made Ewan's gut tangle into an unyielding knot. Not because she wanted a little wild and kinky sex, but because she'd wanted it with someone other than him.

"Put me down."

Sasha pressed her palms against his ass and pushed herself upward. Ewan's jaw squared and his jaw clenched so tightly that he felt the enamel on his molars grind. He deposited her to her feet and she took a stumbling step back as she pushed against his chest. She bumped into the foot of the bed and reached out to steady herself on the footboard, rattling the leather cuffs secured there in the process. Ewan couldn't help but picture her laid out on the coverlet, her ankles and wrists secured in place, helpless to do anything but lie there while he pleasured her. His cock stirred behind his fly and his gut clenched as a wave of white hot lust shot through him. He'd agreed to get close to Sasha to protect his other secrets from Gregor. He tried to convince himself that she had no effect on him. That she was nothing more than a curiosity he'd needed to work out of his system. Sasha wasn't a curiosity. She was a fucking drug and Ewan was on the road to becoming an addict.

"What in the hell are you doing here?"

Ewan was taken aback by Sasha's indignant tone. His lust was quickly replaced again by anger. He turned and locked the door before coming back to face her. The last thing he needed was some randy asshole barging in to try and join in the fun. "What am *I* doing here? What in the hell are *you* doing here?"

"I don't need your permission to go anywhere or do anything." Sasha's eyes flashed silver, an indication that her temper was about to crest.

"Oh really?" Ewan knew better than to take her on, but he couldn't help himself. "Did you, or did you not, proclaim that I was your *mate*? Do you often make such claims before seeking out other males to fuck?"

Sasha's eyes went wide. She gripped onto the footboard and leaned forward for emphasis. Ewan's mouth went dry as he looked at her. Her expression, livid eyes bright with silver, face flushed, her breasts pressing against the tight tank top she wore and threatening to spill over the deep V of the neckline. "You sent me away!"

"You bit me!"

Sasha let out a bark of disbelieving laughter. "*Vampire!*" She jabbed a finger at her chest. "It's sort of what we do."

"What? Sink your fangs into your victim's throats without asking permission?"

Sasha's brow furrowed with hurt and Ewan felt a stab of momentary regret. She was right. What she'd done was simply what was in her nature to do. He couldn't fault her for it and yet, centuries of hate and conditioning had convinced him to do just that. Quiet settled between them, so thick and heavy that it nearly suffocated him. Ewan fought the urge to rub at his chest and instead crossed the space between them and put his mouth to hers.

Ewan had fucked Sasha, but he'd yet to kiss her. Her lips were as soft as he imagined, full and silky as she yielded to him. Ewan deepened the kiss, slanting his mouth over hers, forcing her lips to part with his tongue. She kept her grip on the footboard, creating space between their bodies, and a growl built in Ewan's chest. He didn't want an inch of space between them. He wanted her hands on him. Any reservation on her part wasn't acceptable.

As much as he hated to break their kiss, Ewan pulled away. Just enough to speak against her mouth. "Touch me."

Sasha leaned back in a show of defiance. "No."

Ewan's frustration mounted. Passive aggression wouldn't do anything to calm the temper that simmered just under the surface of his control. Before he'd insulted her that night in the stockroom, Sasha hadn't been able to keep her hands off him. Now, as punishment, she withheld what he wanted. Ewan didn't respond well to aggression of any kind. Nor punishment. Hell, he'd defied his own leader, the most feared warlord in supernatural history. He expected nothing less than total surrender from Sasha. There was a time and a place for playing games. Tonight, however, Ewan wasn't in the mood.

That piece-of-shit shifter had taken Sasha's hand and placed it on his cock. He'd pushed her when she didn't want to be pushed. The bastard was lucky Sasha had stayed Ewan's hand, otherwise that particular piece of him would have been the first to go. Maybe it wasn't wise to make demands when she'd been faced with unwanted advances only moments before. Ewan wanted to be understanding and gentle and all of those things he expected more sensitive males were, but it simply wasn't programed into his biology to be any of those things. He was burly, demanding, insensitive. Selfish, gruff, and rough around the edges. Hell, maybe he was every bit as bad as that piece-of-shit shifter. The only difference being that in the short span of two encounters, he already felt a possessive instinct when it came to the spirited vampire. He didn't want another male's hands, lips, or anything else on her. Didn't want another male to so much as look at her with interest.

Ewan wanted Sasha for himself. And that all-consuming, insufferable want was sure to be his undoing.

He wouldn't force her. Wouldn't take her hands and put them where he wanted them like the shifter did. But neither would he plead for the favor. A warlord never bowed to anyone, not even a lover. If he truly was her mate, it was a fact Sasha would have to come to terms with.

He kissed her again. He wouldn't force her, but he'd sure as hell do his best to persuade her to do what he wanted. Ewan had a tactical mind and he was more than prepared to win this battle of wills. She wanted him. The rich perfume of her arousal invaded his nostrils. She was simply too proud to admit it after being hurt.

Her grip on the footboard tightened as though she needed it to keep her from reaching out. She might not have wanted to touch him, but Ewan wasn't about to impose those kinds of restrictions on himself. He closed the space between them until his body pressed against hers. Gripped the back of her neck with one hand and let the other slide around her back to cup her ass.

Ewan thrust his hips and Sasha allowed an indulgent moan. He abandoned her lips. Kissed the corner of her mouth, across her jawline, to the base of her ear. "Touch me," he demanded once again.

Her response was nothing more than a murmur. "No."

She punished him for rejecting her bite. If he didn't want her fangs at his throat, she wouldn't give him the satisfaction of her touch.

"If you won't touch me, then maybe I should tie you to this bed?" Ewan slid his hands down to circle her wrists. "Maybe it'll satisfy that stubborn streak of yours." He took her earlobe between his teeth and bit down gently. "Or maybe it'll frustrate you to the point that you beg me to let you touch me."

She let out a soft snort that didn't carry half the confident weight he expected she wanted it to.

His grip tightened and she let out a slow breath as she melted against him. So she liked the prospect of being bound and at his mercy? It would certainly keep those wicked fangs of hers at a safe distance. Heat gathered in Ewan's gut at the memory of that sharp sting followed by a rush of delicious heat. For something so reviled among their kind, the act certainly hadn't been a hardship to suffer through. That didn't mean Ewan was about to entertain disaster by letting it happen again.

He was more than willing to push his boundaries with

Sasha. She was a female who knew her mind and what she wanted. If she didn't like what he was about to do, he had no doubt she'd make it known.

He moved his hands from her wrists to her waist and tossed her over the footboard and onto the mattress. She let out a gasp of surprise but didn't move a muscle as he rounded the bed to stand beside her. He braced his arms on the mattress and bent over her. "Touch me." She knew what he wanted and he'd warned her of what the alternative would be.

Sasha bucked her chin in a defiant show. Gods, that stubborn streak of hers drove him wild. Her eyes met his and flashed with feral silver. "No."

"All right. Have it your way." Ewan reached over her and hooked his fingers in the waistband of her leggings. "You asked for it."

Gods, Ewan turned her on.

The last thing Sasha wanted to do was admit to him that she was more than prepared to beg for whatever the hell he wanted her to. She wanted to touch him so badly, her hands shook and her limbs quaked. When he'd threatened to tie her up, a thrill raced through her. So intense, she thought she might come from his words alone without him having to lay a single finger on her.

She'd showed up here tonight in search of excitement and found that nothing compared to the feelings Ewan evoked in her. But being here with him—in this place that overwhelmed her senses with sex and desire—was almost more than she could take.

Sasha let out a slow, shuddering breath as Ewan rounded the bed toward her. His hungry gaze devoured her as it raked from her feet, up the length of her body. As he braced his arms on the bed and leaned over her, Sasha's heart raced. Her breath quickened and her senses became awash with his scent, his body, his sheer size as he leaned over her. "All right. Have it your way." His fingertips slid against her skin as they dipped beneath her waistband of her leggings and Sasha's stomach muscles twitched in response. "You asked for it."

Her breath stalled in her chest as he pulled abruptly away. He reached for her feet and pulled off both of her ankle boots, tossing them to the floor along with her socks. Sparks of electricity ignited along her nerve endings as he once again went for her waistband and pulled her leggings and underwear down the length of her legs, stripping them off in one fluid motion. He grabbed her left foot and secured one leather restraint around her ankle. Sasha's breath left her lungs in a rush. Wet warmth spread between her legs as anticipation sent chills over her bare thighs. He rounded the foot of the bed, seized her other ankle, and secured it with the other restraint. She'd thought he was full of shit when he threatened to tie her to the bed, but she should have known a male like Ewan would never bluff.

"This is why you came here, isn't it?" His gaze burned through her as he strode with slow, measured steps to the head of the bed. "To be restrained. To be pleasured. To be fucked."

She'd come here to find a male who'd make her forget Ewan had ever existed. To banish the memory of him once and for all. Instead, Fate mocked her—as usual—by throwing them together once again.

He gripped the hem of her shirt and stripped the sheer, V-neck tank from her as well. He reached beneath her and a smirk tugged at his lips as her back arched to allow him access to her bra. The clasp came undone with a tick and he pulled that from her as well, discarding it somewhere beside him as he took her hand in his and guided it above her head so he could fasten the leather restraint around her wrist.

She barely knew Ewan. He was a berserker. A sworn enemy. She couldn't trust him and yet, she allowed him to tie her to the bed frame. Sasha wasn't helpless. It's not like a few leather straps could actually restrain her. But that was the point. All part of the game. She could break free at any time. It was a test of her control. Her submissiveness. Her resolve. Would she allow Ewan dominance? Or would she fold and take back her power?

Her will was just as strong as his. Stronger. She'd show him what stubborn was. She wouldn't ever beg for the privilege of touching him. Instead, he'd plead for the favor of her touch.

"Answer me."

She looked up to find his stern gaze trained on her face. The soft waves of his light auburn hair fell over his forehead and she was possessed with the urge to reach up and brush the locks away. It wasn't wise to provoke a berserker's anger but that's exactly what she was about to do. Sasha raised her right arm to the headboard and wrapped her fingers around the metal in anticipation of being bound.

"That's exactly why I came here," she said low, and did him one better as she added to his list of lewd acts. "To be bound. Used. Pleasured. Licked. Sucked. Fucked."

Dark shadows passed over his gaze like storm clouds blocking out a golden sunset. He rounded the bed and bound her other wrist, tightening the leather strap until she felt the bite of the restraint on her skin. "Who here touched you, vampire? Who so much as laid eyes on your bare skin? How many here used you tonight?"

Vampire. As though addressing her in such a generic, impersonal way would somehow hurt her. Ewan had cut her deeply once already. She steeled herself against his words. He wouldn't cut her a second time. His attention wandered from her face in favor of a slow perusal of her body. Suddenly very aware of her nakedness, a chill stole over her, coaxing goose bumps to the surface of her skin and causing her nipples to pearl. The rich musky scent of Ewan's arousal bloomed around her and she breathed deeply of the intoxicating aroma.

Sasha wanted to call him out on it. To point out that it wasn't fair for her to be completely naked while he was fully clothed. But she knew that any protestations would fall on deaf ears. He wanted her to believe he was in charge. Sasha could play along. For now.

She bucked her chin up and met his gaze with a defiant stare. "Aren't we supposed to establish some sort of safe word before we get started?"

"Safe word?" Ewan smirked. "Oh love, there isn't a word in existence that will keep you safe from me."

He wanted to scare her, but all his posturing managed to do was excite her even more. Everything about him raised the stakes. Took Sasha out of her comfort zone. She'd play this game as long as he wanted to. Anything to keep feeling this way.

Ewan stroked a finger from Sasha's belly button upward, between her breasts, to the hollow of her throat. She let out a quiet moan as she squirmed against the restraints. "You didn't answer my question." His gaze darkened once again as he leaned in close. "How many males have had the pleasure of your body tonight?"

She allowed for a slow seductive smile. "What if I told you I've been here every night for a week and have lost count of how many males I've allowed between my legs?"

Ewan didn't take his eyes from hers. He reached between her legs and gently dragged his finger through her slick folds, settling at the knot of nerves at her core. Sasha's back arched as a sharp stab of pleasure shot through her. Her lids fluttered as her hips pressed upward toward his touch.

"I would say that you're lying to me," Ewan said darkly.

"Because your wet, swollen flesh tells me the last time you were satisfied, it was me to do it."

Arrogant bastard. He was right, though. Try as she might, she couldn't bring herself to even think of anyone else, let alone allow another male to touch her. She wouldn't give him the satisfaction of honesty, however, whether he knew the truth or not. He'd turned her away. Treated her bite as though it repulsed him. He didn't deserve her honesty, her compliance, or anything else.

Sasha didn't look away. Instead, she kept her gaze locked with his.

"The only reason that shifter is still breathing is because you willed it so."

Ewan placed his palm on her lower abdomen and slid his hand up her torso and over the swell of one breast. Sasha's breath caught as he gently plucked at one pearled nipple. Another jolt of electric pleasure shot through her and Sasha swallowed down a whimper. Gods, he knew exactly how to touch her. How to tease her. As though he were completely wired in to what she wanted and needed. Was it the tether that made it so? Or something else altogether?

"I made a concession for you tonight, Sasha, and it's the last time I ever will. If I find you in the company of another male with his hands on you in that way ever again, I'll kill him before he can take his next breath."

Her gut knotted with indignant anger at his possessive show. He had no right to make any claim on her after outright rejecting her. His palm wandered to her other breast and he cupped the flesh there before plucking at that nipple as well. Her anger dissolved under the intense sensation and Sasha pulled at her restraints as her back bowed off the bed.

"You don't own me, berserker." Sasha's words held little conviction as she strained toward his touch.

Ewan chuckled. The sound carried so much masculine confidence that it made Sasha grit her teeth in frustration. He'd barely touched her and she was already reduced to a panting, squirming mass of nerves.

"Oh no?" His fingers hovered over her. Not quite touching. The barest whisper of contact. Sasha arched toward him and he pulled back. "Your body tells a different story."

Her own body betrayed her. All Sasha had wanted was to get him out of her head once and for all. But now, he'd managed to work his way so far under her skin she knew it would take nothing short of a stake through her heart to get him out of her system.

So much for taking charge. Sasha was lost. To him.

CHAPTER
12

Ewan didn't know how much more of this he could take. He'd wanted to teach Sasha a lesson, show her exactly who was in control. But the sight of her on the bed, limbs outstretched and secured, her gorgeous body bare and presented like an offering, pussy glistening and on display, pushed him dangerously close to his breaking point. As did the way she tried so hard to provoke him. He liked a female with fight and Sasha had it in spades.

"Tell me you want me to touch you."

So far, she'd yet to submit to him. It shouldn't have mattered, but he wanted it from her. Wanted her at his fingertips ready and willing to do or say anything for the reward of his touch. She had a strong will and he admired that defiance. Made the challenge of breaking her that much more appealing. Wild creatures like Sasha rarely came to heel. If she did so for him, it would be a heady thing indeed.

"If you're looking for someone who'll beg, go find some other female. I'm sure there are plenty of them here who would gladly mewl for your favors."

He'd never gain her submission by barking out commands. No, Ewan would get what he wanted through silence and touch. And likewise, he didn't need her to beg him with words. Her body pled with him equally well.

Ewan was a seasoned warrior. He knew wars were won one battle at a time. He needed to strategize and focus on the immediate situation. He couldn't tame the wild vampire in one night and he didn't plan to. But if he played his cards right, she'd be eating out of his hand in no time at all.

Just like Gregor wanted.

Weakness wasn't tolerated in his world. The weak were picked off one by one. Sasha was a casualty of war, a sacrifice that had to be made for the greater good. Ewan's good. Drew's good. And according to Gregor, their entire clan's good. Using her for Gregor's gain was the only way to protect his own secret. Right now, all Ewan wanted to feel was Sasha's bare skin against his.

He stripped his T-shirt and discarded it to the floor. Music filtered in through the walls as did the moans and cries of pleasure from throughout the club, creating a soundtrack of sex that only served to whet Ewan's appetite and intensify his lust. Sasha's eyes tracked his every movement, the dark irises rimmed with brilliant silver. Her chest rose and fell with her quickened breath and she shifted on the mattress, causing her pert breasts to bounce with the motion.

Ewan bent over her. He put his mouth to the flat plane of her stomach, just above her belly button. He kissed her there just before he delivered a gentle bite that elicited a low moan from Sasha's lips. She squirmed again, arching her back to press her stomach to his mouth. It was as good as any pleading words and it drove him mad with want.

He let his mouth wander. Wet, open-mouthed kisses that ventured over her hip, her belly, her torso. Between her breasts and over the swell of one as he worked his way to the center and the stiff nipple that he drew into his mouth and sucked. Sasha gasped. She pressed into the contact and let out a desperate whimper as Ewan used his teeth to tease the pearled tip to an even stiffer peak. She pulled against her bonds. Her hips bucked. She twisted from one side to the other but the cuffs held her secure. The scent of her arousal intensified and still she didn't speak a single word.

He moved to her other breast and paid it the same lavish attention before venturing along her collarbone and then to her throat. Sasha turned her head away to elongate her neck and Ewan let his teeth scrape along the skin there. She shuddered. Curious, he bit her again, harder. Her body went rigid and she let out another low moan.

Apparently vampires liked to be bitten as much as they enjoyed being the one doing the biting. The thought gave Ewan a rush that caused his cock to throb hot and hard. It shouldn't have turned him on. His jets should have been cooled in an instant. Rather than pull away, he bit her again, almost hard enough to break the skin. Sasha cried out and pulled against her bonds.

"Oh gods." The words were nothing more than a desperate whimper. "Oh gods, Ewan, that feels good."

Finally, a verbal response. His chest swelled with masculine pride that he'd managed to elicit a reaction from her. It made him want to spend hours at her throat. Biting, licking, sucking. Whatever it took to continue to coax those words and sounds from her lips. She nearly made him forget they were hardly alone in this building and that soon, their privacy might be compromised, locked door or not.

Ewan straightened and quickly shucked his boots, jeans, and underwear. He'd be damned if he didn't have her and he didn't want to wait another second. His gaze wandered to her bound wrists and then her ankles. He could release her, revel in the sensation of her touch, but he was determined to teach Sasha a lesson. He was in control. And that she'd gone this long without breaking free on her own told him that she was more than willing to follow his instruction.

Sasha's gaze raked the length of his body and settled between his thighs. His cock was so damned hard it almost pained him and Ewan took his erection in his fist and stroked its length once, squeezing the base to relieve some of the pressure. Sasha watched, rapt, and took her bottom lip between her teeth. Her dainty fangs pierced her bottom lip and her tongue flicked out at the blood that welled from the punctures.

Gods. It should have repulsed him, but Ewan found the act so damned erotic that it caused his heart to hammer against his rib cage. Silver swallowed the dark brown of her irises and she bit down on her lip once again and licked the blood away.

She needed it. Blood. How long had it been since she'd fed?

Ewan climbed onto the bed. Sasha went still as her hungry gaze followed his every movement. A lick of heat traveled the length of his body at her undivided attention. Her hips rolled up toward him as her back pressed into the mattress. Ewan's gaze dropped between her legs at the soft, glistening flesh there. So ready for him. He reached out and circled the pad of his thumb over the swollen knot of nerves of her clit. Sasha responded with a desperate whimper that caused his stomach muscles to tighten as the sound vibrated over every inch of him. Gods, he wanted her. And he wasn't going to wait another second to have her.

Sasha's head rolled back on the pillow. Ewan braced one arm beside her as he took his erection in the other hand and guided it to her opening. He sucked in a breath as the sensitive head met her slick heat and Sasha's back arched.

"Look at me," he commanded through clenched teeth. She might have refused to tell him she wanted him, but he'd be damned if he let her be completely detached.

Her eyes met his. The wild heat in her gaze nearly stole his breath and he drove home in a powerful thrust. Her inner walls clenched around him, satin smooth and tight. He pulled out and thrust once more in order to feel the delicious intensity of sensation again.

She felt so damned good.

It didn't matter if a single word was spoken between them. Sasha's gaze was locked with his. Her panting breaths caressed his face and throat. The tight points of her nipples grazed his chest as she arched her back. Her body trembled with every touch and despite her considerable preternatural strength, she didn't attempt to break her bonds, instead opting to submit to him. They didn't need words. Her body spoke volumes.

Ewan kept one arm braced beside her to shoulder the bulk of his weight as he continued to move with achingly slow strokes. Fucking Sasha was an indulgence. Something to be savored. Ewan had never considered sex as anything but perfunctory. A need to be sated like eating or drinking. He got an itch and went out in search of someone to scratch it, end of story. Besides, it wasn't like many females were tripping over themselves for a night with a berserker. The warlords were famed for their strength, speed, strategic minds, and fighting prowess but little else. They were the most feared creatures in the supernatural world.

Sasha wanted him. He knew it by her scent, her eyes, the beat of her heart and dripping wet pussy. He wondered that she might crave him to the point that she desired not only his body, but his blood. Part of the mate bond she so emphatically believed in? Ewan couldn't deny it made him feel damned good. He let his face drop to the silky strands of her dark hair as he breathed in deep. Following through on Gregor's orders to gain Sasha's confidence in order to betray her might be harder than he'd thought.

Sasha wasn't embarrassed to admit she'd fucked her way across L.A. over the course of the past several months. Encounters meant to fill the void of her missing soul and temper her heartache over losing someone she'd never truly had. She'd had some great nights. Wild nights. Hours of what she'd thought was pleasure. But none of them compared to even a few minutes with Ewan.

She'd wanted to submit to him. Wanted to follow his every command and beg for every little touch. Wanted to do any damn thing he wanted for even the smallest favor. But she couldn't let herself give in completely to him. She couldn't give him even an ounce of ownership over her. He already owned her soul. She couldn't lose any other part of herself to him.

Too late, Sasha. You're already half gone.

He fucked her in such a languid way it was downright lewd. As though he were unconcerned with anything other than drawing out their mutual pleasure for as long as possible. He enjoyed her body and asked nothing in return. Hell, she'd been bound for the entirety of their encounter. She couldn't touch him, caress him, put her mouth on him . . .

Maybe that was the point? Her bite had disgusted him. Had he tied her to the bed to keep her fangs at a safe distance? The thought sent a momentary pang of sorrow straight through her chest and she fought to push the sensation away. Feeding wasn't simply necessary to a vampire's existence, it was something that fortified and strengthened the tether as well. Her muscles tensed as her own damned bothersome thoughts pulled her out of the moment. Away from Ewan and the way he made her feel . . .

"Sasha. Look at me."

His tone was gentle yet commanding. She met his golden brown gaze and her heart stuttered in her chest. Whatever assumptions she'd made melted under the heat of his stare. Her own fears and insecurities evaporated as he brought her back into the moment. What he thought or felt didn't matter. All she needed was for him to keep looking at her as though she was the only thing on the planet worthy of his attention. As long as he kept making her feel as though her pleasure was his one and only concern.

Sasha's hips rolled up to meet his. The heady musk of his arousal intoxicated her. The delicious scent of his blood as it pumped through his veins ignited her thirst. Her secondary fangs throbbed and she swallowed against the dryness in her throat. His blood was the sweetest thing she'd ever tasted and since the night she'd taken his vein, she couldn't bear to drink from another. Lucas had offered his wrist to her tonight. He'd sensed her mounting thirst and, nice guy that he was, had offered it up to her with a kind smile and zero romantic inclinations. She'd considered it for half a second before turning him down. She'd wanted Ewan's blood. No one else's would do. And he was so repulsed by the act that it appeared Sasha would have to force herself to take another vein or starve to death.

She couldn't let herself overthink it. In fact, it would be better if she didn't think about anything at all, ever again. Sasha needed to live in the moment and leave her worries by the wayside. Otherwise, what did any of this mean? If she didn't stick to the path she'd set herself on, she was committing the ultimate betrayal. Tether or not, this was about liberating herself. Ewan was a means to an end and she needed to remind herself of that. He'd tethered her, but he didn't own her. Sasha belonged to herself.

Ewan gave a slow thrust as he ground his hips against hers. Sasha lost herself to pleasure. To sensation. To the glide of his rigid shaft against her inner walls and the friction against her clit that sent tiny pulses of sensation dancing through her body. Her back arched as she let out a slow, indulgent moan. Ewan kept his measured pace, building the tension until Sasha wasn't sure how much more she could take before she broke apart into myriad pieces. She reached up and wrapped her hands around the nylon cords that secured the leather cuffs to the bed as though they were the only things grounding her to the earth.

Sasha's body wound tight and she resisted the urge to close her eyes and simply *feel*. Ewan drove her out of her mind with want. She refused to beg, to ask him for any favor, but she needed to come and he was in complete control of her body. He could choose to be generous, or he could simply get himself off and leave her tied to this damned bed.

Sasha didn't doubt for a second that Ewan could be vindictive if he wanted to be.

He thrust home, harder this time, and she answered with a sharp gasp that ended on a groan. A few more strokes just like that and she'd be good to go. At least one of her hungers would be sated . . .

"Do you want me to finish you off, Sasha?" Ewan's darkly murmured words caused her stomach to clench. *Damn him*. He obviously wasn't through playing with her. He slowed his pace and switched to shallow strokes that did nothing more than tease her. "All you have to do is ask."

His right hand settled at her breast. Almost absently, he caressed her nipple. He touched her as though he'd known her body for centuries and spent every single night learning its secrets. He used her desire against her. He wielded pleasure like a weapon. Sasha should have known better than to go up against a warlord. She had to face the fact that she might have to concede this battle. It was either that or launch a counterattack.

Maybe if she gave him something he wanted . . . he'd give her something in return.

"I want it." Sasha could be subversive and strategic as well. She'd get what she wanted from him by coaxing it willingly from him. "Please, Ewan. I need to come."

Rather than give her what she wanted, Ewan stopped entirely. A sardonic grin curved his wicked mouth as he brought his head up to look down at her. "If you're going to put on a show, I think you can do much better than that performance."

Gods-damn it. There was no way for her to win. It didn't matter what she did or didn't say. Ewan wanted her to know the rules changed when and where he saw fit. She'd surrendered power and it was up to Ewan whether or not she'd get an ounce of satisfaction here tonight. Her thirst raged as the need for blood nearly surpassed her need for physical satiation. Manipulation obviously didn't work with Ewan. Neither did sweet talk. She had no choice but to be honest with him.

"I want you hard and deep and I shouldn't have to beg for it." She thrust her hips in an effort to show him exactly how she wanted him inside of her. "I want my fangs buried in your throat because my thirst is out of control and as my mate, it's your fucking obligation to see me fed. I want to come with your blood on my tongue because it's a pleasure that has no equal. Is that straightforward enough for you?"

Ewan's gaze darkened and a crease dug into his forehead where his brows drew together over his eyes. Butterflies took flight in Sasha's stomach, half excitement, half fear. A low growl gathered and vibrated in his chest and she sensed they were at some sort of turning point. Gods, if he stopped now and walked away from her, it would gut her.

Not because she held any measure of affection for him. But because she didn't know if she could go another second without feeling some sense of completion whether it was from sex or feeding. She didn't care at this point. The stagnation was driving her out of her mind.

He thrust hard and deep. Sasha cried out as sensation flooded her. His hand abandoned her breast to cup the back of her neck as he fucked her with wild abandon. Sasha's cries became sobs of pleasure as he brought her close to the edge.

"Don't stop!" Gods, if he quit now, she swore she'd burst into tears of frustration. "Gods, Ewan, don't stop."

His mouth came to rest at her ear. He took the lobe between his teeth and bit down before growling, "Bite me when you come, and not a second sooner."

For once, she'd do exactly as he told her to.

Ewan's breath sawed in and out of his chest as he fucked her. A groan accompanied each deep thrust that wound Sasha even tighter. Her hips bucked and her back arched as her body seemed to twist and coil in on itself. She sucked in a sharp breath and exhaled as the orgasm exploded through her with an intensity that caused her limbs to quake and chills to break out over her skin. The pleasure ebbed only to crest again and Sasha buried her face against Ewan's throat. She bit down and as his blood flowed over her tongue, the wave crested once again, as overpowering and intense as it had been when the orgasm started.

Ewan's fingers curled around the nape of her neck as he held her head tight against his throat. She took long pulls from his vein as she was swept up in the euphoric bliss. Ewan let out a low groan as his hips bucked wildly.

His muscles went rigid as he settled against her. The base of his cock pulsed against her pussy and Sasha was flooded with heat as he came. He collapsed against her and Sasha's tongue flicked out to close the punctures at his throat.

"Don't ever visit this place again, Sasha." The words left Ewan's lips between pants of breath that tickled Sasha's ear. "Do you understand me?"

She didn't know what to make of his possessive tone but for the second time tonight, she had no problem doing as he asked. "I won't."

"Keep your word. I don't take broken promises lightly."

Sasha was in way over her head with the berserker, and thanks to their tether, there was no getting out.

CHAPTER
13

The days bled into weeks.

Sasha's tongue made lazy passes over the punctures in Ewan's inner thigh. He rolled to his side and she used his leg as a pillow. He reached down to caress the silky length of her dark hair, letting the strands slip through his fingers. Ewan's nights had become an endless haze of fighting and fucking and he no longer cared about the rumors that spread about him. Apparently, Ewan had created quite a stir in the supernatural underground. The berserker warlord, arena fighter, and skilled killer, who'd taken a vampire as his lover. Fortunes were made and lost on his fights and afterward, he'd spend the hours till sunrise being pleasured by Sasha, pleasuring Sasha, and seeing to every single one of her needs.

His appetite for her was insatiable. As was hers for him.

He no longer had an aversion to her taking his vein. On the contrary, its erotic effects seemed to intensify with every feeding and Ewan welcomed her bite. Gregor would have his balls if he found out, but what the berserker king didn't know wouldn't hurt him. Drew, on the other hand, had formed some very unsavory opinions about who Ewan chose to keep company with lately. He'd quit voicing those opinions once Ewan told his cousin to keep his fucking mouth shut or he'd nix his cut of the arena winnings.

What Ewan did with Sasha was no one's fucking business. And he planned to keep it that way.

"I can't believe you're not passed out right now." Sasha gave a lazy laugh and the husky tenor rippled over Ewan's skin. "You have to be exhausted."

Berserkers were bred to be nearly inexhaustible. Coupled with his superior healing ability and strength, he was surprised the battle master still allowed him to fight in the arena. The odds were always in his favor. Hardly fair.

"I can go all night, love." Ewan brushed the hair away from her temple. "And all day. Give me the opportunity to prove it to you."

Her heartbeat kicked up in her chest and Ewan smiled. Gods, he loved her responsiveness, the way the simplest words affected her. She rolled onto her stomach so she could look up at him. Her coy smile revealed the dainty tips of her fangs and Ewan's gut clenched at the memory of those fangs piercing the flesh of his inner thigh only moments ago. Her passion was unparalleled, her appetites, insatiable. Every night presented a new challenge and Ewan couldn't wait to rise up to it.

Gods, she was beautiful.

Sasha's finger traced a pattern from his thigh, up and over his hip. "Lucky for you, I'm out of commission at sunrise. Otherwise, I'd put you to the test."

Her finger roamed from his hip to the trail of crisp hair that ran from his belly button to his cock. She reached the base and traced the length of his shaft, stirring the needy bastard to attention in an instant. Her lips quirked in a seductive half smile and silver flashed in her hungry gaze. They'd been at it for hours and she was ready for more. Talk about inexhaustible stamina . . .

"Keep touching me like that and if I have to, I'll yank the sun right out of the sky for a few more hours with you."

Her gaze went liquid and her lips parted on a breath. So responsive.

She'd rented a one-bedroom apartment on the outskirts of the city and they'd spent all of their nights there since the night he'd found her at the sex club. They might have been fucking every chance they got, but Sasha hadn't let her guard down enough to allow Ewan access to her coven. Gregor wasn't a bit worried about the situation or concerned about the pace at which their supposed relationship was developing. With every hour spent together, Ewan gained another little piece of Sasha's trust. He was the perfect double agent, poised to take the vampires down from the inside. Ewan looked away as a momentary twinge of guilt tugged at his chest. He used Sasha's own nature against her, a mate bond he knew nothing about and couldn't feel. Would she be surprised by his betrayal? He was reminded of the story about the frog that trusted the crocodile and accepted a ride on his back, only to be shocked that the croc had planned to eat him all along.

She knew what he was. It wasn't his fault if she didn't do anything to protect herself.

"You have to be starving. You haven't eaten all night."

Ewan grinned. "I'm starving all right. But it isn't for food."

Sasha's gaze slid to the side. It amused him that she could still act shy and embarrassed, considering the long list of incredibly dirty things they'd done over the past several weeks. There wasn't an inch of her body that he didn't know. Hadn't explored. He'd fucked, licked, sucked and then some. He couldn't help but think about the hours they'd just spent in this bed. How he'd turned her into a wet, shuddering mass of flesh and want and need. How she'd begged, moaned, and writhed while he feasted on her pussy, allowing his finger to wander down the crease of her ass and into that sensitive region that had driven her to scream when she'd finally come for him.

"I'm being serious." Her words pulled him from his sensual reverie. She looked at him from beneath lowered lashes and gods, did that coy expression ever turn him on. "You need to eat. What do you want? I can order a pizza or we can get Chinese."

Her concern for him sent a warm rush through his limbs. Berserkers were hard, compassionless creatures who cared little for the well-being of others. As long as you could fight, you were good to go. It hadn't always been that way. But it had been so long since they'd known empathy, Ewan could scarcely remember what it felt like. By small degrees, Sasha reawakened those lost feelings in him and it worried him far more than it probably should have.

"I'll eat when I get home." The word soured in Ewan's mouth.

"Home" was a run-down shithole that wasn't fit for an animal to live in. And breakfast would consist of whatever scraps from the previous night he could scrounge up. There were times when Ewan wondered if what Gregor's hatred of the vampires really stemmed from was their seemingly endless wealth and extravagant lifestyles. Historically, they were the aristocrats of the supernatural world. Their covens amassed wealth and only their outcasts didn't benefit from their affluence. Ewan's life had always been hard. Cold. Hungry. Wanting. Even before the wars and the slaughters, he'd known hardship.

Berserkers had always been considered outliers. Shunned and feared. Perhaps that stigma was what fed Gregor's need for vengeance. Ewan sighed. Did it matter one way or the other? It wouldn't change his lot in life or the current situation.

"I don't think I've ever seen you eat . . ." Ewan shifted onto his back and Sasha crawled up the length of his body and settled herself on top of his chest. "Do berserkers have some sort of weird food hang-ups?"

He chuckled at her teasing tone. "I don't have the luxury of being able to snack during sex like you do. I doubt you'd be so forgiving if I reached over for a slice of pizza while you were straddling me."

Sasha swatted at his chest. Her laughter rang out around him, music to his ears. "If you don't like it, I could always ask someone else . . ."

Ewan reached out and snatched her wrist in his hand. He didn't mind her teasing him, but there were some things he wouldn't joke about. "If you ever so much as *think* about allowing another to feed you, whoever it is will meet a swift end."

The thought of Sasha's lush mouth on another's body caused a violent surge of jealousy that rivaled battle rage in its force and power. Ewan wasn't used to feeling possessive of anyone or anything. The foreign emotions nearly choked the air from his lungs.

"You don't have to worry about that." Sasha's voice went low and soft. "After tasting your blood, there's no way I could stomach anyone else's."

The heat in her gaze seared him. It filled him with a perverse sense of pride that he had something no one else could provide her. That she depended on him for her very survival. No one had ever depended on Ewan for anything that wasn't derived from violence. He wasn't sure he was equipped to properly care for her.

You're not. And besides, that's not what you're here for. Ewan needed to remind himself that caring for Sasha wasn't his reason for being here with her. The moment he let their time together become something it wasn't was the moment he'd secure both of their deaths.

Gregor didn't tolerate insubordination or betrayal. Those who crossed him met violent and painful ends.

"I'm glad I have something you need." Sasha was a means to an end. Nothing more.

"Oh, you do." Her eyes sparked with mischief. "No doubt about it."

Attachment wasn't an option. Because their blissful nights of passion would come to an end all too soon.

Sasha had never felt as free as she had these past several weeks. Having her own space away from the coven and the autonomy to be with Ewan—however she wanted—made her feel as though an invisible weight had been lifted from her shoulders. She answered to no one. Had shucked all of her responsibilities. Of course, she knew it couldn't last forever, this vacation from her life. She couldn't avoid Diego or Saeed for much longer. Ewan would no longer be her secret once she was forced to come clean. And when that happened, the peaceful bliss she'd found with him would disappear.

She wasn't ready for that to happen yet.

"What about you? Is blood the only thing you need or could you go for a slice of pizza every once in a while?"

Sasha rested her chin on Ewan's chest. Over the past several weeks, they'd gone from quick encounters where they sated their physical needs and parted ways, to post-sex conversations, to entire nights spent together. She'd tried to convince herself that she needed nothing more than her soul to be returned without any sort of relationship to go along with the tether. She'd thought she could keep it impersonal. But with every passing day, she came to realize impersonal might not be possible. Ewan fascinated her and that was a huge problem.

"Pizza's okay, but I'd kill for a bowl of mac-and-cheese."

"So you can eat?"

The intensity with which he watched her coaxed chills to Sasha's skin. "I can." Sasha paused. She worried her lip between her teeth and the point of her fang nicked the skin. Her tongue flicked out to lick the blood away and Ewan's gaze focused on her mouth. She wanted to open up to him, to foster some sort of intimacy between them. But doing so could be disastrous. He was a mortal enemy to vampire kind and by simply being with him, Sasha was a traitor. "I need blood to keep my organs functioning, though. Without blood, my heart won't beat, my lungs won't expand or contract. My stomach can't digest food."

Ewan's brow furrowed. "So blood is like a supplement?"

Sasha laughed. "I guess you could say that. Dhampirs need blood but much less frequently than vampires do. I'm not a biologist, but I'm guessing our bodies don't produce something we need and the drinking of blood takes care of that."

"I've always wondered."

Had she said too much? It's not like whether or not they could eat actual food was some deep, dark secret. It didn't reveal some hidden weakness the berserkers could exploit. Still, she couldn't help but feel as though she'd done something wrong. Gods, why couldn't she have been tethered by a shifter or werewolf? She would have gladly settled for a warlock or even a fae. Hell, she would have considered herself blessed to have been tethered by a dhampir. Instead, Sasha found herself inexorably bound to someone whose entire existence revolved around wanting her kind dead.

"I like ice cream, too. And chocolate."

Ewan's lips quirked in a half smile. Sasha's stomach did a backflip and she tried not to stare. His expression rarely broke a scowl, but when it did, it took her breath away. "So you have a sweet tooth?"

"You could say that."

His grin faded and his lips thinned as he studied her. "What does my blood taste like?"

Sasha swallowed. His absence of humor reminded her why it was a good idea to remain wary of him despite their tether. "It's unlike anything I've ever tasted." Sasha averted her gaze. Somehow the admission made her feel vulnerable. "Heady. Sweet. Like warm honey. The scent of your blood calls to me. I crave it."

A shadow passed over his gaze. "All blood does this to you?"

"All blood is palatable," Sasha replied. "But yours is the sweetest. The most fragrant."

The storm clouds passed and his eyes once again shone bright golden brown. "I see."

Sasha's lips puckered. She couldn't tell if he was happy with her response or not. One of the things she enjoyed about being with Ewan was his unpredictability. It kept her on her toes and added a layer of danger to their relationship. If you could call whatever this was between them a relationship.

Fatigue pulled at Sasha's eyelids and she stifled a yawn. Sunrise wasn't far off and she needed to get back to the house before she succumbed to daytime sleep and was forced to stay in the apartment—where she was more vulnerable—until sunset. She never slept here. Not when Ewan—and possibly every berserker in the city—knew where she was. Sasha wasn't stupid. She knew how to protect herself. She might have craved Ewan like a drug, but she also knew the dangers of addiction.

"I should go."

She pushed away from Ewan's chest and instantly missed

the warmth of his body against hers. As usual, he didn't move to stop her. Didn't ask her to stay a little longer. Sasha didn't want to admit it hurt a little. Deep down, some part of her wanted him to want her. To crave and need her like she did him. She hated that there was a part of her that was dependent on him. That the tether could only be felt by her.

She didn't want to want Ewan. But she was coming to realize there was nothing she could do to stop it.

He folded his arms behind his head and he watched in silence as she dressed. She used to find his undivided attention a little unnerving but she'd quickly grown to enjoy having his eyes on her. From the corner of her eye she took note of the hills and valleys of muscle that constructed his torso, the sheer strength of him that she knew so intimately. Her attention wandered to the unkempt mass of light auburn curls that fell across his forehead and the shadow of a beard that covered the sharp angles of his jaw. The supernatural world feared Ewan, but Sasha desired him with an intensity that left her shaken.

She finished dressing and grabbed her bag. Without a word she turned to leave.

"Tomorrow night?"

She paused at the doorway. Her stomach twirled as a pleasant rush of heat suffused her. "I'll be here." She didn't bother to look back as she left the bedroom and headed for the door.

The cool night air helped to clear Sasha's head as she headed for her car. With a little over an hour till sunrise, she'd be squeaking in just under the line. Every night she pushed it a little further, stayed a little longer. Her attachment to Ewan wasn't healthy. It wasn't even close to sane. As though she had no control over her own body or actions, she continued on the path to ruin night after damned night. She was obviously a glutton for punishment.

The sharp tang of sulfur hit Sasha's nostrils a moment before a large force shoved her against the passenger door of her Audi. She spun away from one hulking body, only to find her escape route blocked by another of equal size. Brownish-yellow clouds of sulfur rose around her and Sasha choked on the stench as she was surrounded on all sides. She'd never seen an actual demon up close and personal and she could safely say she didn't want to ever again.

Shit.

They looked like trouble and that was saying a lot considering who she'd recently started keeping company with.

"A vampire in the wild. Who'd have thought we'd ever see one of those again?"

The demon's voice was every bit as abrasive as he was. Sasha wrinkled her nose in distaste as the one directly in front of her leaned down for a closer look. Everyone thought berserkers smelled bad? Jesus. They had nothing on the rotting stench of a demon.

"Find your entertainment somewhere else," Sasha snapped. She'd be damned if she let them intimidate her. "Otherwise I'm going to—"

"What?" The demon to her left interrupted. "Fetch your berserker lover to take care of us?"

Well, shit. She'd known word had spread in the underground about her and Ewan's quasi-relationship, but she hadn't counted on it being common knowledge. She bucked her chin up and bared her fangs. She didn't scare easily. Whatever they wanted, these demons could go fuck themselves.

"You're barking up the wrong tree, asshole." Flippancy might not have been advisable when dealing with demons, but Sasha was out of fucks to give. "I don't know what you're talking about."

The demon in front of her closed his massive hand

around her head and slammed it into her car with so much force, it cracked the window. Wet warmth trickled down the back of Sasha's head and the scent of blood hit her nostrils before the wound began to close. *Ouch.* These guys meant business. Her bravado evaporated under the heat of fear. She narrowed her gaze as she stared the bastard down.

"What do you want?"

He gave her a pleasant smile that revealed a mouthful of yellow, pointed teeth. "Now that I have your attention, vampire, let's talk."

CHAPTER
14

Christian Whalen kept to the shadows, careful to remain downwind. Berserkers' senses were beyond keen. The slightest shift in the breeze and he'd be made. Ever since Gregor's return to L.A., Christian had been twitchy as fuck. Not because he knew Gregor expected him to have found the dhampir he was looking for by now, but because Christian already knew who she was.

Ian Gregor had been searching for Siobhan for centuries and Christian had managed to track her down in a matter of days.

Of course, that had been over a year ago. Months of stringing Gregor along, using his money and resources while pretending to hit one dead end after another. At first, he'd protected her identity because he wanted to know exactly why Gregor was so obsessed with finding her. But since then, Christian's interests had shifted and he was more concerned with protecting Siobhan from anyone who meant to do her harm.

Pussy-whipped much?

Was it possible to be whipped when he'd yet to actually

get his hands on the pussy in question? Gods, he was pathetic. Chasing tail like some untested pup that had his sights set way above his station. Siobhan was out of his league and she never wasted an opportunity to remind him of it. But it didn't stop her from playing with him. Teasing and tantalizing him. Allowing him the pleasure of her mouth on his . . .

Christian gave a violent shake of his head as he tried to dislodge the months-old memory. Her kisses haunted his dreams and every waking minute, only serving to intensify his obsession with her. Too bad she didn't feel the same.

Since that night, she'd made it her goal to taunt him with her presence. He saw her out, every night, haughty and aloof, and completely unavailable. Whereas he used to have easy access to her company, now she brought a bevy of bodyguards with her wherever she went, including that big son of a bitch, Carrig, who was never far from her side. Their relationship had gone back to look-but-don't-touch status and it drove Christian out of his fucking mind.

Worse, Siobhan didn't seem to have any problems with letting others—namely Carrig—put their hands wherever they wanted on her shapely body. Night after night Christian was forced to watch that son of a bitch touch her, put his mouth on her. He watched them feed from one another, and when he was too angry to care and too out of his mind with jealousy to form a coherent word, he dragged his sorry ass back to his suite at the Sheraton Grand and passed out on the damn bed like the pathetic loser he was.

Now that Gregor was back in the city, Christian let his obsession take a backseat to his curiosity. He'd needed the distraction like he needed his next breath. His want of Siobhan ate at him, consumed him. He needed to get her out of his head before he lost his shit entirely.

Gregor ducked into a condemned apartment building.

Christian slowed his pace, careful not to draw the attention of any berserkers who might be standing sentry around the property. He'd known the warlord and his band were squatting somewhere, but Gregor kept his secrets well. Christian had been tracking him for weeks and finally the bastard had led him to his home base.

What a shithole.

The place was a four-story building that took up one corner of the block. Maybe twenty or thirty units, tops. Not enough to house the estimated three hundred berserkers under Gregor's command. Which meant the bulk of Gregor's forces weren't yet in the city. Either that, or he had tasks set out for them elsewhere. The gods only knew what the wily bastard had up his sleeve.

One thing Christian knew for sure: Gregor was hiding something in that building. And he was going to find out what it was.

Security couldn't be stellar with the run-down state of the building. Likewise, aside from Gregor's troops standing guard, there couldn't be much else to keep unwanted guests out. Christian put his nose to the wind and took a deep breath. The loamy scent of the violent creatures floated on the air, but without the intensity that might indicate a large force of them within the apartment complex's walls.

Christian could be pretty damned stealthy when he wanted to. With any luck, he'd get inside long enough to take a look around. He'd have to mask his scent first. Good thing he'd made a pit stop before going out tonight.

He reached in his pocket and pulled out a small vial of liquid. He'd paid a nice chunk of change for the magically enhanced tincture that was supposed to give him thirty minutes of "invisibility" by making his scent impossible to detect. He pulled the cork stopper from the bottle and held it aloft. "Bottoms up." He tipped the vial back and his nose wrinkled at the bitter taste. This shit had better work, or there was a witch in West Hollywood who was going to be on the receiving end of his wrath.

Christian did as the witch had instructed and waited five minutes for the spell to take effect before heading for the apartment building. He lowered his nose to his shoulder and sniffed. It's not like he could identify his own scent, but hey, isn't that what people did in deodorant commercials? Just to be safe, Christian stayed downwind as he headed toward the building. This would've been a hell of a lot easier with backup, but as a rogue, it's not like he was going to be partnering up with anyone anytime soon. The front entrance was a no-go as he caught the scent of several berserkers nearby. He switched up his tactics, and headed for the rear of the building and hopped up on the nearest fire escape.

Where would Gregor feel safest? The lower floors, or at the top of his keep? The sound of muffled voices reached his ears from the third floor. With silent grace, he leapt to the second-floor landing, and then the third. He let his senses guide him, taking a moment to listen and to scent the air.

"What's the matter, Rin? Accommodations not up to your standards?"

Rin? It was true Christian didn't know the names of all of Gregor's cohorts, but he doubted the warlord would speak to any of his brethren in such a way. More to the point, if any of them complained about the state of their lives, Christian suspected Gregor would answer with a fist to their face. Whoever Gregor spoke to was a new player. The berserker certainly had a lot of irons in the fire and Christian was determined to know what each and every one of them was for.

Christian ducked low as he passed beneath a window. The room was dark, but that didn't mean anything since supernatural creatures didn't need light to see, plus, it's not like Gregor would've sprung for electricity or any other amenities. The rumor was that the self-proclaimed berserker king hoarded his money to fund his cause. Truth be told, Christian was surprised he'd managed to get as much money as he had out of Gregor. It just went to show how eager the berserker was to find Siobhan.

He peeked through the window to find the room empty. A slow breath of relief left his lungs as Christian reached for the window and found it unlatched. He almost felt sorry for the careless bastard that forgot to lock it. Because if Gregor found out his security had been compromised, someone's head was going to roll.

"Maybe it's not the accommodations that have you down. Missing your soul?"

Christian paused. Who in the hell did he have in here? The only creatures Christian knew of without souls were vampires. Had the bastard gotten lucky enough to get his hands on one? He didn't venture out of the empty room. There was no point in risking discovery when he could listen from here. But gods, he wanted to get his eyes on this Rin . . .

"You're going to pay for what you've done to me."

Christian perked up at the sound of the unfamiliar voice. The hollowness of the tone caused Christian's wolf to let out a warning growl in his psyche. There was something decidedly not right about that voice. He wrinkled his nose as magic sparked the air. Not a vampire. What the actual fuck was going on? Gregor had a magic wielder as a captive? How was that even possible? Even a low-level warlock should have been powerful enough to free himself from captivity.

The wily warlord certainly had a few cards up his sleeve. Damn it.

Gregor laughed. "In your diminished capacity? I doubt that."

Christian edged his way closer to the door. Curiosity burned as he resisted the urge to get a look at the mysterious magic wielder. Gregor was running so many angles it was tough to keep track of them all. Christian was bound and determined to put all of the pieces of the puzzle together so he could see the full picture.

"Are you ready to tell me about McAlister?"

Holy. Fucking. Shit. Christian was damn near out of his mind with curiosity. For the first time since he'd become involved with the berserker, Christian truly believed Gregor might actually be capable of seeing his plans to fruition.

"You let her destroy my soul." The magic wielder's voice seethed with anger. "I'd rather die than divulge a single detail to you."

"You'd rather die because it would release you from your empty existence," Gregor replied. "That's not going to happen. I'm a patient male, Rin. I've waited centuries for my revenge. I can wait centuries more if I have to. I'll keep you in this state of purgatory for as long as it takes. You'd be wise not to doubt my intentions."

Their conversation created more questions for Christian than it provided answers.

"Cerys is in the city. Did you know that, Rin? Saeed brought her here after he rescued her from the shackles of your slavery."

"Cerys Bain, as well as the vampire, will get what's coming to them." The magic wielder's tone went low and simmered with anger.

Apparently, Gregor had gotten into some serious shit while he was gone. Magic wielders? Vampires? And whatever the hell this Cerys was. On the plus side, Gregor had given Christian something of value tonight. Information was worth its weight in gold. No doubt McAlister would pay a pretty penny for any little bit of it he could provide.

"I couldn't give a fuck about your plans for the vampire. But you lay so much as a finger on Cerys, and I'll make sure every day of the rest of your existence is a living hell."

Whoever this Cerys was, she was important to Gregor. Curious, since she'd apparently taken a vampire as a lover. Gregor had given Christian a jumping-off point, though. The more he learned about Cerys, he suspected the more he'd learn about what Gregor was planning.

"She's coming, Rin. Now that Cerys is free and her strength is regained, Fiona will come looking for her. Especially now that she and McAlister are within touching distance of one another. Maybe I should introduce Cerys to McAlister? What you think? Thanks to you and her treacherous sister, their fates are intertwined. Funny how a simple decision can create so much chaos."

Fiona? Jesus, how many new players had Gregor introduced?

The magic wielder laughed. Again, Christian's wolf let out a nervous whimper at the hollow timbre. "Your overconfidence is going to be your downfall, Gregor. Fiona is wild. She is without allegiance or conscience. You'll be sorely disappointed if you think she'll be so easy to manipulate."

A space of silence passed and the fine hairs on the back of Christian's neck stood on end. He'd lost track of how long he'd been standing here listening to Gregor's conversation. The magic that cloaked his scent had an expiration date. It was better to get the hell out of here now than risk being caught. Especially now that he might have some tangible ammunition against the berserker warlord.

Gregor's voice rang out, "I want a perimeter check! Every corner of every room. Gavin, get on it!"

Time to GTFO. Christian crossed the room and quickly slid through the open window out onto the fire escape. He slid the window closed, careful not to make any sound that might alert one of Gregor's sentries to his presence. He'd risked too much and learned too much to fuck it all up by being sloppy. Rather than cause any undue noise by traversing the fire escape, he launched himself from the third-story landing directly to the ground below him. His feet touched down with a slight rasp of his boots as they hit the pavement and he let out a slow breath as he propelled himself into motion, ducking into the closest alleyway and out of sight.

He watched from the cover of shadow as Gregor's troops fanned out to check the perimeter of the property. Several bodies spilled from the building to inspect outside while he noticed shadows of movement from within the apartment building. His gaze wandered to the third floor and the room he'd just occupied. Gregor appeared in the window as he looked out over the property.

Christian's heart beat double-time as he set his back to the alley wall. He'd pressed his luck, stayed longer than he should have. Hopefully the witch's spell had done its job and masked his scent. Otherwise, he was as good as fucked. Time would tell if he'd been found out. One thing Ian Gregor didn't tolerate was betrayal. He'd have Christian strung up by his nuts in a minute flat if he had any idea what he was up to.

A few more minutes passed before Gregor's soldiers finished up their rounds and headed back inside the apartment building. Christian pushed away from the wall and continued down the alley toward where he'd left his car. He'd hit the jackpot tonight but he wasn't ready to share his spoils with McAlister or anyone else just yet. This was only the beginning. He had a shit-ton more information to collect before he could move on any of it. He'd sell it to the highest bidder. If what he had was valuable enough, he might even be able to buy his way out of the Sortiari once and for all. Who knew what lengths McAlister might be willing to go to in order to find out what Gregor was up to?

In the meantime, Christian needed to form a plan of attack and the first thing on his list was to make friends with a vampire. If he was going to learn anything about this Fiona, who seemed to have everyone shaking in their boots, he needed to get close to the female Gregor seemed intent on protecting from the magic wielder. The vampire's lover. She must have been something to have made the berserker play nice with a vampire.

Shit was getting real. Good thing Christian always looked out for what was truly important: himself.

CHAPTER
15

"Ewan Brún. You've made quite a name for yourself the past few months. Wonder what the male who holds your leash thinks about that?"

Ewan stretched his neck from side to side as he let out a huff of frustrated breath. His fight had lasted longer than he'd intended thanks to being paired against a sylph who managed to elude him most of the fight by becoming an incorporeal burst of air. Not a very useful ability in a fight unless your intent was to actually *not fight*. It had taken a good hour before his opponent had mustered up the courage to face him and not simply run. Once they'd gotten down to business, the male had met a swift end. Ewan gave a sad shake of his head. What desperation drove someone to the point they'd enter a contest they were doomed to lose?

He turned to face the source of the gravelly voice that called out to him, annoyed that yet another obstacle stood in his way of getting to Sasha. He was burning night and too soon, the sun would rise to separate them once again. "Are you trying to pick a fight?" He did nothing to temper the barked words. "If so, talk to the battle master and set up a time to meet me in the cage."

The tang of sulfur burned Ewan's nostrils and he blew out a breath to clean the offensive odor away. Demons. Nasty fuckers. And creatures Ewan tried to avoid at all costs.

"Do you know who I am, berserker?"

The male took a step forward as his gaze narrowed. His eyes creeped Ewan the fuck out. Ice blue—almost white—with a dark ring around the iris. Humans often wore contact lenses to get the same eerie effect. It always struck Ewan as odd that berserkers were so reviled and feared when creatures like demons inhabited the world. The male looked Ewan up and down and his lip curled in distaste to reveal the wicked points of his sharklike teeth.

Ewan dropped his gym bag to the floor beside him, ready to defend himself against the aggressive demon if need be. "Should I?"

The demon let out an amused snort. "Berserkers are such arrogant fuckers. Not sure why, considering you're nothing more than *slaves*."

A common opinion. One that bothered Ewan far more than he let on. His own hatred of Gregor stemmed from the fact that the male's burning need for revenge had indentured their kind to the Sortiari in the first place. The supernatural community viewed them as slaves to the guardians of fate. Shackled for eternity. And when he'd hoped that Gregor had freed them from that stigma once and for all, he'd simply turned the tables and enslaved them all again. This time, to himself. If that wasn't a kick to the nuts, Ewan didn't know what was.

"And demons are nothing more than cowards and bullies who don't have the stones to fight their own battles. So what's your point?"

The demon bristled and Ewan's mouth hitched in a

superior smirk. He had to get his digs in while he could and he was already pissed off that this arrogant piece of shit was keeping him from being naked and buried to the hilt inside of Sasha right now.

"You've cost me a lot of money lately."

And . . . ? Ewan shrugged. Where and on whom the demon chose to bet his money had nothing to do with Ewan. His job was to fight and kill his opponent in the cage. Nothing more. "It's not my fault you're betting on the wrong male. You should have learned your lesson about ten or so fights ago." He took a step forward to show the demon he didn't cower easily. "I don't lose."

The demon's overly large lips spread into a sickening grin. "Don't be so sure about that."

Jesus. If the bastard's intentions were to kill Ewan with his disgusting stench, he was doing a damn good job. He didn't have time for this bullshit. Not when Sasha's soft, willing body was waiting for him at her apartment. He let out a chuff of laughter. "Next time, put your money on a sure thing."

"You truly don't know who I am, do you, berserker?"

Ewan's gaze narrowed as he studied the demon. His ego could give Gregor's a run for its money. It's not like Ewan made a point to acquaint himself with the dregs of the supernatural underground's heavy hitters. Maybe it was time he did, though. It would save him from headaches like this one.

"Again . . . should I?"

"Sorath." The demon snapped his teeth at Ewan. "Learn that name. Remember it. And be sure that you'll see me again."

Ewan didn't respond well to threats. His fists balled at his sides as the powerful onset of battle rage swelled within him. He could put this asshole in his place right fucking now if he wanted to, but he was more interested in letting

Sasha take the edge off for him. Without giving the demon the satisfaction of a response, Ewan bent and retrieved his gym bag. He looked the demon over once more, committing his face to memory, turned his back, and walked away.

Sorath laughed and the confidence in that sound planted a tiny seed of doubt in Ewan's gut that quickly sprouted and grew. He had a feeling he'd tangle with the demon again. Soon. And when he did, it wouldn't be a pleasant experience.

His troubles were beginning to pile up and he didn't like it one damned bit.

By the time Ewan made it to Sasha's apartment, he was wound up tight and desperate to hit the release valve. He walked through the door, ready to get naked and down to business. He wanted to be inside of her so badly he thought he might spontaneously combust.

Sasha sat on a barstool at the kitchen counter with a glass of wine in her hand. "Take your clothes off." Ewan wasn't about to waste another second. "And bend over."

Her lips pursed as she cocked a challenging brow. Her expression spoke volumes and it looked like she wasn't in the mood to play. Pissed he was late? Or something more? Either way, it didn't look like Ewan was going to get the relief he was after anytime soon.

Fuck.

"What's the matter?" Their relationship so far was about sex and little else. Only in recent weeks had they allowed time for conversation and companionship. It felt strange to ask if something was wrong. As though he had no right to do so. Still, wasn't this what Gregor wanted? For Ewan to get close to Sasha and bring back valuable intel?

"Saeed is grounding me." The hurt and anger in her

tone made Ewan think that whoever this Saeed was, he meant something to Sasha. Or had at some point. "I told him to go fuck himself."

There was definitely something between them. A territorial growl built in Ewan's chest and he swallowed it down. Until Sasha, he'd never experienced possessive feelings of any kind and he didn't like the burn in his chest one damned bit. His temper threatened to flare and he took a calming breath, stuffing that impending rage to the soles of his feet. "Who's Saeed?" The words came with a sharper edge than he'd intended but at this point, he was surprised he hadn't shouted the question.

"Our coven master," Sasha said. "And my maker."

The way her voice went to a low murmur at that last part sent his temper to an even darker place. The intimacy in those words shifted his imagination into high gear and his lip curled. "He has some ownership of you?" What he really wanted to know was how exactly Sasha had been made a vampire by Saeed. Images of his mouth at her throat ravaged Ewan's mind and his gut curled into a tight knot. Had he pierced her throat? Drained her of blood? And then what . . . ?

"He doesn't own me," Sasha said. "But as a member of his coven, I do answer to him."

"He turned you?" Ewan could think of nothing else. His need for answers consumed him. "He drained you of blood?" That much Ewan knew of how a vampire was made. "Then what?"

Sasha's brow furrowed. "He fed me from his vein."

The answer was so guileless that it hit him with the impact of fist to his chest. The air left his lungs as his temper flared to even greater heights. "Your mouth at his throat?" Gods, he couldn't wipe the image from his mind and it drove him mad with unchecked rage. Forming even marginally coherent words seemed impossible.

Sasha looked at him like he'd lost his mind. Maybe he had. Ewan shouldn't have given a single shit how Sasha was made a vampire, who made her, or anything else. He shouldn't have cared who touched her, or talked to her, or who she spent her hours with when they weren't together. But the more he thought about the possibilities, the more Ewan wanted to scrub the images from his mind. He couldn't do a damned thing to stop his irrational behavior, let alone pinpoint why he felt this way.

Fuck!

Every minute spent with her was another minute he lost himself.

"Tell me, Sasha!" His angry shout bounced off the surrounding walls. "What claim does this Saeed have over you?"

Sasha stared at Ewan, dumbstruck. She had no idea what prompted his outburst but it did nothing more than further aggravate her already foul mood. After her run-in with the demons the night before, she'd been on edge. They'd bullied her, roughed her up, threatened her, and tried their damnedest to intimidate her. They thought she held some sway over Ewan. That somehow, their relationship was something more than it was. Sasha had refused to demure and told those nasty bastards exactly where they could stick it. They hadn't taken her defiance lightly and had left her with a little parting gift to show her what was in store if she didn't play ball.

Her forearm still burned like a motherfucker from where one of them had grabbed her. She needed to feed before it would heal completely. Hellfire wasn't anything to laugh at.

Last night had ended on a low note. She'd collapsed into bed and risen at sundown to find Diego waiting for her with the ominous summons from Saeed. Rather than present herself immediately to her coven master, Sasha had taken off. Running from her problems might not have been the best idea, but right now, it was the only coping mechanism she had.

She'd come to the apartment hoping she'd find solace in Ewan's company. That somehow, in the past few weeks, they'd grown closer and he'd help her deal with the shit storm that currently rained down on her. Instead, he only added to her stress with his unfounded anger and demands. Had every male on the planet lost their damned minds? Sasha wondered if there was anywhere she could go to escape the bullshit.

Sasha's own temper exploded as she shot from the chair. "What in the actual hell is wrong with you, Ewan?"

He leveled his gaze and his eyes darkened, a sure indication that a storm was coming. The barest hint of fear tickled at the back of Sasha's brain but she ignored the warning. Ewan could rage all he wanted. She refused to be afraid of him.

"Answer me, Sasha."

"*No male* has claim on me." She leveled her gaze and met him look for look. "Including you."

Black bled into his irises, transforming Ewan into the creature so many feared. She didn't understand that part of his nature. It seemed so apart from who he truly was. She swallowed against the dryness in her throat and the nagging thirst that flared from her weakened state. Sasha was as much a predator as Ewan. When cornered, a predator fought back.

Ewan reached out and snatched her arm. His fingers dug in where the demon's hellfire burned her and she couldn't quell the sharp gasp of pain. The black retreated from Ewan's gaze in an instant and a deep crease of concern marred his brow. He slid his grip to her wrist and yanked up her sleeve with his other hand.

"What happened? Who did this to you?"

Sasha drew her lip between her teeth. She didn't want him to know anything that had happened last night but he'd smell the lie on her if she tried to hide it. *Damn it.* Why did he have to show up angry and wanting to pick a fight? All she'd wanted was a break from reality. To fuck and feed and replenish her strength. Instead, all she'd managed was to further complicate her already fucked-up life.

She met his gaze and found the words he wanted from her weren't easy to provide. She wanted to protect Ewan. But from exactly what—and how—she had no idea.

"Why haven't you healed?"

"Hellfire." Sasha nearly choked on the admission.

"Motherfuckers!" The word burst from Ewan's lips in an angry shout that made Sasha flinch. "When? Where?"

He seemed more angry than surprised, which made Sasha think that Ewan had already had a run-in or two with the demons himself. Great. She'd hoped their tactic was to put pressure on her alone but they obviously didn't trust her to convince Ewan to play ball on her own.

"Last night," Sasha said with a sigh. "Right after I left here."

Ewan didn't release his grip on her. With the pad of his index finger, he traced the skin around the burn with such gentle care it made her breath hitch. His duality fascinated her. The combination of violence and tenderness that always seemed at war with each other.

"I'm going to gut that son of a bitch and then choke him to death with his own entrails."

That painted quite the mental picture. Ewan giving in to his temper was exactly what the demons wanted, though. It would show them they'd managed to get under his skin and that he could be compromised.

"I'm okay." Sasha didn't know if that's what he wanted to hear but she didn't know what else to say. "I can take care of myself. A supernatural burn is going to leave a mark. It weakened me, that's all. Once I feed, I'll be fine."

"What do they want from you?"

Compliance. "To scare me." Not the whole truth but enough of it to placate him, she hoped.

"To get to *me*," Ewan insisted.

Also true. Sasha didn't know why that truth bothered her so much. It seemed ridiculous the demons would come to the conclusion that she had that sort of sway over Ewan at all. No one knew about the tether but her, Ewan, and Ani. No way would her best friend talk. The rumors that had been circulating pegged them as lovers, nothing more.

As far as Sasha could tell, the tether that bound them went one way. Ewan had no attachments to her whatsoever. Sex was their only connection. He used her for a few hours of pleasure every night and in return offered his vein as payment. Sasha cringed at the thought that her relationship with Ewan reduced her to that status. A blood whore, trading her body for something vital to her: the blood of her mate.

The tether weakened her. Made her dependent. It undid everything she'd tried to build in her life since becoming a vampire. So far, the return of her soul had been nothing but a curse. "They said they wanted to talk to me about you and I told them to fuck off." That part had been true as well. Which was why they'd burned her with hellfire. To let her know they meant business. "I don't think they're used to getting the brush-off."

What Sasha didn't tell Ewan was that the demons had given her one hell of a sales pitch. He'd made some serious waves in the supernatural underground and those who'd bet against him weren't happy about the money they'd lost. Sasha had laughed in their faces when they'd told her what they wanted her to do. Ewan couldn't be controlled any more than a hurricane could be steered. Her influence meant nothing.

"What did you tell them, Sasha?"

Ewan's gaze darkened once again and indignant fire sparked in her gut. He thought she'd roll over so easily? That perhaps she'd spilled her guts and given the demons something they could use against him? What a bunch of bullshit.

"Nothing." She tried to pull her arm from his grasp but he held her fast. "What the hell could I possibly tell them?" She'd tried to come to terms with their casual-sex relationship. But the realization that she didn't know a single thing about Ewan outside of the battle arena stung. They weren't even friends with benefits. "I don't know a single gods-damned thing about you!" She didn't mean to shout but she'd kept her emotions bottled for far too long.

The anger melted from Ewan's expression and he stared blankly at her before he hauled her close and put his mouth to hers. The kiss was crushing, urgent. Full of heat and desperation and something Sasha didn't understand. He thrust his tongue past the barrier of her lips, demanding that she open for him. He deepened the kiss and her knees weakened under the passionate onslaught. She hated that he could so easily affect her. Exert such total control over her with so little effort. Sasha wedged her free hand between them and pressed against his chest. She didn't want to be placated or seduced.

She wanted to be loved.

The air left her lungs and her heart hammered against her rib cage. She'd spent months feeding herself lies that she'd swallowed without question. Convincing herself that she didn't want to be cared for or cared about. That she could go from one meaningless encounter to the next in order to find fulfillment. That it was the only way to guard her heart from being shattered into a million pieces once again.

Gods, what a fool she was.

She managed to put enough distance between them to break the kiss. Her forearm throbbed from the supernatural burn that wouldn't likely heal until she fed, but Sasha refused to debase herself by begging Ewan for the favor. His blood might have called to her. It might have fortified her strength in a way that no one else's ever could, but she couldn't allow herself to be used anymore. She didn't think she would survive another broken heart.

"Stop, Ewan. I can't do this anymore." She scrubbed a shaking hand across her mouth as though to banish the sensation of Ewan's lips from hers. "I need to get out of here."

"What in the hell are you talking about?" He tried to keep his grip on her arm but she managed to slide it free. "Sasha?"

His demanding tone only served to spark her ire. As long as he was getting his, what did it matter how she felt? She'd been so stupid to think she had any measure of control over this situation. Things couldn't be more *out* of her control.

So much for autonomy. So much for affection. So much for being a strong, independent female who couldn't be bothered to care. The only thing between her and Ewan was sex and their shared history of violence. She'd been a fool to think there could have ever been anything more.

CHAPTER
16

The door slammed behind Sasha and the sound rammed into Ewan's gut like a fist. He took a lurching step forward before he froze in place. He knew he should go after her, sensed her anger and hurt. But what then? What would he do . . . say . . . when he got to her? That he was sorry? That he didn't mean to hurt her? That he hadn't intended for his temper to get the better of him? Berserkers didn't make apologies. They didn't show weakness. But it hadn't always been that way, had it?

Like every surviving member of their clan, Ewan had done his damnedest to disregard his past and detach from the crippling emotions that only served to weaken him. He'd forgotten some of his own instincts. Letting Gregor's revenge and anger become his own. He'd given himself over to rage and sorrow and allowed it to change him. As a whole, the berserkers had lost themselves. Let time and grief erode what made them who they were like water wore away at rock to make deep canyons.

Gregor's vendetta had damned near destroyed him and Ewan wouldn't stand for it. He'd been fighting for so long, killing in the arenas in order to secure his freedom when what he should have been doing all along was inciting a revolution. Maybe it wasn't too late to make a change. But one thing Ewan knew for certain: He couldn't do it without Sasha.

Over the past several weeks, she'd become his solace. His safe space. And he'd shown his appreciation by keeping her at arm's length. It seemed impossible, but Sasha had reawakened something in Ewan. Something buried so deep its presence felt foreign. He'd tried to convince himself that he came here night after night out of some sense of duty. To protect Drew and his own damned secrets and machinations. That somehow, Sasha didn't figure into the equation at all save being something warm and inviting for him to stick his dick into. He'd tried to convince himself that she didn't matter. That she meant nothing to him. He no longer believed his own lies, however. Sasha mattered. She mattered in a way that was almost incomprehensible to him.

She was the light home. Ewan still didn't know what that meant exactly, but he knew it to be true. And because of that—because of her very existence—her life was in danger. From Gregor. From those loyal to him. From those fucking demons who thought they could get to him through her. From her own gods-damned coven. Talk about star-crossed. If they got through this without permanent damage, Ewan would be shocked.

Sasha was important. Without her, Ewan realized he had no chance of getting back what he'd sought to reclaim for decades: himself.

For centuries, the Sortiari had used them as their guard dogs. Three hundred years ago, in the guise of priests, they'd purged Europe and Asia of vampires and whatever else their leaders determined were a threat to the course of fate. They'd allowed their instincts to be dulled and replaced with the Sortiari's magic and weaponry. Ewan let out an angry huff of breath as he began to pace the confines of the tiny living room. He himself had been a weapon long before the Sortiari came along. He didn't need magic or anything else to make him deadly.

The battle arenas had reminded him of that.

Gregor knew too much. Expected too much. Ewan's only option was to keep Sasha close. As much for her own safety as to protect his own secrets. He'd set something in motion that night when he'd approached her, so full of himself, high on the win, and determined to have her. He had to see whatever this was through to the end. He couldn't let Sasha walk away. It was too late for that. They were both in too deep.

As he locked up Sasha's apartment and headed for his car, he was struck by the thought that he wasn't the only berserker that had lost touch with his natural born instincts. If Gregor had even an ounce of sense, he'd realize Ewan could help him systematically take down each of the city's covens with little to no effort without Sasha's help, whether indirectly or not. Through their shared time together, Sasha had ingrained tiny bits of memory and experience into Ewan's DNA. Berserkers didn't recognize their mates in the same way other supernatural creatures did, but nature made up for that by allowing them to bond in other ways. Scent, touch, sex—anything he'd experienced with Sasha that involved his senses—helped to build a database that integrated with every tiny particle that constructed him. He'd simply forgotten how to access and utilize that information.

Sasha had awakened something in Ewan and he wasn't about to discount the importance of it.

Time and history had maligned the supernatural world's opinion of berserkers. They'd been painted as brutes. Killers. Violent. Mindless beasts. Creatures of war. But beyond

that, *before* that, they'd been protectors. They kept safe at
all costs what belonged to them. Ewan was beginning to
believe that in some small way, Sasha was his. His to protect. And he wasn't going to let Gregor or anyone else stand
in the way of that.

He squeezed into the tiny beat-up Civic and started the
engine. The damned thing coughed and spluttered like it
was on its last leg and Ewan cursed under his breath. He
put it into gear and pulled out onto the street as he emptied his mind and let instinct guide him. Sasha's routines
would be etched in Ewan's subconscious without him even
realizing it. All he had to do was let that part of his brain
take over and lead him where he needed to go.

Forty minutes later, Ewan pulled up to a vast estate nes-
tled on a nice chunk of property just outside of the city. A
large iron gate, complete with guard station and high fenc-
ing, enclosed what he surmised was just over two acres of
land. The main house was an enormous Spanish-style
mansion, big enough to house a few dozen vampires and
dhampirs. He pulled off onto a side street a hundred or so
yards away and killed the engine. He didn't doubt the vampires were serious about security, but he could negotiate
almost any security without being detected.

Ewan moved like a wraith through the night. A shadow
carried on a breeze, he didn't stir a single blade of grass
as he leapt over the perimeter fence. He moved with blurring speed to the front door and paused. It would take little
effort to simply kick the door down and find Sasha. But a
little diplomacy probably wouldn't hurt. He put his fist to
the heavy oak door and knocked.

A berserker paying a visit to a vampire coven. Hell had
indeed frozen over.

The door swung wide and Ewan was met by a tall, muscular vampire with dark skin and eyes. An air of authority

surrounded the vampire and Ewan couldn't help but wonder if this was the male who'd turned Sasha. The male's brow furrowed with momentary confusion, as though his brain couldn't reconcile what his eyes told him. The confusion turned quickly to shock and then outrage as he took a defensive stance and bared his fangs.

"I don't want any trouble. I'm here to see Sasha." Ewan almost laughed at how ridiculous that sounded. He didn't want any trouble? All his kind had done for the past several centuries was stir up trouble with vampires.

The vampire's gaze went bright silver as he let out a low hiss and attacked.

Well, fuck. Ewan should have expected a little hostility. The vampire was faster than Ewan expected. It had been a long damned time since he'd been face-to-face with one in a volatile situation. He'd been fighting lesser creatures for the Sortiari for the past two hundred years, various supernatural creatures in the ring for the past few months, and none of them could hold a candle to the strength and speed of the male who came at him now.

A whoof of breath left Ewan's lungs as he was slammed into the stone arch of the breezeway. It spoke to the quality of construction that the damned thing didn't crumple down on top of them with as hard as the vampire threw him into the wall. Ewan wasn't looking for a fight. The last thing he needed was to piss Sasha off even more by hurting a member of her coven. Even if he did want to beat the fucker to a pulp at the thought of him allowing Sasha to feed from his vein.

He didn't want a fight, but that didn't mean Ewan wasn't going to defend himself.

"How many more of you are there?" The vampire wedged his arm against Ewan's throat. His strength was impressive as he exerted enough pressure to cut off Ewan's airway. Not exactly a solid plan if the male was expecting an answer, but then again, if this had actually been an ambush, it would've taken a hell of a lot more than a chokehold to get him to talk.

"A-lone," Ewan managed to force the word from his constricted throat. "Here . . . for Sasha."

"You'll die before you get even a finger on her."

If he could have, Ewan would have laughed in the vampire's face. He'd gotten a hell of a lot more than a finger on her. And she hadn't exactly complained about it. Ewan reached between them and with an upward swipe, knocked the vampire's arm away. He dragged in a deep breath and held it in his lungs before shoving at the vampire, sending him stumbling backward several paces. Ewan's fists ached to swing out but he needed to establish that he'd come in peace. A hard pill to swallow for any vampire. Ewan could definitely use a little help to convince him.

Her name left Ewan's lips in a forceful rush. "Sasha!"

She was here. Her scent permeated his nostrils and awakened his senses. His stomach muscles knotted, urgency rose up within him, and adrenaline dumped into his bloodstream. He needed her calming presence. Otherwise, he'd succumb to the battle rage that threatened to overtake him and he'd kill the vampire without even realizing what he'd done.

The vampire rushed at him again and pinned Ewan to the cold stone archway. He braced his hand against Ewan's chin, forcing his head to one side. Fuck, the bastard was strong. From the corner of his eye, Ewan noticed the male's lips pull back to reveal the wicked points of his fangs. Armed with the only weapon at his disposal, it was obvious what he intended to do: rip Ewan's throat open and hope he'd bleed to death on the front steps before he had the opportunity to heal.

How very vampiric of him.

Fuck it all. Looked like he was going to have to bring the pain. He only hoped Sasha would forgive him . . .

"Saeed, stop!"

Sasha's heart lodged in her throat as she rushed to the foyer. Ewan might have been a virtually unstoppable killing machine, but in the confines of the coven, he was seriously outnumbered. Saeed was formidable in his own right. A skilled assassin and warrior, and old enough to have fought many wars before Ewan was likely even born.

Saeed froze. He looked over his shoulder at Sasha, his expression one of utter shock. He loosened his grip on Ewan, but didn't fully release his hold.

"Step aside, vampire, or I'll move you myself."

Shit. Ewan's dark tone proved he was more than ready to throw down. Sasha raced to intervene, inserting herself between the two males before their encounter devolved into violence. Not in her wildest dreams could she imagine a worse scenario. What was Ewan doing here? How had he found her?

"Ewan." She placed her palm on his chest, hoping that somehow the contact would calm the rage that built within him. His eyes darkened and his muscles tensed beneath her fingers. She didn't know much about a berserker's battle rage, but she did know that its all-consuming darkness terrified her. "You need to calm down. Please." She'd seen him fight in the arena enough times to know that once that rage consumed him, he'd be impossible to stop.

"Sasha." Saeed's voice went low and deadly. "Move."

Gods, the male ego. Sasha was almost tempted to do as they asked and allow them to beat each other to death. But the only thing a fight would accomplish would be to alert the other thirty-plus members of the coven who might be on the property to come to Saeed's aid. His was one of the largest covens in the city. Ewan wouldn't survive.

"*Dios mio*, Sasha! Get out of the fucking way!"

"Dear gods" was right. Sasha rolled her eyes at Diego's frantic shout. She braced for impact as he raced from the formal living room to the foyer, nothing more than a smear of color, ready to protect her from the deadly berserker who managed to infiltrate their coven. In a knee-jerk reaction, she squeezed her eyes shut and waited for the freight train.

Instead of getting knocked on her ass, strong arms encircled Sasha. Ewan spun her, leaving himself vulnerable to attack while he protected her from the brunt of the impact. His frame was unyielding iron. A cage that surrounded her. Diego slammed into Ewan's back at the very moment he spun away, with such force that it slammed him into the opposite wall. He let out a grunt as his arms cracked the stone, and still Sasha was barely jostled as he kept her safe.

"Are you all right? You're not hurt?"

The warm timbre of his voice in her ears coaxed goose bumps to the surface of her skin. Superman had nothing on Ewan Brún. Her earlier anger melted under the scorching heat of his presence. That he put himself in the path of danger to protect her caused Sasha's chest to swell with emotion. The tether that bound them gave a slight tug and she shrugged the sensation away. She didn't have time to deal with warm, fuzzy feelings right now. The shit had hit the fan.

"Saeed?" A warm female voice joined the mix. Cerys, Saeed's mate. Great. "What in the hell is going on?"

It was only a matter of time before multiple bodies converged on Ewan. Sasha needed to get him the hell out of here now. And the only way to call off Diego, Saeed, his mate, and possibly the rest of their coven was to tell the truth. So much for keeping her mate bond a secret. *Shit*.

"He's my mate!" Sasha shouted above the din of panicked voices, praying everyone under the breezeway had the presence of mind to listen.

Time came to a screeching halt. Or maybe it just felt that way. Her declaration was answered with the sort of still silence that froze dust particles in place. Sasha held her breath as she gazed up at Ewan from lowered lashes. A crease dug into his forehead just above the bridge of his nose as his gaze delved into hers. Gods, if ever she wished she could hear someone's thoughts . . .

"It's impossible." Saeed was the first to speak, to break the spell of her shocking revelation. "Berserkers are—"

"I dare you to finish that sentence, vampire." Ewan cut Saeed off without taking his eyes off Sasha. "Your speculations and misinformation aren't going to get you anything but killed."

Sasha's ears pricked as multiple footfalls echoed from the hallways and upper levels of the house. Supernatural hearing made discretion nearly impossible, even when soundproofing measures had been taken. Things were about to go from bad to worse.

She couldn't see. Ewan refused to move even an inch and his massive frame caged her in against the cracked stone wall. He hadn't moved a muscle, hadn't removed his arms from the indentations they made, or even tried to protect himself. She had no idea what sort of attack was coming and there was little she could do to stop it.

"Saeed, he's done something to her. She doesn't know what she's talking about."

Of course, Diego would assume Sasha wasn't strong enough to take care of herself. The assumption that Ewan had somehow tricked her into thinking they'd been tethered made her fangs itch.

"It's you who doesn't know what you're talking about, Diego!" Sasha stood on her tiptoes to try to look at him but Ewan was so gods-damned big it was impossible to see over his arm and shoulder. "My soul was returned and he anchored it. Do you doubt me, Saeed? Are you going to stand there and say that you didn't instantly recognize your tether when Cerys returned your soul to you?"

A space of silence passed and she couldn't help but feel a little smug. The mate bond was sacred. It trumped everything. Whether Saeed liked it or not. He had to respect and recognize Sasha's tether. Nothing in their world was more important.

"I don't understand how this could have happened." The grief in Saeed's tone cut through her. As though his heart broke for the situation she'd found herself in. She knew how he, and Diego, and the others would view it: as a death sentence. Bound for eternity to her most hated enemy and unable to cut the strings that tied them to one another.

They didn't know Ewan, though. A sharp pain hollowed out her chest. Gods, she didn't know him, either. Not really. Her soul knew his, though. It wouldn't have secured itself to him without good reason. She had to trust in that bond. He could have killed her a hundred times over. Tonight, he chose to protect her even when he had to have known that neither Saeed nor Diego would ever harm her. There was more to Ewan than what their history painted of him. Sasha refused to believe anything different.

The footfalls grew louder as dhampirs gathered in the great room, the foyer, and spilled out onto the breezeway. Sasha's stomach tied into an anxious knot and she sent up a silent prayer that the gods would see fit to let this conflict end peacefully. Ewan closed his body in on hers. Closer. Tighter. Forming an impenetrable barrier between her and everyone that stood beyond them. Would a heartless killer—a sworn enemy—behave in such a way?

No.

"I want everyone except myself, Cerys, Diego, Sasha,

and her *guest* off the property until sunrise." As coven master, Saeed's command was law. The distasteful sneer in his tone when he referred to Ewan sent a fresh wave of anger washing through Sasha. No wonder the supernatural world considered vampires and dhampirs as classist and elitist. "Anyone who disregards this mandate will be subject to my authority and punishment. Do you understand me?"

A murmur swept through the small crowd of dhampirs and Sasha wished she could see their faces right now. The gossip was going to spread like wildfire. More than only the underground would know about their relationship after tonight.

Several tense moments passed as the dhampirs scattered. Not a single one of them dared to pass through the foyer, instead opting for one of the several other exits throughout the massive estate. Sasha didn't blame them. A couple of months ago, she would have rather yanked her fangs out with a pair of pliers than to walk past a berserker warlord. Ewan was an intimidating creature. A mountain of sheer strength and unchecked rage.

When the sounds of the last door closing from the east wing of the house echoed into silence, Saeed spoke. "Diego, Cerys, and I will be in the study. Meet us there when you're ready."

His tone was all business and Sasha cringed. This wasn't going to be a pleasant conversation by any stretch of the imagination and she'd be surprised if by the end of the night, Mikhail Aristov himself wasn't involved. So much for keeping her tether on the down-low. In the span of a few minutes, Ewan had blown that secret wide open. *Great.* As if she didn't have enough to worry about . . .

"Sasha." The deep timbre of Ewan's voice resonated through her. "Are you hurt? I know you're weak. Your arm—"

"I'm fine." Her arm still burned like a son of a bitch and

the skin was raw and puckered where it had yet to heal. But the effects of the hellfire were the least of her worries right now. "I need to talk to Saeed. I've put it off for too long and there's no getting out of it now. You can leave if you want. There's no reason for you to stay."

"I'm not going anywhere." Ewan's tone invited no argument. "I'd like to see them try to make me leave."

So would Sasha. Amusement tugged at her lips as Ewan relaxed and pulled away to look down at her. He truly was a magnificent male.

And she belonged to him.

CHAPTER
17

Ewan could think of no other situation more uncomfortable than his current one. He walked into Saeed's stuffy, pristine, and precisely decorated study already feeling the weight of the considerable chip that rested atop his shoulder. Ewan had centuries under his belt. Countless battles won and trials endured. He followed Sasha into the study, feeling as though he were some untested, impoverished youth about to ask for the privilege of courting an aristocrat's daughter.

And he didn't like it one fucking bit.

"Before you start in on me, Saeed, you might as well know that whatever you say isn't going to make a difference." It appeared as though Sasha wasn't in the mood for her maker's show of authority, either. "I'm tethered and there's nothing you can do about it."

"Sit down, Sasha."

Her defiant reply fell on deaf ears. Ewan didn't appreciate the show of disrespect and a growl gathered in his chest. Saeed's gaze met his and the vampire cocked a haughty brow. Too damn bad. Ewan wasn't going to pretend

he was domesticated simply because it offended the
vampire's sensibilities. He was in this room right now
because it was what Sasha wanted. If he had it his way,
he'd take her as far away from here as possible and tell the
entire world to fuck off.

"Speak to her in such a way again, vampire, and I'll
show you why the supernatural underworld cowers in my
presence." Big talk? Probably. But it wasn't untrue. Ewan
wanted Saeed to know exactly who he was dealing with.

Saeed's expression remained calm. "Do you think I'm
afraid of you?"

"I don't give a shit if you are or not. I'm just stating a
simple fact. Treat Sasha with disrespect and you'll deal
with me."

A glimmer of amusement passed over Saeed's expression. As though he were pleased with Ewan's show of protection and somehow backed up Sasha's claim that he was
her mate. Too bad Ewan didn't give a single shit about
proving anything to Saeed or anyone else.

Rather than do as Saeed instructed, Sasha remained
standing at Ewan's side. She tucked her arm—the one that
had been burned by hellfire—behind him as though to
hide the injury. Ewan angled his body toward hers. It was
obvious she didn't want anyone to know about the burn
and he wouldn't betray her confidence. This bullshit with
the demons was their business and no one else's.

"I find myself in a rather difficult situation." Gods, were
all coven masters so stuffy and formal? "By all rights, you
should be dead. I can't allow you to leave here knowing
the location of our coven. It compromises our security."

So damned civilized. Probably why their kind had been
nearly eradicated in the first place. Had Ewan been in
Saeed's position, he would've attacked first and asked
questions later, mate bond be damned. Nothing was more

important than the protection of those under your care. At least on that, they could agree.

"Then kill me." Ewan shrugged a casual shoulder. "Or at least try to. I told you, I'm here for Sasha and nothing else. Believe that or don't. I'm not going to waste my breath trying to convince you of anything."

Saeed looked to Sasha. She mimicked Ewan's actions with a shrug of her own. "He's tethered me, Saeed. Would you take my side over Cerys's?"

Ewan didn't miss the hurt that sliced through Sasha's tone as her attention fell on the red-haired female that sat at Saeed's right side. This was the male Sasha had once had feelings for. Jealousy punched through his chest and he swallowed against the bitter burn. In the beginning, he'd convinced himself that his attraction to Sasha was nothing more than physical. But now that he'd realized she'd managed to awaken lost instincts and feelings, he feared the permanency of that change and the ripple effect it would have within his clan.

"The tether is absolute. You know I would never argue the validity of that."

Ewan wondered if the members of Saeed's coven often fell asleep while he rambled on. Ewan certainly felt a nap coming on.

"Then why am I here?" Sasha asked.

There was definitely more to Sasha's relationship with Saeed than she let on. He'd hurt her. Deeply.

Saeed's eyes went wide. "For months I've entertained this wild streak of yours. Allowed you to shirk your responsibilities and duties, and allowed Diego to see to our security. Looked the other way while you partied your way across the city. Held my tongue while you made reckless decisions and compromised not only your safety, but the safety of this coven. I turned a blind eye to your carelessness, and a deaf ear to the rumors that circulated. I let you come to terms with your transition in your own way and it's a decision I regret."

High-handed motherfucker. The last thing Sasha needed was for anyone to tell her how to live her life. Ewan knew far too well what that felt like and he brought up his right fist as he took a lurching step forward. But Sasha stayed his progress by tugging on the back of his T-shirt. She looked up at him and her expression said, "I've got this." Despite his need to protect her, Ewan knew Sasha could protect herself.

"You abandoned me." Sasha didn't need to shout to convey her rage. It vibrated through her into Ewan. "You turned me because it was convenient for you. You left me here to pick up the pieces of everything you'd shattered. You came back with your soul intact and a mate at your side. I was broken, and you were whole, and you didn't care enough to see it."

Her voice cracked with unshed tears and the depth of emotion slammed into Ewan's chest like a fist. She'd walked out on him tonight because their lack of intimacy frustrated her. He'd never stopped to consider that Sasha had a past because he'd never taken the time to actually have a conversation with her.

"You didn't give a single shit what I did as long as I was out of your hair. And now that you think your precious coven is compromised, you're ready to care again?" Sasha let out a disbelieving bark of laughter. "I'll save you the worry. I don't need to be here. I'm not dependent on you anymore."

Like berserkers, werewolves, and some shifters, vampires were communal creatures. Though Ewan didn't know all the intricacies of their group dynamic, he did know vampires and dhampirs were interconnected and needed one another to survive. It was a fact Gregor had drilled into their heads over the decades. Vampires existed as myriad small parts of the whole. In order to kill one, you had to kill them all. What would happen to Sasha if she broke from her coven? Ewan needed answers, and he doubted he'd be getting them anytime soon.

"This isn't about you, and me, and what has transpired between us, Sasha." Apparently Saeed wasn't interested in airing their dirty laundry in front of guests. "A berserker stands in our home." His silver gaze met Ewan's. "How many of us have you slaughtered, slayer? How many vampires' and dhampirs' hearts have you pierced with your silver-tipped stakes?"

Sasha stiffened beside him. Among the things she and Ewan never talked about, their shared brutal history was one of them. He refused to soften the blow for her benefit. It would be an insult to her intelligence. "Hundreds." The word left Ewan's lips without emotion. "Perhaps more."

Saeed's attention turned to Sasha. "If he has indeed tethered you, then Fate has made a terrible mistake. I never should have turned you. I have condemned you to an existence far worse than death."

The insult stung more than Ewan wanted to admit. There were two sides to every story and if you asked a berserker for their version, it was the vampires who would be painted as the villains.

He fixed his gaze on Saeed. "Insult me again, vampire, and I'll add one more of you to my number of kills."

Saeed bared his fangs. The aggression Ewan felt toward the male had more to do with his relationship to Sasha than his heated words. Ewan didn't give a shit what he—or anyone else—thought about him. What got under his skin was the knowledge that this male had, at one time, meant something to Sasha.

The female who had remained quiet at Saeed's side lunged toward Ewan. The curls of her flame-red hair cascaded over her shoulders and her strange light eyes grew bright with anger. Power sparked the air and Ewan's muscles tensed as the foreign magic zapped him like a Taser. He was unfamiliar with her origin, but whatever she was, her magic sent a ripple of fear through him.

"Cerys." Saeed reached out and gathered her close to him. "Don't."

She was his mate. Ewan recognized Saeed's protective tone and body language. The way his heartbeat spiked with concern when she'd rushed at Ewan. He glanced at Sasha just in time to see the hurt that sliced through her expression. She'd been in love with Saeed. And he'd broken her heart.

And for that, he wanted to make the vampire bleed.

There had been a time when Sasha would've given anything to have Saeed treat her with the kind of concern and care he showed to Cerys. Her heart ached as much now as it had in the months before he'd turned her. She thought she was over him. Over the heartache of losing him. But some small part of her heart had held on.

Gods, she was so sick of feeling humiliated.

Ewan's intense gaze met hers and Sasha's stomach leapt up into her throat. So quick to anger, it didn't take much to set him off. Her inability to read him frustrated her. In the end, everything translated to anger: frustration, worry, affection, concern. It seemed the only time Ewan wasn't angry was during sex and even then, he was always close to the edge. She wanted to clear the room. To tell Saeed, Cerys, and Diego to get the hell out. But even then, would she have the guts to ask him how he truly felt? Or would she brush her curiosity under the rug in order to protect her own damaged heart?

"Just let me go, Saeed." Sasha had grown too tired to fight. "You don't want me here any more than I want to be here. You're not obligated to me. You don't owe me anything. Let me walk out the door and I promise, your conscience will be clear."

"You don't know what you're saying." Saeed's brow furrowed with concern. He didn't love her. She knew he never had. It was his sense of honor and need to protect that wouldn't allow him to let her go. "You are a part of this coven. Nothing is going to change that."

Sasha cocked a brow. "Oh no? Not even my tethered status?"

Historically, covens were welcoming of mates. Of course, during a time when the world was populated with vampires, they hadn't found their mates outside of their own species. It was a different world now. Ironically enough, this new dynamic was created by the same misguided individuals who thought to change the course of fate by eliminating them in the first place.

"He returned your soul, yes," Saeed began. "But it gives him no ownership over you. You have no obligation to him, Sasha. You owe him nothing."

Tension vibrated from Ewan in palpable waves. Perhaps it was because of the tether that Sasha seemed so in tune with his mood. Or maybe Saeed just chose to ignore the danger signs. No one like to be talked about right in front of their face and Sasha's own temper mounted that Saeed would show such disdain and disrespect for her mate no matter what he might be.

"For some reason, this conversation keeps swinging back around to obligation. So we're agreed, you're not obligated to me, I'm not obligated to Ewan. Understand this, Saeed, if I leave this coven, it's because I *choose* to do so. No one is forcing me, or manipulating me, or planting a suggestion in my head. My tether might be unorthodox, but I'm not going to stand here and let you treat the return of my soul as though it were some sort of horrible mistake."

"Sasha." Diego stepped forward, apparently ready to add his two cents. Perfect. All she needed was one more dissenting voice in her head to fuel the doubt that already lingered there. "No one is saying the return of your soul was a mistake."

Saeed let out a derisive snort. "Speak for yourself, Diego. I refuse to believe Fate could allow for something like this to happen."

When had Sasha's life become a dysfunctional family drama? She wasn't some stupid kid dating a boy her parents didn't approve of. She'd walked the earth for centuries. Lived through wars and the near eradication of her race. She was intelligent, self-sufficient, and capable. She'd managed the safety and security of their coven for two hundred years. And yet, the two males who knew her best treated her as though she were the most helpless creature to ever exist.

The air continued to thicken with Ewan's quiet anger. It sucked all of the breathable oxygen from the room, leaving Sasha's lungs tight and aching. When he pulled the cork, shit was going to get messy real fast. She needed to get him the hell out of here.

"If you care at all about keeping me a part of this coven, you'll watch what you say about Ewan."

Saeed's eyes widened a fraction of an inch. "You're quite familiar with him, aren't you?"

She rolled her eyes. He could be a disdainful prick all he wanted, but she wasn't going to tolerate his elitist attitude for another second. An insult to Ewan was an insult to her. How could he not see that? It wasn't Ewan's anger Saeed should be wary of anymore. Sasha's own had reached its breaking point.

"Listen to yourself, Saeed!" Sasha did nothing to temper her angry shout. She couldn't turn her feelings into words. Couldn't bring herself to tell him how devalued he made her feel. How unworthy. Like she wasn't good enough to be tethered by anything other than a lowly berserker. Tears stung at Sasha's eyes and her chest burned with the excess of emotion. She'd given Saeed ownership of her feelings for far too long. "You know what? I'm better than this. I'm better than what you think of me and I don't have to stand here and take this from you. I'm leaving."

"With *him*? Sasha, it's not safe."

"He tethered me weeks ago, Saeed. And don't you *dare* lecture me about safety. You haven't given a single shit what I've been up to the past few months and believe me, safety hasn't exactly been my number-one concern."

"Sasha, don't leave." Diego wanted to be the peacemaker. The lone voice of reason to keep the family together. "Everyone just needs to calm down. We can talk this out and—"

"I don't have anything more to say." She was through wasting her breath. All she'd done for decades was fill Saeed's sails with words of adoration. She'd offered her undying loyalty and bent over backward for him. No more. "And I'm not interested in anything he has to say, either. Ewan?" She turned toward him to find his posture relaxed, expression smug. "Wanna get out of here?"

He wound his fingers with hers. "Absolutely."

"Sasha, wait!" Diego wasn't going to let it go. She was so done with all of it and wanted nothing more than to let her past—all of it—go.

Her step faltered. Ewan urged her to follow him out of the study and toward the front door. She let him take control. Let him lead her and gladly followed. Oh, she was still plenty pissed off at him, too, but she wanted Saeed to see her leave with him. To know that he'd fucked up so royally that she chose a berserker over loyalty to her maker. To her own coven. Petty? Sure. But Sasha wanted to hurt him. And even though she knew he'd never hurt like she did, it made her feel like she was reclaiming the part of her heart he'd stolen and mishandled by doing this. She was using Ewan to get under Saeed's skin. She was willing to risk the karmic payback if it helped to heal her some small bit.

Sasha had left her heart unguarded for far too long. And she wasn't going to let anyone hurt her that deeply ever again.

She didn't need tenderness or affection. Love or intimacy. She'd been upset tonight because Ewan refused to open up to her. Well, he was off the hook. Tonight proved why it wasn't a good idea to let anyone get close to her ever again. All it led to was hurt. Sasha didn't want to hurt ever again. She didn't want to feel anything. She could have sex with Ewan. Companionship. But nothing more. She'd harden herself to affection of any kind. Saeed thought the berserkers were cold, cruel creatures? He hadn't seen anything yet.

CHAPTER
18

Arrogant fucking vampires.

Ewan vibrated with anger as he led Sasha out the door and through the fancy-as-fuck breezeway. Her car was parked at the edge of the driveway and he hung a right toward it. Sasha resisted and he turned to look at her. Worry shot through his gut as he took in her hollow expression. The apathy there shook him and he squeezed her hand as though it would somehow wake her from her stupor.

"Sasha?"

"How did you get here?"

Even her tone had an empty quality to it that he hadn't heard before. Another jolt of worry shot through his bloodstream. What in the hell was going on? He was supposed to be the detached asshole, not the concerned, emotional one.

"I drove here." He'd nearly forgotten about the piece-of-shit Civic in his haste to get Sasha out of here. "I'm parked down the street."

"Okay. Good."

Sasha changed course and headed toward the driveway. "Hey." Ewan tugged at her hand but she wasn't stopping. He fell into step beside her as she hustled toward the main gate. "We can take your car and come back for mine later."

"The coven's money paid for my car," Sasha said. "I don't want it. I don't want anything that's connected to Saeed."

She was hurt and rightfully so. It took every ounce of willpower he had not to march back into the house and beat that smug motherfucker to a bloody pulp. A red haze of anger and jealousy clouded Ewan's vision. Different from the battle rage that consumed him, this kept him painfully lucid and feeling so gods-damned helpless that it made him want to throw his head back and shout his frustration to the sky. He didn't know how to help her. How to fix things for her. Ewan knew only one thing: how to kill.

He'd been fighting for months in order to create a way to leave his clan while Sasha had been cast aside by those she'd hungered for attention from. They were the same and yet, so different. Ewan wasn't accustomed to dealing with soft emotions. Hell, emotions of any kind, really. This was foreign territory.

"My car is . . ." *A piece of shit. Old as fuck. Barely running.* "Not as nice as yours."

Sasha's brow furrowed as she gave him a sidelong glance. "Do you think I care about that? Those sorts of things don't matter to me. I wouldn't have given a shit if you'd told me you rode here on a bike. I still wouldn't drive my car out of here."

Ewan appreciated the sentiment, but he hated the emptiness that remained in her tone. She had no idea what she was setting herself up for. Ewan had lived centuries in poverty. At the beck and call of someone else. Dependent on others for even the barest necessities. Sasha had always

been privileged. Had always been provided with everything she needed and more. She'd lived a life of luxury.
She was giving all of that up to salvage her damaged
pride. She had no idea how hard her life would be from
here on out. Hell, she probably hadn't even contemplated
who'd pay the rent on her apartment now that she'd left
the financial security of her coven behind.

She didn't have anything but the clothes on her back.
She'd regret her decision to leave once she got a healthy
dose of reality.

As they neared the gate, Ewan hesitated. He'd used
stealth to get past security and who knew what Saeed had
told his people after they'd stormed out. Sasha urged him
forward this time, her shoulders thrown back, head held
high.

"They won't dare touch you," she said.

"Why? Because they're afraid of you?"

Sasha laughed. "No. Because they're afraid of *you*."

Ewan had no idea how many vampires were in Sasha's
coven. It was only part of the intel Gregor had wanted him
to collect. He'd only seen three including Sasha and he assumed that had there been more in the house, Saeed
would have summoned them to provide additional backup.
Which meant the remainder of their coven probably con-
sisted of weaker dhampirs. Easy to overpower.

Sasha released Ewan's hand and marched straight up to
the gate. She turned to face whoever manned the guard station. Her eyes flashed feral silver. She didn't speak a single word. The gate remained closed and she slowly turned
her head to look at Ewan, directing the guard to follow her
gaze.

Ewan stood his ground. His eyes met the dhampir's and
he waited. Seconds later the gate swung wide with a me-
chanical hum. Gregor wouldn't be too happy if Ewan's
presence here tonight caused the vampires to pull up camp

and move. Ewan suspected that wouldn't happen, though. Saeed would keep this a secret until he could secure Sasha's safety. The vampire knew he'd hurt her and would want to somehow make amends.

His guilt was Ewan's saving grace.

Sasha led the way past the gate and down the driveway. She didn't so much as cast a glance over her shoulder as she walked away from her home. A protective urge spiked within Ewan. It tightened his skin on his bones and caused his heart to beat a little too fast. Sasha cradled her right arm in her left as she walked, drawing his attention to the wound that had started them down this road tonight.

"You need to feed." Ewan picked up his pace to catch up to her. She tilted her head to the left but gave no other indication that she heard him. "The burn hasn't healed."

"I'll live."

It had been one hell of a night and apparently it wasn't over. Ewan wasn't interested in yet another fight, but it looked like he was going to get one whether he wanted it or not. "I know you'll live. That's not the point."

"Then what is your point?" Sasha hung a left and headed down the street to where Ewan's Civic was parked. Rather than hustle to catch up, he hung back. If they were going to get into it, he'd rather it happened out of Saeed's earshot.

"Nothing. Never mind."

Sasha whipped around at his dismissal. *Great*. He couldn't catch a fucking break tonight. He'd spent the first half in the battle arena and the second half deep in hostile territory. All he wanted to do was take Sasha back to her apartment where he knew she'd be safe and call it a godsdamned night. The sun would be up in a few hours and there was a lot to take care of at the apartment before then. Sasha had never spent the day there before. Nothing had been done to protect the space from encroaching sunlight. Fucking hell, did she not consider her own safety and well-being *at all*?

The spark in her silver eyes and set of her jaw told him she was ready to throw down. "Get in the car, Sasha." It wasn't going to happen here. Period. "Now."

"You might have tethered me, Ewan, but don't think that gives you the right to treat me like property."

Good gods. Ewan rolled his eyes. She was going out of her way to goad him. She wouldn't be happy until she got what she wanted: a knock-down, drag-out verbal brawl. Awesome. Ewan was a stubborn bastard, though. He'd be damned if he gave her what she wanted.

"You're right. Far be it from me to force you to do anything." He yanked open the driver side door and stared at her from over the hood. "The apartment's what . . . a good fifteen or so miles from here? You're welcome to walk it if you want. Sunrise is still a couple hours off. You'll make it with plenty of time to spare."

She could make it back to her apartment in fifteen minutes or less thanks to her supernatural speed. But Ewan suspected she didn't want to go on foot. If she had, she wouldn't have gone to his car in the first place. She just wanted to push his buttons. *Push away, baby.* He was unshakable.

Sasha would learn soon enough that going head-to-head with him wasn't a good idea. She'd lose. Every time. Ewan only hoped that in the process of teaching her a lesson, he didn't push her away from him as well.

Sasha was itching for a fight and it pissed her off that Ewan refused to give her one. Almost every male she knew had managed to earn a spot on her shit list and she was about three seconds away from asking Ewan to drive her to Pasadena so she could spend the night with Lucas's coven.

Anywhere was better than here. In fact, Pasadena probably wasn't far enough away. Right now, a place on the freaking moon would be too close to Ewan and Saeed and Diego and anyone else who thought to cross her. She wanted to put her fist into both of their guts, though for two totally different reasons.

Were they really different, though? Maybe her reasons for being annoyed with them were more similar than she wanted to admit.

Ewan gave her one last disdainful look before settling into the driver's seat and closing the door. Sasha glanced at him through the window and fought a bout of laughter. He barely fit in the tiny compact car and it made his frame seem even larger and more imposing. Like a grizzly bear shoved into a golf cart. Her lips twitched, threatening a smile and she locked that shit down. She wasn't ready to let go of her foul mood.

She climbed into the passenger seat and shut the door. "How did you find me?" It had been nagging at her ever since he'd shown up. Berserkers had keen senses, but he couldn't have possibly picked up her scent over fifteen-plus miles.

"Does it matter?"

His elusive bullshit was what had started the ball rolling tonight. Because Sasha had allowed herself to *care*. All caring did was open her up to hurt. He didn't want to share? Fine.

"I guess not."

He glanced at her from the corner of his eye as he turned the key. The engine coughed and spluttered before dying and Ewan turned the key once again as he pumped his foot on the gas pedal to encourage the old car to start. His scent soured with his annoyance and Sasha wrinkled her nose. It bothered him that the car wouldn't start. Maybe even embarrassed him? Sasha had meant what she'd said. She didn't give a crap what his car looked like or how old it was. Material possessions meant little to her.

Though she had to admit, her Audi had never managed to break her heart . . .

Ewan said a curse under his breath. He turned the key once more and though it resisted his efforts to get it going, it finally whined and whirred to life. Sasha suspected he'd gotten the engine to turn over by sheer will alone. She knew Ewan well enough to realize he didn't take defeat lightly. Which was why she couldn't believe he wouldn't let her goad him into a fight. Aggression was what he did best. She wasn't thrilled with his passivity.

He pulled out onto the street and pushed the ailing car as fast as it would go. Why the urgency? They had plenty of time to make it back to the apartment by sunrise. Ewan took a hard left and Sasha reached for the "oh shit" handle above the door. "Where's the fire?"

Ewan glanced up at the rearview mirror. His jaw squared as his hands gripped the steering wheel tight. "We're being followed."

Followed? "What? By who?"

Ewan gave her a look. "If I knew that I wouldn't be hauling ass to get as far from your coven's home base as possible. It could be a coincidence, but I don't think so."

A knot of worry gathered in Sasha's stomach. She was angry with Saeed and needed space but that didn't mean she wanted anything bad to happen to the members of the coven. A seed of doubt sprouted in her mind. One that ate away at her like acid. Had she somehow allowed Ewan to easily find her tonight and thereby given the berserkers the location of their coven? Worry turned to panic as Sasha envisioned an ambush. One she'd narrowly escaped. Their security had been her responsibility. One she'd shirked in order to party her life away. Gods, if anything happened to them, she'd never forgive herself.

"What did you do, Ewan?"

The accusation left her lips before she could think better of it. Old habits died hard, it seemed. She couldn't help but throw her suspicions in his face. He kept his attention on the road, his concentration solid as he veered off to a side street in order to shake whoever followed them. At least, that was the impression he gave. For all Sasha knew, Ewan was playing a part for her benefit, appearing to elude their pursuers. She'd been petulant and angry at Saeed, ready to dismiss every word out of his mouth for the sake of being contrary. But what if she was wrong about Ewan? What if their connection—the moments they'd shared the past several weeks—meant absolutely nothing to him?

What if he were leading her into a trap?

Doubt gnawed at her. Fear scraped at the back of her mind like a dull knife. She considered bailing but she'd burned a bridge with Saeed tonight and likewise, Ewan knew where her apartment was which eliminated hiding out there as a possibility. She could try to make it to Lucas's or take shelter with Ani for the day, but Sasha wasn't interested in bringing trouble to either of their doors. She was left with only one option: stay right the hell where she was and weather the storm. And pray she lived to see another night.

"For the record, berserkers wouldn't be so blatant." Ewan's response chilled Sasha's skin. "An attack would come out of nowhere. They'd strike silently and kill you before you had a chance to process what was happening."

Sasha let out a breath. "Is that supposed to somehow make me feel better?"

Ewan shrugged as though he couldn't care one way or another how it made her feel. "I'm just laying it out for you since you suddenly think I've somehow betrayed you."

It was nearly impossible to get anything over on a supernatural creature. Sasha's scent gave her away, as did the beat of her heart and the small tells in her body language that indicated she was on edge. Ewan cut to the right, back-tracking the way they'd come. The Honda's tired engine protested and the car spluttered as he put the pedal to the floor. Definitely not the ideal vehicle for a high-speed chase.

"Ewan, look out!"

Sasha caught sight of the projectile from the corner of her eye. It hit the pavement twenty yards in front of them and exploded into bright orange, blue, and green flames.

Hellfire.

Well, she guessed that ruled out the berserkers as their pursuers. Ewan jerked the wheel to his left and the tires screeched as the car went into a skid. They narrowly avoided the explosion and Sasha cupped her palm over her burned forearm. Hellfire wasn't anything to mess with. The flames burned hot enough to melt metal and couldn't be extinguished by water. Some demons could even coax hellfire to spring right from their hands. Sasha had been on the receiving end of one of those particular demon's not-so-gentle touch. And she never wanted to experience anything like it ever again.

Ewan straightened the wheel and the car righted itself. "Fucking demons!" Rage resonated in his gravelly tone and Sasha didn't need to see his eyes to know that inky black bled into the whites and irises. "I'm going to kill every last one of them!"

He brought the car to a screeching halt that nearly sent Sasha through the windshield. Yeah, Ewan was pissed. She was shaken up, weak, and it was too close to sunrise for this sort of melee. She wasn't prepared to stand and fight. Did that matter to Ewan? Sasha doubted it even crossed his mind. Berserkers were war machines. Fighting was in-grained in their DNA. They didn't know fear. They didn't retreat. There was no other option for Ewan but to stand against his attackers. Running wouldn't even cross his mind. And by default, Sasha would have no choice but to stand and fight as well. Or more to the point, defend herself as best she could and try not to get burned to a crisp in the process.

Was it too late to ask for a do-over? Because this night was officially fucked.

CHAPTER
19

Ewan was going to destroy every single one of those low-life bastards. Those piece-of-shit sore losers had messed with the wrong male. After the fucked-up night he'd had, Ewan was more than ready to blow off a little steam. If they wanted a fight, he'd sure as hell give them one.

"Wait in the car."

He might have wanted to deliver unimaginable pain to the demons who thought they could bully him, but he wasn't about to risk Sasha's safety in the process. He reached for the door handle and stopped as Sasha grasped his arm.

"You're kidding, right?" Silver laced her disbelieving gaze. "You think I'm actually going to sit here and watch while you go out there and get yourself killed?"

Her lack of faith in his fighting prowess left little to be desired. He'd deal with that later, though. In the meantime, he wasn't about to let her step foot outside the car. Not that it would do much to protect her from hellfire, but if it came down to it, she could at least beat a hasty retreat.

"You're injured and weak, and you're not getting out of

this car. Do you understand me, Sasha?" Ewan's gaze drilled into hers for emphasis. Her stubborn expression filled him with a dark foreboding that did nothing for the anxious energy that cycled through him. The odds were against him and he needed every ounce of focus he could muster. Distractions would only help to get them both killed.

"I'll stay in the car if you do."

Ewan clenched his jaw so tight that the enamel of his teeth ground from the force. Gods, she was a stubborn pain in the ass. "I don't have time to argue with you. Stay in the car, Sasha. Slide over to the driver's seat and if shit goes south, hit the gas and get the hell out of here."

She met him look for look. "No."

Sasha frustrated the *fuck* out of him. He opened his mouth, ready to tell her he'd kill her himself if she didn't do as he said, when several dark figures emerged from the flames. Impervious to their own hellfire, the demons strode toward the car, dark outlines against the bright backdrop. Their time had run out.

"Let me take point. Don't engage unless you have no other choice. And for the love of the gods, Sasha, don't piss anyone off with that mouth of yours!" Ewan had no choice but to stand and fight and hope Sasha would come to her senses and stay where she'd be safe.

He let out a frustrated huff of breath as he got out of the car. All he needed was one more complication in the current clusterfuck that was his life. Apparently, Sorath hadn't been too pleased about Ewan brushing him off earlier tonight. He wanted to get his point across and wasn't above sending his henchmen to throw supernatural fire across the city to get it done.

It wouldn't be long before the local fire departments were deployed to the scene. The oncoming clash would be fast, furious, and violent. Over before it barely had a chance to begin. Scuffles like this were common when secrecy was tantamount. The supernatural world fought their wars subversively, many times under the guise of human conflict. That the demons chose to set off a hellfire explosion in the middle of Los Angeles was as careless as it was stupid. Ewan didn't have time for this shit. The sun would be up soon and he needed to get Sasha out of here ASAP.

"Spread your hellfire!" Ewan shouted over the roar of the flames. "The Sortiari will have your heads for it!"

Laughter echoed over the din. It seemed the demons weren't frightened by the guardians of fate, their laws, or anything else. "Without their berserker war dogs to enforce their rules, who gives a shit?"

The male had a point. For centuries, the secret society had used Ewan and his brethren to stir fear in the hearts of supernatural creatures all over the world. Gregor had known when he staged his little coup that breaking from the Sortiari would decimate their credibility and authority. Ewan had been doubtful, but no longer. He bore witness to the fracture and it sent a tremor of fear through him.

A world without order was what Ian Gregor sought to create, and he was within touching distance of achieving his goal.

Fucking chaos.

"And yet," Ewan shouted back. "Here you are, about to have your asses handed to you by a *war dog*."

The car door slammed and Ewan's eyes drifted shut for the barest moment in an effort to calm the hell down. Knowing Sasha was out here, even more exposed, sent a rush of adrenaline through his bloodstream. He kept his position between the encroaching demons and Sasha, his senses tuned in to her every movement. She stepped to the left and Ewan mirrored the motion. To the right, and he shifted in kind. His consciousness split into a dual awareness. One that focused on the threat in front of him, and the other on his mate who needed his protection.

Mate?

The thought came out of nowhere and Ewan quickly banished it from his mind. Every crunch of the demons' footsteps skittered along his senses and his muscles tensed as he readied himself for the coming fight. They might be armed with hellfire, but that wouldn't put him down. Nothing short of severing his head from his shoulders would kill him, and Ewan wasn't about to let the bastards get close enough to try.

Behind him, Sasha stepped to the side. Ewan moved in tandem, completely in sync with every motion. The demons stepped from the cover of shadows, the yellowish pallor of their leathery skin intensified by the flames behind them.

"You owe my employer fifty large, berserker." One demon stepped from the ranks of the other four and approached Ewan. The wicked points of his sharklike teeth glinted in the firelight as his lips pulled back into a contemptuous sneer. "And he's not the sort who likes to be kept waiting when it comes to debts being repaid."

Assholes. It wasn't his fault they refused to bet on a sure thing. "I don't owe your boss or anyone else a gods-damned cent!" His hands balled into fists at his side. Sasha took three steps toward him and one to the left and he mirrored her actions to keep distance between them. "Tell the male who holds your leash to go fuck himself! He deserves to lose his money for betting against a warlord."

Gods, Ewan was sick of big talk being used as a battle tactic. Why couldn't someone just try to stab him or pull a gun or some shit? He'd much rather fight than beat around the fucking bush.

"We could take payment as a pound of your flesh," the demon suggested. He craned his neck to look past Ewan and his hackles rose. "Or maybe take it from the flesh of your lover."

Power flooded Ewan's body in a wave of angry heat that caused sweat to bead his brow. Rage blanketed his thoughts until nothing remained but a violent urge to send these bastards straight to the underworld where they belonged.

"Take even a single step toward her," Ewan warned, "and I'll tear your throats out before you can utter another word."

The demon's derisive snort only served to further ignite Ewan's temper. He glanced Sasha's way once again and his lips spread into a sinister smile. "How's her arm?"

Ewan's gut tied into an unyielding knot. This was the son of a bitch who'd burned her? He took a lunging step forward before he checked himself. The demon was trying to goad him into making the first move. He wanted Ewan enraged and off balance. He needed to keep his fucking cool and maintain the upper hand.

"You won't get close enough to find out."

The demon's smile didn't fade. Nor did his attention wander from Sasha. Intentionally goading Ewan by showing him exactly where—and on who—they planned to launch their attack. Fucking cowards knew they couldn't take him in a fight and so instead, they'd go for his one weakness.

Sasha had quickly become Ewan's Achilles' heel and the realization kicked him straight in the gut. The demons knew it and he suspected Gregor knew it as well. Would have been nice if he'd realized it himself before tonight. He'd only recognized the hold she had on him after she'd walked out of her apartment tonight, forcing him to go out in search of her. There was no turning back now. She was under his skin. And now he had no choice but to defend her at all costs.

Ewan stepped into the demon's line of vision. It was ill

advised to be the first to attack but that's exactly what he was going to do. "Stay back, Sasha!" He hoped that for once, she'd heed his damn warning. He drew on the power that pooled in his gut like molten lead and let it overtake him. The bright-colored flames of the hellfire transformed to shades of gray and black. A low growl built in Ewan's chest as his thoughts grew hazy. His feet dug into the soles of his boots and he propelled himself forward with an angry shout.

It was time to send a message. Anyone who sought to harm Sasha Ivanov would meet a violent end. Ewan would make sure of it.

Sasha stood in awe of Ewan. The ferocity with which he attacked stole her breath. She'd seen him fight in the arena but it didn't hold a candle to what she beheld now. He embodied everything she'd ever been taught to fear. Berserker. Force of destruction. Violent. Mindless. Bringer of death.

He was all of those things and none of them at the same time. Ewan was a force of nature. A storm that couldn't be stopped until it ran its course. He was beautiful and graceful. Every step precise as though choreographed. His focus seemed singular, and yet, Sasha noted that he never moved far enough away from her to leave her vulnerable to attack.

Gods, he was magnificent.

The demons scattered under the onslaught. He moved with blurring speed, knocking one off his feet a split second before he barreled into another, sending him flying into the concrete piling that braced a section of highway above them. The force of the impact vibrated in a loud boom that echoed over the din of the still burning hellfire and sent chunks of concrete flying around them. Shit was about to get messy and Sasha hoped no innocent souls would be caught in the crossfire.

A brawl of this magnitude in such a public place would be frowned upon by all factions. She couldn't believe the demons would sanction something like this. The fallout could be disastrous. Obviously, not Ewan or the demons he fought gave a single shit about discretion.

"Sasha, stay behind me!"

Good gods! He had bigger things to worry about than where she was standing. Did he really think she'd just hang back and watch while he fought? The demons weren't going to hurt him—or her—no matter what Ewan thought to the contrary. Sasha knew what they really wanted and this production was just to help convince her to play ball.

"Your berserker lover is going to die either way." The demon's words from last night resonated in Sasha's mind. *"He can die in the arena and keep you safe, or you can both die slowly in a torture pit. Take your pick, vampire."*

They wanted Sasha to sign Ewan's death sentence. Or more to the point, convince him to sacrifice himself in the arena so they could walk away with a fortune. Their flaw was in thinking she cared so much about her own safety that she'd so willingly sacrifice his. Fifty thousand dollars wasn't even close to what they stood to gain if Ewan lost in the arena. They goaded him tonight and made their ridiculous demands to agitate his temper. They knew he'd never willingly sacrifice himself. No one with an ounce of sanity would! No, their strategy was to push, and push, and push some more. Threaten Sasha and put them in one dangerous situation after the next until Ewan was out of his mind with worry and desperate to do anything to protect her.

The problem was, the demons assumed Ewan was in love with her. That she meant something to him. Boy, did they ever have it wrong. Sasha didn't know what this was between them, but it sure as hell wasn't love.

All of this was a waste of energy. And aside from coming clean with Ewan about what the demons wanted—which wasn't going to happen—she had no idea how to stop him. They'd played Ewan and he let them. Greedily swallowed their bait. Sasha rolled her eyes to the sky. The only way this would end was if she intervened.

He was going to be pissed, but she'd deal with the consequences later. Ewan thought he was the biggest, baddest creature around and that might be true. But Sasha wasn't completely helpless and it was time Ewan realized it. She'd been taking care of herself just fine before he came along.

Sasha dodged to the right and as though a length of rope connected them, Ewan echoed the motion. How in the hell was he able to focus like that? Especially with her behind him where he couldn't see her? The shift made his left side vulnerable to attack. The demon smirked as he dusted himself off and opened his fist, palm facing toward the sky. Hellfire sprang to life in his hand, the flames eager as they danced.

"We both know you're not going to do anything with that, so why don't you and your cronies fuck off and go home!"

Her snarky words were wasted on the two stubborn males. Figured. The demon used Ewan's shift as an opportunity to attack. This might have been a scare tactic, but they were going to get their licks in any chance they got. He pulled back his hand and pitched the ball of fire straight to Ewan's exposed side. Sasha knew the excruciating burn of hellfire and without even thinking, she launched herself at Ewan, determined to intercept the ball of flames before it hit him.

Ewan caught her in midflight. He jerked her against his

body as he turned to his right, taking them both to the pavement before the hellfire could hit either one of them. His reflexes were unlike anything Sasha had ever seen, even in a berserker. Almost precognitive, as though he knew what she was going to do before she did it. He caged her in with his massive arms and cradled the back of her head with one palm, taking the brunt of the impact as they rolled.

"Gods-damn it, Sasha," Ewan ground out from between clenched teeth. "Are you out of your fucking mind?"

Her? He was the one who thought it was a good idea to act like a living shield! Sasha pushed away from Ewan, too worried about a second fireball to respond. The sound of retreating footsteps barely registered over the din of hellfire that still burned thirty yards to their left. A car door slammed and tires squealed as the demons sped away. Cowards. They never would've beaten Ewan if they'd stood and fought.

The frantic beats of her heart slowed and Sasha's worry was replaced with anger. Ewan's carelessness made her want to take him and shake some damned sense into him. "That was stupid, Ewan!" The words left her mouth in a thoughtless rush. "They could have burned you to ash!"

In a motion that defied gravity, Ewan rolled and managed to bring them both to a standing position without releasing his grip on Sasha. His core muscles must have been constructed with steel rods. It was no wonder the supernatural world feared the berserkers. They were ultra-supernaturals. The most extraordinary creatures on the planet. Sasha had no doubt that gods would bow at Ewan Brún's feet. But not even his magnificence would distract her from her anger.

"They could have burned *you*!" Ewan steadied Sasha before he put her at arm's length. His eyes went wide and his jaw, slack. "What the fuck were you thinking by putting yourself in the path of that fireball?"

"I was trying to protect you!" She brought her finger up and poked it at him. "You're not indestructible, Ewan!"

His gaze went to the sky and he let out a disbelieving bark of laughter. "Look who's talking! Jesus, Sasha! I would've survived it a hell of a lot better than you would have."

The sky lightened from navy blue to hues of gray as they stood beneath the damaged underpass. Hellfire burned in the distance, inextinguishable until the fire ran its course and burned out on its own. Sasha's skin tingled with the coming dawn and exhaustion pulled at her muscles and tugged her eyelids downward. Her apartment was still a good ten minutes away and the tiny Honda wasn't going to do much to shield her from the sun once it rose. Somehow, winning this argument with Ewan seemed much more important than finding shelter.

"I'm not the one with the death wish!" The faint howl of sirens in the distance meant they wouldn't be able to stand here and argue for much longer. "I mean, seriously! Since the night I met you, all you've tried to do is get yourself killed!"

Ewan averted his gaze. She'd hit a nerve. "You don't know what the hell you're talking about."

The calm levelness of his voice was more disturbing than any shout. Sasha wanted to take back her words, or at the very least take back the intent behind them. Why had she let her temper get the better of her? Damn it. She didn't know why Ewan was so upset, but it didn't bode well.

"Ewan, I—"

"Sun's rising." He turned and headed for the car without saying another word. "We need to go."

Sasha fell into step behind him. All the fight and anger drained out of her and all that was left in its place was regret. So far, her plan to remain detached and emotionless was working out just like she thought it would.

In complete and utter failure.

CHAPTER
20

He had a death wish? He wasn't the one about to be fried to a fucking crisp by the sun! No creature on the face of the earth could push his buttons like Sasha did. He fought the urge to grab her, throw her over his shoulder, and toss her in the damned car. Instead, he turned on a heel and walked away. His decision to let her follow on her own wasn't doing anything for the urgent sense of worry that was about to lay him low, however.

Gods. Did she not understand that sunrise was only a few minutes off?

Unspent energy pooled in Ewan's muscles causing an acidic burn that he was desperate to work off. Fucking coward demons didn't have the balls to stay and fight. Instead, they'd run off with their tails tucked between their legs. They weren't going to get money—or anything else—out of him. And if one of them so much as turned a caustic eye Sasha's way ever again, he'd make them eat their own hellfire and watch as they burned from the inside out.

Gods, he needed to blow off some steam.

He reached for the door handle of the Civic and gave it

a solid yank. The door ripped from the hinges and hung in Ewan's grip. *Fucking hell!* Like the damned thing wasn't already a piece of shit. Thanks to his preternatural strength, it now looked like something that had rolled out of a junkyard.

From behind him, Sasha cleared her throat. The sound carried a little too much humor for his taste and Ewan's lips curled into a disdainful sneer as he turned to face her. "I'm sorry." He cocked a brow and kept his tone even and clipped. "Did you say something?"

Any amusement that might have been present in Sasha's expression faded in an instant. The petulant pucker of her lips would have been sexy as hell if he weren't so pissed off at her. She gingerly opened the passenger side door and just as delicately settled herself into the seat. If she was trying to further aggravate him with her dramatic show, it was working.

In the distance, the demons' bonfire still raged and the flashing lights of the approaching fire trucks bounced off of nearby structures. Ewan could only imagine what sorts of conclusions the humans would jump to when they assessed the unquenchable fire. Hazmat crews would be called in. The area would be shut down and blocked off. Not to mention the damage done to the overpass that probably wouldn't support the weight of the upcoming morning commuter traffic.

Bastard demons had really fucked a lot of shit up tonight. Way to be discreet, assholes. There was nothing Ewan could do about it. It wasn't his mess to clean up and he was more concerned with Sasha's vulnerable state.

"Don't you think you should buckle your seatbelt?"

Ewan fought the urge to bang his head against the steering wheel. Seriously? It's like she wanted to drive him insane. He turned the key in the ignition, silently daring the fucking car not to start. The engine groaned but turned

over on the first try and Ewan let out a slow breath of relief.

"Worried I might fall out?"

Sasha's face remained passive. "Something like that."

"Well, don't. I've lived through too much to worry that
something as minor as a little road rash is going to do me
in. I haven't managed to die yet."

Sasha's brow furrowed. Her eyes flashed with feral silver as her temper flared. "Not for lack of trying, I'm sure."

On the western horizon, the sky brightened from shades
of light gray to peach. Ewan's jaw clenched as he put the
car into gear and stomped his foot down on the gas pedal.

"Nope." The more Sasha pushed, the more he wanted
to push back. "Probably not."

Things had been simpler when their relationship was
nothing more than hookups. If they were fucking, they
sure as hell weren't fighting. But now that they'd moved
past that, it opened up the door for all sorts of complicated
bullshit. Like fighting. And passive-aggression. Fan-fucking-
tastic.

Ewan sped in the direction toward Sasha's apartment
building. His teeth gnashed together. Tension tapped at his
chest like some sort of torture technique and grew more
unbearable with each mile. The sky transformed from light
peachy orange to vibrant pink and the steering wheel
creaked with his grip. They weren't going to make it.

"Sash—"

She slumped in her seat and Ewan's heart stuttered in
his chest before taking off to five hundred beats per minute. The car swerved as he let go of the wheel to try and
straighten her in the seat. As though her posture was somehow the deciding factor between life and death.

Jesus fucking Christ, Ewan. Get your shit together!

He'd always been cool under pressure. Calm and com-
posed. His thoughts focused and sharp. He could handle

any hostile situation with ease, but this . . . He forced himself to take a breath. The thought that something was seriously wrong with her caused his brain to freeze up and cease function. He couldn't form a coherent thought, couldn't focus on anything but the worry that overtook him with the force of a hurricane. These foreign emotions were unwelcome and equally uncomfortable. It made Ewan feel like a squatter in his own skin, a stranger to his own thoughts and experiences. He wanted it gone. All of it. And he worried that the damage that had already been done was irreversible.

"I'm okay." Her exhausted tone juxtaposed to her previous shouts. In the space of a few seconds, she'd gone from alert and feisty to quiet and lethargic. "The sunrise. Need to sleep."

He knew vampires slept during the day. That the hours of sunlight left them vulnerable. But he had no idea it would debilitate her in such a way. For all of Gregor's research, the knowledge he'd drilled into their heads over the centuries, there was so much about the vampires they didn't know. Gods, what fools they all were.

"Just hang tight." Helplessness wasn't a feeling Ewan was accustomed to, and he hated it. There was nothing he could do for her aside from getting her indoors and away from the sun. "We're almost home."

Sasha offered a lazy laugh. "Home." Her soft snort was almost a snore. "Is that what it is?"

He scowled at her bitter tone. "Fine. We're almost to your fuck pad." If she wanted uncaring and crass, he'd give it to her.

"Better." She slumped in her seat once again, and knocked her head against the window.

"Sasha?"

"Mmmm?"

She tried to respond, but all that came out was a jumbled

mess of syllables that made no sense. Ewan stomped his foot down on the gas pedal and the car protested. The engine clanked and the frame shook. He'd drive the damn thing into the ground if he had to. Five more blocks. And now, it was a race against the sun.

By the time they pulled up to Sasha's apartment building, the sun had crested the horizon. Ewan jumped out of the car and hustled to the passenger side door. He nearly pulled that one off its hinges as well before he ducked inside and gently cradled Sasha in his arms. She weighed nothing. Spun sugar in his hand. She betrayed the illusion of strength because Ewan knew that in reality she was fragile and delicate. The sun continued its ascent and he took a stumbling step as wisps of steam rose from Sasha's exposed skin.

Jesus fucking Christ! It was burning her!

Ewan got his ass into gear. Without any thought to his carelessness or who might see him, he crossed from the parking area to the entrance of the apartment complex in the space of a few seconds. His finger shook as he punched the code to unlock the main entrance into the keypad. A loud buzz signaled as the lock disengaged. He pushed open the heavy glass door and rather than waste more time waiting for the elevator, raced up the flights of stairs to Sasha's third-floor apartment.

Keys! Where the fuck were her keys?

"Sasha?" He gave her a not-so-gentle shake. "Where are your keys so I can get you inside?"

Her arms flopped toward her legs as though the slender limb weighed hundreds of pounds. "Pocket. Probably."

Good gods. *Probably?* Ewan rolled his eyes. He shouldered her weight with his left hand while he felt against her jeans pockets for an outline of the key. Of course it would be in the pocket closest to his body. The hardest one to get into with their positioning. His arm didn't want to bend the way he needed it to and his fingers were too large and clumsy to negotiate the denim that clung to her like a second skin. When he finally managed to work the key free of her pocket, he was out of his mind with frustration and damn near sweating. He shoved the key into the lock and carried her into the apartment, kicking the door closed behind him. Thank the gods the blinds were all shut. Still, it didn't completely black out the space. Ewan carried Sasha into the bedroom as though she were made of hollowed-out eggshells, and set her on the bed. He pulled the throw blanket from the foot of the mattress and crossed to the window, draping the heavy cover over the blinds. Darkness settled over the morning-bright space and for the first time since they'd been hijacked by the demons he allowed a breath of relief.

One window down. Six or seven more to go.

Sasha awoke to the sensation of her skin burning. She sucked in a sharp breath and sat upright as she brushed her palms over her arms in an attempt to extinguish the non-existent flames.

"Sasha, you're okay."

Strong arms gripped her shoulders and another wave of disoriented panic swept over her. She fought against the hold, desperate to break free. But his grip was iron and his arms carved from marble. She couldn't move him if she tried.

"Burning." Her thoughts were muddled, her mind slow with the dregs of sleep. She remembered the demons, their taunting violence, and her own frustration as she'd thrown herself into the path of one of those supernatural fireballs. "Hellfire."

Warmth soaked into her skin from the hands that held her still. Her breathing slowed and the quaking in her limbs subsided. A throbbing pain still plagued her right forearm, but no longer did she feel the lick of flames against her flesh. She shook out her hands, fingers, splayed and limp, and let the panic drain from her on a slowly exhaled breath.

"Are you always this disoriented when you wake at sundown?"

The rich timbre of Ewan's voice vibrated through her. The tether that bound them gave a gentle tug at Sasha's chest and she brought her palm up to rest over her heart. "Yes. I mean, no. I'm just weak. I haven't fed and . . ." Gods, she could barely string two words together to make a sentence. She needed to get it together. Her fangs throbbed in her gums and her throat burned with thirst. The last thing she needed was to let Ewan see her behaving like some stereotype of what her kind had been painted to represent. Creatures ruled by madness, lust, and thirst.

"Then take what you need." Ewan turned her in his grasp so Sasha was settled on his lap. He tilted his head to one side, elongating his throat.

"I could . . . I mean . . . Your wrist would be—"

"No." His demanding tone sent a delicious shiver down her spine. "You'll drink from my throat."

Okay. His tone let her know, plain and simple, that he expected her to do as he commanded. And whereas most of the time Sasha would've responded by doing opposite of what he wanted, she was too damned thirsty and too damned weak to fight back.

As though she had no choice, Sasha nuzzled his throat. The scent of his blood called to her, intensified her thirst a thousand-fold. Her secondary fangs elongated as she put her lips to his flesh. Her mouth opened wide as her tongue flicked out and Ewan shuddered against her. Despite her need for apathy, her self-coached detachment, she wanted him. The tether had returned her soul, but as payment it had made her weak and dependent. Gods, would there ever be a time that she didn't want him? She forced every torturous thought from her mind and bit down, allowing the sharp points of her fangs to break the skin.

His blood flowed over her tongue and Sasha allowed an indulgent moan. His taste had no equal and she wondered after so many times of doing this very thing, how in the hell she ever had the willpower to stop.

Ewan's hand came up to cradle the back of her head. He held her tight against him as though worried she'd pull away. They were like a couple of junkies. Each one dependent on the other for something and knowing the only cure for their addiction was to go cold turkey. And yet, neither of them possessed the strength necessary to do that. The first time she'd pierced his vein, Ewan had been repulsed, disgusted by the act. And now, he craved it as much as she did. His hold on her, his demand that she drink from his throat was proof enough. The tether that bound them tightened. Saeed mourned for Sasha and perhaps he had reason to.

Sated, Sasha tried to pull away. Ewan refused to let her. The blunt pads of his fingers pressed against the back of her skull. "No." The word was nothing more than a guttural sound. "Don't stop. More."

She'd been on the receiving end of a vampire bite enough times to know it was a euphoric experience for both parties involved. But the euphoria usually faded. Everyone came down from the high eventually. Was it that Ewan hadn't come down yet? Or was he greedy to hold on to the sensation?

Sasha's tongue flicked out at the punctures, though it was hardly necessary. Vampires possessed a venom in their fangs that kept the wounds open in quick-healing supernatural creatures and their saliva was the only thing that could close the punctures. Not so with Ewan. Berserkers were beyond supernatural. The tiny openings she'd made would close on their own, but that didn't stop Sasha from laying the flat of her tongue against his flesh just the same.

"It will weaken you if I take any more," she murmured against his throat.

"No, it won't." His masculine confidence coaxed a smile to Sasha's lips. "I'm strong enough."

She didn't doubt his strength for a second. It was her own that she worried about. It was Sasha who had to break the contact before she let herself go too far. Before she lost herself to him.

"Even the big bad berserker warlord only has so much blood in his body. I've taken enough. How about you replenish those stores for the next time I get hit with hell-fire?"

"It won't happen again." He spoke with such arrogance. So sure of himself. "Because I won't let it."

Yup. So damned overconfident. "Going to take on the world, huh?"

"If I have to."

This was why Sasha couldn't allow herself to get close. Because beneath his crass, rough exterior, behind his tough words, brutal fighting prowess, and cruel countenance, Sasha knew there was an honorable male. Someone she could admire and perhaps even . . . love.

Sasha couldn't afford to give her heart to Ewan or any-one else. It was already so damaged, the slightest mishandling would destroy it completely. Ewan could crush it with little effort. At one time, Sasha had given Saeed the power to crush her and she refused to give it to anyone else. Even her own mate.

She breathed deeply of his alluring musky scent and held it in her lungs before pulling away. His grip on the back of her head loosened and he reluctantly allowed her to sit upright as she brought her forearm up for his inspection. "See? All better."

Ewan's gaze burned with that same intensity that both frightened and attracted her. No longer dark with rage, his irises were light golden brown. Beautiful and fathomless. Dusk gave way to night, the windows are covered that made the bedroom seem unfamiliar. Sasha never slept here. It was simply a place where she could meet Ewan in private. Well, she guessed her privacy was shot to shit now that Saeed and the entirety of her coven knew her little secret.

He cradled her arm in his grip and put his mouth to the spot where the burn had been. The kiss was gentle, his lips soft and pliant. Her stomach curled into a tight knot as a delicious rush of pleasure cycled through her. He affected her with even the slightest touch. It was hard to remain detached and stoic when he could take command of her body with the simplest of acts.

"Sasha." He said her name like it was a prayer. A holy word only to be uttered in a holy place. Her throat tightened as she willed the tender emotions that threatened to overtake her to the soles of her feet. He kissed his way up her arm, pausing only long enough to strip her shirt up the length of her body and over her head. Kissed the dip at the opposite side of her elbow. Her upper arm. Her shoulder. He kissed along her collarbone to the hollow of her throat.

Feeding and sex often went hand in hand. It was a necessary act but also a sensual one. Foreplay. And the gods help her, Sasha didn't want him to stop.

His tongue lashed out at her throat and Sasha sucked in a breath. Hot, wet, it swirled against her skin for a languorous moment before he grazed her flesh with his teeth. A shiver of anticipation danced over her skin. "Again," she said on a breath. "Harder."

Ewan's muscles tensed beneath her. The heat of his tongue met her skin as though in preparation for the sharp sting of his bite. A rush of heat spread between Sasha's thighs and she gripped Ewan's shirt in her fists as she held him close.

She may not have wanted to lose herself to Ewan, but she was starting to realize that she might not have a choice.

CHAPTER
21

Ewan was starved for Sasha. For her body, her soft skin, the taste of her, the tight wet heat that held him so perfectly. His want of her went beyond the need for temporary satisfaction and that scared the shit out of him. She'd been dead to the world for the past ten or so hours. He could have driven a stake through her heart. Ended her existence as he had countless other vampires in the course of his life. He could have made Gregor proud and given up the location of a vampire coven for their clan to ravage. He could have betrayed her. But he didn't.

Instead, he'd watched over her. Protected her while she was weak.

He was at odds with himself. Had been since the moment he'd laid eyes on her dark, savage beauty. He didn't know who he was anymore. His future, his very existence was uncertain and it scared the shit out of him. And it was that fear that drove him to find solace in Sasha's arms. He wanted to forget the things that plagued him—for a little while at least. Outside of these walls, the world faded away. Inside this room with her, an alternate reality existed.

Her scent drove him wild. The urgent longing in her sultry voice hardened his cock to stone. He bit down, harder like she wanted, and she let out a quiet moan. "Do you like that, Sasha?" He couldn't help but ask for confirmation. His ego demanded it.

"Gods, yes." The words left her lips in a breathy rush. "I love it."

"Does it make you wet?" He bit her again, harder.

She sucked in a sharp breath. "Yes."

His chest puffed with smug pride. He wanted her as mindless with passion as he was. As desperate for escape, for pleasure, for abandon. The hours she'd slept had crept by like days. Ewan couldn't believe it was impossible to miss someone who was in the same room, but he'd counted the minutes until sundown when she'd wake.

"Get naked."

Too many clothes separated them. He wanted bare skin and he wanted it *now*.

Sasha scooted off his lap and climbed off the bed. Gods, her beauty stole his breath. Her dark hair was tousled from sleep and a blush of passion painted her cheeks. Silver rimmed her irises, lending a wildness to her otherwise serene countenance. She reached around her back and slowly unhooked her bra. Her gaze held his as she dragged the straps down her arms. Slowly. She brought her arms in front of her and it pressed the enticing swell of her breasts over the cups for a torturous moment before she discarded the garment to the floor. Ewan's gaze was drawn to the soft, pale roundness of her breasts and the delicate pink pearls of her nipples. She toed off her socks and her pants went next. Clad in nothing but a pair of lacy white underwear, she paused as she fiddled with the waistband.

A sweet, guileless smile curved her dark pink lips. "These, too?"

He'd never seen this playful, teasing side of her. Ewan

himself had never been a lighthearted male and he found he didn't quite know how to react. His world was made of hard edges and cold, focused, strategic thought. Strength and force. He didn't know softness. Playfulness. Only since he'd met Sasha had he experienced the sensation of tension melting from his body. She fiddled with the lacy waistband, urging the fabric over her hip, giving him a teasing glimpse of the junction where her hip met her thigh. She eased the fabric back into place and waited, her expectant gaze holding his.

Ewan swallowed against the lump in his throat. "Those, too. Now."

Sasha's expression heated and her lips parted on a breath. She reached for her underwear and stripped the garment from her thighs and stepped out of the legs. Ewan's stomach clenched as she drew her bottom lip between her teeth. One sharp fang nicked the skin and she licked the blood away. Gods, he'd never known something so simple could be so erotic. "I have a lot less clothes on than you do now."

"True." And he was going to take care of that right fucking now.

"Think you might want to join me in the no-clothes movement?"

Again, she teased him and Ewan had no idea how to react. There wasn't a playful bone in his body. He climbed off the bed to the opposite side and quickly stripped. For a quiet moment, they stared at one another, the bed separating them. Ewan was a fighter. A soldier. His world was about giving and following orders. Though he had to admit he'd never been much of a willing follower, as evidenced by his recent rebellious streak. He was more comfortable leading. He wanted to command. And he expected to be obeyed.

"Get on the bed."

Sasha's gaze smoldered. A corner of her mouth curved upward and without a word, she did as he asked, laying herself out on the mattress. Ewan's cock throbbed as the memory of Sasha bound and tied to the bed at the sex club invaded his thoughts. Gods, she'd driven him wild that night. And how he'd loved her submissiveness. She understood his need to be in charge and didn't fight it.

She raised her arms above her and gripped the slats on the headboard as if she'd read this thoughts and wanted to return to that night as well. She shifted, her thighs rubbing together and Ewan's attention wandered to the slick, glistening flesh of her pussy.

"Spread your legs."

Her knees fell open.

"Wider."

Again, she complied without a word of protest.

Ewan moved to the foot of the bed. The image of Sasha stretched out on the bed, his to do with what he wanted, burned itself into his memory. He climbed up onto the mattress and slid his hands beneath Sasha's ass, cupping the round curves in his palms before pushing her upward toward his waiting mouth.

Her hips bucked and she cried out as his tongue slid against her sex. Soft, easy passes not meant to do anything other than stoke the fires of her passion. Ewan wanted a slow build. He wanted her writhing and begging. Mindless with need. He wanted to brand her with the pleasure he gave her so she would know without a doubt no other male would be able to give her what he did.

According to Sasha, her soul was already bound to his. But Ewan wanted *more*.

He continued his unhurried assault, careful to keep his pace slow and even. The pressure of his mouth against her was just enough to guide her to the edge but not enough to push her over. Her panting breaths and tight moans spurred him on. The slats of the headboard creaked as she gripped them tighter. The muscles of her thighs twitched against his cheeks as he dipped his tongue inside of her to fully taste the honey sweetness.

He couldn't get enough of her. She was incomparable. He knew that a relationship between them would be impossible. Too many obstacles stood in their way. But he also knew that he would set the world on fire before he'd ever let her go.

The sound of her heartbeat echoed in his ears, soft whooshing pulses that somehow calmed the inborn rage that always simmered beneath the surface of his skin. He'd never known the sort of peace that being with Sasha provided. She was shelter from a storm. Warmth on a cold night. Water to quench his thirst and sustenance to satisfy his hunger. His tongue swirled over her clit and she let out a whimper. He sealed his mouth over that same spot to suck gently and her whimper transformed to a decadent moan. He spread her wide with his fingertips to graze the tight bead with his teeth and a violent shudder wracked her body. She balanced on the razor's edge and he could give her what she needed with nothing more than a little push.

He wanted it. Wanted his senses to be awash with her pleasure. Wanted her to come against his mouth, to bathe his tongue in her sweetness. It didn't matter whether or not she could wait any longer. Ewan couldn't.

He laid the flat of his tongue to her clit and reached up with his right hand to cup the roundness of one breast. His fingers plucked at the pearled nipple at the exact moment he swirled his tongue over her pussy. Sasha's body tensed as she drew in a sharp breath that she released as several shuddering sobs of pleasure.

Her pussy pulsed against his tongue and Ewan drew out her pleasure until she could take no more. He kissed her swollen lips, drew them into his mouth, ran his tongue along the insides of her thighs, up and around one hip to her stomach, along her torso to one breast. Up and over the swell to her nipple that he took into his mouth and gently sucked. Then to her chest, collarbone, jawline, the corner of her mouth, and finally her lips that he seized with a greedy hunger that she answered with equal enthusiasm.

"I need you inside of me, Ewan." The words left her lips between pants of breath. "Now. Please. I can't wait."

She squirmed beneath his weight. Her hips rolled up to meet his. He understood that desperation all too well. It burned within him like hellfire. Inextinguishable and unnaturally hot. He settled himself between her thighs and drove home, bathing his cock in her wet heat. A shiver of pleasure danced over his skin and Ewan let out a groan as he adjusted to the tight hold on his shaft.

He could never, *ever*, let her go. And his selfish want of her was bound to destroy them both.

Just when Sasha didn't think the sex could get better between them, Ewan went out of his way to prove her wrong. How could each night spent in his arms be more intense, more pleasurable, more . . . *everything*? He constantly surprised her. Never acted in the way she anticipated. That unpredictability sent a rush of excitement through her veins. Kept her on her toes. She got off on that spontaneity.

There wasn't a male on the face of the earth who could compare to Ewan.

She might have wanted to keep a stoic emotional distance from him, but that didn't mean they couldn't have a purely physical relationship, right?

She'd be sure to file that under Lies I Tell Myself. She'd deal with her emotional baggage later. Right now, all she wanted was to feel. To enjoy this moment with Ewan. And to share in the pleasure that only seemed to increase in intensity every time their bodies came together.

Sasha loved the weight of Ewan's body on hers. He braced the bulk of it on an elbow and slid his free hand under her ass as he thrust home. Her back arched off the mattress and her blood quickened at the deep groan that rumbled in his chest. He filled her completely. Beyond a simple physical satiation. She felt full on a soul-deep level, the tether that connected them making its presence known. No matter what Sasha did or didn't want to happen between them, there would always be that spiritual connection. It couldn't be severed. Ever.

"Harder, Ewan." She needed him to make her forget the things that plagued her mind. "Deeper." It seemed those two words were always on her lips when their bodies joined. She couldn't get enough of him. Always needed just a little bit more than either one of them was capable of giving. He pulled out and thrust again, doing as she asked, and Sasha's head rolled back on the pillow as she let out a contented moan. *Yes.* This was what she needed. To be fucked without mercy until she was too gods-damned exhausted to think about anything other than how good she felt.

"Tell me you want me, Sasha." The deep rumble of Ewan's voice coaxed chills to the surface of her skin. He pulled out and thrust home again. "Tell me you need me."

She wanted to say the words. But saying them out loud would only turn the emotions she repressed into something tangible and real. "I do." It was as much of an admission as she could force herself to make. Her hips rolled up to meet his as her back arched off the mattress. Not long ago, all she'd wanted was for Ewan to open up to her. Now, all she wanted was for things to go back to the way they'd been. Cold. Emotionless. Purely physical.

"Look at me."

She'd closed her eyes without even realizing it. Ewan's demand that she look at him heated her blood as much as it scared her. She feared the intimacy she'd once welcomed. Shied from his intensity. How could she admit to him that she wanted and needed him when doing so made her utterly powerless? Admitting it gave him ammunition against her. It transferred power.

Ewan must have sensed the shift in her focus. His pace slowed and the thrust of his hips became shallow and easy. "Sasha. Stop."

His tone carried with it the barest hint of anger. Her eyes came slowly open to find his expression dark and serious. This was the male who had tethered her soul that night in the warehouse. The male who'd ordered her into the bathroom, bent her over, and taken her simply because he wanted to. Because he could. Because she'd wanted him to. Without apology or reason.

"Come back to the moment." Even now, he sought to ground her when all she wanted was to overanalyze her own thoughts and feelings to death. "Don't think. Just feel."

That was the problem though, wasn't it? She felt too much. His demands on her pushed her to a place where her brain fought with her heart. "Distract me from my thoughts." A temporary fix, true, but she'd take what she could get. "Until the only word I know, the only one I can speak, is your name."

His gaze heated as he claimed her mouth in a ravenous kiss. The raw hunger, the base need, sparked Sasha's own instinctual desire for completion. His tongue thrust past her lips to deepen the kiss at the exact moment he drove forward with his hips. This was what she needed from him. Heat. Passion. Urgency. With no words to disrupt or distract them. The thoughts that plagued her left her mind as though blown clear by a breeze. Ewan kissed her like he fucked her, with complete abandon.

Sasha gripped his shoulders. Her nails dug into his flesh and he let out an approving growl. His pace increased as did the force of his thrusts, which jarred Sasha with the impact and left her breathless and desperate for release.

Her legs fell open, wider. Ewan adjusted, breaking their kiss as he hooked his arms under her knees to bring her legs up to either side of him. "Gods." His voice was a primal growl that vibrated over her skin. "You feel so good, Sasha. Come for me. I want to feel it."

Sasha's muscles grew tight. Her body seemed so small and insignificant in comparison to what she felt. Her throat burned with thirst and the urge to sink her fangs deep into Ewan's flesh overwhelmed her. She arched up and buried her face against his throat. Her fangs broke the skin and his rich, sweet blood flowed over her tongue. The orgasm exploded through her and Sasha pulled away with a start. "Ewan!" His name burst from her lips, exactly as she'd wanted it, as wave after wave of intense sensation crashed over her. "Don't stop!" There seemed to be no end to the pleasure as it only built with each one of his hard, unforgiving thrusts.

"Bite me again." His tone carried all of the urgency that Sasha felt and more. "Do it now."

She complied without argument and bit down at the junction of where his neck met his shoulder. He let out a low growl as his body went tense. His thrusts became wild, his cock swelled against her sensitive flesh, and Sasha was filled with delicious warmth. They rode out their pleasure as one, breaths mingling, bodies moving in tandem. Wild and intense, and then slower as the storm that swept them up began to ebb. Sasha closed the punctures in Ewan's skin and ran the flat of her tongue along his neck to capture every last drop of blood she'd spilled. He let out a slow sigh as he settled against her, remaining deeply rooted inside of her.

"You are mine, Sasha." His hot breath in her ear caused her to shudder. "Understand that I will not share you. I won't hesitate to kill anyone who tries to take you from me."

He'd never spoken such words to her before and never with such grim finality. He wanted her to understand, but she didn't. She didn't understand any of this, let alone her own opinions on the matter.

"Anyone?" The word was barely a whisper. Sasha could forget a lot of things, but who and what Ewan was wasn't one of them. "Even Ian Gregor?"

His muscles tensed and a space of silence passed. If Gregor knew about Ewan's relationship with Sasha, the berserker warlord would demand he turn her over to him. Either that, or he'd command Ewan to kill her himself.

"Anyone." The word was heavy with anger and grated in his throat. Were his proclamations simply an attempt to claim ownership? Or something more?

"I understand." She hoped he couldn't smell the lie in her words. She'd never been more confused, her emotions so torn.

"Say it."

She knew what he wanted, but gods, the words were harder to utter than she thought they would be. Not because of her own fierce need for independence, but because it forced her to admit what she already knew. She'd belonged to Ewan since the moment he'd tethered her soul.

"I'm yours," she said through the thickness in her throat. The truth of it nearly choked her. "No one else's."

For the first time in a long time, Sasha was truly afraid. Not of Ewan, though, or even of Ian Gregor. No, the future was what frightened Sasha the most. Its uncertainty and her place in it. If she stayed with Ewan, allowed herself to truly become his, what would that make her? A traitor? Betrayer? With every passing day, she lost a little more of herself. How long would it be before she became completely unrecognizable, even to herself?

CHAPTER
22

Ewan made no apology for his brash, cruel mandate. He knew how it made him sound. Selfish. Possessive. Cold and abrasive. He'd never pretended to be anything else. He meant what he'd said. He wouldn't allow any creature to take Sasha from him, including Ian Gregor. He'd play by the rules, give Gregor whatever fucking information it was that he wanted, and hold up his end of the bargain in order to protect Drew. But Sasha was nonnegotiable. Ewan didn't care if Gregor killed every last vampire on the face of the earth. But the second he set his sights on Sasha, Ewan wouldn't hesitate to destroy him.

He rolled away from her and a chill settled over his skin at the absence of her heat. He wanted to soften the blow of his words somehow, but he had no idea how, or where to start. He listened to the sound of Sasha's breaths as they began to slow and become more even. The quiet settled over him like a heavy mantle. His own thoughts were too loud in his head and made him anxious.

"Tell me something." Sasha's voice was small and unsure, and it made his stomach clench. "I don't care what it is. Just something real."

Ewan gathered her in his arms and pulled her close to his body. There wasn't much that he could tell her that wouldn't inadvertently bring her pain. So much of their history was shared, and so much of it embroiled in violence but he couldn't expect her to give herself to him in the way he wanted and not offer anything in return. He was an asshole, but not completely unreasonable. She didn't care what he told her as long as it was the truth.

"At one time, there were seven separate berserker clans. Seven kings reigned over us and met each year for a High Council. Grievances were aired and settled, contests were held as well as festivities. Requests for marriages were heard and ceremonies performed."

"Berserkers don't recognize mate bonds." The sad realization in Sasha's tone lodged in a tight ball in Ewan's chest. "I'd hoped . . . I mean, I thought that maybe . . ." The words trailed off into disappointed silence.

Gods, why was it so hard to articulate his nature to her? It would be impossible for anyone other than another berserker to understand, and maybe that was part of the problem. Their differences were so many.

"How did you recognize the tether, Sasha?"

She let out a slow breath. "It's hard to explain. Being turned, it's . . . traumatic. Painful. The transition is jarring and when it's done, you're filled with this sense of emptiness that's overwhelming. There is no solace. The Collective offers ghosts of emotion that torture more than they comfort. Everything you once felt becomes diluted. After a while, you get used to the apathy. But then, the tether crashes over you like a wave. I felt close to bursting, so full it nearly brought me to tears. The emptiness was gone. The apathy disappeared. I saw you, and I *knew*. The scent of your blood called to me, and I *knew*. The first time I fed from you, it filled me with power, and I *knew*. The certainty is inborn."

"Exactly. We don't have a tether, and we may recognize our bonds through ceremony instead of feeding, but it's not much different. I will admit that it's not immediate. Our bonds grow through shared experience and instinct. Our instincts are ingrained in our DNA. What you call a mate bond speaks to us on a subconscious level. There's . . . an awareness that wasn't there before."

A space of silence passed. Ewan sensed Sasha wanted to ask him something but feared the answer. She took a deep breath. Held it. And let it out in a rush. "How did you find me last night? I know it wasn't by scent."

Not what she'd wanted to ask. Her own scent soured and Ewan wrinkled his nose. Perhaps she'd opted for a question that wouldn't invite a disappointing answer.

"No. It wasn't by scent. The more time I spend with you, the more connected we become. Like your tether, it's hard to explain. Your essence—the very thing that makes you who you are—has attached itself to my DNA. And in turn has changed *my* essence—the very thing that makes me who I am—to become instinct. Does that make any sense?"

Sasha shifted and laid her hand on Ewan's chest directly over his heart. The warmth of her palm radiated over his skin and he marveled at the difference in her body temperature after taking his vein. "So basically, you're saying you don't know how you found me. That blind instinct led you and you followed."

It was the simplest explanation. "Aye. Because you had been to your coven many times, traveled the route over and over. Because it was your routine, it was now mine as well."

Again, her scent soured with worry. "Wow. Not gonna lie, that's pretty trippy."

Ewan let out a chuff of laughter. "That's one way to put it."

"And it's scary as hell."

He sensed her fear and wished there was something he could do to assuage it. Lessening the blow wouldn't change the facts, however. Like her tether, this melding of their life forces was inevitable. He could no more change it than he could change the shifting of the tides.

"What's the Collective?" He didn't want her to dwell on her fear. Besides, she owed him. He'd shared something about his nature and it was time for her to reciprocate. Perhaps he could find something in what she told him to offer Gregor. Some small inconsequential piece of information that would keep him placated and far away from Sasha.

"It's our memory. All vampires are connected by blood. A single bloodline created us, and it flows through all of our veins. Contained in that blood are the memories of every vampire that ever existed. Upon our transition, we inherit those memories."

Gods. Ewan couldn't even imagine what it would be like to suddenly have his brain stuffed full of the memories of every berserker. How was there room for her own thoughts and memories? How did she separate her own experiences from those that didn't belong to her?

"They're with you all the time?"

He felt her nod against him. "The memories are overwhelming at first. Hard to ignore. They call to you, like ghosts seeking company. It's one of the most difficult things to overcome post-transition. And if we don't learn to resist the pull of the Collective, we risk falling victim to madness."

Ewan let out a slow breath. It sounded horrible. "Was it hard for you?" A ripple of worry vibrated through him. Did she struggle with the Collective? Did it weigh heavily on her mind?

Sasha answered with a bark of sarcastic laughter. "Not

at all. It was unusually easy for me to resist the Collective's pull. I think that's why Saeed chose me. He knew my mind and knew I could withstand it."

"He turned you against your will?" Anger toward the male who had hurt Sasha so deeply surged fresh and hot in Ewan's chest.

"No." Sasha was quick to answer. "He would never do that. He might've strongly urged me," she added. "But ultimately, the choice was mine."

"Did it worry you?" Ewan knew he was pushing his luck by asking so many questions when he was supposed to be the one giving all the answers. But he found himself greedy for every bit of information he could gather from her. She fascinated him.

"I worried more over the loss of my soul than I did the Collective."

"Why?"

Sasha traced a lazy pattern on Ewan's chest with her fingertips. The sensation of her gentle touch rekindled the dying embers of his lust and caused his cock to stir between his legs.

"I worried that I would never be tethered. But I agreed to be turned in the hopes that—"

She abruptly cut herself off and a finger of dread stroked down Ewan's spine. "What? Tell me, Sasha."

Her fingers paused in their lazy pattern and she turned her head away from him. "I hoped that Saeed would tether me."

Jealousy choked the air from Ewan's lungs. "You are in love with him?" He'd known she held some measure of affection for the vampire but knowing she loved him made Ewan want to run a stake through the bastard's heart.

He sat upright on the bed. His heart raced in his chest and raw, untamed rage swelled within him. With it came a rush of power that caused his limbs to quake. Sasha was *his*. Anyone who tried to take her from him would meet their end.

"Ewan?" Sasha's tentative voice didn't push past the haze of jealous rage that clouded his mind.

"Answer me." The tiny, insignificant bit of reason that clung to his mind tried to tell him to back off but he wasn't listening. "Do you love the vampire? Am I perhaps meant to make him jealous? I don't like games, Sasha. And I won't play them. Tell me the truth before I return to that coven and beat the answer out of Saeed instead."

His words and actions would do nothing but push her away. And the gods help him, Ewan couldn't do anything to stop himself.

Sasha's heart jumped up into her throat as she sat up beside Ewan. His moods turned on a dime, without warning or reason. She'd been honest with him, not realizing her words might hurt him. But how could they? How could anything hurt such a strong, stoic, unfeeling male?

She'd given him honesty. And she would continue to do so. "I loved him. Once. I bared my soul to him and he rejected me. He turned me for his own selfish reasons and left me to mind his flock while he went in search of his true mate."

She brought up her hand to rest on Ewan's back. He flinched at the contact but she didn't shy away. His breaths were heavy, pulsing in and out of his lungs and through his nostrils as though he fought to control his rising temper. He could be truly terrifying when he wanted to be and though some part of Sasha knew he would die before ever hurting her, it was Saeed she feared for in this moment. Ewan could easily turn the location of their coven over to Gregor. An ambush would be devastating.

His muscles tensed beneath her palm. He was unyielding marble, chiseled and smoothed to perfection. "When he returned with Cerys, I knew that everything he'd told me was true. I wasn't his and he wasn't mine. Our souls were never meant for one another. I'd been devoted to him for so long. Doted upon him. Worshipped him. Respected him. I'd done everything he'd ever asked of me without question or complaint. I gave up my life for him. I became a vampire for him. Centuries wasted. A lifetime forfeit. I needed to reclaim myself and heal my heart. And so, I went out looking for life. And that's when I found you."

Ewan turned toward her. His brow furrowed as his gaze searched her face. He had to know the truth of her words. And whereas she admitted her love for Saeed, she could not in turn, admit her affection for Ewan. She'd fallen victim to the weakness of love and she wouldn't let it happen again.

"What is your purpose within his coven?" He steered the conversation away from emotions and Sasha wasn't sure if she was disappointed or relieved. "What made you valuable to him?"

"I was head of security up until the time he turned me." Her voice fell. "After that, I became more of a diplomat."

Ewan studied her. "You were a warrior?"

Of course that's the conclusion he'd come to. "Not really. At least, not in the way you might think. My father was a warrior and a strategist. He had no sons. He taught me how to fight and that my mind could be as effective a weapon as a sword. Saeed served under my father during the wars. He was a famed assassin and deadlier than any dhampir I'd ever met. I studied hard, trained even harder, in order to impress him. I saved his life." She looked away as a pang of regret shot through her chest. "Only the two of us know that." She turned back to look at Ewan. "Three of us now."

"How?"

Ewan's focus was unwavering and Sasha squirmed

under the scrutiny. Opening up to him felt like a betrayal of everything she was and had been. She never should have mentioned saving Saeed's life.

Sasha tucked her legs up against her body and hugged her arms around her legs. The darkness that surrounded her made telling the story a little easier. Comforting somehow. "We were losing momentum." She refused to look at Ewan, to see the dark emptiness of his eyes, a reflection of the horror the vampire and dhampir races had endured. "The berserkers weren't limited to fighting only at night and it was up to the dhampir forces to hold them back in the daylight hours. We weren't as strong. Or fast. We healed too slowly and drinking blood only did so much."

Reliving these memories merely served to remind Sasha that Ewan was the enemy. He'd admitted without an ounce of guilt to Saeed the night before that he'd killed countless vampires during the Sortiari's attempt to wipe the vampires from the face of the earth. It made being here with him even stranger and the tether that bound them seem even more impossible. Gods. They were mortal enemies. Sworn to kill one another.

Ewan didn't speak. Sasha was still too afraid to look at him, to try and gauge his mood or thoughts by the expression on his face. His scent was clean, masculine, without even a hint of anxiety or anger. Did that mean it didn't bother him to hear talk of the wars from her perspective? Or that perhaps he had no remorse over the part he'd played in it?

"Before sunrise, my father told me not to leave the stronghold. He didn't want me on the battlefield. There was no one to protect me and we were weak. I promised him I wouldn't go but . . ."

"Saeed left to fight." Ewan finished the thought for her and the dark undertone of his words sent a shiver over Sasha's skin. "And you were concerned for his safety."

Her chest ached with the admission. "Yes. I found him not far from the stronghold. Berserker forces were advancing and gaining ground. My father—all of the other vampires inside the keep—were put down by the sun and vulnerable. Saeed refused to let anyone die. He was the most honorable male I'd ever known. Brave. Caring. His sense of duty astounded me. If we lost him, I was sure we'd lose everyone. I couldn't leave him unprotected."

"He must be quite a male to have someone so fiercely loyal at his back." Ewan's tone left a tannic taste in her mouth. "We should all be so lucky."

Sasha wasn't going to sugarcoat any of this for him. He'd asked about her feelings for Saeed and he was going to get an honest answer. If he didn't like what he heard, then that was just too damned bad.

"They should have retreated," she continued. "But Saeed has always been stubborn and pressed on. He was surrounded by three warlords and losing momentum in the fight. They would have killed him if I hadn't intervened. It was easy. They were focused on killing him. He was the biggest threat on the field. If they took him out, the stronghold would fall before sundown. I beheaded the first with my sword before he even realized I was behind him. The second was prepared for me and his strength overpowered me. But together Saeed and I managed to kill the two that remained. After that, we retreated and waited behind the safety of the wall until nightfall."

"What city was this?" Ewan's voice tightened with his words.

"Kiev." It was the last vampire city in what was then Russia to fall before the coven retreated into Europe.

He let out a caustic bark of laughter. "I was on that battlefield."

Sasha let out a breath. *Gods.*

Fate truly was an astounding force. Had Ewan been one

of the warlords to attack Saeed, she might have killed him
and her soul wouldn't be tethered now. Of course, she'd
seen Ewan fight. The more likely outcome would have
been her death. And probably Saeed's as well. Fate had
seen fit to spare them all that day and Sasha marveled at
its foresight. The Sortiari were fools to think they could
bridle and steer something so out of their control. So
misguided in their efforts to set things right.

"Do you love him still?" Ewan's voice quieted to a dangerous simmer that was far more menacing than a shout.

Sasha waited a beat too long to reply. "No."

"Are you sure about that?"

His doubtful tone convinced her to turn to face him.
Ewan's grim countenance sent a shiver of dread down
Sasha's spine. He was as deadly a creature as she'd ever laid
eyes on. Why did it matter what she did or didn't feel for
Saeed? Ewan had made no promises to her. No proclamations of love. He considered her property and nothing
more. A toy he wasn't willing to share.

He pushed himself up from the bed and began to dress.
Sasha's heartbeat picked up its rhythm in her chest and she
took several breaths to try and calm the hell down. She
couldn't keep up with his sudden mood swings. At one second passionate, and the next agitated. Calm and almost
gentle and then stoic and brutal. She could do nothing but
sit there in stunned silence and watch him throw on his
clothes. She knew better than to try and understand his
mood, his reason for leaving, or anything else. Gods, why
did she even bother with him? Each day spent together became more difficult to handle. She was so over the drama.

"Remember what I said, Sasha." Ewan tied the strings
of his boots and headed toward the door. "You are *mine*.
And anyone who thinks to challenge that will die by my
hand."

Like she'd seen him do one too many times already,

Ewan strode from the bedroom with an angry, purposeful stride. Sasha listened as the apartment door opened and she flinched as it slammed shut.

Tears pricked at her eyes but she willed those traitorous bastards to dry. She wouldn't shed a single tear over Ewan Brún or any other male ever again.

She was worth more than her tears.

CHAPTER
23

It might have seemed that Christian had "found" Siobhan, but the fact of the matter was, she let him find her. He had no idea where her coven was located and she always seemed to magically pop up in certain downtown clubs when he happened to be there. The one time she'd summoned him, that bastard Carrig had found him in a private, high-stakes poker game. Not exactly out in the public eye. If he didn't know any better, he'd think she'd found him first and had been keeping an eye on him for a long damned time. He was sick and tired of having to visit every club in the city when he needed to see her. And at the same time, he admired her ability to keep herself—and her coven—protected.

He wanted to talk to her before he went to McAlister with the bits and pieces of information he'd managed to collect. He couldn't explain it, but before he moved forward, he needed her counsel. And in the process, he hoped to arm her with a little information.

He tilted his head up at the black neon sign of Onyx. It

was his last stop of the night. If she wasn't here, he had no idea where else to look.

"See something interesting up there, werewolf?"

Christian pursed his lips. The soft, sensual purr of her voice sent a lick of heat down his spine. At the same time, his wolf gave a disapproving growl in the recess of his psyche. He was supposed to be the predator, and always with Siobhan he felt more like prey.

His wolf was not amused.

"Where'd you come from?" Annoyance bled into his tone.

She stepped up beside him, shoulder to shoulder. Well, shoulder to upper arm. She was a good eight inches shorter than he was but her personality and sheer bravery made up for what she lacked in height. Christian took a deep breath of jasmine and held it in his lungs. The lights of the surrounding businesses reflected off the nearly blue-black locks of her hair. He focused his gaze straight ahead once more as he resisted the urge to get a good, long eyeful.

"Does it matter where I came from?" Her voice was like a caress. "I'm here now."

Yes she was. Christian's wolf stirred once again, its agitation slowly transforming to possessive lust. The stubborn animal believed Siobhan belonged to them. Christian believed the animal was an idiot.

"You know, Siobhan, you have a habit of showing up at just the right moment."

She glanced at him from the corner of her eye. "Is that a bad thing?"

Christian returned her glance. "I'm not sure yet."

One corner of her mouth hitched in a sensual half smile. "So . . . are we going in or do you want to take this little tête-à-tête somewhere else?"

Christian swallowed down a groan. His mind raced with the many options presented by the implication of her words. He wanted to be alone with her, but if that were to happen, they sure as hell wouldn't be talking. Christian glanced over his shoulder at the tiny dive bar across the street. There couldn't be more than ten or fifteen people inside. It seemed like a good compromise.

He jerked his chin as he turned. "Let's go over there."

Siobhan's eyebrow cocked. "Over there?"

He grinned. "What's the matter? Too low-rent for you?"

Her ruby-red lips pursed and Christian's eyes were drawn to the lush display. "Not at all." She turned and fell into step beside him. "Should be fun."

They waited for a break in traffic and crossed the street toward the bar. The sign read *Ray's,* and it looked like the sort of place that catered to day-drinkers. Christian had found himself in places just like Ray's more times than he could count. It was the perfect place to not feel so gods-damned bad about himself. Misery loved company after all. Christian didn't have to feel guilty about not trying to be a better male if he hung out in places steeped in failure and despair.

So basically, he'd be right at home.

"Where's your bodyguard?"

Siobhan smiled. "Carrig? He's close."

Of course he was. Bastard. "You always have a backup plan, don't you?"

"Of course I do." Christian opened the door for Siobhan and she flashed a dazzling smile as she walked past him. "Don't you?"

He tried to. But he was beginning to believe that no one planned better than Siobhan. "Sometimes. I'm not hiding from anyone like you are, though."

Siobhan bristled. She strode past the bar and found a secluded booth at the back of the building. Christian stayed a few steps behind her, too mesmerized by the sway of her hips to do anything other than stare. She slid into the booth, giving Christian plenty of room to join her.

"Maybe not, but you're still looking over your shoulder."

Wasn't that the fucking truth? When you played both sides against the middle with the sort of heavy-hitters Christian was mixed up with, he had no choice but to look over his shoulder. Siobhan had never outright admitted she was the dhampir Gregor was looking for, but the more comfortable she became with Christian, the more she gave away. The tiniest of tells that left a trail of breadcrumbs for him to follow.

He needed her to trust him. To open up to him. But she was a wary, cornered animal. She wouldn't roll over and show her belly. If she felt even a little threatened, she'd fight. Christian had no idea how to deal with her. She was an enigma.

"Gregor's up to something." Siobhan might have liked to play games, but Christian didn't. He cut to the chase rather than engage in their usual banter.

"Can I get you two a drink?"

Christian turned his attention to the cocktail waitress. This place had speedier service than some of the dives he was used to. He was running low on cash after losing a few thousand on a Barcelona match last week. That'd teach him to ever bet against Messi again. Besides, it's not like he'd find any top-shelf shit here. He'd just have to suck it up and drink shitty liquor.

"Bourbon, neat."

The cocktail waitress turned to Siobhan. "And for you?"

She leveled her gaze, expression bored. "Same."

Gods, she was an intimidating female. It totally turned him on. Siobhan's lack of congeniality sent the waitress back to the bar without an ounce of small talk. She focused her emerald green eyes on Christian and her full lips parted to reveal the delicate points of her fangs. "Why do you think I care?"

Time to switch tactics. No games. Time for a healthy dose of honesty. "I don't. I want your opinion before I go to Trenton McAlister with what I know."

Her eyes narrowed and her countenance grew serious. "You want my opinion?"

Wow. If he'd known all it would take to stop her in her tracks was to value her input, he would have asked for her opinion a long damned time ago. "Yes. You know more about Gregor than I do. You know what makes him tick. What fuels him." She opened her mouth to protest but he cut her off. "Don't try to deny it. I tracked him to where he and his loyal troops have set up camp. He's got a prisoner." Siobhan leaned in, almost indiscernibly, and her brow furrowed. Yes! He'd hooked her. "A mage."

She jerked back. Stunned. Christian had never seen the self-possessed dhampir so thrown off her game. This was big. She knew something and it was fucking ominous. Had to be.

"A mage?" She brought her voice down to a murmur. "You're certain?"

A tremor of anxious energy skittered down Christian's spine. His wolf gave a low warning growl in his psyche and he willed the animal to still. There was no use getting bent out of shape until he knew exactly what was going on. And honestly, he didn't have much faith that Siobhan would fill in many of the blanks.

"There's something not right about him, too." The waitress came back with their drinks and he slid his credit card across the table. "Start a tab."

"No." Siobhan slid his card back to him and replaced it with two twenties. "We're one and done tonight." She fixed her stern gaze on the waitress. "And we'd like some privacy."

The waitress scooped up the twenties and straightened. "Can do."

Shit was getting real. This was a side of Siobhan he'd never seen before. Serious. Down to business. Intense. Maybe he'd stumbled on something more important than he'd first thought. If so, McAlister was going to owe him a shitload more than some cash.

Christian was prepared to negotiate for his freedom.

Had Gregor actually found the mage who'd bound McAlister's power? Siobhan was so stunned, a feather could've knocked her over right now. Christian was smarter than she gave him credit for, something she needed to keep in mind for the future. There couldn't be many creatures privy to the secret. McAlister would've made sure to kill anyone who knew his weakness. She was sure Christian didn't realize the precarious position he'd just put himself in.

"I broke into the apartment building. The mage was in the next room and I overheard their conversation."

Berserkers could smell an enemy from miles away. "How did you manage that?"

"I bought a tincture from a witch that masked my scent."

Clever wolf. Siobhan wondered what other surprises Christian had up his sleeve. "What did they say?"

"Nothing that made a lot of sense."

Christian sipped from the edge of his glass and Siobhan's attention was drawn to his mouth as she remembered the delicious sensation of his lips against hers. Now wasn't the time for that sort of distraction, however. She needed to focus and find out *everything* he knew.

"They talked about a vampire named Saeed and his lover. But I got the impression she was something more. Maybe even his mate. Gregor was in Seattle and apparently some shit went down while he was up there. Saeed's female has something to do with the mage. Rin is his name. Rin wants some hard-core retribution against Saeed's supposed mate, and Gregor for something she did to him. From the way he made it sound, she'd destroyed his soul."

Dear gods. Siobhan had been so busy laying low, she hadn't paid much attention to Mikhail's pathetic fledglings. If what Christian said was correct, Saeed had possibly been tethered by a soul thief. The rarest of fae creatures and feared almost as much as berserkers by the supernatural community. Siobhan didn't know all of the details about how McAlister's power had been bound, but the rumor was that an *enaid dwyn* had enlisted the help of a mage to bind McAlister. Was Saeed's mate that soul thief? If so, the game Siobhan had been playing had just dramatically changed.

Gregor was no longer only a threat to vampire kind. He was a threat to supernatural kind.

"What else did you hear?"

Christian studied her for a quiet moment. A golden light flashed in his irises, giving her a glimpse of the animal that lived inside of him. It made him look feral and dangerous. Unpredictable. And so gods-damned sexy it heated her blood.

"They talked about a third party."

Siobhan couldn't help but wonder about Christian's reasons for being so forthcoming with her. The suspicious, guarded part of her worried he was baiting her for someone. Either Gregor or McAlister. The part of her that couldn't stop staring at his full lips and the square cut of his jaw hoped there was something more to it. Some measure of affection, perhaps.

Siobhan hadn't allowed herself to feel anything for anyone in a long damned time. So long, she couldn't remember exactly what it felt like. Tender emotions were a weakness. She couldn't afford to have any chinks in her armor. Especially now that Gregor's threat had grown. It was best to consider Christian as nothing more than a strategic tool for her to use. Anything else would only help to get her killed.

"And . . . ?" She really needed Christian to get to the damn point.

"Gregor called her Fiona. I think she's related to Saeed's mate. Sisters, maybe. From the way Gregor made it sound, Fiona and this Rin were old friends. And he seems to think McAlister is scared shitless of her."

Christian had gathered a cache of information but much of it was incomplete and difficult to fill in the blanks. With a little research, Siobhan was confident she could piece all of it together to see a clearer picture.

"But Rin thinks Gregor is overconfident."

Siobhan let out a derisive snort. Didn't surprise her at all. His overconfidence—his utter inability to consider failure— was what made him such a formidable foe. His faith bordered on fanatic. "I'm not surprised. Doubt won't figure into his plans at all."

Christian gave a nod of agreement. "Rin says Fiona is wild and unpredictable. Without allegiance."

Under other circumstances, Fiona might be the sort of female Siobhan would admire. Maybe even . . . like. But considering her current predicament and need to stay one step ahead of Gregor, Fiona was an unknown variable that could easily turn into a threat.

Christian downed the rest of his bourbon and set the glass down with a forlorn stare. Too damn bad. He wasn't getting another drink. Siobhan sensed that he regularly guzzled gallons of alcohol in an effort to get himself good and drunk. Too bad his supernatural metabolism wouldn't allow that to happen. He was damaged, self-destructive, and self-serving. Trouble. And yet, she found herself wanting to give him what he wanted. Another drink. Whatever.

Anything to make him feel better no matter how temporary the fix.

"Something went down in Seattle between Saeed and Gregor," Christian said after a moment. "I don't know what, but it involved his mate. Rin said he was going to kill both of them. Of course, Gregor said he didn't care what the mage did to Saeed, but that not a hair on his mate's head was to be touched."

Interesting. Of course, Gregor wouldn't care if Rin killed the vampire, but the fact that he was willing to protect a vampire's mate spoke volumes as to the importance of her role in Gregor's plans. "Anything else?"

Christian shook his head. "Gregor's senses are keen as fuck. He got spooked and ordered a perimeter check so I got the hell out of there."

Damn it. It would have been nice if Christian would've been able to get more out of his time in Gregor's stronghold. "So . . ." Siobhan hadn't even touched her own drink. Christian's gaze dipped briefly to the amber liquor and she let out a long-suffering sigh as she slid the glass toward him. He flashed a charming grin that turned her body traitor as heat flooded her. Sexy bastard. "What exactly do you need my opinion about?"

Christian blew out a breath before downing the bourbon in a single swallow. "I want to know how much you think I should tell McAlister."

His eyes widened in response to Siobhan's spluttering laughter. "Are you serious?" He couldn't possibly be considering going to the director of the Sortiari with this. "None of it!"

Disappointment settled on his expression and his brow furrowed. Obviously she hadn't given him the answer he'd been looking for. "None of it?"

"Are you so blindly loyal to the Sortiari that you'd turn this over to McAlister?" For some reason, Siobhan had assumed Christian was a rogue in every sense of the word. Like this Fiona, like *her*, without allegiance.

"Loyalty has nothing to do with it," Christian replied. "Information is valuable. I tend to sell mine."

Fool. Siobhan fought the urge to slap him across his handsome face, if anything, to knock a little sense into him. "You're a slave to money, werewolf." She had eyes on him all the time. Siobhan knew about his proclivity for gambling and the trouble it had gotten him into. "You need to free yourself of those shackles."

His answering scowl told her the subject wasn't up for discussion. "I didn't ask your opinion on that."

"I offered it free of charge." Siobhan made sure to keep her expression serene, her tone light. Whatever emptiness Christian sought to fill, gambling and alcohol weren't going to get it done.

Christian reached for the empty glass and then pushed it away, disgusted. "Yeah, well, don't do me any favors."

His mood had changed and it was a side of him Siobhan had never seen. Brooding. Angry. Disappointed. So unlike the charming, carefree male who loved to bait and tease her. Siobhan didn't like this side of him one bit. It ruined her fun and made her resistant to play. "You want my opinion on the matter? Fine. I'll give it to you. If you tell McAlister any of this, he'll kill you before you have the chance to push yourself from your chair."

Siobhan had had enough of Christian and his foolhardy ways. She scooted out of the booth and stalked toward the exit, prepared to put him and this miserable night behind her. The early-winter air filled her lungs and she let out a disgusted chuff of breath. Gods, how she hated the city. Hated its pollution and heavy air and the fact that the streetlights made it impossible to see the stars . . .

Strong arms spun her around. Christian put his mouth

to hers in a crushing kiss that weakened her knees and quickened the blood in her veins. Forget Gregor and McAlister. Christian Whalen was bound to destroy her before any of her other enemies ever got the chance.

CHAPTER
24

"I've been patient while you let that vampire's cunt distract you. It's time to prove to me that my generosity hasn't gone to waste."

Ewan fought the urge to roll his eyes. Gregor could pretend to be magnanimous all fucking day but it wouldn't change the fact he was a selfish fuck who didn't give a damn about anyone but himself and his own agenda. Ewan was still angry as hell over his conversation with Sasha and ready to do a little damage in order to release the tension that had continued to build through the rest of that night and into the next day. If Gregor wanted to be on the receiving end of that rage, so be it.

"Have you done anything in the past few weeks other than plant yourself balls-deep in the enemy? I've been lax. Let you skip rotations, let you fight in that gods-damned arena like an *animal*." The whites of Gregor's eyes were swallowed by black and a low growl resonated in his chest. "You owe me something, Ewan. And I suggest you pay up."

He didn't owe Ian Gregor a gods-damned thing. Ewan stared their supposed leader down as he took a slow, deep breath. His head whipped to one side as Gregor landed a blow Ewan never saw coming. A loud pop signaled his jaw bone breaking and a flash of white hot pain shot through his face. Ewan let out a grunt as the taste of blood filled his mouth. The split in his lip healed almost instantaneously as he straightened and faced the bastard once again.

Gregor moved with frightening speed and didn't waste a second to remind Ewan of his prowess. He landed another blow to Ewan's face, this time giving him a nasty orbital fracture that left his right eyeball throbbing, his face sagging, and his vision blurred before the bones could mend themselves. He could've taken his beating and let that be the end of it but that's not how Ewan rolled. He went after Gregor, head bowed low, and plowed into him. Gregor dug his feet into his boots, and rather than take him to the floor, Ewan pushed Gregor a good fifteen feet before slamming him into the opposite wall. The force of the impact buried Gregor in the drywall and Ewan used the opportunity to pull back his fist and throw a nasty right hook that connected squarely with Gregor's jaw.

He might as well have struck a brick wall for all the damage it did. Gregor was incredibly resilient, the strongest of them all. Ewan hoped he hurt at least a little. Enough to know not to fuck with him. He wasn't going to lie down and take it anymore. He'd had enough of the bullshit. Enough of vendettas. And enough of vengeance to last him several lifetimes. Ewan wanted out. And if the only way for that to happen was for him to die, then so be it.

Gregor dislodged himself from the drywall and had Ewan pinned to the floor before he even realized he was no longer standing. The air left his lungs in a violent rush and Ewan fought to replace the depleted oxygen. His straining, rasping inhales were ineffective, and Gregor's fist that was wrapped around his throat did little to help.

"You insolent piece of trash," Gregor spat. "You think

you can look at me with open defiance and think I'll just let it slide?" Black swallowed the whites of his eyes, and his native accent grew thicker with his anger. "I've had shits that gave me more trouble than you so don't think for a second you've got one over on me. If you wanted to degrade yourself by dipping into the vampire's tainted pussy, that's your business. When your brothers find out what you've done, a beating is going to be the least of your problems." Gregor leaned in close enough that his hot, rancid breath brushed Ewan's face. "*Qui cum canibus concumbunt cum pulicibus surgent.*" If you lie down with dogs, you wake up with fleas. Asshole. Gregor released his hold on Ewan's throat and in one fluid motion, jerked him up from the floor to stand. "You have five seconds to tell me something I want to hear before I tell your secrets to every warlord within earshot."

Gods, but Gregor was a sorry motherfucker. Ewan could finally take a deep breath and filled his lungs with some much needed oxygen. His many broken bones and contusions healed and he was back at one hundred percent. Gregor he could deal with. An angry mob of his brethren hell-bent on punishing him for betrayal? Not so much. Those blindly loyal to Gregor wouldn't hesitate to rip Ewan limb from limb. And when there was nothing left of him to dismember, they'd rip his head right off his shoulders. He had to play ball. He had no other choice. He wasn't afraid to fight or to die. But Drew would never let him go down alone, and he refused to put his cousin in harm's way.

"Sasha's maker, Saeed, has a mate." Ewan had no idea if this information would be valuable to Gregor but it was worth a shot. "Fae. Unlike anyone I've ever seen. She's powerful, I could feel it."

Gregor broke out into almost maniacal laughter and Ewan wondered if the male had finally lost his mind. "This female who thinks you are her mate, she's part of Saeed's coven?"

Ewan's brow furrowed. How did Gregor know about Saeed? "Aye. There are three vampires that I know of, including Sasha. The rest are dhampirs."

Gregor continued to laugh. "You're utterly fucking useless!" The laughter died to eerie silence and Gregor's lip pulled back in a menacing sneer. His eyes remained black. Onyx orbs that reflected the evil of his soul. "You would have to pick a female from the one coven I want to remain intact, wouldn't you?"

Ewan hid his surprise beneath a mask of passivity. Not since their feud with the vampires began had Gregor ever offered a single coven respite or clemency. Saeed obviously had something to contribute to Gregor's endgame. Either that, or someone close to him did. The fae, perhaps? She seemed the obvious choice.

"I know where the coven is located." It was a huge gamble to offer up that kind of information, especially when Ewan had never had any intention of sharing it. But Gregor's reaction would prove whether or not he truly wanted hands off Saeed and those under his care.

The inky black faded from Gregor's gaze. He raked Ewan from head to toe and his cold disdain would have coaxed goose bumps to the skin of a lesser male. Ewan's desire to protect his cousin from Gregor's misaligned sense of brotherhood had backfired in a big way. He had nothing to offer Gregor. *Nothing.* And Ewan had a feeling he was about to be punished for it.

"That female you're fucking has nothing to offer me in regards to her coven. Stop digging there. I want to know about the others. Where *their* covens are located. *Their* numbers. How many vampires fill their ranks. I want to know about Mikhail Aristov, his bitch of a mate, and the human child that lives with him. Anything else is useless and will only earn you a severe beating. Do you understand me?"

He'd have a snowball's chance in hell of getting Sasha to open up to him about any of that. Especially after their latest fight. "I understand." Ewan spat to his side to clear his mouth of the blood that remained from his beating. His eyes met Gregor's and he didn't even flinch. He refused to cow in the warlord's presence.

"Get the fuck out of my sight."

And with those last seven disgusted words, Ewan was effectively dismissed. He didn't bother contemplating who'd heard their little exchange and subsequent brawl. No one would dare bring it up. Gregor's rule was absolute. No one questioned him. Challenged him. Or otherwise spoke to him unless first spoken to. Likewise, anyone who dared to repeat a conversation had by Gregor with any of them could expect the sort of retribution Ewan had just been on the receiving end of.

He could think of a million better ways to spend an evening other than on the receiving end of Ian Gregor's fists.

Ewan passed Drew in the hallway on the way to his apartment. Their eyes met and his cousin changed course and fell into step beside him. Not a word was spoken between them until they reached Ewan's apartment and went inside. And even then, they were careful not to say too much.

"Jesus, you look like shit." Ewan was so glad Drew was adept at stating the obvious. "Is that your blood all over your fucking clothes?"

Ewan turned to his cousin and cocked eyebrow. He wasn't going to discuss what had just happened with Gregor. Not with him, or anyone else.

Drew cleared his throat and settled down onto a ratty old couch they'd picked up from the side of the road that had a *Free* cardboard sign tied to it. "Haven't seen you around much." He kept his tone conversational and light, but his pinched expression and drawn brows told another story. He was worried, and rightly so. And maybe even a little pissed off. Again, rightly so. But there was nothing Ewan was willing to do about it right now.

"I've had a lot of shit to do." Drew had to have known that Gregor had his tighty-whities in a bunch. "Gregor's had me busy running errands and doing recon."

"Yeah, there's been a lot of shit going on. Everybody's busy. Want to go get a drink?"

"Yeah." If Ewan was going to protect Drew, he was going to have to bump up their timetable. And that meant doing something incredibly unpleasant. "Let's go somewhere quiet and have a drink." Gods help him, Ewan was about to get involved with a nest of fucking demons.

"Sasha. This is a surprise. Come in."

Sasha stepped past the threshold of the enormous mansion that housed the Forkbeard werewolf pack and Chelle Daly's tiny coven of two. Though he seemed surprised to see her, Lucas greeted her with a bright smile and his scent remained clean. It was nice to know she was welcome here since right now, she had nowhere else to go. After Ewan stomped out of her apartment yet again, she couldn't bear to sit there in the still silence, alone. Too much weighed on her mind and without a solution in sight to the worries that plagued her, she decided to grab an Uber and hightail it to the only place she could think to go.

"Sorry to come over without calling first." She was actually surprised Saeed hadn't canceled her cell by now. It wouldn't be long before her credit cards were declined as well. Her dependence on him—and the coven—only helped to show her that the independence she thought she'd gained was nothing more than an illusion. "I need someone to talk to. Do you maybe want to grab a bite to eat or get a cup of coffee?" Might as well do it now while she still had Visa's permission.

"Coffee?" Lucas's good-natured laughter coaxed a wry smile to Sasha's lips. "Are you sure you wouldn't rather have a vodka soda at a club somewhere? I know it's not L.A., but Pasadena has some fun places to hang out at."

Sasha cringed. Gods, she'd been so out of control the past several months. Drinking. Partying. Fucking anything that walked by her. No wonder Lucas thought she'd prefer a crowded club to a quiet coffee shop. She looked around the expansive foyer at the nouveau rustic, yet stylish furniture. Sturdy. Tasteful yet lavish. Supernatural creatures certainly knew how to amass—and spend—their wealth. Which made her wonder about her own financial status. She was hardly an indentured servant. She had her own accounts, money that Saeed as coven master filtered to her. But leaving the coven was sort of like quitting her job. She wouldn't know comfort like this again. She'd relegated herself to a crappy, nearly unfurnished apartment in the Valley.

"Sasha? Is everything okay?"

Gods, she'd totally zoned out. She took a deep breath and choked on the intake as the overpowering scent of werewolf hit her. Wow. "How do you handle the—"

"You get used to it." Lucas cut her off as though he'd read her mind. Then again, she hadn't exactly been subtle in the way she'd choked. He grinned. "It's not that bad."

Maybe she shouldn't have come here. She should have gone to talk to Ani about her problems. Ani already knew her situation and wouldn't be surprised at the way things had gone so miserably south. Ani was rough and wild and unapologetic. She knew the city's underworld. Lucas didn't.

"Maybe that's why you came here, then? Because I don't know any of the things your friend knows."

Sasha's jaw hung slack. She stared, disbelieving, at Lucas. He'd heard her thoughts as plainly as if she'd spoken them out loud. It was impossible . . .

"You know one of my secrets," he said with a sympathetic smile. "So now you can trust me with one of yours."

Holy shit. She'd definitely come to the right place. "I don't have a car." She figured it was a good idea to let him know he'd be driving tonight.

"No problem." He grabbed a key fob from a bowl on a table near the door. "Let's go."

She'd yet to share a single secret with him and already Sasha felt unburdened. But that was the thing about Lucas. You only had to spend a few minutes with him to feel his calming effects. Yep, she'd certainly made the right decision. Because she really needed a dose of that calm right about now.

It wasn't a coffee shop, but it wasn't an overcrowded club, either. The low-key bar a few miles from the pack's estate was the total opposite of the type of place Sasha pictured Lucas hanging out. Dark, a little run-down, a little dirty, with low, old-school country music playing in the background, and no more than two other customers to crowd the space. The bartender looked to be in his late fifties though Sasha bet he was closer to forty-eight. Hard living had no doubt creased his brow, and sagged the skin under his eyes, and prematurely grayed his hair. He had kind blue eyes that crinkled when he smiled at them and he offered up a polite greeting as she and Lucas settled into a booth near the back of the bar.

"Can I get you two anything?" The bartender didn't bother leaving his post, but instead, shouted to them.

"I'll take a beer," Lucas called back. "I'm not picky. Whatever."

The bartender nodded and turned his attention to Sasha.

"Whiskey. On the rocks. And make it a double."

He gave Sasha a knowing look. She figured he was well versed in the art of drinking his troubles away. Like recognized like, and he'd obviously seen the dark shadow on her soul. She'd certainly seen it on his.

Lucas waited to speak until after their drinks were delivered. He took a long pull from the bottle, his fathomless blue gaze trained on Sasha. He wasn't going to press her. Or ask questions. Instead, he waited patiently for her to gather her thoughts. She liked him. Liked his quiet, calming presence and silent strength. He'd make a worthy mate to some lucky female someday. She sipped from her glass and thought about the burn of the whiskey as it slid down her throat. Almost soothing in comparison to the dry heat of bloodlust.

"My life is completely fucked up."

Lucas set his bottle down and gave Sasha his complete attention. "I'm sure it's not that bad."

She cocked a brow. *Oh no?* She was about to prove him wrong. This was definitely a hold-my-beer moment. "I'm tethered to a berserker, left my coven . . . Oh, and there's a gang of demons trying to scare me into convincing my mate to sacrifice himself so they can make a few bucks." She didn't bother to add the bit about said mate being unreasonably possessive and jealous over her one-time love for her maker. Too much drama.

Lucas's eyes went wide as he leaned back in the booth. "You're right. Your life is completely fucked up."

Sasha swallowed down a groan. She wanted to bang her head against the table until it knocked her the hell out and left her blissfully unconscious. "See?"

"You left out the bit about being in love with Saeed,

though." His freaky mind-reading ability really wigged Sasha out! She'd need to be careful what she let float around in her head when she was in Lucas's company. "Not a bad idea," he added with a wink. "You'll get the hang of it soon enough."

"That is seriously off the charts." Sasha drank half of the whiskey left in her glass in a single swallow. "How are you able to do it?"

"A quirk of my transition." Lucas drank as well and let his esoteric answer hang in the air. "I know where you're coming from in regards to Saeed, Sasha. That's why I brought it up. I'm not tethered but I've been in your situation. Sort of. It complicates those feelings that you had such confidence in."

Exactly! She'd devoted herself to Saeed centuries ago. Had always had such undying faith in her feelings for him. Had hoped that someday, he'd return those feelings. After his transition, Saeed had become even more distant. Sasha had failed to tether him and it was like someone had pulled the rug out from under her. And to add insult to injury, she'd found her soul secured to a mortal enemy. How could she possibly trust her feelings ever again when they'd betrayed her for so long?

"I can't help you to not love Saeed," Lucas said. "Just like I can't help you detangle yourself from the berserker. The tether is absolute." A truth repeated among their kind. Sasha was beginning to think it was vampire kind's slogan. "But I can try to help with your other problems. Let's start with the issue with the demons and work our way backward. Who exactly are they, and what exactly do they want?"

She was so glad Bria had thought it a good idea to introduce her to Lucas. She'd been tentative at first. His innocence, inexperience, his nice-guy persona. But Sasha should have known better than anyone that looks could be deceiving and that Lucas showed those around him only what he wanted them to see. There was more to the handsome young vampire than met the eye. He had depth. And secrets of his own. Sasha was glad to call him a friend and thankful to have him in her corner.

"Have you ever been burned by hellfire, Lucas?" She swallowed the rest of her whiskey as she gathered her thoughts. "It hurts like a motherfucker."

Gods, she hoped he could help her find a way out of this mess. If not, she and Ewan both might meet their ends before their respective families had a chance to punish them for their betrayals.

"Calm down," Lucas said. "No one's punishing anyone. At least, not on your end."

It was true that if she was punished at all by Saeed it would be a relative slap on the wrist compared to what Ewan could expect. The leader of his clan was the most feared and remorseless warlord in supernatural history. She worried for Ewan. He was so strong. So confident. But everything and everyone had its breaking point.

Including Ewan Brún.

CHAPTER
25

It took all night and the entire next day for Ewan to track down the piece of shit demons who'd hassled them a few nights ago. Luckily, his success in the battle arena had earned him a few favors and he didn't hesitate to cash in those chits. He planned to take care of his problems one by one and these bastards were unfortunately the easiest on his growing list to tackle. It had been twenty-four hours since he'd walked out on Sasha and it would likely be another twenty-four before he saw her again. *If* he saw her again. He wouldn't blame her if she told him to fuck off and never show his face around her again. Of course, that was assuming she cared enough to tell him to fuck off. For all he knew, she'd already run back to her coven and that motherfucker Saeed.

"Would it matter if I told you this was a monumentally bad idea?"

Ewan looked askance at Drew. It wasn't his first bad idea and it sure as hell wouldn't be his last. "I'll be damned if I let these foul-smelling, hellfire-wielding sons of bitches tell me what I will or will not do." They claimed they wanted compensation for money lost on Ewan's fights, but he suspected they wanted him out of the arena altogether. "And if they think they're getting a dime of our money, they've got another think coming."

Drew let out a derisive snort. "We're already sharing with Gregor; what's one more palm to grease?"

Ewan scowled. "Gregor's *greased palm* was a necessity to buy us some time and a little space. Not going to apologize for it. I'll compensate you out of my cut."

Drew let out a sigh that slumped his shoulders. "Nah. We're good. I'm just sick and fucking tired of being his little bitch and living like a gods-damned squatter."

Ewan felt the exact same way. His need for self-improvement and freedom was what had pushed him toward the battle arenas in the first place. "You and me both. Nothing's going to derail that. I promise."

Drew turned to look at Ewan, his expression sour. "Not even the vampire?"

Fuck. He supposed the subject of Sasha was unavoidable. "It's . . . complicated."

"It's complicated?" Ewan cringed at Drew's incredulous laughter. "What is this, a fucking rom-com? She's a complication we don't need. Find another pussy to stick your dick in."

If only it were that simple. In the past, he'd never had a problem moving from one pussy to the next. Nameless, faceless fucks that meant absolutely nothing to him. An opportunity to blow off some steam and nothing else. But Sasha was different. She was in his blood. His bones. His fucking marrow. He couldn't shake free of her hold no matter how hard he tried. If Drew found that frustrating, it was nothing in comparison to how it made Ewan feel.

"Not gonna happen." Ewan opted for the easiest answer. The one most likely to shut Drew up. "Besides, she's the assignment Gregor's had me on."

"Jesus fucking Christ." Drew's disgust was why Ewan had to keep this business between him and Sasha to himself. "He's finally lost his gods-damned mind."

Finally? In Ewan's opinion, Gregor's sanity had never been intact. The male was a raging psychopath, plain and simple. He was done thinking about that son of a bitch for now, though. He put on his turn signal and pulled into a long winding driveway before coming to a stop at the security gate that barred him access to the demon kingpin's lavish Sunset Boulevard estate.

"This is some swanky shit," Drew remarked. "Gregor should be embarrassed. How can anyone possibly take him seriously when we continue to live like a bunch of assholes holed up in a homeless shelter?"

Drew missed the point. Gregor didn't give a shit about material possessions. He didn't care what the supernatural community thought of him. He didn't wield his power by being flashy with his wealth. Ian Gregor demanded respect through violence. His strength of body, mind, and purpose were his prized possessions. Driven by the ghosts of his past and the burning need for revenge, he'd let them all starve to death and live unsheltered in the forest before he'd abandon his cause.

Ewan leaned out of the gaping hole of where the driver side door used to be toward an intercom mounted on the stone pier near the gate. He pushed the button and unclenched his jaw. "It's Ewan Brún," he growled. "Let me the fuck in."

He didn't get a response, but instead the gate creaked and gave a metallic whine as it slowly opened. Anxious energy gathered in his gut and sent a surge of power through his limbs. There was nothing stopping the demons from killing them both once they walked into the house. Hell, or even once they pulled into the fucking driveway. But Ewan was banking on the fact that the demons needed him. They sure as hell wouldn't make any money by killing him right now.

The long winding driveway that led through the property was almost as ridiculous as the house itself. Gaudy. Extravagant. Completely tasteless. Really, the perfect place for a bunch of classless demon bastards.

"Remember," Ewan said to Drew. "If shit goes south—"

"Yeah, I know," Drew replied. "Get out of there. Fuck you, Ewan."

He let out a soft laugh. At least Ewan could count on his cousin to have his back. "All right, let's get this taken care of so we can get the fuck out of here."

Drew gave a nod and got out of the car. They walked across the breezeway toward the front door, a monstrosity of oak and gold leaf that made Ewan wonder if this particular demon had a hard-on for seventies gangster movies. Jesus. If the demons didn't kill him, their tacky taste would probably get the job done.

The door swung open before he'd even set foot on the last step. It was like some scene from a cheesy haunted house movie, being welcomed by an eerie, empty space. Ewan snorted. If this was an intimidation tactic, it had failed miserably. Ewan was the sort of monster that other monsters had nightmares about. He didn't spook easily.

"I've got a lot of shit to do tonight and you're wasting my time!" he shouted to the room at large. "So let's get down to business or you can take your propositions and shove them up your dank, sulfur-scented asses."

Drew stood stoic, yet alert beside him. He was ready to throw down and kick some demon ass. Ewan wasn't gonna lie, he was more than ready to fuck someone up and he hoped one of them would piss him off to the point that he ignored his better judgment. He was sick and tired of being played, manipulated, controlled. Used, underestimated, abused. Someone was going to pay for his shitty mood and he didn't care much who.

"Gods! Did someone gut a rancid animal, or did a berserker just step into my house?"

Ewan rolled his eyes. Demons went out of their way to get under everyone's skin, he wasn't surprised they were trying to get under his. "I guess if you want to waste time slinging insults, that's your prerogative. But I came here to talk business, and if you don't want to do that, I'm out of here."

The scent of sulfur intensified to the point that Ewan's eyes began to water. He choked on an intake of breath and the dry scorch of his throat. He needed a glass of water. Strike that. He needed a gallon of fucking water. He felt like he'd been drinking all night, climbed out of bed, and emptied a sleeve of crackers into his mouth. Was this how Sasha felt when her need for blood overtook her?

"Do you have my money?" The demon that had first accosted Ewan after his fight stepped into the foyer from a room to the left. It looked to be some sort of formal living room furnished with blood-red leather furniture and every piece draped with ugly, fluffy, white faux fur. Classy. "Seventy-five large, if I'm not mistaken."

Huh. Just a few days ago, it had been fifty large. What a prick. Ewan had a hard time remembering the supposedly infamous demon's name, and frankly, he didn't care. Sorras? Sonath? He just wanted the lousy fucker to tell him what he really wanted so Ewan could plan his next move.

"I'm going to tell you the same thing I told you the last time we talked. You're not getting a dime out of me."

And just like that, demons poured out of the woodwork. From every room, corner, shadow, and crevice, bodies converged on the spot where he and Drew stood. The scent of sulfur filled his nostrils, his lungs. Slithered down his throat and soured his stomach. Drew began to choke on an intake of breath as they were both seized by many pairs of hands and shoved toward the gods-awful red and white living room.

Whatever was coming, it wasn't going to be pleasant. For the first time in a long time Ewan came to the realization that there might be something out there nastier than Ian Gregor. Either way, he was about to find out.

"When I said I would help you, this wasn't exactly what I had in mind."

"Hey, it was your suggestion that we deal with the easiest problems first. This one is easiest."

Lucas pursed his full lips as he regarded Sasha. "True, but it was also my suggestion that we take the diplomatic route first."

Sasha cut Lucas a look. "You can't be diplomatic when it comes to demons. All they want to do is pick a fight."

"That doesn't mean you have to bring them one."

"Yes, it does." Lucas didn't understand. The demons weren't interested in talking, or negotiating, or playing nice. They didn't want to be paid off or placated. They wanted Ewan dead and that was nonnegotiable. And because he was a gods-damned force of nature, unkillable, unstoppable, violent, and ruthless, they knew the only way he'd fall was voluntarily.

Or otherwise under duress.

Sasha had one option and one option only. Take the bastards out before they could do any more damage.

"You don't have to come with me, Lucas," Sasha said. "This is my fight and it has nothing to do with you. I would never expect you to put your life on the line." She'd known all along she'd have to go it alone. And that was okay.

"You're out of your mind if you think I'd let you do this alone." Lucas reached over and grabbed a dagger and a set of throwing knives from a chest in Sasha's living room. "I gotta say, for this only being a crash pad, you've got a nice armory started."

The place might've been sparsely furnished, and the walls devoid of any art or decoration. But Sasha had brought the necessities when she'd first rented this place. She might have wanted Ewan, craved his blood like a drug. She might've been tethered to him. But that didn't mean she'd trusted him. Security was, and always had been, at the forefront of Sasha's mind.

"I don't fuck around."

Lucas laughed. "No, you don't. You definitely have your priorities straight. Do you have any idea where to even find these demons?"

"Not exactly." Sasha might've played around with the seedy underbelly of the supernatural world, but she was hardly an insider. That didn't mean she was without connections. "My friend Ani will know where to find them. At least, I hope she'll know." She hoped her faith wasn't misplaced. The sylph had always seemed so in the know. She kept her ear to the ground and listened even when no one thought she was paying attention. Bartenders had a way of staying beneath the radar and for some reason, no one ever seemed to censor themselves once they bellied up to the bar.

"Okay. That's a solid start. But what then? After we find them? We need to know what we're up against, how many, and what our weaknesses are. An ambush is our best bet, but it's not going to work if we don't familiarize ourselves with our surroundings first."

Sasha paused and studied Lucas for a quiet moment. So much more to him than met the eye. He had a strategic mind and a warrior's reasoning. When she looked in his eyes, all she saw was youth and inexperience which was part of his charm. But beneath that, she sensed a depth and darkness that he didn't allow anyone—even her—to see.

"I don't plan to take them out on their home turf." They'd expect it. Hell, they'd probably already beefed up security just in case. Sasha wanted this to be quiet and stealthy, and at the same time, in plain view of as many eyes as possible. She didn't want to simply take the demons out. She wanted to send a message. If she was going to be on her own from here on out she needed every nasty, villainous son of a bitch out there to know she was someone not to be fucked with.

She refused to live the rest of her life with a target on her back.

"I can fight," Lucas began. "But I'm no assassin."

She didn't need him to be. Sasha had been trained by one of the greatest assassins to ever live. "I just need you to run interference, Lucas. I'll do the rest."

"This changes our strategy a bit." Lucas reached for another dagger and a 9 mm that he tucked into his waistband. "I've a feeling there's going to be very little reconnaissance involved."

"Little to none." Sasha needed to be prepared, but not too prepared. In this case, any careful planning on her part would do nothing more than buy the demons time. She didn't want them to have that. She didn't want them to have an opportunity to plan or think or anything else. She wanted them comfortable. Unaware. Business as usual. So wrapped up in their own greed and lust and violence-mongering that they wouldn't see her coming. And when they were nice and relaxed and feeling so smug and full of themselves, Sasha would strike with silence and end their miserable existences once and for all. "We only have one shot at this." If she failed, it was game over. "If I fuck it up—"

Lucas held up a hand. "You won't fuck it up. But if

something does happen, it's not game over. We'll just find another way."

Sasha smiled. Gods, she hated how he could read her mind.

He smiled back. It was a disarming gesture and for the first time since she'd met him, Sasha noticed how strikingly handsome Lucas was. His smile brightened.

"Hey. Stay the hell out of my brain."

Lucas hiked an unapologetic shoulder. "Stop thinking about things I might want to hear, and I'll consider it."

"You know, you're not as sweet and innocent as you let on."

He smirked. "And you are not as tough and heartless as you let on."

Sasha looked away. She'd worked damn hard to convince everyone she was a cold, stoic bitch. She wasn't about to let Lucas shatter the illusion. "You're lucky I like you, or I would have left your ass home."

"You're lucky I like you," Lucas countered. "Otherwise, I'd have let you leave my ass home."

Sasha laughed, and for the first time in months it actually felt genuine. It was nice to know Lucas had her back. Because once the dust settled, she wasn't sure which parts of her life would be shattered and which parts would remain intact.

CHAPTER
26

"I have no use for that one. Get him out of here."

Rather than be relieved to be saved from what was sure to be a serious ass kicking, Drew lost his shit. Ewan watched as his cousin fought against the demons that held him, his considerable strength ineffective against so many. The demons laid into him, throwing punches after punches, until it drove him to the floor. They didn't stop there. Once he was down, they continued to beat him mercilessly. Boots connected with his gut, his torso and chest. Fists came down to bash against his head, his jaw and shoulders. Berserkers might have been strong and resilient, but they weren't infallible. A beating like that could still hurt like a motherfucker whether you healed instantly or not.

"Knock it the fuck off!" Ewan shouted. The sick fucks had no interest in Drew. This was simply for show. To teach Ewan a lesson. It wasn't just him they could get to.

If he didn't play ball, they'd hurt anyone and everyone he cared about. Which amounted to all of two individuals and one of them was lying on the demon's tacky seventies-style marble floor right now. "He'll leave." Ewan would make Drew go if he had to.

The smug bastard pulling the strings snapped his regal fingers and the bodies that had converged on Drew went still. "How do you feel about having your decisions made for you, berserker?" The demon's words were obscured into a strange lisp due to the sharp points of his teeth. "Do you want to leave? Or do you like the abuse?"

So much for coming here to talk. Ewan should've walked through that open door ready to dispose of moth-erfuckers. Instead, he'd been stupid enough to think he could reason with creatures that'd been shat straight out of hell's ass.

"Drew." Ewan hoped the command in his tone was enough to convince his cousin to get the fuck out. There was no point in them both getting their asses kicked to-night and since Ewan had already taken a beat down from Gregor tonight he might as well let the demons finish the job.

If not for his quick healing, Drew would've looked a hell of a lot worse. But that wasn't saying much. His body still contorted at odd angles where the broken bones had yet to heal. Blood caked his face, ran down his neck, and soaked through his T-shirt. His chest heaved with labored breath and he spit to one side, sending a single tooth across the demon's floor. Black swallowed the whites of his eyes and fanned out over his lids, forehead, and cheekbones. If he didn't calm the hell down, the battle rage would take hold and there wouldn't be a gods-damned thing Ewan could do about it.

"Andrew!" Ewan snapped. "*Seasamh síos.*"

He'd told Drew to stand down and hoped his cousin had the good sense to listen to him. If he reacted, he'd be giv-ing the demons exactly what they wanted. Drew didn't have the control necessary to play their game. Even incredibly resilient creatures like berserkers could be killed. They were outnumbered twenty to one. If it came down to a fight, neither one of them would come out of this alive.

The dangerous black ebbed from his eyes and the bulging tension in his muscles eased. He was by no means any calmer, but he at least showed presence of mind. "Don't do this, Ewan. Don't be a fucking martyr."

He wasn't about to martyr himself. But neither was he going to let these fuckers use Drew against him. This was nothing more than a change in tactics. Sometimes, to gain the upper hand, you had to let your enemy think they were winning.

"It's going to be at least a day or two before you see me again. *Chlúdach dom Gregor.*" He needed Drew to cover his ass with Gregor and to keep him out of this business with the demons. "He's going to be looking for me."

A fist connected squarely with Ewan's gut, doubling him over with pain.

"Don't speak your fucking Highland bullshit language and try to put anything over on me," the demon hissed.

Ewan huffed out a breath. The last thing they needed was for Gregor to go digging around where he shouldn't be and find the substantial stash of cash they'd hidden in the walls of Ewan's apartment. Gods, he had so many fucking irons in the fire he didn't know which one to grab first. All he could do was manage one disaster at a time. Drew pushed himself away from the bodies that crowded him and the resignation in his action let Ewan know he'd comply.

"He's leaving," Ewan said on a growl. "So let him leave peacefully. Otherwise, I might decide not to be so cordial."

The demon's annoying laughter echoed off the marble floors and plastered walls. Whoever the son of a bitch was, he must've been a scary motherfucker because not a single one of the forty demons crowding the room dared to laugh along with him.

"Go." Ewan hoped that in his tone and in his gaze, Drew would realize Ewan wasn't asking him to be a coward. But gods-damn it, he couldn't be responsible for anyone else getting hurt because of his own bullshit schemes.

Drew pushed his way through the crowd of bodies that refused to move for him. His gaze met Ewan's for the barest second before he changed course for the foyer and walked out the door.

"All right," Ewan said as he braced himself for what was sure to be one of the worst beatings of his entire existence. "Let's get down to business, shall we?"

Sasha couldn't remember a time when she'd been so damned frustrated. Ani had provided her and Lucas with several possible locations for where fights might be being held tonight, and so far they'd come up empty. They had one more place to check, a dilapidated structure that had once been a school gymnasium, and if they came up empty-handed, Sasha worried they'd be back at square one.

Several luxury cars lined the parking lot, a good sign. Lucas pulled in and brought the SUV to a stop. He cut the engine and glanced over at Sasha. His tentative expression let her know he'd come to the same conclusion she had. "Are you ready for this?"

She was about to commit premeditated murder. Was anyone ever ready for that? "Yeah. Let's do this."

The sound of raucous cheers and angry shouts drifted to Sasha's ears and she knew they were on the money. Inside the relatively large gymnasium, a battle to the death was already in full swing. A wave of relief crashed over Sasha that Ewan wasn't one of the competitors. That didn't mean he wasn't here though. Waiting in the wings. Ready to send some sorry soul to the afterlife. Hell, for all she knew, the demons had already managed to convince him to lay down his own life for whatever sick, twisted reasons they used to manipulate him. A lot could happen in twenty-four hours. And Sasha's overactive imagination conjured myriad scenarios.

"I'm not seeing any demons," Lucas said as his gaze roamed the vast crowd. "How about you?"

She'd been so preoccupied with her own worries she'd yet to truly focus on her surroundings. The crowd tonight wasn't as big as some she'd seen, but Sasha suspected that had more to do with the size of the venue than lack of interest. She gave a sad shake of her head. The supernatural world was already violent enough. Why go out in search of more?

Sasha focused on the task at hand and forced the troubling thoughts from her mind. She had shit to do and not a lot of time to get it done. The half dome of the silver cage came down over the arena to lock the competitors inside. The crowd went wild, their bloodlust apparent in their wide eyes and enthusiastic cheers. She signaled for Lucas to split off. The plan was for him to distract onlookers with his mere presence. Sasha was a regular, and the rumors of her affair with the berserker were widespread throughout the underground. She was old news, but Lucas was shiny and new. It would give them something to talk about. To speculate on. And even to worry about. A sleight-of-hand to give Sasha the anonymity she needed to slip through the press of bodies and find her marks.

She worked her way from the back of the gym toward the center where the arena had been set up in a meandering spiral. Around the battle arena, through the crowd. Up, over, and around. She let her senses guide her, searched for the faint scent of sulfur. But either her nose betrayed her, or there wasn't a single demon in attendance tonight.

She'd hit a wall and it caused her frustration to mount to an almost unbearable level.

A commotion from the rear of the building drew her attention. She scanned the crowd for Lucas's face and found him directly across from her, his own eyes zeroed in on whatever drew the crowd's focus from the fight. She pressed her way through the bodies that sought to get a little closer, necks craned and angled away from the metallic cage of the battle arena.

Sasha pushed past anything and anyone that stood in her way as her stomach tightened into tiny unyielding knots. The tang of sulfur burned the back of her throat and adrenaline dumped into her bloodstream. The scent increased with each step she took and her worry intensified to the point that it caused her stomach to heave. Lucas must've sensed her rising panic and cut through the press of bodies to get to her. They reached the outer rim of where a large group formed a circle around what appeared to be a limp and lifeless body.

Ewan. Dear gods.

Sasha looked around, frantic, for whoever had done this to him. The scent of sulfur dissipated from the air and disappeared entirely, letting her know the sadistic assholes that had tortured Ewan within an inch of his life had merely dumped off his body and fled. She pushed past the final perimeter of gawkers and threw herself down beside Ewan. The floor cracked beneath her knees from the impact, sending jarring pain from her knees up through her thighs. The discomfort didn't even register. Sasha was too scared. Too worried. Too mindless with concern to care about anything other than the powerful male who had been reduced to a burned and bloodied mass of flesh.

His pain must have been unimaginable.

"Ewan." Her voice cracked with emotion as she put

her mouth close to his ear and spoke. "Ewan, can you hear me?"

He didn't move. Didn't make a sound. Sasha was fearful to touch him, to cause any more pain to the body that had been so thoroughly abused. Not an inch of him had been left unmarred and the fact that he'd yet to heal filled her with icy dread. What in the hell had they done to him? He lay on his stomach, head turned away from her. His back expanded slightly with an intake of breath and Sasha let out a sob of relief as a tear spilled over her lid and trailed down her cheek. She brushed the offending wetness away with an angry swipe and looked up to find Lucas beside her.

"We need to get him out of here," Lucas said. "Now."

He was right. There was any number of creatures in attendance tonight who might capitalize on Ewan's weakness to exact some measure of vengeance on him. The demons weren't the only ones who'd lost money on his fights and likewise, berserkers were reviled by the supernatural community as a whole. Their near indestructibility evoked fear. To see Ewan at a disadvantage like this would create a chink in his armor and embolden others to follow in the footsteps of the demons. Sasha had no great love for berserkers, either, but for this particular one, she would lay down her life to protect.

She was loath to touch him, to do anything that might further cause him pain. Lucas had no such concerns, and reached for Ewan's arm, dragging him up to a standing position. Ewan let out a shout of pain that cut through Sasha like the sharpest blade. A murmur ran through the crowd and her heart stuttered in her chest. The faster they got him out of here, the better. She went to Ewan's other side to bear the other half of his weight, and together she and Lucas carried him out of the building and across the parking lot to his waiting SUV.

Lucas hit the fob and Sasha reached for the back door. She pulled it open and Lucas moved to hoist Ewan inside. "Be careful!" Her voice cracked with emotion. She needed to hold it together at least long enough to get him back to her apartment. But gods, she didn't want to jostle him even a little bit. *The pain he must be in . . .*

"As careful as I can be." The understanding in Lucas's tone despite having been snapped at caused bitter shame to well up in Sasha's chest.

She let out a slow sigh as she allowed Lucas to ease Ewan onto the backseat. "I'm sorry, Lucas. I just . . . I don't know what . . ." She was at a total loss for words. "He should've healed. What in the hell did they do to him?"

She looked up and met Lucas's gaze. He reached out to put a comforting hand on her shoulder as she gently eased the door shut. "It's going to be okay, Sasha. He's going to be okay."

Sasha wished she shared in Lucas's optimism. But she knew firsthand how strong Ewan was. She'd seen him heal almost instantaneously. As she got in the car and fastened her seatbelt, she said a silent prayer to whatever god might hear her. *Please let him be okay. Please let him live.*

Because she knew without a doubt that she couldn't live without him.

CHAPTER
27

Ian Gregor contemplated Rin for a quiet moment. He was a shell of a male. Broken. The essence of what made him who he was, gone. It caused Ian a rare moment of introspection and made him contemplate his own existence. He walked the righteous path. He might've broken faith with those Sortiari bastards, but the ideology that caused him to ally with them in the first place held true. The vampires were unholy creatures. Soulless. Empty. Without essence or substance. They deserved to die, every last one of them.

And he wouldn't rest until they were wiped from the face of the earth.

Rineri de Rege was no different. Vile. Evil. Tainted. He no longer deserved to be breathing the same oxygen as the rest of the world. But Gregor would keep him alive until his purpose was served and then he would wipe him from the face of the earth as well.

"Tell me about Fiona Bain and Trenton McAlister."

Rin glared at Ian, his expression so full of abject hatred that for a moment he could almost imagine Rin still had the capacity to feel something. Ian leaned back in his chair and let out a slow sigh. Contrary to what everyone thought, he disliked resorting to torture to get what he wanted. It was messy, took too much damned time, and wasted energy that could be put to better use.

"Don't make me beat it out of you, Rin."

He'd hardly mistreated the mage during his time as Ian's captive, but his standard of living had certainly taken a nosedive since Seattle. No longer the lavishly wealthy, feared and reviled master of Seattle's supernatural under-belly, Rin's existence had been reduced to a state that no doubt left a sour taste in his mouth. Ian hated elitists. And Rin's attitude made him want to beat the fucker to a bloody pulp.

Rin didn't look away. He kept his dark gaze locked with Ian's, his expression blank. The bastard could be insuffer-ably stubborn when he wanted to be, something Ian found equally admirable and annoying.

Ian brought up the blade of the dagger he held and toyed with the tip, testing a sharp point to the pad of his finger. It nicked the skin, and a drop of blood welled from the tiny cut. He licked it away slowly as he regarded Rin. "Mages need magic to heal. Do I need to remind you that yours is diminished?"

Rin's dark eyes narrowed. The loss of his soul had done more than simply turn him into a husk of the male he'd once been. It had diminished his power, dimmed the light of his magic, and without it he was weaker and more vul-nerable to harm.

"Fiona and McAlister were lovers." The empty quality to Rin's voice bothered Ian a hell of a lot more than the hollow look in his eyes. By destroying his soul, Cerys had turned him into an unholy creature. "He was a new initi-ate to the guardians of fate and had yet to rise up their ranks."

Trenton McAlister was one of the most secretive males

Ian had ever met. A shroud of mystery surrounded him and it was rumored he killed anyone unfortunate enough to discover anything about his past or personal life. Ian felt a perverse amount of satisfaction to have gained any knowledge about McAlister. He would own something no other creature did. Bits and pieces of that sanctimonious fuck's history. And he was bound and determined to use the information to his advantage.

"Keep going." Ian made sure that Rin picked up on the threat inherent in his tone. He'd be damned if he let him stop now.

"He was ambitious and power-hungry but the Sortiari was under the control of da Vinci and his ideological renaissance at the time. Change was on the wind and rumors began to circulate that the organization's seers had foretold of a horrible future in which the world would suffer unless they took action to shift the course of fate."

Ian's brow furrowed. By the time he became entangled with Trenton McAlister and the Sortiari, the male had already been placed at the top of the organizations hierarchy. A century after da Vinci's rule. Had it truly taken one hundred years for them to come to the decision that the vampires should die? Or had McAlister taken over in order to see that grand plan through to fruition?

"In Fiona, he saw a partner who craved power and status is much as he did. They were a perfect match. Each of them ambitious and driven. She pledged her undying love to him. And he betrayed her."

Hell hath no fury like a woman scorned. The berserkers had no females left to revere, but even as a young child, Ian had recognized a power in that gender that his own was somehow lacking. A capacity for something he couldn't feel or understand. He'd always found it amusing that so many missed what he had so easily picked up on. The weaker sex. He let out an amused snort. History's greatest lie.

"He betrayed her with another woman?" Ian found himself enthralled by Rin's story. He was greedy for every detail, no matter how insignificant it might seem.

"Yes and no." Rin's noncommittal answer agitated him but he remained patient. This was the most information he'd been able to get out of the mage since taking him prisoner. He wasn't about to do anything that would cause him to retreat back into stoic silence. "McAlister always loved power more than he could ever love anyone or anything else."

Ian didn't have to hear that from Rin to know it was the fucking truth. Trenton McAlister did whatever it took to get what he wanted no matter how underhanded or dishonest. He took the truth and twisted it. Manipulated. Lied. Blackmailed. Ian had never known the Sortiari's rule under anyone other than McAlister's. He couldn't help but wonder what the guardians of fate had been like with da Vinci—or any of his predecessors—at the helm. Had they perhaps been more honorable? More levelheaded? Perhaps even more skeptical? Had they been brave enough to question the seers that McAlister so blindly obeyed? He supposed none of it mattered. What was done was done and there was no going back to change any of it.

Dwelling on the past wouldn't bring back those Ian had loved. And neither would it resurrect that very emotion he could no longer feel.

"He met an oracle on his travels to Asia for the Sortiari." At the mention of an oracle, Gregor's ears perked up. He leaned forward in his chair, rapt. "I don't know much about the girl because Fiona was loath to speak of her. I only know that her power was without equal and she was an aristocrat. McAlister became obsessed with her, though I don't believe it was in a romantic sense. In her, he saw the path to ascension. And like I said, he loved power above all else. Even Fiona."

Gregor looked to the opposite wall. To the photos, and maps, newspaper clippings, and scraps of this and that affixed to the drywall with pushpins. He followed with his eyes, the thin strings of yarn that connected one thing to another, creating an intricate web of McAlister's business throughout the years. Just when he thought he had all of the pieces to the puzzle, another fell out of the sky to land in his lap. The oracle. A nameless, faceless aristocrat, and powerful beyond measure if Rin was to be believed. Ian pinched the bridge of his nose between his thumb and forefinger. He vowed his patience would endure. He could wait as long as it took to take his enemies down. But with each passing day and each new detail learned, he wondered how much more he could actually take.

He pointed the dagger at Rin's face. "Keep talking. And don't stop until you've told me everything you know."

Ian Gregor walked the righteous path. And nothing—no one—no force upon this earth—would ever stand in his way.

Christian paced outside the elaborate wrought-iron gate as he contemplated his next move. Despite how he'd behaved the other night, he'd taken Siobhan's advice to heart. She was as shrewd and intelligent a female as he'd ever met. He valued her counsel. And whereas he wanted to march straight into McAlister's office with the information he'd gathered and bargain for his freedom, he was wary. If Siobhan thought showing his hand was dangerous, perhaps his bargaining chip wasn't yet big enough. He was already playing both sides against the middle, what would it hurt to add one more to the mix?

Coming here tonight might've been one of his stupidest decisions yet. But it was too late, they already knew he was here. Hell, they'd probably caught his scent long before he'd rung the intercom. As a rogue, he was unwelcome among his own kind. As an agent of the Sortiari, he was unwelcome among most of the supernatural community as a whole.

Damned if you do, damned if you don't.

Christian let out a sigh as he dug a flask from his back pocket. He unscrewed the top and took a swig of the cheap-ass whiskey that burned its way into his stomach. Gods, how he wished he could get good and drunk. The only thing about his humanity that he truly missed. His wolf perked to attention in his psyche and let out a low warning growl. Territorial pain in the ass. This was bound to be uncomfortable for everyone involved, but what the hell. Christian never did pay much attention to his comfort zone.

"Christian Whalen. By the gods, I thought someone was out here playing a joke. But here you stand. You're either very brave or very stupid to have come here tonight."

Probably a little of both. He flashed a charming grin at the werewolf who stared him down from the other side of the gate. "It's been a long time, Sven. How is life treating you?"

"If you ask me, it hasn't been long enough." Sven, cousin to the Forkbeard Pack's Alpha, still bore a hint of his native Scandinavian accent. Vikings. Rowdy, pig-headed, warring sons of bitches, every last one of them. And Christian couldn't help but like them.

"I take it Gunnar declined my request for an audience?" He wasn't really surprised. He hadn't shown up here with any true optimism. He'd just figured it was worth a shot.

"Oh no, Gunnar was just as surprised as everyone else to hear your voice over the intercom," Sven replied with a wily grin. "He sent me out here to frisk you and check you for weapons before he lets you set foot on his property."

Christian gave a chuff of laughter. "Fair enough." Gunnar Falk wasn't a fool by any stretch of the imagination. Honestly, Christian would've been surprised if they'd simply let him stroll right through the gate. He held his arms up and grinned as he spread his legs wide. He didn't utter a word as the gate swung open and Sven stepped up to him. He reached out and swept his hands from Christian's shoulders to his wrists and underneath his arms. "I've gotta warn you, I haven't had a date in a while and that feels pretty damn good."

Sven's fist jabbed at Christian's face and caught him in the nose before he could react. The cartilage popped and blood trickled over his lip before he could swipe it away. He supposed he deserved it for his smart-ass remark, but it was totally worth it for getting a rise out of the bulky werewolf.

Christian remained still while Sven continued to search him. So many sarcastic retorts came to mind but he didn't feel like suffering any more broken bones tonight. It just took too much gods-damned energy to heal.

"Why the beefed-up security?"

It had been a while since Christian had paid a visit to the Forkbeard Pack's home base in Pasadena, but they sure as hell hadn't been so guarded then. Maybe it was the Sortiari setting up camp so close that had the Alpha on edge. In which case, coming here tonight was a *really* bad idea. Or it could have been the internal turmoil that Gregor himself had caused by trying to convince the pack to ally with him. Christian had been on the outskirts of the attempted ambush on a meeting between McAlister and Mikhail Aristov several months ago, and part of Gunnar Falk's pack had been drawn into the fight.

"I'm going to give you a piece of advice, Whalen," Sven

growled. "Don't ask a lot of stupid, unnecessary questions and Gunnar might not be tempted to kick your ass."

Sven turned without another word and Christian fell into step behind him. Walking beside him would indicate that he considered himself at the very least Sven's equal, and as a rogue, that display of dominance would only earn him another ass kicking. His wolf let out a low growl in the back of his mind. The animal knew they were stronger. Far more dominant than any member of Gunnar's pack, save perhaps one. Christian shoved the animal's annoying ego to the farthest corner of his mind where it belonged. Damn wolf didn't know what was good for him. They weren't here to prove anything tonight. And if Christian had anything to say about it, they wouldn't be proving anything to anyone ever again. Fuck that Alpha bullshit and pack mentality. Christian had gone rogue for a reason and he wanted it to stay that way.

The Forkbeard Pack's home base was a marvel of modern architecture. Enormous. Lavish. And at the same time, understated in a way that fit Gunnar to a T. Sven led Christian to a small study where he was instructed to sit and wait. He did as he was told and plopped down on a sturdy leather couch in the corner of the room. His wolf snapped to attention as Sven left the room, stirring the air and bringing with it a scent that Christian recognized in an instant. *Vampire*. What in the hell was Gunnar Falk up to?

"Christian Whalen. I'd say I was glad to see you, but of course, you'd know that was a lie."

The Alpha of the Forkbeard Pack entered the room with all of the menacing presence expected of a Viking lord and Alpha werewolf. Jesus. Gunnar seriously needed to update his look. He might as well have stepped right out of a history book—or more to the point, a History Channel show—with his head shaved on either side to showcase his ancient tattoos, leaving a swath of long, straight hair that

cut down the center of his head, and his bushy, yet mani-
cured beard that covered the regal cut of his jaw. Gunnar's
bright blue eyes zeroed in on Christian, who looked to the
floor despite his wolf's desire to do otherwise. They weren't
here to challenge an Alpha. The gods knew he didn't need
any more drama in his life.

Christian waited for Gunnar to take a seat before he
brought his gaze up. "Gunnar. Thanks for seeing me."

"So," Gunnar said as he shifted in the desk chair and
leaned his elbows on the rests with his fingers steepled in
front of him. "What sort of shit did you get yourself into
this time that your powerful benefactors can't get you
out of?"

Benefactors? Christian swallowed a snort. Jailers was
more like it. "Believe it or not, Gunnar, I'm not in any shit.
Currently." Gods knew he'd be neck deep in it soon enough,
though. "I don't need help. I have some information that
I'm not sure what to do with. On the advice of a friend, I've
decided not to tell the Sortiari what I know. Instead, I'm
telling you."

Gunnar laughed. The sound was so utterly stereotypical
of the mirthful Viking that Christian rolled his eyes. "You
don't have any friends, Whalen." Also true. "Which
means . . ." Gunnar fixed him with a contemplative stare
that coaxed Christian's wolf closer to the surface of his
mind. "You're working an angle and you think somehow,
I can fit into it."

"Yes and no." There was no point trying to deceive a
werewolf. They could smell even a half-truth from a mile
away.

"Does this *information* somehow compromise me or
any of the members of my pack?"

Gunnar had made his allegiances perfectly clear the
night of Gregor's attempted ambush. He wanted no part
in the berserker's or the Sortiari's business. Again, the faint

scent of vampire hit Christian's nostrils. Maybe Gunnar's allegiances weren't quite as clear as Christian had thought.

"Ian Gregor—"

"Get out." Gunnar cut him off and stood from his chair. "Now. I want nothing to do with that bastard."

"Ian Gregor has taken a mage hostage. One who helped to bind Trenton McAlister's power." The words left Christian's lips in a hurried burst. "He's made a deal with a vampire—I think—and he has a powerful fae—a soul thief, maybe two of them, in the city."

Gunnar froze, his icy blue gaze trained on Christian's face.

"He's going to set this world on fire and watch it burn if he gets his way. We'll all die in the name of his holy vendetta."

"Why not tell McAlister, then? You're one of his after all."

Christian's lip curled. No one outside of the Sortiari understood the roles of those under the leadership's thumb. Christian was hardly "one of them." He was an indentured servant, plain and simple.

"I don't belong to any male. Nor any pack or any faction." He fought to keep his tone level, but his wolf felt nothing but aggression and it bled through in the growl that rose in his throat. Christian kept his ass planted in his seat, gaze cast up at Gunnar, despite the animal part of him wanting to rise up and challenge the Alpha. "No one knows about McAlister's power. Or the soul thieves. One of them is very dangerous and has ties to him. The rumor is that McAlister isn't above killing to keep his secrets in regards to her and his power."

"But you wanted to tell him . . ." Gunnar steered the conversation back to Christian's original point. "Why?"

He let the question hang. It was up to Christian to decide how much he wanted to divulge. He had no interest in becoming a member of Gunnar's—or any other—pack. He just wanted his gods-damned freedom. "I want out," he said. "And I thought what I knew might buy my freedom."

Gunnar settled back down into his chair and Christian let out a slow breath as he fought to calm his agitated wolf. "For what it's worth," Gunnar began, "I agree with your *friend*." Christian's eyes narrowed at the way Gunnar stressed "friend." Asshole. "Tell me everything you know."

It was a start. Whether good or bad was yet to be seen. Christian settled back into his seat and allowed a smile. "Got anything good to drink around here?"

He was going to be here a while. Better make the best of it while he worked to either improve his life or throw it in the shitter. But if he were being honest, he really hoped he wouldn't have to add tonight to his long list of regrets.

CHAPTER
28

"Are you sure you don't want me to stay?"

Sasha practically pushed Lucas out the door. He'd helped her to get Ewan inside and onto her bed. But now that was done, he needed to get the hell *out*. It wasn't that Sasha didn't appreciate his help. She didn't know what she would've done without him tonight. But it was for his own protection that she needed him out of here. Ewan was a feral creature. Wild. He was injured and probably traumatized. When he woke, he'd have the mentality of a cornered animal. He'd go after the first visible threat and that would be Lucas. She could handle Ewan on her own. She'd been doing it for weeks. He didn't scare her, not even a little bit.

"I'm sure. I can handle it from here. Thanks, Lucas." She eased him over the threshold and pushed the door closed. Lucas put his foot in the way to block her and she let out an exasperated sigh. She didn't have time for this overprotective crap. She might've looked harmless, but Sasha was fierce. She didn't need protecting. Not from anyone and especially not Ewan. "I'm serious. I've got this."

His eyes narrowed as he contemplated her. "If you need anything . . ."

"I know." She was grateful she could call Lucas a friend. "You'll be the first person I dial."

"Good." He leaned in and put his lips to Sasha's forehead.

Lucas froze. Sasha sensed a presence at her back and the fine hairs on her arms stood on end. She resisted the urge to groan. Shit. Damn it. *Fuck my life* . . . Of all the shitty timing . . .

"I have *got* to quit getting caught between females and their mates," Lucas murmured against her forehead. A low growl sounded from behind her and Sasha cringed. "I think this is definitely my cue to leave. Call me later."

Sasha's eyes drifted shut. Well, she guessed the question of whether or not Ewan would regain consciousness was answered. The door closed almost soundlessly as she let out a breath and turned to face Ewan. She should have known that not even hellfire could put him down for long.

She opened her eyes. For the first time since she'd met him, she got a glimpse of the creature that other supernatural beings feared. Ewan's lips pulled back in a snarl and black swallowed the whites of his eyes. His ripped and bloodied T-shirt stretched taut across the bulge of his muscles and his nostrils flared with breath.

"Tell me, Sasha. Exactly how many males follow in your wake? I should give up the battle arena completely and devote my time to killing your admirers instead."

Gods, but he was a frightening sight. Angry red welts and large blisters raised his flesh. Dried blood from injuries that had long since healed stained nearly every inch of his clothing that was torn from where daggers no doubt had pierced through cloth and muscle, down to the bone. Sasha cringed. Her body ached with the ghost of pain he'd endured at the hands of those sadistic bastards. If she could, Sasha would kill every last demon on the face of the earth. Her anger, her indignation, her need for vengeance burned through her. If not for Ewan's weakened state, she would've geared up, and gone out to hunt down the creatures that had done this to him.

Ewan looked like the walking dead, and all he was concerned about were the males Sasha kept company with? Good gods.

"I think you should be more concerned with the demons that burned and beat you bloody tonight."

"Who is the male, Sasha?"

Sasha swallowed down an exasperated growl. She'd never known a more stubborn creature than Ewan Brún. "You should be in bed, resting. Not worrying about whoever the hell I choose to be friends with."

A deep groove cut into Ewan's forehead and Sasha could practically feel the heat of his rising temper. She shouldn't have to explain herself to him. About anything. She didn't have to justify who she chose to be friends with, male, female, or anything in between. They weren't a couple. They weren't anything. Ewan had tethered her soul, but for the most part he acted as though he couldn't care less. The bond between them meant nothing to him. So why did he give a single shit who Lucas was?

"Who—is—he?"

Had he not already been beaten half to death, Sasha would've been tempted to do the deed herself. He aggravated her like no other could. Sparked her ire. Ignited her desire. Her heart ached for him, for everything he'd endured, his undoubtedly harsh existence. And on the rare occasion he graced her with a smile, her chest felt full to bursting and she nearly choked on the flood of emotions he invoked in her. She didn't know if she loved Ewan, but right now she definitely didn't like him.

"Lucas is my friend." In truth, she didn't owe him any explanation. But she needed him to calm the hell down and get his ass back to bed so he could start to heal. "He helped me get you back to the apartment tonight."

"He was with you? At the battle arena?" He took several menacing steps toward her and Sasha's heart leapt up into her throat. He'd been unconscious by the time she'd gotten to him, but apparently he'd been awake and aware before the demons dumped him off at the battle arena. "What in the hell were you doing there, Sasha? And what was he doing there with you?"

"I was looking for you." She could hardly tell him the truth. That she'd planned to hunt down the demons that had threatened them and kill every last one.

"And you needed your *friend* to do that?"

He took another step toward her, and another. The living room was tiny, barely ten feet across. The length of his stride closed the distance between them until only a couple of feet separated them. An electric charge sparked the air, turning Sasha's blood to smoke as her heart beat a mad rhythm in her chest. No male had ever excited her the way Ewan did. With nothing more than his proximity, a heated look, he could get to her.

"After our last encounter with the demons, I thought it would be a good idea to bring backup."

"Is that so?" His tone remained dead serious, but the fathomless black began to fade from his eyes to reveal the light golden brown she loved so much. He took another step closer, and Sasha had to tilt her head up to look at him.

"I don't know what you're trying to get me to admit, Ewan." She hated games, and refused to play his. "Instead of worrying about where I was and why, maybe we should be talking about what happened to you tonight."

His jaw squared. "What were you doing at the battle arena tonight, Sasha?"

Bastard. He just had to be stubborn. Had to be argumentative. Had to be suspicious and make trouble where there wasn't any. Sasha reached back and gripped the door handle. She was five seconds from ordering him to get the hell out. She didn't need this crap. Her concern for him had prompted her to go out tonight. To hunt. To do whatever it took to protect him. And instead of letting it go, Ewan insisted on picking a fight where there wasn't one.

"I already told you, and I'm not going to tell you again."

Ewan leaned in close and put his nose just below Sasha's ear. He inhaled deeply and a shiver raced over Sasha's skin. "You smell of him." The words ended on a low, menacing growl. "Go wash it off."

Seriously? Of all the high-handed, alpha-male bullshit. Sasha bucked her chin up a notch. "No." He was being ridiculous and she wasn't about to reinforce his behavior by complying.

"Don't test me, Sasha. Get in the shower. Now."

"Piss off, Ewan." She couldn't believe she'd been so worried about him earlier.

He reached out and grabbed her, incredibly fast for someone who'd nearly been beaten and burned to death earlier in the night. Sasha sucked in a gasp of breath as he hoisted her up and deposited her over his shoulder. He let out a grunt of pain and for a moment, she almost felt sorry for him. But this was self-inflicted. He didn't need to toss her over his shoulder and carry her to the gods-knew-where for whatever foolish reason. And frankly, she was getting tired of him chucking her around like a sack of grain. Ewan deserved what he was getting. Screw him.

"If you're not going to wash that bastard's smell off of you, I'll do it myself."

What in the hell was wrong with him? He'd nearly been killed tonight, was badly burned and blistered, and the most pressing thing on Ewan's mind was how she *smelled*? "Put me down, Ewan." She was getting pretty damned tired of the way he thought he could just haul her around when she didn't do what he wanted, when he wanted her to do it. "Now!"

He strode through the bathroom door and deposited her in the shower. He turned the knob, and Sasha gasped as the icy cold spray hit her. She stood there, stunned, shivering and unable to move. The water began to warm and she watched as Ewan undressed.

"Take your clothes off. If I have to smell him for one more second, I'm going to hunt him down and kill him. Is that what you want?"

As though she had no control over her own motor functions, Sasha's hands began to move and she undressed. She told herself over and again that Ewan didn't scare her. But that wasn't entirely true, was it? Because despite his childish attitude, he excited her. And it was absolutely terrifying.

Sasha was *his*. And any creature on the face of this earth that sought to take her away from him would meet a cruel and violent end. Tonight had seriously fucked him up. He'd always thought no one could be as nasty or enjoy dispensing pain as much as Ian Gregor. He'd been wrong. The demons had beaten him mercilessly. They'd fucked with his mind. Cut him, nearly bled him dry, stabbed and pummeled him. They'd used daggers, clubs, knives, and their own damned fists. They'd burned him with hellfire. Scorched the skin from his bones and waited for him to heal so they could start all over again. And through it all, they promised him that if he didn't play ball, didn't step into the battle arena prepared to lose, that Sasha's torture would be a thousandfold to what he'd experienced tonight.

She will suffer for eternity. He shuddered at the memory of the demon's hot, seething breath in his ear.

He was in pain, angry, worried, frustrated, and pissed the hell off. So yeah, it didn't do much for his temper to come out of that bedroom, worried sick for Sasha, to find another male leaned in toward her, his mouth on her skin. The vampire's scent lingered on Sasha and Ewan wanted it gone. *Now.* He was out of his fucking mind and nothing short of decimating all of his enemies—whether perceived or not—would calm him down. Then again, Sasha's naked body was a damned good substitute for murder.

His entire life had spiraled out of his control. At least here, with her, he could gain a little of that back.

Goose bumps peppered Sasha's skin and her nipples stood out from the gorgeous swells of her breasts. Ewan quickly stripped, grimacing at the shock of pain as his clothes scraped against his still tender and burned flesh. As the water began to warm, the bathroom filled with steam. Even that little bit of warmth was excruciating but he would endure that and more to feel Sasha's naked body pressed against his. He stepped under the spray and his jaw clenched. It hurt like a motherfucker but godsdamn it, he was going to suck it the fuck up and stay right where he was.

Sasha stared up at him. Silent. Her eyes wide and almost fearful. Ewan wished he could be softer. More gentle. Calm and expressive of his feelings. But he was none of those things and never would be. He was a warlord. Hard. Cruel. Demanding. And right now, he demanded nothing less than Sasha's sweet, clean cinnamon scent. Untainted by another male.

"Stay still." Ewan murmured the words next to Sasha's

ear as he stepped between her and the spray of water and reached past her to grab the bar of soap. He lathered the bar between his hands before he began to wash her. He forced his own pain to the back of his mind as he slowly and meticulously ran the bar of soap over his mate's bare skin.

Ewan paused. *Mate*. It was the second time he'd truly thought of Sasha as such. Any mating instincts had been beaten out of the berserkers centuries ago. The loss of their females had irreparably changed them. Or so they'd thought. With every passing day, that instinct not only returned, but grew. Sasha was his. His to care for, protect, love. She'd gotten under his skin, infused herself into his blood. She was ingrained in the very cells that constructed him. Sasha was his mate. And as such, Ewan's life, his very existence, was sworn to her.

"Ewan." His name left her lips on a whisper. Her body relaxed with every touch, and the tension that had pulled her muscles taut melted away. Her lips parted invitingly and Ewan abandoned the task at hand to put his mouth to hers. The kiss was feather light. A glancing of his lips to hers and it awakened his desire.

"Sasha." He'd never been an articulate male. He was a warrior, not a poet. Didn't share his feelings. He desperately wanted to soften his sharp edges. For her. He wanted her to never have reason to wander away from him. He wanted Sasha to have everything she deserved and more. He had nothing to give her. No possessions. No status. All he could offer was his words. "I wish I could make you understand my nature." He continued to wash her, gentle passes of his hands over her skin, as he spoke low next to her ear. "The only thing that terrifies me more than the scent of your fear, is knowing I'm the one who caused it."

Another twinge of pain fired his nerve endings and Ewan sucked in a sharp breath. Sasha pulled away to look at him, her brow furrowed. "Gods, Ewan." She brought her hands up as though she would touch him but thought better of it. "Hot water on burns? This has to be excruciating."

Sasha turned, quickly switching their positions so the water hit her back. Cool air kissed his naked flesh and he let out a sigh of relief. His gaze wandered over Sasha's glorious body and he watched, transfixed, as the sudsy water sluiced from her shoulders to her feet. He reached out and cupped the weight of one perfect breast in his palm. Sasha's eyes became hooded as he brushed his thumb over her stiff nipple. He was drawn to her like a moth to flame. And as evidenced by his current state, he was willing to endure the burn. Anything for her.

Sasha brought her wrist to her mouth and bit down. The sound of her skin giving way beneath her fangs caused Ewan's gut to clench. Crimson ribbons of blood trickled down her forearm as she raised her wrist to his mouth. "Drink."

Drink? Was she seriously suggesting what he thought she was? Gregor would have both their heads if he knew what she suggested. And yet, Ewan was intrigued.

"It'll help. I think. Your blood is a healing elixir to me, why shouldn't mine be one for you?"

He'd never considered it. Hell, it had never even crossed his mind. He worried, not over the effect it would have on him, but rather that Gregor would smell it on him. He couldn't afford to do anything that would further put Sasha in the path of danger. "I shouldn't." But gods, how he wanted to. Some wanton part of him needed to know her taste. Wanted to experience the thing she needed to survive.

"What's the matter?" A corner of Sasha's mouth curved into an enticing smile. "Afraid?"

He couldn't help but smile. He fucking loved her fire.

Without another thought to the consequences, Ewan snatched her wrist in his grip and brought it to his lips. He kept his gaze locked on hers as he opened his mouth and sealed it over the punctures. Sasha's head rolled back on her shoulders as she let out an indulgent moan. Ewan had never realized drinking her blood could be as pleasurable for her as drinking from another. Her blood flowed over his tongue, not quite sweet but not as tannic as he expected. He increased the suction and the thick warmth of her blood coated his tongue. Ewan swallowed as his grip on her wrist tightened. He swayed on his feet, lightheaded, as a pleasant buzz settled over his brain. He felt like laughing. Shouting his elation to the sky. He was fucking drunk. Drunk on Sasha. Drunk on the blood she offered him and the euphoric rush it gave him.

The pain that wracked his body, his many injuries, and every worry that plagued him disappeared. His mouth left her wrist as he pulled her tight against his body. His free hand went to the back of her head, which he urged against his throat. He didn't need words to convey what he wanted. Her fangs struck out and pierced his flesh and Ewan's cock throbbed in time with his racing heartbeat. Fire ignited in his veins, along his nerve endings, bathing him in intense pleasure. With every powerful pull of her mouth he lost himself further. To her. To the moment. To the sensations that crashed over him. He never wanted it to end.

"I need to fuck you, Sasha. Now."

He couldn't wait another gods-damn second. If he didn't take her, didn't feel her warm, slick heat encase his cock, he'd go out of his mind. He reached for her ass, prepared to hoist her up against the shower wall and fuck her soundly. Sasha reached up between them and put a staying hand on his chest, so gentle as she continued to feed from his vein. Ewan stilled. His chest heaved with breath and he trembled with need. But Sasha wanted him to wait. And he'd wait for as damned long as she wanted him to.

She owned him. Body. Mind. Soul. And even . . . his heart. Ewan was in love with Sasha, and the realization shook him to his core.

CHAPTER
29

Ewan had fed from Sasha's vein. It didn't matter that it wasn't necessary for his survival, it had solidified the bond between them. Secured their tether and made it unbreakable. She'd felt the change almost in an instant. Any hope she'd had at keeping Ewan at a distance was obliterated. The tether was absolute. Sasha was a fool to have ever thought she could simply put her emotions on a shelf and disregard him.

He wanted her. Now. She sensed his urgency without the words to back it up and yet she dared to place a staying hand on his chest. Since the night they'd met, they'd been slaves to their urgent need for one another. Each and every time, Sasha had given herself to him with abandon. For once, she wanted to take things slowly. She wanted to be in control. And she wanted to take her time in pleasuring him.

Sasha pulled away to inspect Ewan's many burns. Remnants of fear trickled into her bloodstream at the realization that such a seemingly indestructible creature could sustain such damage. The blisters had already begun to heal, and the angry welts that marred his skin were no longer red and were finally fading. Sasha didn't know whether or not her blood contributed to it. She was simply glad to see an improvement.

He might've been healing, but she didn't dare touch him. She didn't want to do anything to undermine the progress he'd already made and neither did she want to cause him pain. Sasha eased him to the rear of the shower where the spray barely touched them. Their eyes met for a quick moment before she lowered herself to her knees in front of him. Ewan was built like a god, and Sasha was eager to worship him.

She took the rigid length of his cock in her hand and stroked from the swollen tip to the base. Ewan sucked in a breath and she looked up at him from lowered lashes to find his golden brown gaze alight with an intense fire that nearly stole her breath. She leaned in, and her tongue touched all of the places her hand had just been as she licked from the base all the way up to the tip.

"Gods, Sasha. That feels so good."

The deep gravel of Ewan's voice spurred her on. She came up higher on her knees, closed her mouth over his erection, and sucked deeply. Ewan's hips bucked and he let out a groan. Sasha savored the taste of him as she pulled back before sliding her mouth down his length once again. She allowed the points of her fangs to lightly scrape along his sensitive flesh and he shuddered. A satisfied smile curved her lips. Pleasuring Ewan was a high unlike any other. A rush that had no equal. A deep, throbbing ache settled in her pussy and she didn't need to reach between her legs to know she was slick and wet with desire. Simply being in Ewan's orbit was enough to turn her on. He didn't have to do a single thing, didn't need to speak a single word to ignite her passion.

She settled into an easy rhythm, enjoying the slide of

him against her lips. She placed a tentative hand on one thigh, careful to keep her touch light. The muscles bunched beneath her palm, sculpted marble. With her other hand, she gripped the base of his cock and gently squeezed as she swirled her tongue over the satin smooth crown.

"Fuuuuck." The word was a drawn out moan that shot straight between Sasha's legs. "Suck me deep, love. Gods, do it now."

Love. Emotion bloomed in her chest. Ewan's words were half command and half desperate plea. Sasha was helpless to do anything but comply. His fingers threaded through the wet tendrils of her hair as he urged her where he needed her to go. He was careful not to exert too much pressure. Not to thrust too deep. It was perfect. He was perfect.

He belonged to her and no one else.

Sasha would make sure he never had reason to think of another female ever again. She wanted him to crave her touch as she did his. Wanted to twine herself into his soul the way his had wound with hers. The flood of emotions she'd held back for so long crashed over her. Everyone deserved to be wanted. Needed. She'd gone too long being someone's second choice. Hell, really not even a choice at all. She wanted to be someone's first choice. Someone's only choice. She wanted to be Ewan's choice.

Sasha's fang nicked the flesh near the hood of Ewan's cock. He gripped Sasha's hair tighter and a low growl gathered in his chest as he thrust deep. The natural salty taste of him mingled with the sweetness of his blood as Sasha's mouth was flooded with jets of warmth. She bit down again, just enough to open another tiny puncture and Ewan's hips bucked wildly as she greedily sucked him.

Ewan's ragged breaths quieted until the only sound was that of the water splashing on the fiberglass floor of the shower. He reached down and pulled Sasha to her feet, putting her back to the wall as he kissed her deeply.

"Gods, you drive me crazy." Ewan broke their kiss and put his mouth to the sensitive skin just below her ear. His teeth grazed the skin there and Sasha drew in a breath. He reached between her thighs and lightly stroked her pussy. She shuddered against him and her hands went up to his shoulders as she steadied her careening world. "I need to be inside of you, Sasha. Let me fuck you."

Again, the plea in his tone nearly pushed her over the edge. "Yes." She could barely push the word past her lips she was so out of her mind with desire. "I need you, Ewan. Right now."

He reached down to cup her ass and hoisted her in his arms. Her legs wound around his waist as he pressed her against the shower wall. The head of his cock probed at her opening and Sasha let out a quiet moan at the shock of delicious heat. He pushed into her, agonizingly slow, and she pulled him closer, urging him to take her hard and deep.

She couldn't wait another damned second to have him.

A sense of intense relief flooded over Sasha as he buried himself to the thick base. The feeling of fullness, of finally being complete shook her as it did every time they were together and she let out a low breath that ended on an audible sigh.

"Just like that." She didn't want slow and easy. She wanted Ewan in all of his glorious intensity. "Don't stop until I come."

He buried his face in the crook of her neck and fucked her exactly how she wanted it. How she *needed* it. Ewan Brún was incomparable.

Pressure built within Sasha's body. A coming storm ready to unleash its fury. The world expanded around her until she felt as though she were nothing more than a speck of dust floating in a vast and endless universe. She dug her heels into Ewan's ass, desperate for release. He sensed her need and obeyed the cue, thrusting hard and deep, his pace unrelenting.

"Bite me, Sasha. Gods, do it now."

It didn't matter how many times he asked her to do it, nothing compared to the rush of adrenaline that surged through her when he demanded her bite. Her mouth came down over the swell of muscle near his neck and the skin popped beneath the pressure of her fangs. His blood, rich and sweet flowed over her tongue as the orgasm swept her up and away from herself. Deep pulses of sensation rippled from her core, outward to her limbs and heat infused her veins as she continued to feed from Ewan.

His thrusts became harder. Faster. Wild and disjointed. Sasha disengaged her fangs and closed the wounds, pulling away so she could see that moment of rapture on Ewan's face. Sasha rested her head against the shower wall as she took in every detail of his harsh, but striking face. His brows were drawn, jaw clenched. The deep, expressive brown of his eyes darkened slightly with his passion and Sasha stared in awe of his dark beauty. Her hand came to rest on his cheek, rough with russet stubble. He was the most breathtaking creature she'd ever beheld and somehow, Fate had deemed her worthy of him.

"Come, Ewan." Sasha's gaze locked with his "I want to feel it. All of that heat. I need it."

Gods, how she needed it. How she needed *him*. Ewan was her one and only weakness and she knew without a doubt their enemies would use that against them.

Sasha took his breath away. Cheeks flushed, lips swollen and parted, the tiny points of her fangs barely visible. Her molten gaze trained on his, so full of heat, intensified his pleasure. Lent an intimacy to the moment that damn near shook him to his foundation. He'd never felt as raw and vulnerable as he did with Sasha. Exposed. His soul, naked. And whereas that should've prompted him to have his guard up, it had the opposite effect. He lowered all of his walls for her. Anything for her.

She wanted him. Wanted to own this moment with him. Wanted to own his orgasm. She had all of that and more. Fuck, she'd owned him from that very first night when she'd let him bend her over the bathroom counter with hardly a single word spoken between them.

The orgasm exploded through him. Pulse after powerful pulse that made his thighs quake and caused every muscle in his body to go rigid. Sasha's expression softened as her lids drooped almost imperceptibly. Her jaw went slack, parting her lips invitingly. Ewan couldn't resist their soft lusciousness and leaned in to kiss her as he came down from the high. "Sasha." He spoke her name with the sanctity of a prayer against her lips. "Sasha." Another kiss, his offering to the goddess in his arms. "Sasha." He deepened the kiss, parting her lips to allow his tongue to slip between them. There were so many things he wanted to say to her. So many confessions sat at the tip of his tongue. But he was a gods-damned coward. Unworthy of all of this perfection in his arms. And so, he remained silent and hoped she would understand some measure of what he felt for her in the gentle, yet insistent kisses he rained down on her.

Ewan wasn't a communicator. He didn't share. He took his feelings and buried that shit deep. He was a fighter. A warrior. A killer. Sasha deserved so much better than him.

He continued to kiss her until the water ran cold. Sasha shivered, bringing Ewan back to reality. He reached to his left and turned the knob to cut off the spray before lifting Sasha to set her on her feet. The moment her body left his a physical ache settled in the pit of Ewan's chest. The harsh

reality of the past twenty-four hours settled over him. He
was a berserker, in love with a vampire whose life was
threatened by a gang of angry demons, not to mention the
ruthless male he answered to. And Ewan would do anything to protect her.

He'd gladly die for her.

He hadn't meant for things to turn so gods-damned
somber. He took his worries, his concerns and insecurities, and shoved them to the farthest recesses of his mind.
Stepped out of the shower and grabbed a towel from under
the sink. He went back to Sasha and gathered the wet tendrils of her hair into the towel, drying it before wrapping
her body in the terrycloth.

"You're cold." The gruffness of his own voice surprised
him. He cleared his throat and tried again. "Let me take
you to bed."

"Mmmmm." The smooth timbre of her voice was enough
to warm him through the coldest of winters. "That sounds
like a good idea." The dreamy quality left her expression
and she fixed him with a serious stare. "I'm not that cold.
But you're not completely healed. We need to take care
of you first."

He didn't deserve her selflessness. Her kindness and
concern. Didn't deserve any gods-damned part of her. His
wounds seemed inconsequential in the aftermath of their
passion. All Ewan wanted to do was get her into bed and
tuck her naked body against his.

"I'm fine." He brushed her worry aside. His skin could've
been hanging from his bones and he wouldn't have noticed in the presence of Sasha's raw beauty.

"You're not fine."

"I will be. Your blood helped." He still couldn't believe
it. His brain continued to buzz from the rush. The unequiv-
ocal high. He'd been energized, revitalized, and the bone-

deep pain that had raced along his nerve endings dulled. "Right now, let me take care of you."

Sasha unwound the towel from her body. She draped it over Ewan's head and gently dried his hair. "I'm not the only one who's cold and dripping wet."

He let her towel him dry from head to toe. No one had ever taken such care of him and he felt awkward and out of place. In truth, he didn't know how to respond to kindness. "You don't have to do that."

"I know." Sasha's voice was soft, almost a whisper. "I want to."

Ewan scooped Sasha up in his arms. This simple, quiet moment between them threatened to lay him low. He needed to act, to do something to break the spell before he lost himself even more to her. He crossed to the bedroom and pulled down the covers before depositing her on the mattress and sliding in beside her. Sunrise was still a few hours off, but he needed these quiet moments with her before the sun came to steal her from him.

"Talk to me." Sasha fitted her body to Ewan's, putting her back against his chest. He wrapped his arms around her and held her as he put his mouth close to her ear.

"About what?"

"Anything." Her voice took on a dreamlike quality and Ewan wanted to do something to keep her awake. He wasn't ready for her to fall into that deathlike sleep caused by the fucking sunrise. "I like the sound of your voice."

His gut clenched and his chest puffed with the compliment. He wanted to please her. Bend over backward, do whatever the hell she asked. Anything to make her happy.

"I'd never met a vampire before . . . the wars." Berserkers never referred to their attempted eradication of vampire kind as a war. Gregor called it a "cleansing." They were ridding the world of something vile and pestilent. He didn't want Sasha to know that ugliness, though. And so, he referred to it as she had, by calling it "war," even though it was nothing more than prejudice-driven genocide. "We stayed close to the highlands, kept to ourselves. It wasn't until Gregor began dealings with a vampire lord and traveled across the sea to Ireland, that we found the trouble we'd be trying to avoid."

He didn't know why he chose this story out of all the others he could have told. Maybe he was trying to justify himself to her. The lives he'd taken. His part in her own horrific history. Sasha covered his hand with hers and squeezed. The reassurance was all he needed to continue.

"Gregor only took a few warlords with him whenever they ventured over the water to meet with the vampire. To this day, I don't know what it was he did for the vampire or vice-versa. Anyone who might have known is dead. All I know is that they quarreled and the lord accused Gregor of betraying him. The vampire was infamous for his cruelty, was thought to be mad, and he took Gregor and those with him as captives. He held a trial of sorts and pronounced judgment."

Sasha remained quiet, only the sound of her breaths reached Ewan's ears. She snuggled up closer to him and a tremor shook her. She reached back and cupped the back of his neck and Ewan couldn't help but to place a kiss on the fragrant skin beneath her ear.

"The vampire lord, Aodhan Reámon, played judge, but he left the job of sentencing punishment to his daughter. A young dhampir, not more than seven or eight years old. A child. He wanted to teach her a lesson in how not to forgive your enemies. He let the choice fall on her: punish the berserkers by killing all of their young, or all of their females. He explained to his daughter that without our young, it would be centuries before our numbers replenished. But without our females, we could no longer propagate at all. You were only as strong as your enemies were weak, he'd reasoned with her. And he asked her, 'Which sentence would make their coven—their kind—stronger?' "

Sasha drew in a sharp breath and held it in her lungs. Ewan wondered how many among those still living knew how all of this had started. He'd been there from the beginning and even his knowledge of the events as Gregor told them was vague at best.

"Is this true?" Sasha whispered.

"It's the truth as I know it." It was the best he could offer her. "It's the truth as Gregor told it to us. The Sortiari promised Gregor retribution. Vengeance for what we'd lost and would never get back. They promised us justice, but what they made us were slaves.

"We killed for them. Fought their wars that went beyond vampire-kind. We intimidated anyone who dared to stand against them. We became the weapon they wielded. And never once, in all of those hundreds of years, did they offer us freedom."

Sasha turned in his embrace to face him. "Ewan." Her voice bore so much sadness and tender emotion that it damned near gutted him. Her wide eyes searched his face. "Ewan, I'm so sorry."

Sorry. He'd killed her kind. Ran stakes through the hearts of countless vampires in the name of a holy war he'd known virtually nothing about. He'd done it without apology or remorse and she was sorry? Gods. She was incomparable. A shining star in the endless dark of his universe. The only bright point in an existence so steeped in bleak bullshit that he'd gladly stepped into the battle arenas again and again, not caring if he lived or died. Not caring about a gods-damned thing.

Sasha Ivanov had made him care about something. *Her.* He was lost to her and there was no going back.

CHAPTER
30

Sasha stared at Ewan. It seemed that since the day they'd met, he'd struck her speechless time and again. This was something different, though. It wasn't his sinful good looks, or smoldering gaze. It wasn't his harsh, demanding nature. Not his power and darkness or his masculine charisma. No, it was the sorrow in his tone that struck her this time. The story he'd told her that was different than the story she knew. The story that tied them together. That tied vampires and berserkers together as sure and tight as the tether that bound them now.

Her heart broke for him. For what he'd endured and what he'd been required to do. He'd agreed to kill to avenge those he'd lost. How could she blame him for that? Just tonight, she'd vowed to kill every demon that walked the earth in retaliation for what they'd done to him. And in return for his loyalty to his leader, his brethren, and the memories of those lost, he'd been enslaved and required for centuries to kill beyond the wrongs done to him.

"Don't, Sasha." His voice broke and the sound sliced

through her like a blade. "I don't deserve any gentle words from you."

How could he possibly think that?

"You think you're the only one with blood on his hands?" Sasha braced herself on an elbow so she could look into his face. "I've killed."

"You defended yourself." Ewan's gruff voice vibrated through her. "There's a difference."

He could try to paint himself the villain all he wanted, it wouldn't change her opinion of him. Sasha let out a rueful bark of laughter. "I know you don't truly believe that. In times of war, no one is innocent."

"You call it a war." Ewan's gaze darkened. He reached up and cupped Sasha's cheek. "It was anything but a war."

Sasha gave him a soft smile. "If what you say is true, then wasn't it a vampire who struck the first blow? Wasn't it a vampire who is guilty of being the aggressor? Wasn't it Gregor who was provoked?" If Saeed or any other of her kind heard her words, she'd be considered a traitor. But weren't there two sides to every story? Didn't Ewan deserve the benefit of the doubt?

"There are only two souls left alive who know the entire truth." Dark clouds gathered in Ewan's eyes and in his ominous tone. "Ian Gregor and the dhampir who pronounced the death sentence."

Sasha sat up a little straighter. "She's alive?" If what Ewan said was true, then somewhere within the thirteen covens, hid the now grown female who'd started them all down this dark path.

"Gregor believes she is." Ewan fiddled with her hair, suddenly lost in thought. "He searches for her, night after night. All of his machinations intended to lead him to her so he can capture her and make her suffer for her sins."

Talk about a vendetta.

"And by our very existence, we are a part of that

endeavor. He won't stop." Ewan sat up to drive his point home and gripped Sasha by the shoulders. "He won't give this up until every last one of you is dead."

Why did it have to be that way at all? Sasha had been alive to witness the carnage, the hate, the indiscriminate killing. She'd known fear and panic. But why couldn't the past be left in the past where it belonged? Why did Gregor have to hold on so tightly to his hatred?

Because this wasn't something passed down through generations. Supernatural creatures didn't let go of the past because it was always with them. It molded and shaped them. Followed them through centuries of existence. They weren't simply stories of hardship passed down through generations. Wounds were as fresh now as they were when first made. Long-lived creatures had the memories to match their physical endurance. Gregor would never forget. He would never forgive. Ewan was right. He wouldn't stop until he had his vengeance.

"Where does this leave us?" Sasha had refused to believe there was ever an "us" to consider. She'd thought she could exist apart from the tether. Apart from Ewan. She'd been stupid to think she could keep herself away from him. There was no way they would ever escape their pasts, who they were, what they were, and how they fit into the grand scheme of that sadistic bitch, Fate's plans.

Ewan leaned in and kissed her. Slowly. His full lips moved over hers and Sasha sighed into his mouth. "Gregor will never lay so much as a finger on you, Sasha," Ewan murmured against her mouth. "I promise you that."

His words were a fist that squeezed her heart. She didn't want to love him. Didn't want to open herself up to the possibility of being hurt again. But gods, how could she not love him? How could she not lose herself completely to this magnificent male who vowed to defy his family, his history, the very events that made him what he was, in order to keep her safe?

"Don't make promises you can't keep." Sasha reached up to stroke her fingertips along the stubble that edged his jaw. Though hadn't she tried to do the same for him tonight? She'd hunted the demons that harangued him, determined to end their miserable lives.

His tongue flicked out to trace the seam of her lips. "Believe me. It's the only promise I would never dare to break."

For a moment, Sasha allowed herself to become lost. To the moment. To him. To the sensation of their mouths meeting, their tongues sliding against one another. She lost herself to his scent. His taste. The strength of his embrace as he crushed her body against his. It was so easy to let the world and all of their problems fade into the background. So easy to let her world revolve around only him. Her arms wound around his neck and they collapsed back to the mattress. Sasha's heart pounded. Her clit throbbed in time with her pulse and her thighs grew slick with renewed desire. She wrapped one leg around him and thrust her hips, letting out a low moan as the length of his erection slid between her swollen lips.

Ewan flipped her onto her back and spread her legs wide as he thrust home with a groan. Sasha gasped at the delicious intrusion, the intensity of being filled as his cock slid against her inner walls. She couldn't form a coherent thought to save her life. There was so much between them that hadn't been shared. So much they still needed to discuss. But for the life of her, Sasha could do nothing but *feel*.

"You are mine." Ewan's voice was a territorial growl in her ear. He thrust hard and deep to drive his point home. "Say it."

"I'm yours," Sasha replied on a breath. How could she possibly belong to anyone else? He'd owned her from that very first glance. "And you are mine." She needed him to understand she wasn't willing to share any more than he was. Ewan had tethered her soul. He was her mate. The bond was absolute and nothing but death could sever it. "Say it."

"Yours," Ewan agreed. "Above family. Above allegiances. Above all else."

Emotion clogged Sasha's throat as her back arched up from the mattress. His words were sacrosanct and she knew making such promises to each other would only hasten them to their inevitable ruin.

He fucked her with all of the intensity of his words. Every thrust sending her closer to the edge of her restraint. No other male had ever affected her in the way that Ewan did. With nothing more than a look, the deep tenor of his voice, a simple touch, he awakened her passion. Her body coiled tight moments before the orgasm exploded through her. Her nails dug into his shoulders as she threw her head back and cried out, each wracking sob matching the waves of sensation that rolled over her.

"That's it, love." Sasha shuddered as Ewan's hot breath brushed her ear. "Give yourself over to it. Let it take you."

"Come with me." Sasha managed to form the words through the blinding pleasure. "Please."

Ewan drove into her harder, faster, deeper. His jaw squared and the bright silvery gray of the oncoming dawn lent a strange otherworldly sheen to his golden eyes. The change was almost indiscernible but it was there. Like oil over water. Or the glow of the northern lights. His brow furrowed as though he'd come to some sort of realization and then he threw his head back and let out a roar.

"Sasha!"

The base of his cock pulsed against her pussy and Sasha

was flooded with warmth. Her breath raced. Her heart pounded. Every inch of her trembled against him and she kept her grip on his shoulders as though he were the only thing anchoring her to earth.

Ewan pulled out slowly to the tip and slid back in just as agonizingly slow. Sasha swallowed a groan as he continued with his easy thrusts to bring himself down from the high. He rested the bulk of his weight on an elbow as he settled against her. The only sound in the room was that of their mingled breaths that became one. Exhaustion tugged at Sasha's eyes, weighed down her limbs, and she cursed the coming sun. Hated that she had no choice but to succumb to sleep. Hated that it would separate her from Ewan until it retreated beneath the horizon once more.

She never wanted anything to come between them ever again.

Ewan had never felt so at peace. He listened to the sound of Sasha's breaths and let it ground him. Focused on the way she felt beneath him. Soft. Warm. Yielding. He'd never known comfort like this could exist. And he'd found it in the arms of a sworn enemy.

So many years lost. So much energy wasted on unfounded hatred. On helping to further a cause he knew so little about. Believing a truth simply because he'd been told to do so. For months, he'd been trying to find a way out. Looking for an escape. For forgiveness. For absolution for so many fucking sins he'd lost count. When all along, his salvation had been right under his nose.

Sasha was his freedom. His absolution. His *everything*.

The gray dawn lightened in the confines of the bedroom, causing Ewan's stomach to clench. He hated the sunrise like he never had before. Hated the way it took Sasha from him, the hours always more than he thought he could endure. He placed featherlight kisses to her forehead, her temple, across her cheek to her jaw. The corner of her mouth. And her luscious lips, so soft and pliant.

A tome of words sat at the tip of Ewan's tongue. He wanted to tell her she was beautiful. Fierce. Loyal and smart. Strong and full of fire. He wanted to tell her that he loved her. Cherished her. Would never let anything happen to her. Would never let anyone come between them. So many gods-damned words. And he was too much of a fucking coward to say a single one.

The muffled sound of his cell brought Ewan out of his reverie. He knew the ringtone and didn't move an inch, despite what ignoring Gregor would mean. Sasha lifted her head and he rolled to his side, settling Sasha in against him. The ringing stopped and immediately started up again. Ewan swore it sounded angrier. Louder than it had just a moment ago.

"I think someone's trying to get ahold of you." Already Sasha's voice was drowsy with sleep. Ewan held his breath and waited for the ringing to stop, only to be assaulted by the offending sound again. Sasha let out a gentle laugh. "I think someone's *really* trying to get ahold of you."

"It's Gregor." There was no point in lying and besides, he didn't want to. "No doubt summoning me to perform some ridiculous task."

Sasha stroked a hand from his shoulder to his wrist and chills danced along Ewan's skin. "You should go," she said through a yawn. "He'll be angry if you don't."

No doubt about that. And Ewan would surely receive the beating to go along with their so-called leader's unreasonable impatience. "He'll be angry no matter what I do," Ewan replied. "The sun's about to rise. I'm not going *anywhere.*"

"That's why you should go." She couldn't put enough force behind the words for anything more than a whisper.

"I'm just going to be here completely zonked out until sunset. You'll be so bored. There's no reason for you to stay."

Zonked out. Ewan gave a humorless chuckle. Dead to the world was more like it. Defenseless. Helpless. At the mercy of anyone or anything that sought to do her harm. And in the past several weeks, the list of those who wanted to hurt her had grown. "That's exactly why I'm staying. You need someone to look after you while you're helpless and at the sun's mercy. To protect you until the sun sets."

She peppered his chest with light kisses that made his heart pound and his breath hitch. "I'm not so helpless anymore. My mate's blood makes me strong. You don't have to worry about me."

The affection in her words stabbed through him. *Mate.* How Ewan loved the way that word sounded coming from her sweet lips. "If you think I would ever leave you unprotected, whether you've had my blood or not, you are in for quite the surprise."

"So you agree?" Her tone became playful. "You're my mate."

"Aye, love." It was the easiest thing Ewan had ever had to agree to. "I am your mate. And you are mine."

"Mmmm. Yes." Sasha stifled another yawn. "I am. Yours. You're stuck with me, forever."

Forever. The word ended on a sigh as Sasha's breathing became deep and even. The windows were blacked out, but he didn't need to see beyond the heavy blankets covering them to know the sun had crested the horizon. His cell began to ring again, insistent in its annoying tune. He eased Sasha from under his arm and left her to rest as he retrieved his phone from the pocket of his discarded jeans.

"Yeah." It was the most cordial greeting he could muster.

"Where the fuck are you and why the fuck haven't you been answering your phone?"

Ewan swallowed the "fuck you" response he wanted to give Gregor and instead took a deep cleansing breath. It would do him no good to pick a fight. At least, not yet. "Wasn't safe to talk. What's up?"

"I don't care if Mikhail Aristov himself had a blade buried halfway through your throat," Gregor growled through the receiver. "When I call, you *answer.*"

Asshole. Ewan stretched his neck from side to side to release some of the tension that pulled his muscles taut. "Roger that." The last thing he needed was for Gregor to send out a search party to look for him. He needed to placate the son of a bitch and keep him calm. "I was with Sasha." It was important for Gregor to believe Ewan's loyalty still rested with him. "She trusts me. I'm sure it won't be long before I know the location of every coven in the city." The fact of the matter was, Ewan had no intention of giving Gregor a scrap of information on any of the covens. The warlord could beat him to a bloody fucking pulp and he wouldn't get shit out of Ewan. He'd made his choices and soon enough, he'd face the consequences for those choices.

"Get back to the building. I had an interesting chat with Andrew just now. I thought I told you to stay out of that gods-damned fighting arena."

Fuck. If Drew had talked, it was because Gregor had beaten it out of him. A surge of anger welled up inside of Ewan, so intense it tightened his skin over his frame. He'd tear Gregor's head from his shoulders if Drew was in anything less than the condition Ewan had last seen him in. "I haven't been fighting. Not for several days." At least that much was true. He'd been too damn busy jumping through hoops for Gregor and dealing with a gang of bloodthirsty demons for anything else.

"Get back here," Gregor snapped. "You've got an hour."

The line went dead and Ewan squeezed his phone so tight the screen cracked. *Fucking hell.* That's all he needed, was to spend what little money he had squirreled away on a new gods-damned phone. He glanced over the bed, at Sasha's still body, and cursed under his breath. If he didn't do as Gregor asked, Drew would pay the price. He couldn't let that happen, no matter how much he wanted to stay here with her.

Ewan quickly dressed. His temper mounted with each passing second until the battle rage collected and pooled in his gut, churning like lava about to unleash its destruction. Indecision warred within him, his desire to protect the two most important individuals in his life playing tug-of-war with his mind and heart. Drew was family, but Sasha was so much more. She was his mate. His life. If he failed either one of them, he'd never rebound from the loss.

"Fuck."

Ewan punched at the air and found it incredibly unsatisfying. He wanted to feel bones crunch beneath his fist, wanted to do the maximum damage. He'd die before he ever got the upper hand on Ian Gregor. Which was probably why the battle arenas had been so enticing. The perfect place to take out centuries' worth of frustration.

He'd run out of time and choices. No one knew about this apartment, except for the vampire, Lucas. Sasha would be relatively safe here. Drew on the other hand, had nowhere to hide. He needed to face the music. Face Gregor. And pray to whatever gods might listen that he'd come out of all of this relatively unscathed.

Ewan finished dressing and crossed to the bed where Sasha slept, her back toward him. He placed a kiss to the top of her head and let his fingers slip through the silky strands of her hair. "Sasha, I have to go. But I'll be back as soon as I can." Gods, he hoped that through her deathlike sleep, she'd heard him. If not, Gregor wouldn't be the only one he needed to explain himself to.

And somehow, he sensed Sasha would be even less forgiving than the infamous warlord.

CHAPTER
31

A silent tear rolled down Sasha's cheek as she came fully awake. Ewan's words as he spoke on the phone were the last thing she'd heard before succumbing fully to sleep. They'd stayed with her through the seemingly endless, dark hours of sunlight that held her in their grip, tortured by the realization that everything she'd thought to be true was a lie. The heartfelt words spoken in the quiet dark. Every gentle touch. His proclamation that she belonged to him. All lies. All constructed to gain her trust so he could help to bring Ian Gregor's twisted plans to fruition.

Some small part of her didn't want to believe it. Couldn't. Not after everything that had happened between them. The things they'd experienced together, the words they'd shared. Tender touches and gentle kisses . . . Sasha's breath hitched on a sob. Ewan's betrayal sliced through her and left a raw gaping wound she feared would never heal. She'd turned her back on her coven, her family, for him. Gods, how could she have been so stupid?

Sasha swiped at the rivulets of salty tears and steeled

herself against the pain. She pushed herself up from the bed, still a little weak and groggy, but determined to get out of here as soon as freaking possible. She needed to warn Saeed, to warn Mikhail and the other covens. She could at least be thankful Ewan hadn't had the opportunity to ask her about the other covens. Otherwise, they'd be in a hell of a lot more trouble than they were now. Vigilance was important, but at least they wouldn't have to pull up camp and move. It could've been so much worse.

She threw her clothes on, refusing to look back at the bed she and Ewan had shared so many times over the past several weeks. She was never coming back to this place. Ever. She'd made so many bad decisions since being turned. She'd been wild, out of control, irresponsible, and immature. And that was saying a lot considering the centuries she had under her belt. It was time to return to her life. The way it had been. Love simply wasn't in the cards for her. It's not like she needed it to live. To thrive.

Snap out of it, Sasha. Just get your ass home. To her *real* home. Not the illusion of home she'd created here. With him.

Fuck Ewan Brún.

Sasha gathered the few meager possessions she had and headed out the door. Her steps were quick and light as she raced down the two flights of stairs, more than ready to catch an Uber and get the hell out of here. She hit the bottom step and white hot pain exploded in the back of her skull. She fell forward and hit the sidewalk face first with nothing to break her fall. Sticky wet warmth trickled down her forehead as her surroundings blurred in and out of focus. Her skull had to have been nearly cracked in two to knock her unconscious. And as darkness settled in to take her, her last unbidden thought was of Ewan's beautiful golden eyes. Gods-damn him.

Sasha's head pounded like someone had repeatedly taken a sledgehammer to it, which probably wasn't far from the truth. She couldn't have been unconscious for too long, her supernatural healing would've made sure of it. She tried to lift her head but she was bound, blindfolded, and secured to the floor by what she assumed was silver netting by the way it pricked and burned her skin. The cold of the concrete beneath her seeped through her clothes, into her bones and she couldn't help but wonder which of her many enemies had done this to her?

"The bitch is moving."

The scent of sulfur reached her nostrils, and Sasha stifled a gag. She supposed she should be grateful the berserkers hadn't gotten to her first. At least as the demons' captive, she was practically guaranteed to only be tortured. Whereas the berserkers would've tortured and then killed her. Yet one more shit storm she'd been dragged into, thanks to Ewan.

Her captors had taken precautions this time around, preventing her the opportunity to fight back. Her wrists and ankles were bound with the same silver cords to keep her from moving too much, while the netting held her in place so tightly she couldn't even move her head from side to side.

"She can't be moving that much," another voice chortled. "You damn near knocked her head off her shoulders when you took her down. Even a vampire needs a bit of time to recover from a wound like that. Besides, she's going nowhere as long as that webbing is on top of her."

Don't be so sure, assholes. Sasha was nothing if not resourceful. And Saeed hadn't put her in charge of his security because she was a gentle little kitten. Sasha was smart. Strong. Fierce. These stupid greedy demons would regret the day they took her captive. Because she was going to kill every last one of them.

As soon as she got herself free.

"What about the berserker? Doesn't do any good to have her without him."

Sasha stilled at the mention of Ewan. She didn't want to care. She should forget about him and leave him to his fate. He'd asked for it after all. But they were sort of in this together. Like it or not, as far as the demons were concerned they were a package deal.

"We'll have him." Sasha wanted to laugh at their confidence. "Once we separate him from Gregor."

Sasha's blood heated at the mention of the warlord's name. She forced her breathing to slow and her muscles to relax. Tension only pressed her tighter against the silver cords that bit into her skin. Still better than hellfire any day of the week.

"That male is as evil as they come," one of the demons replied. "And we know evil, am I right?"

They had a good laugh at that and Sasha gritted her teeth to the point that her fangs nicked her bottom lip. She licked the blood away, wishing she had a donor nearby for a boost of added strength. Ewan's blood would be a super-charge to her system, but since there was no chance of feeding from his vein ever again, Sasha would have to make do with whatever she could get her hands on. Her lip curled in distaste. Unfortunately, the only thing within arms' reach was a disgusting demon.

Probably tasted just as bad as they smelled.

Gods, what a completely fucked-up situation.

"After tonight, there'll be one less berserker in the world, and that's fucking fine by me. They're all a bunch of animals and deserve to be put down."

"What if he won't play ball?"

Sasha held in a snort. She'd found out firsthand tonight that Ewan didn't give a shit about her. These demons were currently holding a useless piece of leverage.

"He'll play. You saw her with your own eyes. What male wouldn't lay down his life for a piece of that?"

Blech. Sasha's stomach turned. If even one of these disgusting demons tried to lay a hand on her, she was going to rip their arms from the sockets. They might've thought Ewan would do anything to secure her release, even sacrifice his own life, but the fact of the matter was Sasha wasn't getting out of here if she didn't take care of it herself.

"We could keep her," one of the demons suggested. "Play with her for a bit. It's not like the berserker will have any use for her once he's dead."

The momentary silence was filled with another round of laughter. "That's not how this works and you know it. He's going to have to see her with his own eyes. Know she's safe before he falls under Aronth's blade. It's the only way to secure a win."

Aronth must've been the male the demons wanted Ewan to fight. Not that it mattered. Ewan would kill him just like he'd killed all of the others in the battle arena. He was unstoppable. A force of nature. Wild, violent. Without remorse. Nothing and no one would stop him.

"How much longer do we have to keep her here?"

Finally, some information Sasha could use.

"Until the others get their hands on the berserker and secure his cooperation. Once that's done, we'll take her to the arena."

If Sasha could just be patient, she'd have an opportunity to escape. They'd have to take the netting off of her. They'd have to remove the bindings from her wrists and ankles to move her. And when they did, she'd attack.

"She's still not conscious. What the fuck is up with that?"

"Don't look a gift horse in the mouth, asshole. Be glad we nearly knocked her brain out of her head. She's a lot tougher than she looks and you'd be wise to keep your distance."

Yes, they all would be wise to keep their distance. Because it wouldn't be long before Sasha got a little revenge of her own.

Ewan hung limp from the ropes that bound his arms and secured him in place. He dangled from the ceiling, strung up like a piece of raw meat, and Ian Gregor was the butcher eager to slice him up. He'd lost all sense of pain hours ago. Gregor wanted to get a point across and he wasn't going to stop until Ewan got the message loud and clear.

Fucking bastard.

Drew wasn't much better off. He'd been cut down after Ewan was forced to look at Gregor's handiwork and then dragged off somewhere in the building to rest and heal. One thing was certain, no one would die at Gregor's hands tonight. Not when he needed every able body to wage his war. No, he'd simply beat Ewan within an inch of his life over and over again. Allowing him to heal only to pick up where they'd left off. He was being taught a lesson. Obey or suffer the consequences.

"You"—Gregor pointed the tip of his dagger at Ewan for emphasis—"belong to me. You eat because I allow it. You have a roof over your head because I allow it. Your lungs take breath because I allow it. And your heart fucking beats because *I allow it!*" His last few words ended on an enraged roar that shook the walls around them. Gregor drove the pommel of his dagger into Ewan's gut. He let out a grunt as his muscles contracted in a last-ditch effort to protect himself. "Do you understand me?"

"Loud and clear."

His sarcasm earned Ewan a slice of Gregor's blade across his left biceps. Blood welled from the cut and spilled over his skin before it began to heal. One of the downsides to being such a powerful supernatural creature: torture could go for days on end. Gregor had bigger fish to fry than Ewan, though. He'd cut him loose soon enough. Once he felt as though his point had been made. It would behoove him to grovel and apologize. To beg for Gregor's mercy. Ewan could put an end to all of this with a few simple words. Trouble was, he'd never been much for throwing in the towel.

"Where's the money?"

Finally they were getting down to the meat of it. What Gregor really wanted was the money Ewan had won fighting. Funds to add to his coffers to pay for his ridiculous war. A war the Sortiari had long since forgotten, defunded, and abandoned. Too bad Gregor couldn't take the hint and do the same. His fist made contact with Ewan's face, breaking his jaw, and sending him swinging from side to side like the punching bag he was. He spat to the side to clear his mouth of blood and wiggled a loose tooth with his tongue.

"Where is the money, Ewan?" Gregor said again slowly and with deadly intent.

Gregor could beat him and cut him into small, bite-sized pieces and Ewan still wouldn't tell him where the money was. He'd worked hard for that money. Drew had gone through hell for that money. He refused to hand it over just so Gregor could waste it on his vendetta.

"So help me, Ewan, if you don't tell me where that money is—"

"You'll what?" Ewan's words were slurred by his broken jaw that still hadn't fully healed.

"I'll kill her," Gregor said on a hiss. "Slowly. And I'll make you watch."

Ewan's heart stuttered and his breath stalled in his chest. He went still as death as he leveled the one eye not swollen shut at Gregor and allowed it to narrow into a hateful slit.

"Do you really think I'm that daft, Ewan?" Gregor's accent thickened with his ire. "You talk a good game, but I know the truth." His lip curled back into a vicious snarl. "I can smell it on you. *Betrayer.*"

In a few short centuries, eons' worth of instinct had been beaten out of them by the Sortiari's cruel indifference and Gregor's single-minded thirst for violence. A mated male could easily be recognized by scent. Ewan hadn't even noticed a change in his, but Gregor had and it told him everything he needed to know.

"You've debased yourself. Soiled and tainted by a fucking *vampire!*" The last word left his lips on a roar that cast spittle on Ewan's face. "You have lain with our sworn enemy!" Gregor continued to rail, his rage so intense he trembled. "Given yourself to her and formed a bond with her!"

Ewan met Gregor's enraged stare with his one good eye. He refused to deny it. Wouldn't. He loved Sasha and he was through playing games. Done with cowing in Gregor's presence. He could beat him bloody every day for the next year and Ewan wouldn't bow.

Gregor stepped up close and put his mouth to Ewan's ear. "I am going to make sure her suffering is *endless.*" The calm of his tone was far more menacing than his angry shouts. "I'm going to starve her. Bleed her. Flay her skin from her with a dull knife." With every word spoken, Ewan's anger intensified. Heat pooled in his gut and flooded his limbs, bulging the veins and muscles beneath his skin. "I'm going to break every bone in her body. Smash them to dust." He pulled back to gaze at Ewan. "I'm going to yank the fangs from her gums and wear them round my neck. Now . . . before you force me to do all of that and more, where is the money, Ewan?"

Ewan let out a disdainful bark of laughter. He could give Gregor the entire contents of Fort Knox, lay Mikhail Aristov at his feet, and it still wouldn't save Sasha's life.

Ewan took a deep, shuddering breath that rattled wetly in his lungs. "What money?"

Onyx swallowed the whites of Gregor's eyes and bled out onto his cheeks to paint a terrifying portrait of rage. Ewan had taken so much damage over the past couple of days, first from the demons and now this. His body was slower to heal and the nonstop beating, stabbing, and slicing was beginning to take a toll. He wasn't going to die tonight or any other night, but that wasn't the point. Ewan had defied Gregor. Time and again. And the warlord king was going to make sure Ewan got what was coming to him for his treachery. First, he'd break him. And then, he'd take everything from him.

Gregor came at him hard. With fists, kicks, slashes, and stabs. Renewed pain radiated throughout every inch of Ewan's body as his resistance waned. Excruciating. Nearly unbearable. Debilitating. He didn't so much as groan. He wouldn't give Gregor the satisfaction. The ropes that bound him dug into his wrists, yanking with each brutal kick Gregor delivered to his torso. A loud pop and a flash of bright heat seared through Ewan's shoulder as it dislocated. He hung there. Limp. Bloody. Damned near lifeless. Bruised. Battered. Broken and mangled. And still, he managed to keep his fucking jaw welded shut.

"Where is the money, Ewan?"

Gregor controlled his battle rage better than most. He could keep himself on the cusp of losing control. Teetering on the brink of that endless black chasm where memory didn't exist. He managed to keep his grip on his mind. The situation. His surroundings. His control was astonishing.

Probably why no one had been able to best him in a thousand years.

"Gregor." A tentative voice called from the doorway. Ewan swallowed a snort. Gavin knew better than to step a foot in the room. "The vampire is gone."

Ewan's stomach knotted tight. He wanted to feel a sense of relief because there was no doubt the vampire in question was Sasha and Gregor had sent his piece of shit cousin, Gavin to fetch her. They'd no doubt hoped to snatch her before the sun set and had failed. Ewan winced as he tried to smile. Looked like he wouldn't be the only one Gregor delivered a beating to tonight.

"What do you mean, 'gone'?" Gregor's voice grated in his throat.

Gavin cleared his throat. "Not gone. Taken."

The knot in Ewan's gut bottomed out. *Motherfuckers.* He didn't have to hear another word to know what had happened to Sasha.

"By . . . ?" Gregor let the word hang and gods-damn, the impact was astounding.

"Demons," Gavin replied. "The scent of sulfur was everywhere. We tracked a small van for a few blocks but lost the scent. They must have used magic to shake us."

Gregor slashed out with his dagger and cut Ewan down. He crumpled to the floor like a puppet whose strings had been cut and sucked in a few ragged breaths as he tried to steady his careening world. Without Sasha, Gregor had no leverage and they both knew it. Ewan would have laughed if he hadn't been so gods-damned terrified. If the demons had Sasha, shit was about to go from bad to worse.

"I'm not done with you!" Gregor pointed his dagger at Ewan as he strode through the doorway, leaving Gavin to stand there, mouth agape.

Gavin threw a disgusted glare Ewan's way for a few seconds before turning to follow after his so-called king.

Thank. Fuck. Now that he was alone, Ewan could get to the business of healing so he could get out of there and find Sasha.

If he couldn't, he had a feeling the only way out of this fucking mess would be to die tonight.

CHAPTER
32

Ewan dug through Sasha's discarded bag, hands trembling. She'd been snatched right off the damn sidewalk in plain sight. Shades of black and white bled into his vision, his unchecked rage threatening to overtake him. It wouldn't do any good to lose control now. He needed to get to that bastard Sorath. He needed to make a deal. And if that meant dying in the arena tonight, so be it. Anything to save Sasha.

"Here." He tossed Sasha's cell to Drew. "Look for a contact named Lucas." The vampire had obviously cared for Sasha and he was a big son of a bitch, certainly capable of protecting her. "If you can't reach him, call Saeed." Ewan loathed bringing the coven master into this, especially after Sasha had walked away from that part of her life. He wasn't even sure Saeed would come to help if summoned. "I'll text you my location after I meet with Sorath."

Drew gave a sad shake of his head. "This is a bad idea, Ewan. I don't like it."

Ewan snorted. Neither did he. But he'd run out of options. "Just do as I ask." Tonight would likely be the last night Drew would ever have to do a favor for Ewan. "Please."

Drew cut him a look but gave a curt nod of his head. "Don't let the bastards push you around."

It was too late for that, wasn't it? Ewan was already up against the wall. "Roger that." But he didn't need Drew worrying about any of that. He headed for the Civic and settled himself into the doorless driver's seat. He turned the key and the engine spluttered to life. He pulled out onto the street and sped off in the direction of the gaudy Sunset Boulevard mansion. The demons had managed to accomplish something Ian Gregor hadn't. They'd taken his mate. And through her, they controlled Ewan. The warlord would be wise to take a page out of the demons' book. Because Ewan was willing to do anything—including sacrifice himself—in order to keep her safe.

Ewan had never feared death. Until now. Never believed there was anything more to this life than pain, violence, and hardship. Until now. He'd never bothered with faith, hadn't believed in any god, or the possibility of an existence after this life. Until now. He'd never known tenderness, passion, or love. Until now.

Until Sasha.

"Promise me you'll watch over her. Give me your oath."

"You need to knock this the fuck off. Now." Drew refused to meet Ewan's gaze after hearing his cousin's words. "You're not dying today."

But he was. His death was the only thing that would protect Sasha. From the demons that wanted to exploit her. From Gregor who wanted to torture and kill her. From his own damned self whose very existence was a threat to her.

"Only one of us is going to walk out of that arena," Ewan said. "And you know what'll happen to her if it's me."

"They're bluffing," Drew replied. "I still can't wrap my

head around how you managed to find yourself mated to
a vampire, but they have to know not even hell could protect them from your wrath if they hurt her."

It was true that Ewan would set the world on fire if anything ever happened to Sasha. He'd leave a bloody swath
in his wake that would make Gregor's vengeance seem
tame in comparison.

"I can't take that chance." He refused to gamble with
Sasha's life.

"Let me at least try to find her. I can track her scent
easily enough." Drew let out an amused snort. "It's all
over you."

That telltale scent of a mated male was what had fueled
Gregor's wrath. As much as he'd wanted to keep his relationship with Sasha a secret, there was no hiding it. Not
from Gregor, Drew, or any of the others. The cat was out
of the bag. Lucky for Ewan, he didn't have to contemplate
his fate or future because of it. He was going to die in the
arena tonight.

"What about her?" Drew wasn't giving up. "Did you
stop to think about what might happen to her if you die?"

Not if. *When.* "She'll be safer without me."

Drew cocked a challenging brow.

It was true Ewan wasn't sure what his death would mean
for their tether. But anything had to be better than living
under constant threat. He could let Drew track her. Try to
beat the demons at their own game. But what then? It
wouldn't change who she was or who he was. It wouldn't
protect her from Gregor and those still loyal to him.

"That's bullshit and you know it," Drew said with disgust. "I left a message for that vampire. He might still show
up. We'll have backup. There's no reason for this. This is a
cop-out, Ewan. You're giving up."

"No." Ewan gave a shake of his head. "This is me finally taking a stand. This is me finally taking control of my life."

"By *dying*?" Drew's incredulous shout echoed in the empty room. "Jesus! Are you even listening to yourself?"

Aye. If it meant dying on his own terms. "Just let me go out there and do what I need to do, okay?" Ewan stepped up close to his cousin until they were almost nose to nose. He reached out and gripped Drew's shoulders. "Give me your oath that you'll protect her."

Drew looked away, disgusted. "*Bhí a saol roimh mianach.*" Her life before mine. "You have my oath."

Ewan stepped away and breathed a sigh of relief. He could leave this world now, knowing Drew would keep Sasha safe.

"So how the fuck does this work?" Drew might've agreed to Ewan's terms, but his tone made it apparent he wasn't happy about it.

"They want a good show. A fight that will raise the stakes and drive up the bets. Sasha will be close, at least that's what I was told by that fucker, Sorath. I'm supposed to drop to my knees once we're both beat to shit. They'll let me see Sasha so I know she's unharmed before the killing blow is delivered."

Drew swore under his breath. "What a disorganized bunch of bullshit. Lucky for you, those demons apparently don't have a brain to share between them. Jesus, Ewan. Drop to your knees if that's what they want you to do. They'll let her go, you'll know she's safe, then you spring up and kill the motherfucker."

The demons weren't as stupid as Drew thought. They'd hedge their bets, have a backup plan in place just in case Ewan tried anything. He refused to gamble with Sasha's life. "It's not that easy, Drew. But I promise you, if the opportunity presents itself and I know we'll all walk away from this unscathed, I'll do whatever I can to live through this." It was an empty promise, but a necessary one.

"Fair enough." Drew headed for the door. "I'll be out on the floor, looking for her. Are you ready?"

As ready as any male about to face his death. "Yeah. Let's do this."

The crowd was particularly rowdy and bloodthirsty tonight. Obviously anxious for a good show. Luckily, Ewan was going to give them one. He wove his way through the throng of bloodthirsty onlookers toward the arena. His nostrils flared as he picked up the faintest hint of Sasha's distinct cinnamon scent. His bones hummed in his body with awareness of her. A bond had indeed been formed between them. She'd woven herself into his very DNA. She wasn't in the building, but she was close. Ewan felt her presence like a single star in an endless black universe. Gods, he hoped she was safe and unharmed.

She'd better be. Otherwise, all hell would break loose.

The demon Ewan was intended to fight waited for him in the arena. He was a big bastard, at least a foot taller than Ewan with cords of thick muscle, sharklike teeth, and skin Ewan knew to be thick and leathery, like built-in body armor. Even if he weren't throwing the fight, the demon would be difficult to kill. In addition to his physical attributes, the demon could use hellfire as a weapon. Ewan suppressed a shudder. He could go a lifetime without being burned by that shit again.

You're in luck, asshole. You're dying tonight. You won't have to worry about it.

As he continued to make his way to the arena, Ewan received pats on the back and words of encouragement from those eager to see the demon fall. He was a sure thing, the famed berserker warlord who dared to take a vampire for a lover. Unapologetic. Violent. Invincible. So many of these poor bastards were going to lose the shirts off their backs tonight.

The battle master gave Ewan a solemn bow as he stepped into the arena. His senses were awash with Sasha, close to the point of distraction. So much so, that Ewan wondered if he'd have to throw the fight at all. It maddened him to know she was so close and yet still out of his reach.

"Choose your weapons!"

The crowd erupted into shouts and cheers. The battle master held the case of weapons aloft for the competitors to choose from. The half-circle dome of silver webbing closed in around them and Ewan couldn't help but wonder, did silver even bother demons? Ewan's blood pumped in his veins with every quick thump of his heart. He scanned the crowd for any sign of Drew, already knowing Sasha wasn't among the crowd of onlookers. At least, not yet. If this were any other fight, he'd be coaching himself to focus and not allow for outside distractions. But what did it matter? He was going to die either way. Focusing on the fight was his priority. If he was about to meet his end, Ewan wanted his mind to be one hundred percent full of Sasha.

Ewan shook his head. Everyone present knew he wouldn't take a weapon. The battle master presented the case to the demon and he, too, declined, sending the crowd into a frenzy. So, no blade with which to behead him? Apparently the demons' plans had changed and it was to be hand-to-hand combat to the death. What a way to go out in a blaze of glory. The demons certainly had their dramatic show planned to the last detail. Tonight's fight would become the stuff of legends. As in all legends, there would be a villain. Unfortunately, Ewan would be the one to fill that role.

His opponent attacked without warning. Ewan took a

fist to the gut that might as well have been the branch of a redwood. He stumbled backward several feet and landed flat on his ass. Not a great start. Rather than the usual excited cheers, the building echoed with boos and cries of dissent. Yup, a lot of sorry bastards were going to lose some money tonight.

The demon was fast, but Ewan was faster. He propelled himself up to his feet, pulled back his arm, and threw the heel of his palm into his opponent's solar plexus. The demon folded, bending at the waist as he gasped and fought for breath. Ewan capitalized on the demon's distress, and delivered a roundhouse kick to the bastard's head. He might be letting the demon win tonight, but he was damn well going to make sure the male earned it.

Ewan was going down, but it wouldn't be quietly.

Sasha was two, three blocks at the most, from the fight venue. She heard the roar of the crowd, but more than that she felt Ewan's presence in the threads of the invisible tether that bound them. It gave a tug at her chest and she wished she could rub the sensation away. But thanks to the piece-of-shit demons that held her captive, her wrists and ankles were still tied and secured to the floor.

Not for long, though.

"We need to get her moved."

Sasha was having a hard time telling one voice from the other, but did it really matter? She was just grateful for the opportunity to escape the smell of sulfur. First things first, she needed to get free. Then, she needed to find a weapon.

"Sorath won't want her there a second early," one of the demons groused. "He'll have your head if she is."

"It's gonna take a minute to get her out of that damned netting."

Sasha kept her breathing even and shallow. If they were foolish enough to believe she hadn't regained consciousness yet, she wasn't about to correct them. It would be hard enough to take down two demons on her own. She didn't need them being prepared for an attack.

"All right, then. Let's do this. Fucking silver," one of the demons muttered under his breath. "Makes me break out into a rash."

Better than raw burns and angry welts.

More than being untied, Sasha couldn't wait to be rid of the blindfold. She imagined this was how humans felt trying to find their way around in the dark. The blindness drove her freaking crazy. She needed all of her senses if she was going to get out of this mess.

Footsteps shuffled with a sandy scrape on the concrete. Sasha forced herself to relax despite her prone position. *Breathe in. Breathe out. Relax.* The weight of the silver netting lifted from her and with it the annoying prickles of pain along her exposed forearms and the small of her back where her T-shirt rode up. It was a minor discomfort in comparison to the blistering heat of hellfire, however.

"Watch out!" Sasha jumped at the barked warning and prayed no one had noticed. "If she rouses, and you're too close, she'll rip your throat out."

True. She wouldn't waste an opportunity to put her fangs to use if one presented itself. Despite her vow to never drink from anyone but Ewan, she needed to fortify her strength. Then again, she guessed that vow meant little in the realization that Ewan had never cared for her. So many promises made that meant nothing now. Gods. Sasha's heart ached and she forced the hurt to the back of her mind. She needed blood. Any vein would do.

"I clocked her good with that steel pole. Nearly split her head in two." Sasha suppressed a growl. The bastard wouldn't be bragging when she was done with him. "You think she's healed up already? Without being able to sink her fangs into the nearest throat?"

The demon's misconception that Sasha was too weak to heal worked in her favor. She could play the helpless female and when his guard was down, she'd attack.

"The fuck should I know?" the other one snapped. "Do I look like a gods-damned vampire to you?"

Good gods. Sasha wished they'd hurry the hell up. While they were standing around contemplating whether or not she was strong enough to fight back, Ewan was about to lose his life in the battle arena.

Sasha's breath hitched. Despite his betrayal, despite her broken heart, she couldn't simply let him die. True, his death would send her soul back into oblivion—a fate she didn't think she'd survive—but beyond that, beyond her broken heart, she knew she'd never be able to live with herself if she condemned him to death. She was not Ian Gregor. She was not the demon kingpin. Her compassion and empathy made her who and what she was. Nothing would change that part of her nature no matter how badly she'd been hurt. She'd save Ewan despite his betrayal because she was better than all of them. *Damn it.* Why couldn't she be cold and ruthless and only interested in saving her own damn neck?

"Just get her up. Sorath will put your head on a pike if you don't get her where she needs to be when she needs to be there. Leave the silver cords behind, but keep her wrists and ankles cuffed. It'll weaken her enough that she won't be able to put up much of a fight."

Son of a bitch. A thousand vile curses against these and every other demon in existence ran through Sasha's mind. They certainly weren't going to make this easy for her. True, the silver cuffs would weaken her. But with any luck, it wouldn't be enough to make a difference when she made her move. She'd fight through the pain. Push past the weakness. A little silver wasn't going to come between her and her mate.

Nothing would.

Sasha relaxed by small degrees as the tension from the silver cords that held her to the floor loosened and slipped away. One obstacle down. Two to go.

A noxious cloud of sulfur settled over her as the demon bent low. Sasha stifled a gag and wondered how she'd ever force herself to pierce the demon's vein when push came to shove. His blood had to taste like the seventh level of hell. Gag. Not an experience she was looking forward to.

The demon hoisted her up with an unceremonious heave, and deposited her on his shoulder. The angle wasn't great—right now her best plan of attack was to bite him in the ass—but if she could manage to twist her body up and around, she could at least try for his upper arm. The neck would be ideal, though. Demons had particularly thick skin. From the looks of them, that skin was more delicate at the throat. Sort of a flaw in their anatomy in Sasha's opinion.

"All right. Let's get the hell out of here before she wakes the fuck up."

Patience. Breathe. Calm. Bide your time . . .

Sasha let the words be a mantra as she waited for the demon to get her outside of wherever she'd been held and outside. There was no use breaking free now when the building might be protected by magic that refused to let her leave. Demons were tricky bastards. Wily. And they weren't taking any chances with Ewan's fight tonight. She could wait. A few more minutes and she'd have her chance . . .

The demon's lumbering gait jostled her against his shoulder as his heavy footsteps beat a grating rhythm against the concrete floor. Was he going out of his way to dig his shoulder into her rib cage?

"If I had it my way, she'd be dead already." The other

demon was several feet ahead from the sound of his voice. Problematic, but not disastrous.

"Not gonna happen. Sorath wants the berserker dead before she's dealt with."

Of course. Sasha gnashed her teeth together and her fangs punctured her bottom lip. She quickly swiped the blood away with her tongue, lest the demons catch the scent. This Sorath wasn't stupid. He had to have assumed that if Ewan died, Sasha would hunt him to the ends of the earth and beyond to avenge him. He'd leave no loose ends. This was intended to be a lose-lose situation for both Ewan and Sasha. No way out. Too bad for Sorath she didn't accept loss.

"Sort of defeats the purpose to kill her now," the one carrying her grunted. "No leverage against the berserker."

"He'll be dead soon enough, too. One less berserker in this world the better."

Assholes. Sasha wouldn't feel a bit of remorse about killing either one of them.

The whine and groan of a heavy metal door filled her ears and Sasha quelled the elation that flooded her chest. L.A.'s not-so-pristine air wafted to her nostrils and she'd never been more grateful to smell all of that smoggy goodness. They were finally outside, and Sasha wasn't about to waste her opportunity.

She brought her torso up on the demon's shoulder and twisted at the waist, curving her body around him like a scarf. The blindfold was still in place, making it tricky to direct herself but as he stumbled from the momentum shift, it knocked her close enough to his body that she could strike. Fangs bared, she latched on to skin and bit down as hard as her jaw would allow. The demon's skin was tough—like biting into a tree branch—but she managed to penetrate the thick armor of flesh.

"Motherfucker!" The demon's enraged shout sent a

thrill through Sasha that she hadn't felt in a long damned time. She let her own body weight lend momentum to her actions as the demon attempted to toss her from his shoulders and in the process, allowed Sasha to rip the wounds open in his throat. It wouldn't put him down, but it was enough of a distraction to give her a slight advantage before he had the good sense to put his hellfire to work.

She had seconds to escape and they were ticking away too gods-damned fast. Her arms and legs moved slowly, hindered by the silver cuffs. Sasha brought her hand up and tore at the blindfold, unconcerned with her surroundings as she focused on the demon that stood bleeding beside her. A long machete dangled from his waist—real inconspicuous—and she managed to tear it from the holster before he could stop her. She slashed out and caught him in the stomach, spilling his guts to the sidewalk at her feet.

That would slow the son of a bitch down. One demon out of her hair. One more to go.

It felt as though she was running through sludge. Weighed down by the silver cuffs, she dug her feet into the soles of her boots and pushed, propelling her body toward the second demon who was already charging for her. She swung the machete low and the demon shifted in turn, but the movement was merely a feint and she brought the blade up in an upward arc. The effort to swing it was immense and she let out a battle cry as she put every ounce of energy she had into the swing. The blade sliced through the demon's neck, spine, and muscle and his grotesque head rolled down the sidewalk toward his comrade as his body crumpled and bled out at her feet.

Sasha didn't look back. She ran as fast as she could manage, pushing her weakened body to its limit. The sound of raucous cheers and jeers led the way, as well as the tether that inexorably bound her to Ewan as she ducked into a side alley and continued to run.

Hold on, Ewan. Gods, she prayed he wouldn't allow himself to be beaten. *I'm coming. Just hold on.*

Because despite her broken heart, despite everything she knew, despite his betrayal, Sasha knew she wouldn't survive the loss.

CHAPTER
33

Deal or no deal, the demon was the toughest opponent Ewan had ever fought. Resilient. Strong. Skilled and formidable. Quick and agile. Not to mention armed with deadly hellfire. Had this been a true test of skill and battle to the death, it would've been hours—hell, maybe even days—before a victor was crowned. It didn't help that Ewan's attention was divided between the fight in front of him and searching the crowd for any sign of Sasha.

He swore to the gods, if any harm came to her, he would kill every creature who'd had a hand in it.

A fist came out of nowhere and landed squarely on Ewan's jaw. In the past twenty-four hours he'd been beaten, burned, and carved like a Thanksgiving turkey. Twice. His entire world had been turned on its head and he was fucking exhausted. The only positive thing to come out of dying in the arena tonight was the prospect of finally being able to get some gods-damned rest.

Ewan straightened as he shook off the lightheadedness from the force of the demon's blow. He countered with a series of roundhouse kicks and artfully orchestrated hooks that put the demon flat on his ass. He might have agreed to die tonight, but before he did, Ewan planned to get his licks in.

The demon glared up at him with a cruel sneer. Hellfire sprang to life in his palm and he threw a fireball straight at Ewan's face. Ewan dove to his left, narrowly missing the projectile that crashed through the webbing of silver that constructed the dome and into the crowd before it exploded into flames.

Ewan pushed himself up from the floor as he took in the scene of chaos that erupted around him. Well, this wasn't fucking good. The hellfire would burn until it exhausted itself, drawing attention away from the fight. With fewer eyes to watch their performance, less money would exchange hands. It certainly wouldn't make that bastard demon kingpin, Sorath, happy but that's what the son of a bitch got for allowing his fighter to use hellfire in the arena. Ewan had made no agreement to help line the demons' pockets. He'd simply agreed to die.

The hellfire and commotion surrounding the fight added another layer of bullshit for Ewan to try to ignore. He couldn't let it concern him. He needed to keep his head in the game and live long enough to see Sasha alive and well. Ewan centered his focus and went after his opponent before he had the presence of mind to defend himself. He allowed every ounce of anger he felt, all of his heartache at leaving Sasha behind, all of his frustration for the cards he'd been dealt in this miserable life to fuel him as he pummeled the demon with his fists, elbows, knees, and feet. He grabbed the bastard by his shoulders, and delivered a head butt with so much force behind it that it cracked Ewan's own skull.

Tendrils of heat coursed through his veins. Battle rage crested within him, tightened his skin, and flooded his muscles. His vision shifted from full color to black-and-white and he felt the inevitable shift that would soon consume him and turn him into nothing more than a killing machine. *Hold on. Don't let it take you. Stay in control.* Ewan balanced on the cusp of that force that threatened to overtake him. He drew from its power, allowing it to fuel his actions without losing himself completely to its seductive pull. He didn't know how long he could hold on this way. Sooner or later, he'd have to tip one way or the other. And succumbing to the battle rage wasn't an option.

Another fireball flew toward Ewan and he spun away. It caught him in the shoulder before deflecting and spiraling out toward the crowd in another bright orange, green, and blue explosion. He put the various screams and alarmed shouts to the back of his mind. He turned inward from the searing pain that radiated from his shoulder down his forearm. Instead, he focused on the demon's smug expression and vowed to use his fist to wipe it from the asshole's ugly face.

The demon's lips pulled back into a vicious, pointy-toothed smile. "You're going to die screaming, berserker."

Gods, how he hated big talk. As though Ewan's death would be on any terms other than his own. They'd been fighting for a good hour. The momentum continued to toggle between them. Give-and-take, a violent battle dance that held the eager crowd enthralled. Where was Sasha? Why hadn't they brought her here yet? A million scenarios presented themselves to Ewan, none of which had her surviving the encounter. Ewan knew Sasha's nature. Knew it as well as he knew his own. She would've tried to escape captivity. She would've put up a fight. What if she'd been hurt? What if she was already dead and he was doing all of this for nothing? Ewan's heart stuttered in his chest. If that were the case, he'd prefer to die than live in a world without her in it.

Hellfire burned all around him. His opponent circled

him, waiting for the opportunity to land a damaging blow. The crowd cheered, screamed, pressed toward the webbed silver cage of the battle arena as they tried to escape the undying flames. Ewan could think of no better way to go out. He hoped this fucking place and all the greedy creatures within it burned to the ground. The only thing that would make this moment more perfect would be the opportunity to take in the perfection of Sasha's beauty one last time before he checked out.

"Ewan! I see her! She's alive!"

From the right side of the arena, close to the cage, Drew's voice rose above the din to drill into Ewan's brain. He scanned the crowd, frantic for a glimpse of her but unable to find her in the midst of so much chaos. It tore at his heart that he wouldn't behold her beauty again. But she was safe, or at least, she would be when he was dead. She was alive. And that's all that mattered.

Ewan dropped to his knees. The demon's eyes narrowed and a confident smirk curved his lips. *I love you, Sasha.* His only regret was that he'd never been able to say the words she deserved to hear aloud. *I love you.* Ewan's eyes drifted shut as he waited for the killing blow. Time to leave this miserable life behind . . .

"Ewan!"

Sasha's voice was a beacon that reached out to him. Ewan's eyes flew open and he scanned the crowd. *There!* She wound her way through the press of people, alone. She waved her arms above her head as though to gain his attention. Silver cuffs circle her wrists but she showed no other sign of captivity. Not a single demon held her, stood near her, or followed her.

"Ewan!" she shouted again. "Fight, gods-damn it! Don't you dare die!"

She was free? How? The demon came at him, hellfire blazing in both of his palms. Ewan didn't have time to contemplate the hows and whys of Sasha's apparent freedom. She wanted him to fight. And gods-damn it, that's exactly what he was going to do.

Battle rage surged within him as Ewan rolled to his left, narrowly avoiding the demon's killing blow. His opponent let out an angry snarl that only served to encourage Ewan as he allowed the battle rage that built within him to once again take hold. He held the strongest pull of it at bay, refusing to completely lose sight of Sasha. He was prepared to end this miserable bastard—and every last demon who meant to do them harm—but he had to know she remained safe. He'd take care of the threat in front of him first, and one by one eliminate every last one of Sorath's minions, including the kingpin himself, when he was done.

He had so much life left to live, and he planned to spend every minute of it with Sasha.

"You're going to pay for this, berserker!" the demon shouted. "You and that bitch vampire!"

The demon's insults only fueled Ewan's rage. His focus sharpened as he rushed at his opponent and took him down to the floor in a full-body tackle. The tables had turned and the crowd knew it. Those spectators unconcerned with the hellfire surrounding them roared and shared their approval as he laid his fists into the demon's face, chest, and torso. Ewan's arms moved in a blur of motion. The force behind each and every punch was meant to disable, to cripple, to debilitate. The demon was resilient, but not half as resilient as Ewan. Not half as strong. He lacked Ewan's conviction. His need to persevere. Ewan was inexhaustible. Unkillable. He was a berserker warlord.

He didn't know how to lose.

The scent of Sasha's fear invaded Ewan senses. He looked up from pummeling the demon to death to find her engaged with the very same creatures that had taken her captive. She swung out with a machete, showcasing the abilities of a trained warrior. Ewan had never been so in awe of her, or so fucking scared for her. She needed him. Time to end this bullshit and protect his mate.

Ewan reached down and grabbed the demon's head. He gave it a sound twist and the bones cracked as skin and sinew teared. The demon went limp beneath him as one last ragged, wet breath rattled in his lungs.

He was the king of the battle arena. Invincible. And now, he would make an example of the demons and show every soul present why he was a male worthy of not only their respect, but their fear. And with any luck, Gregor would hear about all of it and learn to fear him as well.

Ewan didn't wait for the cage to be lifted. Instead, he reached for the webbing of silver bars and spread them apart with brute force until he'd made an opening wide enough for his body to slip through. He rushed through the crowd, shoving at any creature who got in his way. No doubt the outcome of tonight's fight had pissed off a good chunk of the supernatural underground's population. He'd deal with those bastards, too, if they had a problem with him. Later. Right now, he had more demons to kill.

Sasha's heart had leapt into her throat as she'd watched Ewan go to his knees, prepared to die. For her. He couldn't possibly have been willing to sacrifice himself and at the same time betray her to Gregor. Could he? There had to be an explanation for it all and she was more than willing to hear him out. They simply had to survive the night first.

The stench of sulfur floated around her and Sasha's senses switched to battle mode. She'd disrupted the de- mons' plans and no doubt they'd try to kill her for it. That wasn't going to happen, though. Not tonight. Not any night. Sasha refused to bow. She refused to give up. And she refused to accept anything other than victory. She was the daughter of a warrior. The protégé of an assassin.

Sasha Ivanov would show her foes why they should fear her. She was the bringer of death and these demons were her prey.

Sasha held the machete aloft as she adopted a defensive stance. In the background, Ewan fought for his life and she had to trust he'd come out the victor. She had faith and that's all that mattered. Together, though separate, they would eradicate this threat.

"Fucking bitch! I'm going to gut you before I burn you to ash!"

The demon she hadn't managed to kill on the street came at her, hellfire blazing in his palm. He threw the orb of supernatural fire at her and she narrowly missed it, though she felt the lick of flames on her cheek. The fireball smashed into the far wall of the building, erupting into a third fire that only added to the chaos around her. Spectators began to flee the building, most of them unwilling to risk being burned to death in order to witness the outcome of the fight.

Smart. The more of them that evacuated the space, the better.

Several more demons joined the melee, and Sasha prepared for the attack. She was outnumbered, but the odds didn't bother her. She'd been in dicey situations like this before. She could handle this.

"Sasha!"

She looked to her left to find a shock of blond hair moving toward her from the crowd that flowed in the opposite direction. Lucas pushed his way through the obstacles that separated them, armed with a pair of daggers and an angry expression that made him look anything but innocent. She let out a sigh of relief as she said a silent prayer of thanks. She had no idea how Lucas had found her, but she was damn glad he had.

"Aim for the throat!" she shouted over the roar of flames

and commotion of the crowd. "They're most vulnerable there!"

The demon advanced on her with a wide sweep of his arm. Sasha ducked and jabbed with the machete, catching him in the gut for the second time that night. They were strong and resilient, but demons weren't exactly the best fighters. They should've stuck to wielding hellfire and left their weapons at home. She pulled back her arm and swept the blade to her right in an uppercut, driving the blade through the throat of a second attacker. The male's eyes went wide with surprise and the hellfire died in his palm as he crumpled to his knees. Sasha wasn't about to leave him simply wounded and able to heal. She let out a shout as she sliced the blade through the thick muscle of his neck, severing his head from his shoulders.

"You're going to die, vampire!" the demon she'd gutted twice in one night shouted.

She spun with a wide sweep of her arm and cut his head from his shoulders as well.

Sasha hated shit-talk.

The scent of sulfur flooded her nostrils. Hellfire raged around her, incinerating everything in its path. It wouldn't be long before it consumed the building entirely, but it didn't stop the demons from attacking. They were immune, after all. Sasha had only one choice: stand and fight. She only hoped she didn't burn to death in the process.

Lucas entered the fray, fast and nimble, the silver of his daggers glinting off the bright, multicolored lights of the fires. He jabbed and parried, swung wide and cut down with his massive arms, bringing as much damage as possible to the two demons that had converged on him. Sasha didn't have time to watch the show, however. Trouble was headed her way. Three more demons attacked, and outnumbered, she needed every ounce of focus to keep from getting burned or sliced open with one of their wide-blades.

A battle dance ensued. Sasha was more agile, quick, and graceful, able to deflect the demons' blades as well as avoid their hellfire. She rolled away from the attack and scooped up one of the dead demon's machetes. A weapon in each hand would be much more effective even if the machetes were awkward and cumbersome. It was tough to fight with any finesse, but did it matter? Survival was more important than providing a good show.

"Lucas! To your left!"

The fireball came out of nowhere. Lucas dove to his right, narrowly missing the hellfire, but it put him in the path of an oncoming demon. The male's blade sliced along Luca's torso and Sasha cringed as crimson bloomed from the wound to stain his shirt. The wound appeared superficial. He'd heal, but a few more cuts like that and the blood loss would take its toll. Sasha needed to cut down as many demons as possible so the odds were more even. They wouldn't last for long, outnumbered by at least five to one.

Pain exploded down Sasha's left side as the sharp edge of a blade sunk between her ribs. She'd been preoccupied and missed the demon who'd come from behind to ambush her. He leaned into the act, his face mere inches from hers as he drove the blade deep. Sulfur burned Sasha's nostrils as his lips spread in an evil smile that showcased the sharp points of his yellow teeth.

"You've fucked with my plans, vampire," the demon seethed close to her ear. "Now your lover is going to watch you die."

Sasha brought up her right hand to deliver a downward cut with the machete when the demon twisted the blade in her torso. She cried out as it tore through skin, muscle, and scraped over bone. The machete fell from her hand as blood gushed from the open wound. *Damn it!* She'd been so careful. So vigilant. That the demon had gotten the drop on her hurt more than the damned hole he'd opened up between her ribs. She doubled over and went to one knee as she dragged in ragged gulps of breath. He'd missed her heart, thank the gods. She'd heal. She just hoped the wounds closed up before he was able to deliver a second blow.

A fist connected with the demon's face, sending him sprawling a good ten feet away. Sasha brought her gaze up, up, *up* to find herself staring into the face of the most enraged berserker she'd ever seen. Ewan was magnificent in his anger. Black consumed the whites of his eyes and bled onto his cheeks. His muscles pulled the skin that ran with bulging veins tight over his frame. His breath heaved in his chest as his lip pulled back in a snarl. He was the embodiment of death. Destruction. And the demons would be wise to leave the city and never come back.

He took her breath away.

Sasha hugged her right arm around her waist. The wound had begun to heal and she regained sensation in her arm. She was diminished, but not out of the fight, so she scooped up the discarded machete, prepared to give Ewan whatever backup she could.

The sound of urgent shouts and the clash of blades drew Sasha's attention. Bodies swarmed through the outcroppings of hellfire toward where she, Ewan, and Lucas fought. Saeed, Diego, Cerys, and countless dhampirs flooded the space to join the fight and put the demons down. Sasha drew in a shuddering breath as emotion swelled in her chest. After everything that had happened, all of the bitter words and anger, they'd come to her aid. Her family hadn't turned their backs on her. They were here for her. And maybe even for Ewan.

The tables turned in an instant. No longer the outnumbering force, the demons quickly fell. Not even their hell-fire could protect them. A renewed burst of energy cycled through Sasha's veins as she reentered the fight. Her blades sang through the air as she hacked, cut and stabbed. Ewan's ferocity knew no limits as he ripped demons to pieces with nothing more than his bare hands. Gruesome. Violent. She'd seen him fight this way in the ring countless times. As though he were possessed, unable to control his own actions and running on autopilot.

One by one, the demons fell until not a single one was left alive. The building had emptied of casual spectators and all that remained were four vampires, twenty-five dhampirs, and one very enraged berserker.

Whatever force held Ewan in its grip had yet to release its hold. The demons were dead but the fight hadn't drained out of him and as Saeed approached Sasha from her right, Ewan charged at the vampire and took him to the floor. Sasha raced to Ewan's side desperate to keep him from killing Saeed, who was more than prepared to drive his blade into Ewan's throat as retaliation. Panic overtook her, made her lightheaded, as Sasha gripped Ewan by the shoulders and shouted, "Ewan, stop! You're going to kill him!"

Nothing could stop him. Not even her words. He was lost to the battle rage and Sasha feared there was no bringing him back.

CHAPTER
34

"Ewan, stop! Please!"

Words reached his ears as though spoken through a long tunnel, or from under water. Muffled and unintelligible. Incomprehensible to the singular focus of his mind. Ewan stared down at the male whose throat he gripped, seeing, but not comprehending. His was simply another body to put down. Another foe to decimate. Another threat to eliminate in order to protect his mate. Battle rage held Ewan in its grip.

Kill. Kill. Kill.

"Ewan!" Again a voice tried to break through the endless black and instinct that drove him. "Listen to me! You've got to snap out of it! Saeed isn't a threat! Don't make him hurt you!"

The words had more form this time, but Ewan was unable to grasp their meaning. His grip tightened, constricting the throat under his palm. He'd tear the male's head from his shoulders and move on to the next. One by one until his mate's safety was guaranteed.

"Ewan! *Gods, listen to me!*"

The urgency of the tone spoke to a part of his brain that had been switched off. He recognized his mate's voice and some shred of awareness returned. Ewan gave a violent shake of his head in an effort to bring himself back into the moment. Sasha was trying to convey something to him, but his mind had shifted into autopilot a while ago and taken him to that dark place where memory and cognizant thought didn't exist. He was in the full grips of battle rage and bringing himself out of it was a feat he wasn't sure he could accomplish.

"Don't hurt him! Please!"

His mate pled for someone's life. Ewan gave another shake of his head as his eyes began to comprehend exactly what they were looking at. He held the vampire Saeed in his grip. A slight twist, and Ewan could separate the vampire's head from his shoulders. His rival for Sasha's love would be dead. Gone forever. Nothing would stand between them . . .

"Saeed, please!" Sasha tugged at Ewan's fingers in an effort to loosen his hold. "He doesn't know what he's doing. Don't hurt him! Ewan, listen to me! I'm safe. We're safe. But we won't be for long. You've got to come back to me! We've got to get out of here. This place is burning to the ground!"

It wasn't the vampire's life Sasha begged for. It was *his*. A grayish white glint of metal caught Ewan's eye and he looked down to see the tip of a dagger pressed against his throat. The vampire was poised to drive the blade home. A quick slice would partially sever Ewan's head. It wouldn't take much for the vampire to finish him off. Sasha implored the vampire to spare him even though Ewan had his fists wrapped around the male's throat.

Color bled into Ewan's vision as conscious thought returned. The tendrils of heat that coiled within him retreated. He released his grip on Saeed's throat and fell

backward as the battle rage began to ebb and drain from
his body. Sasha's cry of relief drew his attention as he
turned toward her. A small crowd had gathered around
them. Sasha, Lucas, the other vampire and dhampirs from
Saeed's coven. Drew kept a safe distance from them all as
he watched tentatively from the battle arena and the silver
cage that began to melt as the hellfire ate away at it.

Gods. What a fucking mess. The bodies of demons lit-
tered the floor. Blood and carnage surrounded them. Ewan
let out a shuddering breath as he took stock of Sasha's
disheveled form and the blood that stained her shirt and
crusted her hands and arms.

She could have been killed. He could have lost everything that meant something to him tonight. Fear punched
him in the chest and stole his breath. They'd come out on
top, but if the vampires and dhampirs hadn't shown up, the
outcome would have been completely different.

Ewan pushed himself to stand and reached for Sasha.
She flinched and took a tentative step back, her brow furrowed. Afraid? Her scent soured as her heart rate increased.
He'd always known that once she saw what he truly
was—witnessed the unchecked beast that lived within
him—that she would run from him. Hurt sliced through
him, sharper than the vampire's blade. Sasha should
have let Saeed kill him. Because there was no way he
could live with her fear and revulsion.

Lucas pushed his way toward the center of the circle
and began to shove the gawking bodies of curious dhampirs toward the front of the building. "This place is coming down around us! We need to get out of here!"

The iron rafters creaked as they melted under the heat
of hellfire. A section fell just beyond the battle arena and
Ewan's gaze met Drew's as his cousin turned and ran for
the exit. He was in the midst of hostile territory and Ewan
didn't blame him for cutting a hasty retreat. Sasha might

have been terrified of him. She might not have wanted to have anything to do with him. But that wasn't going to stop him from getting her the hell out of here. Whether she liked it or not, she was his mate. And he was sworn, bound, dedicated to protect her.

"Everyone out!" Ewan's voice boomed. "Now!"

Bodies scattered at his command. He reached for Sasha, unconcerned with whether or not she wanted his hands on her and scooped her up in his arms. The building's integrity disintegrated under the hellfire's supernatural flames and it began to collapse as each rafter gave way. Ewan held Sasha tight against his chest as he dodged the rubble that rained down on them. He shifted, turned, bent his body over Sasha's as a chunk of glowing red iron struck his back and sent him to his knees.

Sasha's grip tightened on his shoulders as he let out a grunt of pain. Her gaze met his and for a moment, he almost thought her expression was one of concern. He pushed himself up, determined to get them the hell out of there. The molten iron burned like a motherfucker but it didn't compare to the lick of hellfire on his skin. He'd be all right. He'd heal. He just needed to get Sasha to safety.

"I won't let anything happen to you, Sasha," he said close to her ear. "I promise."

Her grip on his shoulders tightened and the tension in her muscles relaxed. He pushed his battered and exhausted body as hard and fast as it would go, close on the heels of the dhampirs and vampires who were in full evacuation mode. The ceiling continued to fold, threatening to overtake them and Ewan pushed harder. The entrance to the building was nothing more than flimsy metal frames now empty of glass and Ewan pushed off, throwing his body through one of the openings as he held Sasha close to his chest.

He spun midair and landed hard, the asphalt scraping

the skin from his back as he skidded to a stop. He kept his arms tight around Sasha, protecting her. He'd be damned if she sustained so much as another scratch tonight.

"Are you okay?" Ewan murmured between labored breaths. The exhaustion of days of torture, physical exertion, and battle rage threatened to lay him low. "You were wounded . . ."

In the background, the building collapsed completely, engulfed in supernatural flames. Not even glamours put in place would protect this place from the prying eyes of humans for long. The Sortiari were bound to get involved now. They wouldn't tolerate any creature violating the sacred secrecy of their world. Sasha didn't meet his gaze. She didn't stir. Didn't utter a single fucking word.

"Sasha?" Fear rose hot and thick in Ewan's throat. "Sasha? Talk to me."

"I-I heard you." Her voice barely broke a whisper. She trembled in his arms and the scent of her fear burned his nostrils. "On the phone. With Gregor."

Fuck. Ewan pushed himself upright and set Sasha on her feet. No wonder she was terrified of him. She'd thought he'd betrayed her. He cursed Ian Gregor. Cursed his birth, his very existence, and the vendetta that had caused so much pain and suffering. Ewan put Sasha at arm's length so he could look into her eyes while he spoke to her. So she could use every single one of her senses to recognize the truth in his words.

"What you heard was a lie." Ewan reached up to lay his palm to her cheek and she flinched. Her fear, her doubt, gutted him and he was desperate to assuage it. "Gods, love. I could never hurt you. I would never betray you. My life, my allegiance, everything that I am is yours. If you doubt that, doubt the sanctity of this vow, or my love for you, then take your blade and run it through my throat. Believe me when I tell you that death is the only option to living without you."

Sasha brought her gaze up to meet his. Her lips parted and her brow furrowed. "You love me?"

He'd been a fool not to tell her sooner. Had wasted countless opportunities to make sure she knew—without a doubt—how he felt and what she meant to him. But he'd been a coward. Scared of his own gods-damned heart. Silenced by emotions he'd thought destroyed over the course of centuries of suffering. No longer. The only thing that frightened Ewan was the prospect of a life without Sasha in it. And he'd be sure to tell her every day for the rest of their lives how he felt about her if she'd let him.

"I love you, Sasha." Ewan took her hand in his. "I love you more than I've ever loved anyone or anything."

Sasha's chest was close to bursting. Only the return of her soul rivaled the warmth, the fullness that Ewan's words evoked. He wanted her. Over everyone. Over anything. Over everything else in his life. She was first. She was his choice. He *loved* her.

"I love your strength and your fire. I love the spark of life you carry within you that never dulls. I love your wit and your intelligence. Your prowess in battle, your independence. Your fierce loyalty and the way you protect those you care about. I love your sense of honor. I love your gentleness. Your compassion. I love your beauty, inside and out. I'm lost to you, Sasha, and there's no going back."

His words stripped her bare. Everything she'd ever wanted to hear from him and more. To her right stood Saeed, Diego, and members of her coven. The family not of her birth, but of her choosing. Ewan was her family now as well. She chose him. She loved him. And if Saeed, or any of the others loved her at all, they would accept Ewan as she accepted him. For the male he was and not the history that shaped him.

"I love you, Ewan. So much. More than I ever thought could be possible. I love your heart and your soul. Your protectiveness and every gruff inch of you," she said with a smile. "I love the parts of you that you might not like. The parts you try to hide. The tether might have connected our souls, but I fell in love with *you*."

Ewan took her in his arms and crushed her body to his. Sasha felt the rapid beat of his heart against hers and she held him tighter. Gods, she never wanted to let him go.

"I almost lost you tonight and it scared me half to death. Don't ever do that to me again, Ewan. We're in this together. Where you go, I go."

"Where you go, I go." He spoke the words against her temple. Kissed her there before moving to her cheek, across her jawline, to her mouth. He kissed her gently. Slow and soft. And through the simple act, Sasha felt all of the love he had for her and more.

"I hate to break up the lovefest, but we should probably get out of here." Lucas stepped up beside them, tentative, as he kept an eye on Ewan. "I don't know about you two, but I'm not interested in waiting around to see who else might show up."

Ewan glanced over at Lucas and Sasha was relieved to find not an ounce of animosity in his gaze. "You're right. We need to get out of here. I'm not interested in tangling with any more demons . . ." Ewan paused. "Or anyone else."

What he omitted spoke volumes. Sasha didn't need to hear the words out loud to know Ewan worried Ian Gregor might show up with a squad of warlords at his back. She glanced at Ewan and then quickly at Saeed and then Lucas. Her apartment was compromised. They'd find no safe haven there. Sasha and Ewan were officially outcasts. She had no idea where to go.

"Come home, Sasha." Saeed stepped forward. He was a little worse for the wear, his usually pristine clothes tattered and stained with blood. It'd been a long damned time since they'd fought side by side and Sasha couldn't help but find it a little bittersweet. Saeed's gaze wandered to Ewan and back to Sasha. "Both of you."

Relief flooded Sasha. Hope coaxed a smile to her face. Maybe instead of thinking of this as the end, she needed to remind herself that it was merely a new beginning. For all of them. "Thank you, Saeed." Emotion cracked Sasha's voice.

"Thank you." Ewan's rough tone vibrated against Sasha's chest. "For your offer of shelter, for your help tonight, for protecting her."

Saeed gave Ewan a smile that didn't quite reach his eyes. She didn't expect them to become one big happy family overnight. But maybe, this was a good start.

Sasha awoke with the setting sun. Saeed had boosted security at the estate, bringing in a private firm for the next couple of months. It was a necessary precaution, one Sasha agreed with. And whereas she didn't think the demons would pose a threat in the future, the same couldn't be said for Ian Gregor and his band of warlords.

"Now that you're awake, you should feed."

Sasha's lips curved into a smile. "Concerned for my well-being?" Her voice was still heavy with sleep. "Or more concerned with pleasure?"

Ewan gathered Sasha in his arms. His naked body against hers was an indulgence she'd never tire of. "Both, love." He put his lips to her forehead. "Always both."

The previous night felt like a dream. Or rather, a nightmare. Sasha still couldn't believe how close she'd come to

losing him and a tremor of fear settled in the pit of her
stomach.

"Why are you afraid?" The comfort of Ewan's voice
calmed her.

"Just thinking about last night," Sasha said with a guilty
laugh. "We were lucky."

"That we were." At least she could count on Ewan to
never sugarcoat anything for her. "But we are here now.
We are alive. We are safe. And we're together. That's all
that matters."

Gods, how she loved him. "You're right. And I won't
ever let a second of our time together go to waste."

Sasha rolled and settled herself atop his chest. Her
legs straddled his hips as she let the slick warmth of her
pussy slide against his shaft. Ewan's gaze heated as he
groaned. His hands came to rest at her hips and he lifted
her as he thrust upward and slid inside of her.

Ewan sat upright on the mattress. His arms went around
Sasha and held her tight. The roll of her hips was slow.
Precise. Languorous. There was no more reason to rush.
Their nights together were no longer numbered. Doubt no
longer lingered between them. Their tether was secure and
Sasha basked in the warm confidence of Ewan's love.

"This isn't feeding." Ewan kissed her throat. Her collarbone. Over her shoulder. "You took some serious damage
last night. I want your strength fortified."

If Ewan thought she could get through this interlude
without burying her fangs into his flesh, then he didn't
know her very well. "Have you ever known me to resist
the call of your blood in these moments?"

She pulled away to look at him and he flashed a rare
smile that squeezed her heart like a fist. "No, love, I
haven't. And I hope that never changes."

Pleasure radiated through her as she continued to ride

him. Her breath hitched in her chest and she let her head fall back on her shoulders. "Never," she promised him. "Now, fuck me harder so I know you crave me as well."

"Always." Ewan held her tighter. He thrust his hips and drove hard and deep, just how she liked it. "Not a day will go by that I won't crave you. Your scent. Your taste. Your body. Your fierce beauty. I crave you like a drug, Sasha. I won't ever get enough."

Sasha bent over Ewan and nuzzled his throat. Her tongue flicked out before she sealed her mouth over the vein and sucked gently to coax it to the surface. He kept his unhurried pace, each thrust of his hips meeting the roll of hers. A satisfied groan rumbled in his chest as her fangs broke the skin and the euphoric bliss of feeding from her mate's vein stole over her.

She could stay this way forever. Each powerful draw of her mouth caused Ewan's body to tense along with hers. Her muscles tightened, her stomach coiled tight. Her clit throbbed and her pussy squeezed his shaft as the orgasm burst over her, tingling and pulsing, each wave more powerful than the last. Sasha pulled away as deep sobs of pleasure built in her throat. Ewan braced his arms behind him as he met her passion with wild, desperate thrusts. He leaned forward and swallowed her cries as he put his mouth to hers and fucked her harder. Deeper. Each drive of his hips more powerful than the last.

His body went rigid as he came. Sasha took him as deep as he could go, reveling in the sensation of his shaft pulsing against her and the wet warmth that flooded her and bathed them both in the aftermath of their passion. Sasha bent to Ewan's throat. The punctures had healed, but she returned to catch the remaining rivulets of blood on her tongue. Ewan let out an indulgent moan as he kissed her shoulder, to the swell of her breasts, upward. His hand came to rest at the back of her neck and he guided her mouth to his and kissed her with all of the passion they'd just experienced and more.

Sasha had never dreamed she'd find a love like she'd found in Ewan. And likewise, she never dreamed she could feel so content. So complete. So utterly sated and spent. She was boneless, helpless, in his arms. Lost to him. And she hoped she was never found.

"I love you, Ewan." She'd tell him every opportunity she got for their rest of their lives. So many obstacles lay before them and even though their differences seemed insurmountable, she knew they could conquer anything as long as they were together.

"I love you, too." His golden brown gaze met hers and in it Sasha saw the proof of his words. His lips quirked into a mischievous smile. "Should we venture out from your bedroom tonight? We haven't had any excitement in twenty-four hours. Stirring up your coven seems like it might fit the bill."

No rush on this earth equaled the thrill she got from just being in Ewan's orbit. He was the ultimate adrenaline rush. The perfect drug. Everything she'd ever needed and more. "I think that's a great idea," she said. "You know what'll really get the ball rolling? Drink the Cokes Diego has stashed in the fridge."

Ewan laughed. "That's one way to break the ice."

Every night from here on out would be an adventure, and Sasha couldn't wait to experience each and every one.

CHAPTER
35

"Saeed. We have a serious problem."

Ewan looked up from his plate of chicken fettuccine Alfredo to find one of the dhampirs on security duty standing in the doorway to the dining room. He, Sasha, Saeed, Cerys, Diego, and several dhampirs had been in the middle of what could only be described as an awkward dinner when the male burst into the room. It wasn't every day you sat down to break bread with your enemy. But it was the best meal Ewan had eaten in months so he wasn't about to complain. Vampires didn't fuck around when it came to food. Despite the decadent grub, Ewan was glad for a break in the tension.

Saeed set his napkin aside. "What is it?"

The dhampir cast a tentative glance at Ewan. "There's a berserker at the gate. He's demanding you turn over the fugitive you're harboring."

Ewan swore under his breath. He knew it would only be a matter of time before Gregor came to fetch him home. Two days of respite since the battle arena had burned to the ground and already, he was about to be cast back into a fight. Ewan let out a slow sigh. Was there to be no end to the strife? He pushed his chair out and Saeed held up a staying hand.

"This is my coven. I'll take care of this."

It might have been his coven, but it was Ewan's clan—or more to the point, their clan's *leader*—who caused the problem. "I'm not one to let another male fight my battles." He was working on being more cordial and less gruff but so far it wasn't very successful. "I can handle Gregor."

Saeed cocked a brow. "What makes you so certain it's Gregor?"

Ewan gave him a look as though to say, "Come on." It couldn't be anyone else. Ewan knew some sort of bargain had been made between the coven master and berserker king. And besides, after so many monumental fuckups on Ewan's part, Gregor wouldn't trust anyone else to fetch him home.

"All right." Saeed's dark eyes showed the slightest hint of amusement. "We'll go together then."

Ewan could live with that.

"I'm coming, too." Of course Sasha would refuse to stay back.

"No," Saeed and Ewan said in unison. At least he wasn't the only one who wanted her to stay put. He appreciated the vampire's concern for his mate but that didn't stop Ewan's protective—and possessive—instinct to rear its ugly head. He tamped down the heat of battle rage that gathered in his gut and forced himself to calm. Baby steps. If he was going to keep company with Saeed, he'd need to learn to keep his jealousy in check. Sasha loved *him*, not Saeed. Ewan knew that.

Save that rage for a real fight.

Which, if Ian Gregor was here, wouldn't be too far off.

"You're both crazy if you think I'm just going to sit here and wait," Sasha said with a disbelieving laugh. So stubborn, his mate. It was a quality that both infuriated and impressed him.

"Of course not." Ewan could play her game. "You'll come with us." He gave her a stern look. "But you *will* stay thirty feet back."

"No way!"

"Or you won't go at all," Ewan said. "Take your pick."

Sasha's eyes narrowed. She was put out but not angry. Besides, it's not like Ewan trusted her to do as he asked. He full well expected her to march right up to Ian Gregor and point her finger in the bastard's face. Something that would certainly amuse Ewan under different circumstances.

"Fine."

Sasha pushed out her chair and followed Ewan, Saeed, and the dhampir out the door. Ewan's lip quirked even as his stomach gave a nervous roll. He could smell the lie on her and she knew it. Ewan wouldn't put it past Gregor to pull something shady. He'd already said he'd hurt Sasha to punish Ewan. But he also knew Saeed's coven somehow fit in to Gregor's master plan. Was punishing Ewan more important than seeing his end goal? He guessed he'd find out soon enough.

The walk from the house to the security gate at the bottom of the driveway felt like miles rather than steps. Thirty feet from the gate, Ewan stopped and turned toward Sasha. "Wait here."

Her jaw took a stubborn set. "Come on, you had to have known I was never actually going to agree to that."

Of course. That didn't mean he wouldn't try to make her see reason. "I don't have to tell you how dangerous he is," Ewan said. "I know you can take care of yourself, that's not the point. If you won't stay here, will you at least hang ten feet back? For my peace of mind?"

Sasha let out a huff of breath. She was stubborn, but not unreasonable. At this point, Ewan would settle for five feet of distance between her and Gregor. He just needed a cushion. A bubble of space where he could insert himself between her and Gregor if the need arose.

"Ten feet," she agreed. "But no more than that."

Ewan gave a nod. They continued toward the gate, and with each step, Ewan's gut knotted tighter. His heart beat faster. His anger gathered and built. Ten feet separated them from the security gate and Sasha came to a tentative halt. Ewan reached out to take her hand in his and he gave it a reassuring squeeze before he walked away and her fingers brushed his as they slipped out of his grip.

"Gregor." Saeed approached the gate slowly, his demeanor almost serene, his hands folded behind his back. "I can't say I'm pleased to see you. House calls aren't a part of our agreement."

Curiosity burned. What sort of deal had Saeed made with Gregor? Whatever transpired between them had to be huge for Gregor to lower himself to making any deals with the vampire.

"You're harboring a fugitive." Gregor stabbed his finger at Ewan. "Which has nothing to do with our agreement."

Saeed countered Gregor's anger with a serene smile. The vampire certainly knew how to push his buttons. "Ewan is tethered to a member of my coven," Saeed replied. "Therefore he is now a member of my coven. Under my protection."

A presence at Ewan's back drew his attention and he watched from the corner of his eye as Saeed's mate made her way down the driveway to Saeed's side. Like Sasha, Cerys took no shit.

"Everything okay?" Her saccharine sweet tone belied the deadly glint in her eye. She stared Gregor down, daring him to show even an ounce of hostility.

Gregor's jaw squared. Saeed's mate was powerful. Her unique brand of magic rippled along Ewan's skin like tiny pinpricks. She made him nervous and put him on edge. He couldn't help but wonder once again if she was the reason Gregor had formed a tentative truce with Saeed. A tense moment of silence followed before Gregor dragged his gaze away from Cerys and focused it on Ewan.

"You're a fucking traitor, Ewan Brún." Gregor's seethed words carried the burden of accusation. "You've turned your back on your clan to lie with the enemy."

So many centuries of hate. Of strife. Of seeking vengeance for a wrong that could never be undone. Ewan had had enough. And he wasn't the only one. There were others, like he and Drew, who wanted their freedom. Wanted to rid themselves of this centuries-long strife. "Sasha is not the enemy." It took all of the self-control he could muster not to fly at Gregor in an angry rage. "Saeed is not the enemy." He pointed at Diego and the dhampir whose name he'd yet to learn. "They are not the enemy. They have committed no offense against us or ours. I refuse to continue to dole out punishment to innocent souls."

Gregor's eyes practically bulged from his head. "They have no souls!" His laughter echoed in Ewan's ears. "They are *abominations*. You have given yourself to an abomination!"

Never before had Ewan wanted to kill Ian Gregor as much as he did right now. Gregor's hatred was fueled by his own ignorance as much as it was grief. He had no interest in learning about his enemy. He had no interest in trying to understand. His hatred was blind and it would remain so until someone finally managed to put the bastard down. The insult to Sasha—to all of them—wouldn't stand. Ewan took a step forward, prepared to launch himself over the gate and put the nefarious warlord out of his misery once and for all.

"Ewan, don't." Sasha's voice was gentle in his ear. She came up from behind him and reached out to take his hand in hers. "None of us can change what's happened. But we can change how we react to it going forward."

Wise words from his mate. For the hundredth time since he'd met her Ewan marveled that Fate had seen fit to bring them together. He certainly didn't deserve her. Even so, he'd never let her go. "You're right, love." He would never change Gregor's mind. Nothing he could ever do would soften the hate that had festered and hardened within him. "Sasha is my mate," he said to Gregor as he pulled Sasha close. "We are tethered. I am hers, and she is mine. *Is é ár banna naofa.*" Our bond is sacred. Such bonds had been recognized within their clan through ceremony and vows. Ewan spoke these words to Gregor now knowing he would recognize the importance of them whether or not he wanted to actually acknowledge it. "I love her, Gregor. I will not raise a hand against her or anyone she holds dear. Ever."

Sasha couldn't be any more in love with Ewan than she was at this moment. Pride swelled in her chest as she stood by his side while he proclaimed his love for her, his devotion, and offered his protection to everyone she cared about. He faced the most feared berserker warlord in supernatural history and made his heart, his convictions known despite the impact of that perceived betrayal. He'd taken a stand. His bravery astounded her. He was an extraordinary male. And he belonged to her.

Gregor's eyes narrowed into hateful slits and his jaw squared. His lip curled with disgust and he spat at his feet. "*Tá tú ag caitheadh amach, Ewan Brún!*" Sasha didn't need to understand Gaelic to know the words Gregor spoke were grave. "Banished! For your betrayal of your clan, you have accepted your enemy's fate."

Sasha's heart clenched. Ewan had been cast out from his family and Gregor had effectively put a price on his

head. He'd be shown no clemency in battle. Killed on sight.
She hated that it had to be like this, and if she could, she
would change it all for him.

Ewan gave a shallow nod of acknowledgment. "What
about Drew?"

Gregor smirked. "Unlike you, he returned to his family.
Made his amends, and accepted his penance."

Ewan relaxed beside her. He bowed his head and remained that way for a quiet moment. Sasha gave his hand
a reassuring squeeze. It was all she could do and she hoped
it was enough. It was obvious she was missing a frame of
the bigger picture and she hoped Ewan would seek solace
from her and open up about all of it. She wasn't sure what
Drew's role in all of this was, but she knew he meant something to Ewan.

"I think your business here is settled, Gregor," Saeed
said coolly. "I trust you won't show up unexpected again."

Gregor's lips spread into a slow, cruel smile. "I forgot
to mention, Saeed. Rin sends his regards to you both."

Sasha's brow furrowed. She had no idea who this Rin
was, or how he or Ian Gregor for that matter, were connected to Saeed, but she intended to find out. Now that she
was home, she planned to take back her role as head of security. And after what had just happened, it wasn't a position she would take lightly.

Saeed turned and the small group that had amassed
turned and followed him toward the house. Sasha kept
Ewan's hand in hers as they fell into step beside Saeed.
"Do you want to tell me what that was about?"

Saeed offered a reassuring smile. "No. At least, not
right now."

Sasha pursed her lips. She didn't like getting the brush-
off but she'd accept his clipped response, for the time
being.

Despite the wrought-iron gate between them, turning

her back on Ian Gregor sent a shiver of trepidation down Sasha's spine. She didn't fear him. She feared what would happen to Ewan if Gregor ever got his hands on him.

Ewan let go of Sasha's hand, instead putting his arm around her to pull her against him as they walked. The solemn group returned to the house, all of them lost in their thoughts, crossing the breezeway to the front door.

Saeed stepped up to Ewan and paused. "I want you to know that I appreciate everything you said to Gregor. The sanctity of the words you spoke weren't lost on me."

"And the same goes for you," Ewan replied. Sasha sensed his discomfort at having such an intimate conversation with Saeed. "What you said was appreciated and I won't take your hospitality for granted."

Saeed smiled. He reached out and took Cerys's hand, leading her out in front of him. "Ian Gregor certainly knows how to ruin a dinner, doesn't he?"

Ewan's lips twitched. "That he does."

Sasha hung back and let Saeed and the others filter back into the house. She wanted a private moment with Ewan and those were few and far between in a communal living situation. He turned to face her, his brows raised in question. "Is everything all right, love?"

Love. She'd never get tired of hearing that word on his lips.

"Gregor gave up pretty easily, don't you think?"

Ewan shrugged a shoulder. "He's a very calculating male. Everything he does has a reason and purpose behind it. I don't think he expected Saeed to turn me over. Or for me to leave willingly."

"Then why come at all?" That's what worried Sasha the most.

"To be seen, for starters," Ewan began. "To make sure we know he's watching."

"Who's Rin?" Curiosity ate at Sasha. While she'd been

sowing her wild oats, so much had happened and she needed to get up to speed.

"I'm not entirely sure," Ewan replied. "He's Gregor's captive. He returned from Seattle with him."

"Seattle?" Saeed had been in Seattle for weeks. A piece of the puzzle clicked into place but it was far from complete. "Saeed was in Seattle."

"Figures," Ewan said with a snort. "Gregor told me that Saeed's coven was temporarily under his protection. I have a feeling Saeed's mate has something to do with that."

"Funny," Sasha said. "I had the same feeling."

"Gregor doesn't do anything that doesn't serve his end goal. If she's valuable to him, it's because she has something or can do something that will further his agenda."

"That's crazy." Sasha couldn't quite connect the dots. "She's mated to Saeed. She wouldn't turn against him, the coven, or any vampire."

"Gregor wants his vengeance," Ewan said. "But he wants so much more than that. He wants the Sortiari to burn as well."

"I didn't think of that." Ewan could bring so much insight into what they needed to do to protect themselves. "Cerys might be ammunition against them."

"That's my guess." Ewan put his arms around Sasha and let his hands rest at the small of her back. "We have a lot to talk about, don't we?"

"Yeah, we do." They'd been so swept up in each other, and then the drama with the demons, that so much had fallen through the cracks. "It's going to take us a few weeks to play catch-up."

"A few weeks?" Ewan cocked a brow as one corner of his mouth hitched. "I don't plan on letting you out of bed for at least a month. I don't think we'll be talking much. At least not about Gregor or Cerys."

Sasha couldn't help but smile. "A month? That's pretty

ambitious. There isn't anything else that might demand your attention?" She didn't want to ask about the battle arena but it weighed on her mind. Something had driven him there night after night. Was he ready to walk away or was he still chasing that high?

His expression became serious. "Like what?"

She averted her gaze. "The arenas."

"Sasha." Ewan placed his forefinger under her chin and directed her face up to look at him. "I won't be returning to the arenas. I'm done fighting."

Relief cascaded over her. "Are you sure?" She would never deny him whatever he needed to bring him peace. She'd seen him in the grips of battle rage. If what he needed to keep that part of him satisfied was to fight, then she'd come to terms with it.

"I'm sure. I fought for money so I could get free of Gregor. I don't need that anymore. I have my freedom. You gave me that. Now that I have you, I have everything I need."

Sasha's stomach flipped. She wondered if there would ever be a day when even the smallest word or gesture from him wouldn't affect her so viscerally. She knew there would be more trials to face. The road was bound to be bumpy when a berserker tethered a vampire. But as long as they had each other, Sasha was certain they could overcome any obstacle that lay before them.

"You can do anything you want now." Sasha could only imagine how liberated Ewan felt. "You have hundreds of options. What do you want to do?"

"Right now?" A mischievous glint sparked in Ewan's gorgeous golden brown eyes. "I'm going to go heat up that delicious plate of fettuccine that's probably cold, thanks to Gregor's interruption."

Sasha laughed. "And after that?"

His smile grew. Feral, predatory, and so damned gorgeous it stole her breath. "After that . . ." Ewan pulled Sasha close and put his lips to hers in a gentle kiss. "I plan to take you back to bed and shut the world out for a while."

She couldn't think of a better way to spend the night. "Or . . ." Sasha came up on her toes to kiss him as he'd kissed her. Her voice went low and breathy as she spoke against his mouth, "We can take the fettuccine back to my room and eat in bed. I'm pretty sure there's tiramisu for dessert. I'll make sure we have extra whipped cream."

Ewan groaned. "Gods, you're a wicked female, Sasha Ivanov. And I love you."

"Just as you are a wicked male, Ewan Brún. And I love you, too."

She'd though her life had begun anew when Saeed had made her vampire. But she'd been reborn the moment Ewan tethered her. Through their journey, she'd found herself, and with him at her side, they were capable of anything.

The world and all of its possibilities were theirs.

Crave more?

**Don't miss these other books in
Kate Baxter's True Vampire series**

THE LAST TRUE VAMPIRE

THE WARRIOR VAMPIRE

THE DARK VAMPIRE

THE UNTAMED VAMPIRE

THE LOST VAMPIRE

Available from St. Martin's Paperbacks